ALL THE BEAUTIFUL SINNERS

STEPHEN GRAHAM JONES

Also by

STEPHEN GRAHAM JONES

The Fast Red Road—A Plainsong

RuggedLand

RUGGED LAND | 276 CANAL STREET · FIFTH FLOOR · NEW YORK CITY · NY 10013 · USA

RuggedLand

PUBLISHED BY RUGGED LAND, LLC

276 CANAL STREET · FIFTH FLOOR · NEW YORK CITY · NY 10013 · USA

LIBRARY OF CONGRESS CONTROL NUMBER: 2002117807

PUBLISHER'S CATALOGING-IN-PUBLICATION
(PROVIDED BY QUALITY BOOKS, INC.)
Jones, Stephen Graham, 1972-
All the beautiful sinners / Stephen Graham Jones. —
1st ed.
p. cm.
ISBN 1-590-71008-8
Texas—Fiction. 2. Indians of North America—Fiction. 3. United States. Federal Bureau of Investigation—Fiction. 4. Missing children—Fiction. 5. Abduction—Fiction. 6. Suspense fiction.
I. Title.
PS3560.05395A66 2003 813'.6
QB133-1102

Book Design by
HSU+ASSOCIATES

Photography by
JASON FULFORD

RUGGED LAND WEBSITE ADDRESS: WWW.RUGGEDLAND.COM

PRINTED IN THE UNITED STATES OF AMERICA

APRIL 2003
1 3 5 7 9 10 8 6 4 2

for Nancy, always

God have mercy on the man
who doubts what he's sure of

—Bruce Springsteen

some of the names have been changed

15 MAY 1991

BETHLEHEM, NORTH CAROLINA

THE birds. He told her he wanted to see the birds.

'They're not pretty,' she said.

'But still,' he said.

She touched his face to see if he had looked away, if his eyes were open. Being in the dark like this was like wearing a mask. His face was just there, slack. He was ten. She was twelve.

'Okay,' she said.

They stood together in the van, holding onto each other with one hand, touching the carpeted wall with the other. The carpet was thick to absorb sound, and black, for stains. There were no windows, no door handles, no window jacks, just the dark, polycarbonate glass. It could take the impact of a 9-mm slug.

They moved to the front of the van, walking along the top of where the frame would be. It kept the cab bushings from creaking. They'd learned that four hundred miles ago. Tied to the rearview mirror was a plastic war bonnet, red white and blue. The boy touched it and the girl understood: for five days now, it had been the only thing moving, a metronome for the two of them, sitting with their backs against the twin cargo doors, their knees tucked under their chins, arms hugging their shins, eyes open.

For the twentieth time, they checked the nooks and crannies of the console, the blank spaces under the seat, the ashtray. There was nothing, though. There wouldn't be.

They had maybe six minutes now until He finished eating.

And it had to be here, *this* truck stop.

The boy sat in the passenger seat and kicked the glove compartment until the simple lock gave. He didn't kick in the middle, where the metal would bend, but at the top, where the chrome button was. The girl stood behind and watched, her fingers hooked into the plastic molding that traced the inner contour of the van, separating back from front. It was for hogwire. She shuddered when the glove compartment opened like a mouth. Now there was no turning back.

She helped the boy wrench the glove compartment door off. It took longer than it should have. Its corners were rounded perfectly, though. Because she was stronger, she sat sideways in the passenger seat, wedged the rounded corner down as far as she could under the base of the window, into the inner parts of the door, set her feet against the armrest, and pulled. For long seconds it didn't work—nothing, nothing, nothing: *four* minutes—but then she threw her head back, baring her throat to whoever wanted it, whoever needed it, and the ledge of metal below the glass groaned back towards her maybe an inch. It was just enough for the boy to force his arm down into the workings, hook his index finger around the vestigial latch.

He looked to the girl to see if it was all right, if they were really going to do this.

Her legs were trembling against the armrest. She nodded, once, *yes*, and he did it, opened the door, only she was still pushing against it. It slammed out and took him with it, his bare feet pedaling the air. The delicate bones of his forearm were a wet sound in the parking lot. The only sound. He didn't cry, though, just looked back to the girl. In turn, she looked to the diner for a reaction, for a tall man in a brown hat to stand up from His meal, a fork still in His hand, but nothing happened. Nothing *was* happening.

'Okay,' she said to the boy, and stood on the cold running board, pried him up from the door. His arm flapped loose behind them as they ran. She knew how to splint it, how to set it, how to lick it clean if she had to, but there wasn't time. They just had to run then, each of his footsteps falling into hers, hers set into the warm road toe after toe, no heel. *Like deer*, she thought, and smiled. The bottle caps and glass embedded in the asphalt glittered underneath them like snake eyes. They touched the mailboxes as they passed them—a game—and at one ramshackle house a large black animal rose up against a section of white clapboard, its eyes pale yellow.

They broke stride, stood panting in the road.

'It's a dog,' the girl said.

'I know,' the boy said. 'I remember.'

He was staring at it, holding his arm close to his side.

'We don't have time,' she said.

'I know,' he said, but stepped forward anyway. Just to pet it.

It came out to the end of its chain, wetting its nose so their smell would stick better. So it could taste them.

'Hello,' the boy said, offering the back of his numb hand.

The dog flattened its ears, was just reaching forward when a light in the house clicked on.

The girl ran, the boy close behind, his eyes still large from the dog.

'I remember,' he said to the girl.

Instead of tying the boy's arm up into a sling, they folded it back against the bicep, fastened it there with a plastic bag from the ditch. Because you needed your balance. It was turning black at the fingertips, though, under the nails.

'You okay?' the girl asked him.

The boy nodded, his eyes empty.

Two years ago, he hadn't been dead like this.

Maybe the birds would bring him back, though. The way they *flew*. She'd told him about it on accident one night and he'd held onto it after everything else was gone: the birds, lifting, all at once.

They ran until they fell, until their feet bled, until the sun threw their shadows alongside them, and then they hid in the trees and refuse of a rest stop. It was like a diorama for them, an exhibit: the pale mothers leading their pale children to the restrooms then standing by the door, watching every man who went in, imagining knives and burdizzos and worse strapped to their clammy torsos. You didn't need all that, though.

Just a brown hat, a glance in the mirror, a smile. An empty stall.

They meant to sleep, but didn't.

'Do you remember?' the boy said.

The girl looked at him.

Yes. No. A man with a cigarette leaning down over a birthday cake. A rolled-up diaper lying on the carpet in front of the television.

Her lip shook.

No.

There was an ant crawling on the boy's broken forearm, its antennae slashing the air before it. The girl pinched it off, the boy's skin rising with it. So she killed it. The boy's skin fell back down, but there was a ridge for a few seconds: dehydration. Night fell around them like a curtain.

'It was a good dog,' the boy said.

The girl nodded.

They ran, one behind the other, eyes set ahead, breathing in through their noses, out through their mouths. The girl made them run on the yellow line, trying to get to each reflector with six long steps. Once, when the boy let go, she looped back and found him squatted on the ground, studying the face of a watch set into the black rock. It was still ticking. He looked up at her and smiled, and she nodded, and they looked at it for eighty-nine seconds—one complete revolution and almost half of another—then rose into the headlights slouching around the corner.

They faded to opposite sides of the road.

It wasn't Him, though.

The truck whipped past.

They ran in the silence it left, and when she led them off the road, she held his hand so he wouldn't get lost. His palm was hot, from fever. She pulled him as much as she could, tucking him into her wind drag, or the idea of it.

'The birds,' she said, when he stumbled.

His head was lolling on his shoulders.

They had to see.

5

The clock in the road had said one o'clock. They made the campsite she'd told him about two hours later, maybe, then stood small among the hulking RV units, the propane tanks balanced on their noses like a deathwish.

Yes, she knew this place. When there were fewer eyes. When the floor of the van was white from overspray, and red underneath.

There was no one standing at the glowing embers, so they did, three palms held out to it, in memory of other fires. A man leaning down over a birthday cake.

But don't think about that.

The girl dipped her hand to the ashes, brought it up pale.

'Like this,' she said.

The boy stared.

They walked out past the brick restrooms and the barbecue pits buried in the ground. They were holding hands again, the girl saying *here*, *here*, *here*. She wasn't sure it was even her voice anymore.

'Did you see that?' the boy asked.

The girl looked to him.

They went back.

In the last barbecue pit was a dog head. Yellow eyes. It was smiling, the pupil of the eye they could see blown wide. The girl stepped back, got a black-and-white flash of the two of them standing at this pit. They were small, though. Like someone was watching them. Like He was here.

The world reduced itself to a heartbeat.

She closed her eyes, opened them.

'We have to run now,' she told the boy, and they did, the boy stooping to pick up a beer bottle, its neck choked grey with ash.

The girl looked back when he let go of her hand, but he just stared, and she stared back, and they ran.

The birds.

Maybe they weren't even for him anymore, but her.

When the trail curved, the girl shot through, over the berm, continuing the line they'd been on, then cut hard left, slid to the ground. The boy followed. They watched behind them, their hearts hammering. Nothing. They would never see Him, either. Not Him.

'You sure?' the boy said.

The girl nodded: He was here.

They moved from shadow to shadow, the moon gibbous above them, the leaf litter inconstant, shuffling with inattention, and, forty yards from the trail, they saw them, the other children, the ground beneath their feet rustling, the tree above them bent. It was an oak, one of the old ones, that had been tied over from the top when it was a sapling, back before America was America. An Indian tree, a marker. It made an arch. This was a holy place.

The boy hesitated, staring.

'No,' he said.

The children were white like the girl remembered them. Just not moving.

The boy's beer bottle fell from his hand and a small breath of ash rushed up out of the mouth, resettled.

The girl looked over to him. His lips, pale, drawn. A dog loping through the woods after them, no head. A diaper in the blue afterglow of the television.

'This way,' she said.

Together, they stepped from tree to tree, tacking in to the white children, so that they resolved bit by bit. The moon was still harsh enough to catch the dead girl's face. It made it look wet, shiny. Like the clothes she wore, had been *dressed* in. And the boy one, Daniel. That was his name. Daniel, whispering under the stairs. Daniel and Marlene.

The girl stepped forward, almost into the level place where the children were. She hadn't known they would be this white still, that the shellac or lacquer or water sealant or whatever would have lasted this long.

Daniel and Marlene had changed, though. Under their hard shells.

Their heads were larger now, bulbous, their jutting cheekbones filled with wax then heated up with a torch and pressed back in, in different shapes. Their noses filed off, so that there were just two slits, their eyes sewed over with catgut, so they couldn't see what was happening to them. Their hair was sandy blond, glued on, left to blow, the strands clumped together now with uric acid. They were short now too. Ten and twelve again. The stitches circling their legs and arms were like the lace of a football, and just as even.

Later, the forensic men would find rebar hose-clamped to the bones of their legs. It went in straight, but then would only bend with heat—electricity, introduced at the shin. It cauterized the muscle around the rebar into a leather sheath. The girl remembered Daniel's femur, extracted under the floodlight while it was still steaming, then sawed in two places near the center, the straight section lifted out, spilling marrow, the remaining parts fastened back together, caulked shut. To make him short again. Like he had been. Daniel.

'No,' the boy said again, 'I don't want to anymore—' but the girl stepped forward anyway, and then it happened: the ground rushed up into the sky. Birds, the birds, and under them weeks of black seed, poisoned to blind them, making them stay to catch the only food they could anymore.

'Look,' the girl said to the boy.

Like this was all for him.

He was on his knees.

She smiled—allowed herself a smile—and reached for Daniel's new hair.

She still remembered what he looked like, how he sounded in the darkness of the basement, whispering that this would happen, that even when you got away, you didn't. That he was only letting you run. But it felt good, God.

The moon was shot through with the small bodies of blind sparrows.

Behind her, the boy looked to the girl. To Marlene. Marly. She was smiling, the soldering wire molded into her lips, the flesh of her cheek, the one dimple pulled through with a piece of thread, tied to her second molar. The scissors used to cut the thread would show up in a trashcan back at the campsite. Along with an empty can of the sealant used on her face. They would be in a stratum that would get labeled MARCH 15TH. There would be no prints on her, though, not in the shellac around her arms, where she'd been lifted, *placed*, not on her own fingertips, even.

The boy shook his head no at Marlene, no no no, but then when he stood to run it was into a denim shirt. Far above, a brown hat.

The girl looked around slow.

'Father,' she said. 'Look what we found.'

'Yes,' her father said. 'Good, good.'

The boy looked up at Him and hugged himself into a ball, still shaking his head no, and his father carried him back to the road like that, the girl trailing behind, holding the fingers of one hand in the other, behind her back, her smile fixed like the children's had been, her eyes glazed with wonder.

PART ONE

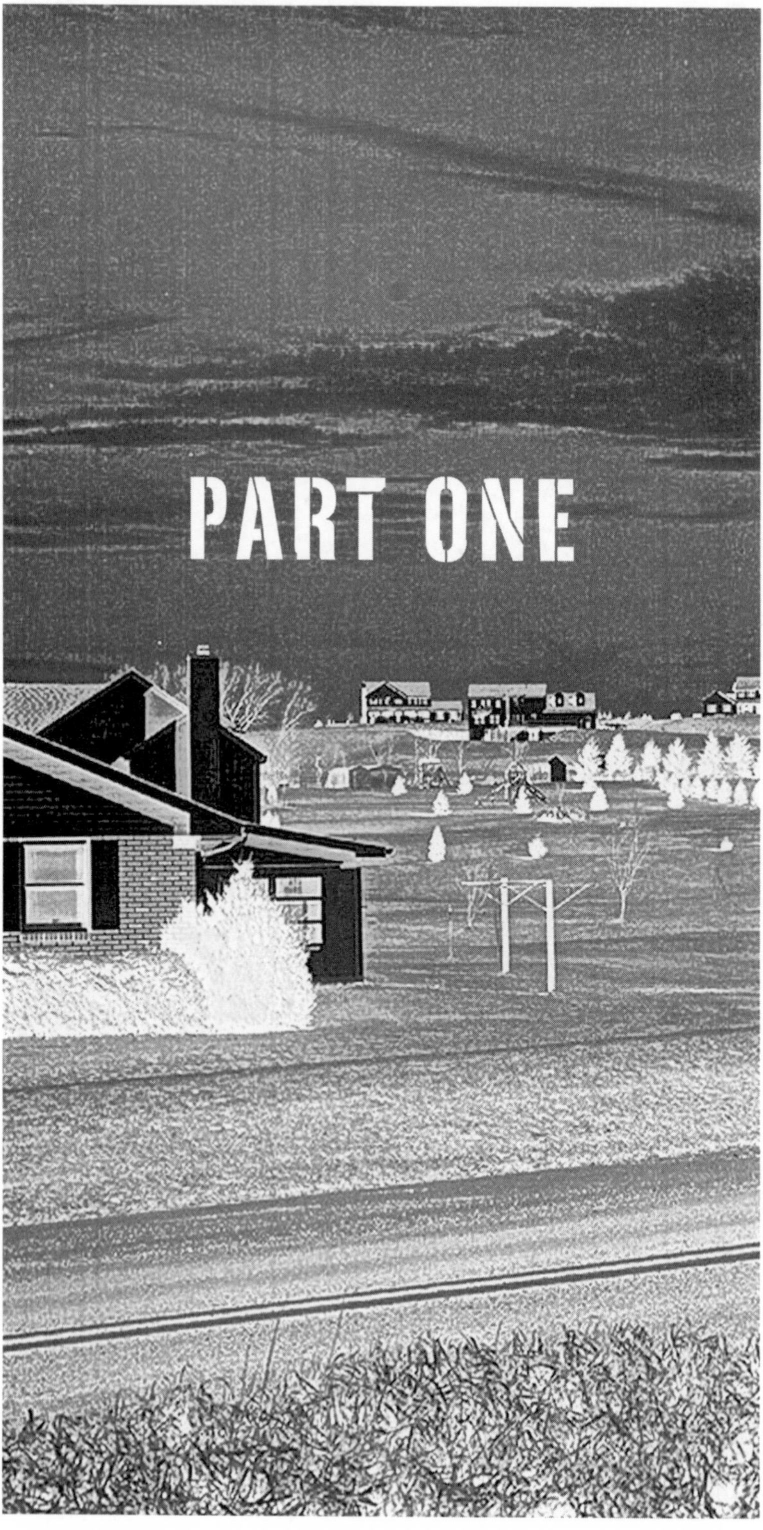

1

21 MARCH 1999

NAZARETH, TEXAS

SHE was walking in the ditch, along the road that went away from the high school. It was two-thirty. She was wearing a skirt that hugged her legs. It came down to the tops of her boots. Jim Doe smiled, closed his eyes, opened them. She was still there, against the backdrop of the baseball field. He coasted alongside, the gravel dancing behind him. Past her and all around her to the north was a dryline. It had been building for four hours now. Jim Doe had been watching it even before he came on shift.

He rolled the passenger side window down.

'Deputy Sheriff,' she said, looking at him once, and not head on.

'Going to rain,' Jim Doe said, easing through the tall grass.

She smiled. 'Guess I'll have to get wet then.'

Terra. Her name was Terra, Terra Donner.

Jim Doe told her to get in, and she did. The Bronco was pointed out of town already, into the miles of scrub land nobody lived in because nobody wanted to. Through the windshield the sky was blue and heavy, and, looking through the line of tint that ran level with the rearview, Jim Doe could see what the clouds would look like by four, with the sun burning into their backs: worse. He looked over at Terra, snugged into her seat belt. It crossed between her breasts like a bra commercial. They met like this sometimes, on accident, but not. He was twenty-five. He'd been warned.

'So what about prom?' she said.

Jim Doe smiled. They were easing up county road 526 now, with the high tension wires, the caliche dust hanging behind them for too long in the damp air, then becoming dirt when they crossed 614—the roads Jim Doe had grown up on—then almost catching up with them when they dog-legged over to 527 along with the wires, down to 608. Still standing there, on the left, were the black metal ribs of a barn, and, just before them, four broken-down houses, for the hands the barn had once made necessary. They were all in a row, the houses, each with a utility pole behind it. Full of birds now, and worse. The walls showing chickenwire behind the stucco. An old, rounded refrigerator dragged out of one of them, laid on its back to rust. Jim Doe liked it here because it was the highest place around, the barn, the houses, what his father had always taught him to look for, because H_2S gas couldn't collect there like it could in the low spots, killing everything that walked into it. Jim Doe hadn't believed it until his father took him out of school one day to show him: a nearly perfect circle of dead animals. Rabbits and moles and ground squirrels and pack rats and birds. It had been unholy. His father had made him look, remember. Touched Jim Doe's sternum with the side of his hand when Jim Doe started to step in. He hadn't said no, though. That was why Jim Doe still remembered. Instead it had just been *not yet*.

Jim Doe could still hear it, when he didn't try: *not yet*. And see his father sitting up here too, watching the sky over his steering wheel, the child Jim Doe used to be walking soft through the empty houses, placing his weight on each foot with care, so it wouldn't push through the floorboards into whatever was underneath.

Not yet.

He leaned forward, clicked the two-way radio up. Because, technically, he was on duty. But this was Nazareth, on a weekday.

'Look likely?' Terra asked, lifting her chin to the north.

Jim Doe shrugged.

Below them a four-wheel drive Case, still shiny from the showroom floor, was pulling a four-bottom breaking plow across three hundred and twenty acres of winter wheat. That was the way you could tell it was March again: large blades slitting the earth open.

'About prom,' Jim Doe said, 'yeah.'

Terra looked to him. Her seat belt was off now, rolled back up into its nest by her head. The lines above them humming with tension.

'Just as chaperone,' she said. 'Protect me from those . . . Mitch and Jacob and them.'

'Still,' Jim Doe said. Last week he had pulled the prom car into the grocery store parking lot over in Dimmit. It was a 1982 Corvette, its nose and taillights almost touching. The telephone pole it had slammed into had hooked the plastic of the passenger side door panel onto the ball of the gear shifter, nevermind Molly Jankins, who had been sitting there. In Jim Doe's day, he'd stood in the parking lot of the grocery until dawn sometimes, with his friends, careful each time to leave their beer cans on the lip of the trailer under Molly's door, like they owed her that.

'You know why they take your picture?' he asked Terra. Both his arms were folded over the wheel, his fingertips touching the plastic housing the speedometer and tach were set in.

Terra stared at him. He could feel it. 'At prom, you mean?'

Jim Doe nodded.

'I've never been,' she said.

'But you know.'

'Because your mom's dressed you all up,' she said, finally. 'Done your hair for like two hours.'

Jim Doe was still nodding. 'It's because everybody thinks you're going to die that night.' He looked at her. 'They just want one last picture.'

Terra breathed out through her teeth. Like this had happened before: Jim Doe.

The windows were fogging up on the inside. After she was gone, Jim Doe would be able to see the individual hairs of her head in the passenger side window, where she was leaning against it now. The sheriff's department had been pulling that Vette around for nine years already. Jim Doe had been doing it for three, ever since Gentry signed him on.

'What class are you missing?' he asked Terra.

'Geometry,' she said. 'They're all the same, though.'

'Wilkins?' Jim Doe asked.

'Wilkins,' Terra said.

Jim Doe wondered what the dryline in front of them would look like on Doppler, or thermal-enhanced from a satellite. It was rolling now, more black than blue. The Case below them was stopped, the farmer standing out on the fender, his hat lifted so he could see the lightning better. It was like static electricity under a blanket at night. You wonder if it's been like that forever. What your grandparents thought about it, what they didn't.

For a moment the radio under the dash flickered with static: a truckdriver barreling down 27 out of Amarillo. He was talking about the hail. It was dime-size, coating the road white.

'Think it'll make it here?' Terra said. The hail.

'Hope not,' Jim Doe said. 'Better now than later, though,' he added, nodding down to the Case. 'For him, I mean.'

'Don't you ever think about me?' Terra said.

Jim Doe didn't answer. He was trying to dial the trucker back in.

Terra hitched her elbow up on the armrest. It was always like this. Jim Doe looked up to her.

'Sometimes,' he said, and then the dial rolled across Sheriff Gentry's voice.

'—Chief?' Gentry was saying, *'Chief?'*

Jim Doe shook his head in wonder. He palmed the mike.

'This is an open line, you know,' he said. '*Sheriff*.'

'I'll call you a damn red-ass Indian on the six o'clock news, if you want,' Gentry said.

Jim Doe smiled, clicked back on. 'I'm here,' he said.

'Where?' Gentry asked back.

Jim Doe was still looking at Terra. There was space between the top of her boots and the hem of her skirt now. No hose. Behind her was the mesh that separated the truck into front and back, safe and unsafe, cops and robbers.

'Chief?' Gentry said.

Jim Doe held his finger over his mouth for Terra not to say anything.

'Out past the school,' he added. 'North.'

Gentry keyed in just to laugh. So Jim Doe could hear him laugh.

'Looking at all the pretty clouds on county time?' Gentry said.

'Something like that,' Jim Doe said.

He was one of only two deputies on duty. Gentry was a friend of his father's. Had been, anyway.

'Well,' Gentry began, so that Jim Doe could see him in his cruiser, leaned back in the seat the way old men do, like that gives them more baritone, carries their voice deeper into the wire, across the air. 'It's like this. A blue—'

Jim Doe missed the rest: Terra, running the knob of the two-way along the side of her finger.

I didn't say *anything*, she said with her lips. Not with her eyes, though.

Jim Doe looked over to her, pulled his lips back from his teeth, and switched the rig to his other hand, so he could guard the dashboard.

'Say again,' he said into the mike.

There was a long, impatient pause.

'. . . sure you're ready?' Gentry asked.

Jim Doe nodded. For radio.

'This guy, Nebraska plates. Blue sedan. Mary says he pocketed something at the Allsup's. A candy bar, maybe.'

'Dimmit?' Jim Doe said.

'Josie,' Gentry said back. She worked the counter in Dimmit.

'If we start arresting people for candy bars . . .' Jim Doe said.

'You have to live here to get away with it, anyway,' Gentry said back. 'But here's the deal. He's Indian, I don't know what kind. White-tail, black feet, something.'

He paused, holding the line open so Jim Doe couldn't say anything. Jim Doe's father, Horace, was seventeen fifty-seconds Piegan—Blackfeet. With papers, like a dog or a horse.

'And . . ?' Jim Doe asked.

'And he's got one of those damn chicken feathers hanging from his rearview,' Gentry said.

'Eagle,' Jim Doe said.

'Just thought you might want to be there,' Gentry said. 'Go back to the blanket with him or something. He's heading your way, up one sixty-eight.'

Jim Doe ran his tongue against his lower lip, side to side.

Terra was waiting for him to say something back to Gentry.

He didn't. Instead he just asked did Gentry need him there?

'It's a boring day, is all,' Gentry said. 'What is it, Tuesday?'

'Wednesday,' Terra said.

Jim Doe looked at her. He could hear Gentry smiling through the mouthpiece. 'I can take it if you want,' he said.

'Hell, he'll likely be gone by the time you get her back to school,' Gentry said, his voice strained from some turn he was making, the steering wheel rasping across the gut of his shirt. 'From, y'know, *wherever* you are.'

Jim Doe shook his head, trying hard to figure how this could have gone any different.

'Town and Country?' he said, signing off.

'Five o'clock,' Gentry said back.

They never made it.

Gentry hit the sirens just past the Episcopal church, where the highway flattened out. It was his favorite place. He had his radio locked open—the Nazareth version of back-up.

'Can he hear us?' Terra whispered.

No. Jim Doe nodded anyway. Just to keep her quiet, let him think. He held his index finger over his lips.

Gentry was reading the plates off to Monica, back at the office.

His car was stopped now, too, you could tell. No more road whine, no more wind through the open window, no more sirens. Just the lights, probably. To keep people from rear-ending him, or slapping him with their mirrors.

'Don't forget the camera this time, Tom,' Monica said.

Gentry laughed, said something hard to catch, and scratched over the steering wheel again, hit the record button. The heads under the passenger seat squealed in protest, then rolled, rolled.

Monica read the plates back just after Gentry stepped out.

They belonged to a black farm truck from Nebraska. They hadn't been registered since 1952.

Jim Doe studied the radio. 1952?

'Look,' Terra said.

Jim Doe did. It was the cloud, opening up. Streaks of blue sifted down like corn pollen, but there were streaks of white, too: hail. Pale and slight in the distance.

'Watch the corners,' Jim Doe said. 'The edges.'

That was where the rotation usually started. Like eddies left behind.

But 1952. Jim Doe said it again, in his head, then keyed Monica open, to get her to run the plates a second time. Beside him, Terra clicked her seat belt open. Jim Doe didn't even know she'd put it back on again. The metal head reeled across her chest. She leaned forward to see the edges of the cloud, and Jim Doe was watching her but thinking about an old black truck, rambling down the road, past the Episcopal church, one of its tires slinging rubber.

'Tom?' he said into the mike, holding his hand out for Terra not to say anything, *please*, and four miles away Gentry looked back to his car, into the camera mounted on the dash, then hitched his pants up on the left side, kept walking.

The longhair's car was a blue sedan, a 1985 Impala.

He hadn't needed the cherries, either, the lights—the car had already been slowing, guilty—but had turned them on just for Mary Watkins and her sister Janna, crossing the church parking lot early for choir, like they'd done every Wednesday for twenty-two years. They'd waved to Gentry as he drove past, then tied their scarves down tighter over their heads, leaned inside. Gentry had smiled, raised a finger over the wheel to them, and hit the siren too, just to see the Watkins girls jump, just to hear them later on the phone, complaining about the *screamers*. It was their word. Gentry liked it.

Behind him, on the dash, he'd drawn a black cross on the notepad suction-cupped to his windshield. It meant he'd stopped at the church again. He liked to take them as far as the litter barrel, to empty his ashtray, but this Indian had too much candy in his pockets to even make it that far. Gentry smiled, leaning down the slightest bit to be sure the chicken feather was still there, on the rearview, *impairing vision*, endangering the lives of every other motorist for miles around. It was.

The Indian stood from the Impala when Gentry was still even with the bumper.

'—no, no, son,' Gentry said, his elbow already cocked out, the butt of his service revolver set in his palm.

The Indian was a longhair in faded jeans, a blue sleeveless flannel shirt open at the chest, a concert T-shirt underneath. Def Leppard. It figured.

'You want to be careful now,' Gentry said. 'This isn't Nebraska.'

The Indian just stood there.

Gentry smiled.

Maybe he was one of those mutes. Kawliga.

'You know you can't do that,' Gentry said, hooking his chin in at the rearview.

The Indian just stood there.

'Got some identification, then?' Gentry said.

The Indian raised his head as if just hearing, just tuning in, then shrugged, leaned down into the car, across to the passenger side. Gentry stepped forward, shaking his head no, saying it—'Son, no, you can't'—his elbow cocked again, but then the Indian stood, holding something out to him. It was white, but wrong: a snub-nose revolver wrapped in masking tape or some shit.

He was pointing it at Gentry.

Gentry took a step back, lowering his hip to get *his* revolver out faster, but it wasn't enough: the Indian stepped forward, pulling the trigger.

Gentry shuddered, felt the grill of his car digging into his back, heard his gun clatter to the ground, wondered what the Watkins sisters were singing just now—for him—and said his wife's name: Agnes. And that he was sorry.

But then he raised his hands, just to see what his insides looked like after all these years.

They were clean.

He looked at his shirt.

It was clean too. Dry.

The driver's snub-nose had misfired. They were both looking at it now.

Gentry's hat touched the hood once when it blew off his head, the storm pushing in, and then it was gone.

He grubbed around in the gravel for his gun, came up with it, walked behind it to the driver, the longhair, and calmly took the snub-nose, set it on the peeling vinyl roof of the Impala. And then he went to work. With his hands, and his knees, and the sharp brass bead on the topside of his pistol, and the blunt, checkered plate of the handle, and the heavy door of the Impala.

The longhair was on his knees, then on his stomach, then pulled to his knees again, then slammed into the side of the car, his hands cuffed behind him. He sagged to the ground, some of his hair catching around the post of the antenna, holding his head up at a wrong angle, the rest still hiding his face.

Gentry leaned into the Impala for more guns, then, evidence, a *reason*, and when he ripped the feather from the rearview, the mirror came with it. He stood from the car with the keys in his hand, walked close enough to the longhair to knee him in the chest, and popped the trunk.

It took his eyes—his mind—a few breaths to make sense, and then he backed up, dry-heaving.

It was two children. They were dead, decayed, staring.

The smell.

Gentry steadied himself on the hood of his car, the large, early drops of rain leaving wet spots on the dusty rear window of the Impala.

He followed his hands along his hood to the dummy light of his cruiser, to call this in—the Army, the Navy, the National Guard—but stopped at his door, the skin on the back of his neck tightening with knowledge, awareness of the Indian balled up sideways on the ground, edging the chain of his handcuffs down the back of his legs, across the soles of his feet, then rising beside the Impala, the snub-nose in both hands.

'Don't—' he said, Gentry, and that was all he got out.

The snub-nose didn't misfire this time.

Down the road, Mary and Janna Watkins raised their voices above the sound and Gentry heard it as the first slug slung him around, then the second. A pirouette, his arms flung out for balance, coming together over the holes in his body, leaving him half on the car, half not.

And then the rain came.

2

23 MARCH 1999

QUANTICO, VIRGINIA

THE bodies were on the wall with all the rest. Dr. Sheila Watts clicked the slide projector and the two from North Carolina came up, as the campers had found them back in 1991. She was walking him through it, Cody Mingus. On a lark, he knew, because he wasn't even supposed to be there, was supposed to be down in his temporary cubicle punching keys, reentering all the Violent Crimes form data from eight weeks ago: brown eyes, not carved, possibly blitzed. It wasn't because the original data had been lost, but because, two years ago—before he even graduated the Academy—a blue-eyed woman had slipped through as hazel-eyed, then wallowed around in the morass of Unidentified Dead long enough for her to be excluded from approximately three thousand five hundred automated searches and one hundred and fourteen manual ones. So now, at the end of each day, Cody was running his data against what was already there, and the Perl module he'd written flagged anything that didn't match, which he then had to trace down in the archives. Because if the analysts on staff didn't have the facts, they couldn't recognize the similarities that would suggest a pattern killer. Cody knew all this. And that this was what he had to do to *be* an analyst, but still. He wanted to leapfrog ahead. It was why he was here, upstairs—why he'd been *called* up here: afterhours, he'd been collating the data on those two North Carolina unidentified dead from eight years ago, lining them up against the massive runaway pools of the late eighties, but then, during a Boolean search with six of the slots asterisked as wild cards, he'd slipped *underneath* the data. And there were bodies everywhere, like North Carolina. All up and down the eastern seaboard.

He'd tabbed away immediately, made himself enter data religiously for four more days, but now they were watching him, the children in the woods, with their sewn-over eyes. He finally wrote them up as ghosts—self-replicating fragments of old files or some other impossible myth—and submitted them to the tech people, but then ITSD sent them back for an analyst, and the analyst had sent them upstairs, to the profilers.

'White Chapel?' Watts had said to him over the phone. An internal line.

It was what Cody had written in the margin of the ITSD form.

'They never solved that one either,' Cody had said back.

The chair he was sitting in now was still warm, too, from all the interviews: VICAP was trying to replace Martin Ronald "Mr." Rogers, who had, as the Bureau tended to put it, gone fishing: retired. Given up. Admitted defeat. Gone to play Boy Scouts with his grandchildren. Which left an empty slot on a senior task force you would need a task force to ever detect: the Three Wise Men. Tim Creed was the other member, after Watts. Or, before her, before *every*body: a legend. He even taught the course at Quantico sometimes, a meandering recollection of the good old days. Cody knew all his cases inside out, too. The file names read like old *Batman* episodes: the Plaid Strangler, the Maniak, Steely Dan, Getty Boy Paul. Some of them were older than Cody was, even, older than profiling itself.

'So what do you see, Agent?' Watts asked, holding on the North Carolina slide.

'Two children,' Cody said. 'Male and female.'

Watts was their forensic psychiatrist, the highest ranking black woman in the Bureau, maybe in all of Virginia. She laughed a little.

'At first we thought they were dwarves,' she said. Cody looked back at her. She was still smiling. 'Did they not look . . . stunted when you saw them at first?'

'They were just—' Cody started.

'Dead,' a man said.

He was standing at the back of the room.

Creed.

Cody nodded: dead, yes. Very.

Creed laughed to himself some.

'They say you graduated top of your class,' he said, stepping forward.

Cody nodded.

'Small class?' Creed said.

'*Tim*,' Watts said. Like a wife might.

Eight years, Cody thought. All he knew about her—Watts—was that she was right more than she was wrong. A lot more. In the halls they called her the Gypsy Queen, because she could see everything, all at once. There was something about *crystal balls*, too.

But Creed. Creed was a god.

Cody nodded, about his class size. 'Two people,' he said, holding his index and middle finger up, then looking at them, changing it to his index and thumb. He looked to Watts. '. . . or, one and a half. The other guy was a dwarf, I mean.'

Watts looked up at the slide. 'If comedy hour's over, gentlemen?'

Creed repeated her word, *gentlemen*.

Cody leaned back and listened.

Eight years before, the first pair had turned up. That had been in North Carolina—Bethlehem. Then it was Pennsylvania—Bethlehem again, just north of 78. The next pair had been in the Connecticut Bethlehem, and then Jerusalem, Rhode Island and Jerusalem, Georgia. Jericho, New York. Back to Connecticut again for Canaan, then down to Virginia, for Ararat. Watts said it before Cody could ask: their man was a biblical kind of guy. Or he wanted them to think that, anyway.

And it was always a male and a female.

'And not dwarves,' Watts said.

'Or midgets, or anything like that,' Creed said.

Midgets. It was a word from Creed's generation.

Watts advanced to the next slide. It was X-ray film of the skeletons of the first pair. The rebar stood out the most, but there was something else.

'You had a radiologist look at this,' Cody said, standing to see better.

'And then another after him,' Creed said.

Each of the long bones in the bodies—the femur, the humerus, the tibia fibula ulna and radius—had had segments removed from the middle. To shorten them.

'Why?' Cody asked.

'To make them look like children,' Watts said.

'They're—?' Cody started, touching the screen. It was warm.

'Old enough that their growth plates have locked into place,' Creed said. 'No more continental drift on their skulls, any of that. And no, we haven't identified the victim pool, yet.'

Cody nodded.

Watts backed the slides up to the bodies, the way they'd been left. The heads were oversized, the fingers too long. Of course.

'And their teeth,' Watts said, clicking forward six slides, to the dental films. 'They're permanent. No fillings, though.'

Cody turned back to her, shielding his eyes from the light.

'How many?' he asked.

'Too many,' Creed said.

Eight pairs; one a year since 1991. Sixteen bodies. That they knew about. All along the Atlantic seaboard. All set within two hundred yards of campgrounds just outside towns with biblical names. And no names for them, either, and no reason, or, no reason *yet*. Cody had heard Creed say it like that in a lecture, once. That everything made sense when you looked back on it. That it made sense *now*, even, just not to them, not from where they were standing. Or how.

Cody sat down. 'Is there more?' he asked, unsure how to phrase it, unsure where to look.

Watts answered by clicking through slide after slide after slide.

'Not enough,' Creed said. 'Now it's all you. Tell us what it tells *you*, Agent.' The formal term.

Cody looked down, at his feet, and deeper, to his Behavioral Science. 'Children are sacred to this guy,' he said, finally. 'That's why he uses adult corpses.' He extended his hand for the slide clicker, and Watts gave it to him. He backed up to the crime-scene photos. 'But this,' he said. 'Number one, he's posing them. And not in his basement or his attic, Norman Bates, but out here. Like he *wants* us to find them. To see them, like he does. Or, to make us see them. Which is why he puts them in this same position time after time—the boy one offering something to the girl one, the girl one looking up at him, waiting for it.'

Cody palmed a marker from beside the projector. The ink in the wick was hot from the bulb, fluid almost. He approached the screen, traced the outline of the boy, the outline of the girl, the felt tip rustling over the textured vinyl, and talked: 'Number two,' he said. 'This isn't anger, or retaliation, or sexual. The ritual mutilation—you know this, right? He cares about them. He does it all after they're dead. Like he's just fixing what's wrong. That they got old. Do we have a cause of death?'

'Absence of life,' Creed said.

Cody shook his head, kept tracing. 'Probably poison. While they were sleeping. Tox?'

Watts waited before saying it: 'Tuinol,' she said. 'Non-lethal amounts.'

Cody stopped with the marker, turned to her. '*Tyl*enol?' he said.

'*Tui*nol,' Creed said. 'Amobarbital and secobarbital.'

'Barbiturates,' Watts added. 'In the same class with Seconal, Amytal, Butisol . . .'

Cody was just staring at her.

'Elvis took them to sleep,' she said, then shrugged. 'They were like . . . Rohypnol before there was Rohypnol. The roofies of yesterday, Agent. Make you real uninhibited. Open to suggestions.'

'Like aspirin in your coke . . .' Cody said.

'Really big aspirin,' Watts said.

Cody smiled. 'It fits,' he said, 'right? His reverence for children.

Or, childhood, I guess. How he only harvests adults to replace his children. He's older, right? *From* that time period, the Tuinol one?'

'Or he wants us to think that,' Watts said again.

'Or he wants us to think that,' Cody said, nodding. 'Meaning we think he's smart. Manipulative. Staging it all for—'

Creed shrugged, interrupted. '. . . could be that we're the ones being too smart,' he said, in a tone of voice that suggested he'd said this all before. 'He could just be one sick, lucky son of a bitch who failed taxidermy school.'

Cody kept nodding, hit the lights. Behind him Watts killed the projector, the fan trying to get it back down below melting.

There on the screen, in wide strokes, was the silhouette of a boy and a girl.

'Probably his children,' Cody said. 'Or maybe his first two victims. The special ones. Fill this in with faces, anyway, and we've got him.'

He set the marker down.

Creed was looking to Watts for something. He got it.

'Top of your class?' he said.

Cody nodded.

Creed looked to the screen, shook his head. 'Give it to him,' he said to Watts.

It was a manila folder, practically cobwebbed over. Cody opened it. There in 8"x10" was the tracing he'd just made.

He laughed. At himself. Looked at the screen he'd just vandalized.

'How much those things run?' he asked.

'About two hundred dollars, I'd figure,' Creed said. 'But we'll take it out of your check.'

Watts spread her hands over the box of folders she'd carried in on her hip. It was a liturgical motion, her hands, her fingers. Like she was offering bread to be broken, files to be opened. Another, better world. One with more facts. The world Cody'd just glimpsed before, suspended under the data.

'We think it's a snapshot he carries with him,' she said. 'Something casual, with the children. He probably even took it himself. It would explain the repetition, the multiple exposures. How he keeps doing this again and again.'

Cody nodded, chewing the inside of his cheek. 'So . . .' he said, unsure, 'this mean I'm on?' He looked from Watts to Creed.

Creed nodded, once.

'What are we calling him, then?' Cody asked.

Creed smiled. 'We're not calling him anything, Agent Mingus. Because we don't know him well enough yet.'

3

25 MARCH 1999

DIMMIT, TEXAS

GENTRY'S funeral glittered with badges. Jim Doe hid behind his sunglasses for most of it, like everybody else. But he was deeper, too. More hollow, since the scramble down county road 612, to Gentry's blood-splattered hood. Holding him like that. The hail coming in glass sheets, leaving the tape he tried to stretch around the car jagged and blowing.

Agnes, Gentry's widow, sat in the front row, her hands in her lap. Her two daughters were to either side of her, and then Randall Garza, the other deputy. The sky above them was empty, spent. If he tried—and it was the only good place to go, really—Jim Doe could remember driving back from the station house finally, after twenty-eight hours, how in each driveway along Bedford there had been a person standing, watching the clouds surge, the leading edge wisping up the grey face, to where it was darker still. They didn't know about Gentry yet, then. About Terra, the lines her hair had pressed into the side glass. Jim Doe had waved, his hand slight against the chrome of his mirror.

And the blue Impala. The luxury sedan. Its junk plate had turned up in a trashcan in Dumas. Dumas was in a straight line north from Nazareth into the panhandle of Oklahoma, all thirty-seven miles of it. Then the road opened up onto the flat grasslands of Kansas, the corn and the wheat and the sorghum swaying like a single, beaten sheet of gold.

The highway patrol had ferried two grim-faced Texas Rangers—

Bill McKirkle and Walter Maines—up to the Texhoma, where 54 crossed, and Jim Doe could almost see them standing there on either side of the blacktop, the butts of their rifles angled into their thighs, their helicopter pilot sitting his rig in the pasture behind them, waiting for the show, his toothpick rolling from one corner of his mouth to the other. It never came, though. The show. The longhair slipped them, maybe sidestepped off the Llano Estecado into the Five Civilized Tribes, the old Indian Territories, Oklahoma proper, where his skin and hair wouldn't give him away. Just the car. And the carrion birds that had to be following him by now. His trunk.

After the funeral, Jim Doe stood awkward, first on one leg, then the other, rolling the brim of his hat and letting it out again. Agnes was still there, the girls gone back to the house. Through the chain link of the cemetery, framed by the white brick of the school, third-graders were sliding on their slides and rushing through the air on their swings. Jim Doe didn't remember ever looking over here when he had been in elementary. It was like it didn't exist, this place. He might have seen himself there, though—now—and done everything different, just let go of the swing one day.

'I'm sorry, Agnes,' he said.

She was standing at the edge of the grave.

When she didn't turn her head up to him, he finally just left, hating that his truck was so loud, that he couldn't at least give her some peace out there. She still wasn't crying, was the thing. It scared him.

Five hours later, he was on the other side of the school, dribbling a basketball into the slick concrete, shooting free throws. They made sense. But then Gentry's oldest daughter Sarah was there.

'If you make ten in a row this time, will none of it have happened?' she asked. It wasn't really a question, more just her showing him that his skull was made of glass, that she could look right in. She'd learned it from her mother.

Jim Doe looked over at her. She was four years older than him, had been in the homecoming court when he was still waiting to get his learner's permit.

'Hey,' he said.

She nodded, took the bounce pass.

'They say he's gone,' she said—the longhair. 'Just . . . poof.'

Jim Doe chased her rebound down, held the ball between his hands.

'I've got a call in to VICAP—' he started, then again: 'the violent crimes people. FBI.'

'What about the video?' she asked.

'You can't see anything, really.'

'Not now,' she said. 'No. Not like it is.'

He shot. 'You've been seeing too many movies, Sare.'

'They have to be based on something.'

'This is Castro County.'

'Jim.'

He looked to her. She had the ball now.

'It won't bring him back either, you know,' he said, trying to use her line against her.

'It's not him I'm worried about,' she said back, chest-passing the ball at him, hard, her thumbnails clicking together on the follow-through, her eyes fixed on him already.

He said it again after she was gone—*it won't bring him back*—but this time it was for himself, so he could hear what he'd sounded like to her, what he hadn't.

He was there before classes started the next morning. Seven-thirty, the audio-visual room. The heaviest, thickest door in the high school. He didn't have the original tape, just one of the copies.

'You want *what?*' Weiner said, his chair skittering across the room on its plastic wheels.

Weiner ran the projectors, the cameras, all of it. He was a sophomore. There early, even.

Jim Doe looked back at the door, then patted Gentry's tape again. It was sitting on the TV cart. He was supposed to have it hand-delivered to Shirl at the post office by three.

'Just enhanced,' he said. 'You can do that, right?'

It was hard to say Weiner's name right, so he was trying to just not say it at all. At any moment Terra could appear in the doorway, too. He hadn't seen her since she'd sat in Interrogation Room B the afternoon of the twenty-first, waiting for her father to pick her up, the hall through the one-way glass full of law—Gentry's friends and family from three counties in either direction, Lubbock to Amarillo, DPS to SID, eighteen to seventy-five. When Jim Doe had walked through, his shirtfront congealed to a dark black, they had quieted, just let him pass. For the moment. He could feel it, though, that they'd already listened to Monica's audio of it. That they knew he hadn't been there. That Terra had been with him.

And when her father had walked in.

Jim Doe closed his eyes to make himself concentrate on Weiner.

'I'll be late for class,' he was saying, taking the tape.

'It's police business,' Jim Doe said back. 'I'll write you a note.'

Weiner turned the tape over, never looked up when he spoke. 'This is the original,' he said, impressed. Then he looked up. 'Thought you were mailing this one off to Dallas?'

'You hear this on the radio, or what?' Jim Doe said, then remembered who he was talking to. All the scanners and shortwave equipment Weiner had in his mother's garage.

'Why not just wait, then?' Weiner said. 'They have better equipment, y'know.'

'Because I wanted you,' Jim Doe said, still watching the door.

And because they might not think to show it to me when it comes back, he didn't say. If he even had a badge still, then.

'He's getting away . . .' Jim Doe said, hooking his chin out to the road, to the north.

Weiner stuffed the tape into the editing machine.

'I can't promise anything,' he said. 'This isn't the movies, you know?'

Jim Doe smiled. 'Pretend it is,' he said.

Weiner shrugged, bent to it.

By ten, he had something. Jim Doe had locked the door a long time ago. A fire hazard, but what the hell. The school hadn't burned down from cigarettes or prayers in forty years already. Maybe this would be forty-one.

Weiner eased the mouse around the tabletop.

The tape was a digital file now. It had taken two hours just to convert forty-eight seconds of visuals. But now they were ready. And it *was* like the movies: Weiner would select a portion of the field, zoom in, repeat, repeat, then let the algorithm smooth the edges until the blurry fabric of Gentry's khaki shirt dominated the screen.

'Try the shooter,' Jim Doe said, leaning over.

'I was,' Weiner said, through his teeth.

He backed up, eased in again. It made Jim Doe think of an inchworm, reaching out, then pulling the ground closer bit by bit.

Finally they got the back of the shooter's head, a real tight shot of hair so black it would had to have been inked blue in a comic book, just to look real.

'Like yours,' Weiner said.

'Back up again,' Jim Doe said.

Weiner did, undoing the Enhance, a Def Leppard shirt coming into focus for a moment—HYSTERIA—then backed the time index up too, to when the shooter was getting back into his car, that fraction of a second before Gentry leaned over the hood to look into the camera, out at Agnes and Jim Doe one last time.

The longhair had looked back to make sure Gentry was staying down.

Jim Doe smiled. Of course: *he* had just risen after being put on the ground. He probably expected Gentry to as well. But he hadn't.

Weiner paused the frame.

'Hollywood,' he said, and inched in, enhanced, inched in some more.

Soon the shadowy shape of the longhair's face filled the monitor.

'Sharpen it again,' Jim Doe said.

Weiner cocked his chin to the side in hesitation. 'Half of it's already made up by the computer, man. I don't know.'

He tried anyway, and the image degraded into watercolors, the vinyl roof of the car leaking over into the longhair's face, both his eyes merging into one raccoon smear.

'Okay,' Jim Doe said.

Weiner backed up, screwed the contrast up some, then did a color-replace on the shadowed part of the face. He used a pixel of the longhair's neck skin as the base. It wasn't bad. It wasn't real—evidence—but it wasn't bad.

'You can print that?' he asked.

'It's anybody,' Weiner said. 'You. With hair, I mean.'

They ran it through the printer anyway, and Jim Doe stood waiting for it, then held the sheet in both hands, fanning it to dry. The longhair. He was an Indian male, twenty-two to thirty-five, no identifying tattoos, indeterminate tribal affiliation. Armed and dangerous. Two corpses in his trunk. Heading north.

Jim Doe walked out into the eleven-o'clock glare, covered his eyes with his glasses again, and held the picture to the light, to see if it looked any better out there. It didn't.

That afternoon, making copies in the new silence of the vacated sheriff's offices, eyes crawling on his back, he got the callback from VICAP's Investigative Support Unit. He took it in Gentry's office.

'Jim Doe,' he said.

The agent on the other end almost laughed. 'Cody Mingus,' he said, around it. 'Just Cody.'

'As in Buffalo Bill—' Jim Doe said, leaving the space blank at the end for *Cody*.

'Excuse me?' Agent Mingus said.

'Nothing,' Jim Doe said.

Papers shuffled in Virginia—ninety-five data elements, faxed instead of entered—and then Agent Mingus was back on the receiver. 'You say your shooter had two bodies in his trunk?'

'What it looks like,' Jim Doe said. 'It was just a partial visual, though. It could have just been one, I guess. I don't know. There was one arm hanging out, anyway. They—or, it—was laying face up.'

'How could you tell that? If it was just a partial visual, I mean?'

'It was a right arm,' Jim Doe said. 'And the thumb, it was closest to the bumper.'

He looked at his own thumb as he said it.

'So . . .' he led off. 'You have anything to match that, or what?'

'Two bodies at once?' Agent Mingus said, like he was writing this all down.

'Yes.'

'Male, female . . . ?'

'*Human*, FBI. Short enough to fit longways in between the wheel wells of a full-size Chevy four-door. If that helps.'

'Maybe they were—?'

'The trunk would have hit their knees when it closed. So, no, they weren't folded. It was like mummies or something, I guess. Kid mummies.'

'So you didn't apprehend the shooter?'

Jim Doe smiled. It was like this was all staged. He told Agent Mingus no, then didn't say that he had been watching the clouds develop with a truant high school girl at the time. That she had been truant because of him.

Agent Mingus breathed out.

'Well?' Jim Doe said.

'We'll have to get back to you,' Agent Mingus said, his tone all about apology. Or trying to sound that way. The way a customer service representative regrets not being able to give you a full refund.

Jim Doe closed his eyes, leaned his head back over the edge of Gentry's chair. His chair now, until the election. Or Garza's.

'Is there *any*thing you can do?' Jim Doe asked.

'We're already doing it, I'm afraid,' Agent Mingus said. Halfway across the country, Jim Doe could see the way the phone was clamped between the agent's shoulder and jaw. How he was already looking at the sheet for his next call.

He gave Jim Doe a number, and Jim Doe wrote down *Buffalo Bill*, thanked him—not genuine, just habit—then sat at Gentry's desk looking at his calendar, all the things he was supposed to have done over the rest of March. As sheriff, husband, father.

At seven o'clock, he called Agnes.

'Indian Joe,' she said through the screen door. It was what Gentry had called Jim Doe the first time he saw him, when Jim Doe was still ten. The post office hadn't even been rebuilt then. Jim Doe stepped in, taking his hat off without having to think about it. There was food mounded everywhere, so Agnes wouldn't starve herself, maybe. Try to feed off her grief and nothing else.

'Sarah?' he asked.

'Beaumont,' Agnes said.

It was as far away as she could get and still be in Texas.

Lisa, the other sister, was standing under the red, slanted awning of the Dairy Queen, soaking up the night. Jim Doe had seen her on the way in. She was with some of the people she'd graduated with. They were looking at each other like dogs in the pound, and drinking cokes through narrow, blue-striped straws. It made their faces longer than they were, their chins flattened out against the plastic lids.

'It's your anniversary,' Jim Doe said.

He had a foil-wrapped present in his hand. The date had been on the calendar on Gentry's desk. He set the present on the mantel. It was nothing.

'I'm sorry,' he said again.

'I know,' Agnes said.

They sat at the kitchen table.

'Is it serious?' Agnes asked, 'at least?'

Jim Doe looked up. 'What?' he asked.

'That girl.'

He looked away. 'It's not like that,' he said, then, just 'No,' quieter, then that he was sorry again.

'You said that already,' Agnes said, touching his hand where he'd left it, on the table before him. 'I *know*, Joe.'

'Jim.'

Agnes smiled.

It was their usual routine.

Jim Doe looked up at her. The tablecloth between them was checkered. Like chain link, and the food, Jim Doe finally got it: for Agnes, the act of cooking would remind her of Gentry, remind her that she was just cooking for herself now.

'I should have been there, I mean,' he said. 'Agnes.'

Agnes was looking right at him. 'Tom carried a gun, Joe. Because he expected somebody to shoot at him someday. He always used to say that. I'm just glad it wasn't anybody from town. Anybody we know.'

Jim Doe nodded.

'He won't get away with it,' he said. 'I won't let him.'

Agnes smiled. 'Thank you,' she said. 'But Joe. Let the state police handle this. Walter Maines said—'

'Tom never hired Walter Maines or Bill McKirkle when it was that or the Air Force, Agnes. Or worse.'

Agnes nodded, looked away. Into the past maybe.

'He told your dad he would take care of you, Joe,' she said.

Jim Doe didn't say anything. His mouth was too full right then. And then a pair of headlights washed across the back of the kitchen curtains, and for an instant he'd never expected, he saw Agnes as she must have been when Tom Gentry married her. As a bride. A young woman waiting for her husband to come home again, like at the end of every other normal, ordinary day. It was the way she held her head to the window. Like those were *his* headlights. Like none of this was real, like everything was going to be all right.

It wasn't Walter Maines at the door, though, with a trophy. Or Bill McKirkle. Either would have been better.

It was Benjamin Donner. Terra's father.

There was just a screen between him and Jim Doe now.

Jim Doe looked back at Agnes, held his hand up for her to stay there, then stepped out onto the porch.

'Ben,' he said.

His hat was back on his head already. Trying to be casual, not hide his eyes.

Benjamin Donner laughed. 'How'd I know you'd be out here?' he said.

Jim Doe shrugged. 'You're telepathic?'

Benjamin looked over at him, away, and when he came back it was with the backside of his thick forearm. It caught under Jim Doe's chin and pressed him up against the weathered clapboard of the front of Gentry's house.

He could have stopped him too, probably. But he didn't. His gun was still on his hip.

'. . . Ben,' he said as best he could, one of his hands on Benjamin's sinewy wrist, the other on his elbow. So his chin wouldn't have to support all the weight.

Benjamin was just staring at him.

Jim Doe's hat was brim-down on the porch. The wind pushed it to the edge, then it cartwheeled off. Benjamin looked up at Jim Doe's hair. It wasn't regulation. By about three months.

Benjamin laughed again.

'Just like him,' he said.

The longhair.

'You probably knew him, right?' he said.

And then Jim Doe saw it, over the padded shoulder of Benjamin's coveralls: the dome light of Benjamin's truck glowing on. The cab was milling with people, three at least. And there were more shapes muttering in the bed. In Texas. Where they'd chased all the Indians out a century ago, and killed all their horses just to make it stick, then sent the sons of the cavalrymen out a century later, to collect the bones on the weekends, sell them in town by the truckload, for soap to wash themselves with.

'. . . Ben,' Jim Doe said, no breath. 'You don't—Terra. It's not what you thi—'

Benjamin pushed forward though, choking off the rest.

'*Don't you goddamn tell me what I think*,' he said, his lips not involved at all.

Jim Doe made himself breathe, breathe, but still: his hand found the butt of his gun.

'You're assaulting a—' he started, then Agnes cut him off.

She was standing beside Benjamin Donner, holding the screen door open with her hip. Gentry's quail gun was nestled behind Benjamin's ear. A Browning 16 gauge.

'*Ben*,' she said. 'Go home.'

Benjamin stared at Jim Doe for long moments, then finally let him slide down the wall.

'Agnes,' he said. 'You of all people—'

'Ben,' Agnes said. 'I'm saving your worthless life here. For Magritte.'

She hadn't taken the gun off him yet.

When Jim Doe slid the catch off his hammer, Agnes shook her head no.

'You too,' she said. 'Inside.'

Jim Doe looked out into the darkness, at the truck, the men waiting for him, all the dry, abandoned places they knew where nobody would ever look, and then he backed inside.

Agnes came in when Ben's truck was gone.

She was crying. Finally.

She went to the cigar box Gentry had always kept on the shelf, by the outdated encyclopedias Sarah and Lisa had plagiarized for all their book reports. She brought it to the table. There was seventeen hundred dollars in it.

She held it out across the table for Jim Doe.

'Take it,' she said. 'You're right. The only way they'll . . . not be like that is if you catch him. And you know if Bill and Walter find him, God. Tom would have wanted him to stand trial, Joe. James.'

'I'll pay it back,' Jim Doe said.

Agnes smiled.

'No you won't,' she said. 'Just come back alive. For Tom.'

Jim Doe looked back at her once, not saying anything, then pushed the door open onto the night, stepped out into it.

4

27 MARCH 1999

LIBERAL, KANSAS

HE'D got the Impala the old way—just led it away from its dirt lot in Jonesboro, Arkansas. Just down from Bethel. It was where the mechanic put vehicles that still had outstanding bills. Nobody would miss it from there for weeks, and when they did, the mechanic would say the owner had an extra key, drove it away one night, *stole* it, and the owner would say that the mechanic chopped it after hours, sold it down into Mexico. Nobody would look for the actual car, though, except the insurance company that finally got stuck with it, and that would be after all the claims got filed, the police reports filled out, and still, it would just be a thing of principle. Because nobody really wanted it. Except him.

He took it because it was Chevrolet, and he knew GM ignition systems. His father had been a mechanic, he thought. Or an engineer. An inventor. He led the Impala out to an oily streetlight. It took him eight minutes to get it started. That was too long, he knew—unacceptable—but he kept blacking out, and his hands were shaking, or his eyes, or the world itself.

He sat in the driver's seat and idled down a half block, lights off, the sole of his sneaker skimming the surface of the road. His other car was there, his Tennessee car. The car he'd left in Tennessee had been the Virginia car, a primered Monte Carlo. The Tennessee car was a Thunderbird, from when they'd been long and heavy. It hadn't been his first choice. But the trunk. He could have kept *eight* children in there, then curled up beside them, pulled the lid down.

He backed the Impala up to the Thunderbird—already facing the other way—and once he'd worked both trunk lids open from the inside, they were a roof for him. He held the two bodies close when he moved them, and for too long, touching their dry cheeks with the inner skin of his lips, whispering where they could hear.

The Thunderbird he left idling, to make sure somebody would take it.

At the first gas station, the first strong lights, he checked under the Impala's hood. The mechanic had put a new fan clutch on it. He should have put a water pump too, while he'd been in there. But it was free. He cleaned the windows, wiped down the handle of the squeegee, then turned the speakers on the back dash upside down, to fill the trunk with music. For the children.

The car was blue, the vinyl top in ribbons.

He thumbed the tape in from the bag he had. They were all the same album, all taken from the same rack set near the front door of one of the drugstores he'd hit. Memphis, maybe. Or Knoxville. They'd had the rollgate down over the pharmacy window, though, meaning no phenobarb, no Dilantin, so he'd had to make do with over-the-counter sleep aids. They were almost enough to keep the seizures down, inside him, so that he was only convulsing *under* the skin. He got some liver pills too, just so they wouldn't be there if anybody needed them.

He drove, and tried not to think.

Arkansas at night was too black, though. Twice he slept; once he skated the chrome bumper of the Impala along a concrete holding wall. He didn't hear it until miles later, when Little Rock was finally spitting him out into a tangle of single-lane construction. It became I-30 after a while, flattening out into farmland, and he told himself it was west, kind of. Maybe. After Virginia, though, he wasn't sure the roads stayed the same if you didn't look at them every foot of every mile, keep track of the yellow lines in your head. A black and white was behind him anyway, pacing. Meaning he no longer had the muscle control to turn the car around. The road was never wide enough, the time never right.

In Texarkana he changed his m.o. on purpose, to mislead anybody who'd noticed him: instead of stealing a Texas car, to fit in—so the cops wouldn't aim their radar guns at him like he was a tourist—he just lifted a set of Nebraska plates from the bathroom wall of a breakfast place, where they were decoration, then watched the blue lid of his trunk as he screwed the two bolts into the rear bumper. There were flies at the keyhole. He drove slow through the rest of town, letting them keep up, the flies, but then they pushed him where he didn't want to go, where he was always going: the firehouse.

He shook his head no, no, his hair tying itself to the faded headrest, making him look. No. He wanted to swallow his tongue on purpose, to hold the lighter to his chest, to do anything but be here. It was like a church he had to go to though, park at, stare into. The firehouse.

He held the wheel with both hands and stared hard at the windshield, just the windshield, and then there was a hand on his shoulder. It was later. There was saliva dry on his chin now, the kind that had been foamy, spit up from deep inside. Medicinal. His first thought was of the flies, then the children. Then the hand.

It was a fireman.

They were all out washing their big red truck.

'You okay, buddy?' he asked.

Buddy.

He stared.

'I'm not Buddy,' he said.

The fireman stared back at him. He was wearing rubber pants with the reflective stripe down the side, the big boots, the helmet, against the distant fire of the sun. Just a white T-shirt, though, the kind you buy folded in a plastic bag. And not any gloves.

It was the no gloves that did it. The hands, the hand, held out to him.

He worked his fingers into his pocket for whatever bottle was there, swallowed a handful of pills dry. His throat bled from it, and he swallowed that too.

'I'm okay,' he told the fireman, making his fingers into a careful okay, then pulled away, the fireman standing there behind him, watching him.

At Greenville, just outside Dallas, there was another cop, a city one. He flashed his lights once in the Impala's rearview then turned around. Like it was a game. Like they were all playing with him. He could feel the miles accumulating inside him, a hard black knot.

He took to the small roads to hide it, to keep it down; skirted Dallas. The Impala heaved from ditch to ditch, drunk with sleep, and he turned the stereo up.

At the truck stop in Weatherford, he ran pink soap between his fingers, massaged it in. He was humming the song from the tape—maybe his father had been a bookkeeper for an auto parts store—content just to wash his cuticles, the hollow space on the backside of his wrist. But then a truck driver approached him in the mirror, his boots heavy like a fireman's, and time dilated around them, the instant blooming open, and he ran out past all the slowed-down people, down the snack aisle, shielding himself from the candy, then past the register girl with the sharp teeth, and finally to the car, but just the passenger side. Because the glove box was open now. Had opened itself. Maybe that's where the flies had all gone, or been hiding.

He walked past the car like it wasn't his, like he could trick it, then crept up again, on the driver's side. The same. He settled into the seat. In the cardboard back of the glove compartment were two things: a black comb, with the teeth getting thinner and thinner towards the end, like piano keys sound, and a set of keys tagged white. They fit the door and the ignition and the trunk. He wired the ignition back in for them—because it looked good to have keys, Officer, especially with out-of-state plates—and screwed the backrest of the backseat in all the way too, because he could just use the key on the trunk lid now, not have to go in the back way anymore.

It took forty-two minutes to get it all done, and then the on-ramp for 20 was right in front of him, the fireman behind, pretending to eyeball the beef jerky in the plastic display case. He took it, the ramp, and flew across the flat land, to 87 heading north. Finally. Making up for Texas.

South of Plainview, though, he saw the sign—Nazareth—and then the fireman rising up from the yellow stripes in his rearview. He was chasing him, his footfalls heavy enough to send great clumps of asphalt up into the night, where they became birds.

'I'm White,' he said into the mirror. 'You don't know me.'

Maybe it would work.

He had found him before, though.

But Nazareth. It was historical, where it had all started.

He walked through its stores, looking for something. He wasn't sure what. Just looking. It was almost familiar. He smiled at the girl with the normal teeth as he lifted the chocolate bar. Not that he would eat it, of course. Do that to his teeth, his gums. He just wanted her to see him take it, was all. Because then she wouldn't see the bottle of Nyquil tucked into his rear pocket, upside down.

She smiled back.

'You kin to that deputy?' she asked.

He narrowed his eyes at her, started to tell her she didn't know him either, that he was White, but then winked instead, extended his fingers to the tile ceiling, lifted himself up onto the roof, climbing down the side of the building on the ridges the day laborers had left in the stucco, careful the whole time to be sure and leave a memory in the girl's head of him walking out the front doors. Which he did too. Like in Weatherford.

They were waiting for him in the car. The children. Just staring.

'Soon,' he told them, and closed it again, and then on the way out of town he passed a border patrol going the other way, and watched in his rearview for the sick-green car to turn around, follow him. Call the helicopters in and describe him on their radio. He slowed down for it to catch him. Out at the church, it finally did, and he understood why it had fallen behind: to change paints, the pale green slipping off, leaving the white underneath. It was a sheriff car now. Still an LTD, though. He smiled, said a name he didn't know: *Gentry*. This had been coming for four states now—all the cops gathering in his rearview, finally balling themselves up into one fat one, with heavy hands. The children were already singing about him. Could the cop not hear? Gentry?

He said the name out loud, trying to imagine where it was from, why he knew it, but then the cop did a thing with his hat which was the same thing you do with a helmet, if you're wearing one and it's night—a yellow helmet, the brim long in back, to keep embers and ash from funneling down your collar.

And his shirt, the brass plaque on his shirt pocket: *Gentry*.

He was already dying.

'Got some ID?' he said.

Yes. Here's who I am.

He leaned into the car, to the passenger seat, for the gun he'd stolen, peeled from the bottom of a cargo van, one side of it sprayed white, like drywall. It was the only thing to do now, but then it didn't fire. Wouldn't. The cartridge in the chamber was gummed up, the white overspray coating the back of the shell, padding it against the firing pin. He should have known.

The whole time the cop was beating him, then, he could hear the children through the metal, saying his name to him, his real name: *A-mos*, *A-mos*, *A-mos*. He closed his eyes and leaned closer to the car, to hear, and then he rose again, his hair in his face, the gun light in his hand, white on one side, black on the other, and said the cop's name out loud.

It was his first time to kill in four years.

It rushed through him, filling the space behind the hinges of his jaw, heating his eyes, and he felt himself smiling, knew it was going to be too late again, soon. That it was going to be too hard to stop again.

He pulled the trigger again after the cop was dead, just to dance him and this was so right.

Pulling away, he leaned down to his side mirror, to see his teeth.

They were all there. He was Amos again.

He smiled, turned the radio up with both hands, the right dragging the left across the dials, the chain glinting between. By Oklahoma his front passenger side tire was throwing sparks. He could see it reflected in the shiny sides of cars he passed at night. He liked it.

5

30 MARCH 1999

GOVE, KANSAS

THE old man was standing in front of the convenience store. It was six o'clock maybe. The fluorescents under the awning made the snow look whiter than it was. The tires of Jim Doe's Bronco crunched it down. He'd been in four-wheel drive for miles, now, the gas gauge diving. He'd been so alone in his lane that he hadn't even had to pull over to lock the hubs. He'd just done it in the road. This was Kansas.

The old man looked up out of his pea coat collar at Jim Doe. He was Indian. Jim Doe nodded. His deputy jacket wasn't thick enough for the wind. Opening the glass door, he lowered his head into the old snow whipping around the corner, but his hat was still in Texas and he got a face full of hair instead. His own. The tip ends bit into his eyes. The old Indian was still watching him.

'What town is this?' Jim Doe called out.

The old man looked around.

'Glove,' he said. Maybe. Or *dove*. The bird. His voice was clipped like the reservation.

'What?' Jim Doe asked.

Love?

The old man pointed at the sign above the store. It read GOVE QUICKSTOP, in flickering neon.

Jim Doe nodded at the old man again, in thanks, and stepped in. Gove. It was up towards 70, on the map. Just west of Trego Center, where nobody'd seen the longhair either. There was no trail, just miles and miles of blacktop spooling out over the prairie. 'Usually snow this late?' Jim Doe asked the girl behind the counter.

She didn't even look up from her magazine. 'Weird year,' she said. 'Like last one y'know?'

Jim Doe nodded: weird, yes. 'Pretty soon this'll just be normal,' he said.

The girl popped her gum in response.

Jim Doe looked out at the old man, still standing there. The Bronco was idling, its exhaust curling up past the tailgate, the snow falling on the hood turning into individual droplets of water. But it kept falling there anyway.

'Who's he?' he asked the clerk.

She still wasn't looking up. 'Who?' she said.

Jim Doe stared at her.

'Coffee's there,' she pointed. At the side of the store, just past the fountain drinks. Her nail was perfect red. Joe followed it, poured one cup, then another, pressed the lids down onto the white foam lips.

At the checkout counter he asked if they got many out-of-towners this time of year.

The girl finally looked up at him. Just her eyes.

'You,' she said.

Jim Doe took out one of the flyers he'd made, unrolled it on the counter for her.

'Him?' he asked.

The girl looked down at the face.

'This a joke?' she said.

'It's not me,' Jim Doe said. He'd had to say it in Montezuma and in Jetmore and in Bazine already. He knew he should have gone to Oklahoma, too. That's where everybody else was, working with the tribal police, stopping every blue Impala with an Indian driver, and hitting the barbershops too. Because maybe he'd changed his appearance. Become Jim Doe. Or maybe he'd been him all along.

The girl was smiling now. 'He supposed to have come through here or something?' she asked.

'Nebraska plates,' Jim Doe said. Which was true, as far as it went.

'You're from Texas,' the girl said.

Jim Doe nodded.

'But you're Indian,' she said.

'Blackfeet.'

She laughed some. 'Let me see your hands,' she said.

Jim Doe did, unsure, keeping his elbows close to his ribs. She pulled his hands the rest of the way across the counter though, turned one over then the other. Shrugged.

'Yeah,' she said. 'One of my boyfriends was from Browning. It's something about the fingers with you *Pie*gan'—she rolled her eyes when she said it, like she'd been trained to say it like that, *pay*-gun—'how they look at certain angles.'

Jim Doe looked at them, his hands.

'What are you doing down here, though?' she asked. 'Long way from Montana, cowboy. Yeah?'

Jim Doe flattened the copy of the face on the counter.

'I was born in Texas,' he said, his lungs full of air. 'My dad was in the—' He looked away though, at the cooler, stopping himself. 'Listen,' he said. 'Have you seen him?'

She smiled, flirting now. 'Your father?'

Jim Doe didn't answer.

She looked down. Shook her head no.

'I should have xeroxed his hands, right?'

She rang up his coffee.

He'd almost told her when his dad signed out of the Air Force, he'd been in Big Springs, that was all—*why*. Like it was an excuse. Like he needed one. Or needed to tell her, explain how he really was Indian, just in Texas.

He held both cups close to his stomach and opened the door with his back, nodding bye to the girl at the last possible instant. He was glad to have the coffee in his hands, too. Because she would have been looking at them.

In the parking lot, the old man was waiting for him.

Jim Doe tried walking to his truck. He could feel the old man watching him, though, measuring his steps. Finally he turned to him.

The old man was smiling.

Gove. Somebody should have warned him about this Gove.

He offered one of the cups to the old man, already shuffling across the parking lot, taking it in both hands. Jim Doe looked away from his fingers. The steam from the coffee caressed the old man's face. He said something in some kind of Indian to Jim Doe.

'No problem,' Jim Doe said.

The old man looked over at the idling Bronco.

'Where you going?' he said. In English.

Jim Doe lifted his cup to his mouth.

'You?' he asked.

One side of the old man's mouth hooked up into a smile. 'North,' he said. 'Home.'

Jim Doe looked north. For no reason that made any sense.

'Sorry,' he said to the old man. For no reason either. That it was a Castro County vehicle and he considered himself on duty here, but that didn't matter. Not this far from the county. And without orders. Without anybody *to* order.

Jim Doe shrugged.

The old man shrugged back.

'Thanks for the coffee,' he said, splitting *coffee* into two words somehow. Like he wanted to make it last.

Jim Doe nodded.

Alone in his truck, then, he sat there, taking small, hot sips.

The old man was just standing there. Waiting for Jim Doe to go south. The way he had to have seen the Bronco just come from.

The girl was reading her magazine.

And the face, the longhair. He was taped on the backside of the glass of the convenience store door, looking out. At approximately the same height he'd looked like from Gentry's dashboard. Jim Doe studied it—*him*—then backed out, slid to a slow, drifting stop, and crawled the Bronco to the front of the parking lot.

He'd already *been* south, was the thing.

He shook his head, said to himself what the hell, clipping the words in his head, and reached over for the passenger side door handle. The wind opened it, flung it as far as the hinge went, but the old man didn't step in. Jim Doe looked in the rearview mirror—empty—so he turned around, to look through the back glass. Nothing. Just the front of the store.

'Old Indian trick,' he said to himself, smiling—it was an Eastwood line, maybe—then popped first gear to close the door, and had to slam the brakes before he could even get the clutch back down.

The old man was standing right in front of him. Still holding his coffee.

The truck was dead, the headlights paler for it.

'That face you're looking for,' the old man said from the passenger seat, two miles closer to 70. 'He's Indian, enit?'

Jim Doe nodded. 'My brother,' he said, half a joke.

The old man looked hard at the shotgun locked in place between them, aimed up at the sky, then raised his cup, took the longest drink in the history of long drinks.

'Only one place to be if you're Indian tonight,' he said, and winked at Jim Doe. 'Put your ear to the ground, you can hear it.'

6

30 MARCH 1999

KALVESTA, KANSAS

HE was throwing up in the ditch now. Amos. The half-digested pills rolling in the dust like punctured ticks, spilling his blood. He was screaming too, a thin line of snot connecting him to the ground, trying to pull him in, under. He raised his head, held his hands over his eyes, but the yellow jacket was there, burned into the backside of his lids. The man in it was holding a long metal pole.

He drove.

He set a fire in the ditch with the lighter from his dashboard, and he *drove*. Maybe the fire would slow him down. Maybe all of Kansas would burn. He poured his Nyquil out the vent window and it clung to the side glass for as long as it could, beading thick against the felt weather-stripping and finally clumping over, into the void behind him. Texas. Oklahoma. Kansas.

What was the metal pole *for?* He'd never had a metal *pole* before.

He had to find a drugstore. This far gone, even straight morphine would do. He would shoot it into his tearduct if he had to, then let the numbness spread out from there. It would be the opposite of crying.

He drove, and drove, and then on one of the turns on 156 the front passenger side tire went and that was almost it, he was almost over, this, *this* was almost over, but then the road on the passenger side of the car banked up for him suddenly, so the car could lean against it instead of shooting off into the ditch, the telephone poles, the fences. Something always saved him.

But the spare. He couldn't get it—the children were lying on it. It would interrupt them to open the trunk. To see him like this.

He could do it, though. He drove on the rim, one side of the car hooked over onto the grass shoulder, where it was softer. Where the rim would last, maybe. He had to hang onto the left side of the steering wheel with both hands, to keep the car straight. It was foolish. He started laughing and turned the stereo up, the tape in the stereo. The mechanized hum of another world. *I crossed my old man.*

A mile marker folded under the car, scraped the oil pan, tore out the belly of the muffler.

It didn't matter.

The handcuffs. He had to get the handcuffs off first. He could do it with a paper clip, he thought, but to get it into the lock he'd have to hold it in his teeth, and the sound of metal on enamel, it would bleed out his ear, and the blood would collect in the dead space over his collarbone, and congeal there, and then everyone would know who he was, what he'd done.

The dry heads of the grass were silk rubbing against the rough Chevrolet frame.

He thought about leaving the car in low then running ahead, holding the chain of the handcuffs in the path of the rim he was pushing. It was sharp and raw. He'd have to tie the steering wheel over with a rag. And set the accelerator somehow. And then pull his arm out before the rim rolled to his shoulder. And then catch the car.

He drove.

Fifteen miles per hour, bits of hot rubber slinging themselves up onto the hood in defeat, or surrender. Once a big truck honked at him the whole time it was passing. He stared after it, trying to memorize the mural that had been on the side. For future reference. For standing next to that particular driver at a long row of urinals, the wall before them not yet splattered with blood and grey matter, the more particular shades of regret.

The next town was two miles away. Kalvesta. It was on the way to

Lydia. Lydia was where he was going. He'd forgotten for a while—driving north and east, fast, away from Texas, *any* way—but now he remembered again: Lydia.

Then, like the tire wasn't bad enough, pushing it through the tall grass and soft earth spun the water pump out, the bearing in there reeling silver angel hair out against the race.

He could hear it, feel all the heat building up in the engine.

Two miles.

The Impala limped into town on three tires, favoring the tender steel rim. He nosed it into a service station, pulled the hood open from under the dash. Steam billowed up into the sky. He still had the handcuffs on.

Before anything else—the station attendant approaching, shielding himself from the steam with a small, red rag—he had to protect the children. He did. He turned into a white person so as not to attract attention—*White*—all his hair telescoping into his scalp, pressing on his brain so that he had to set his teeth against it, hard, then broke the round key off in the trunk lock, using both hands because of the six-inch chain between his wrists. He had his shirt hanging from the chain, wrapped in his hands. Like he'd used it to twist the radiator cap off a few minutes ago, maybe. Probably.

He followed the side of the car around to the open hood. The station attendant was trying to see through the steam. He looked up, the brim of his dingy brown hat framing his eyes. They were blue. The stitching on his shirt read TAYLOR.

'I know you?' Taylor asked, pushing his hat back on his head to see better. The sleeve of one side of his overalls was rolled up the forearm, his hand extended out of it, like to shake, and something about that exact posture changed Taylor for an instant. It started at the fingertips, then went up the arm like oil, thickening the forearm, making the rolled-up sleeve of his coveralls into the oversized cuff of a fireman's jacket.

'No,' Amos croaked, shaking his head no, please. 'You don't know me. I'm White.'

He couldn't look up, at the face.

But the handshake.

There was only one thing to do.

He reached under the hood and placed his bare palm against the radiator cap. The skin sizzled, curling back from the heat, and he fell to his knees, mouth open in a scream, just no sound.

'*Holy*—' Taylor started to say, becoming himself again, then the water started pressuring out from under the cap. It was like a sprinkler head now. In hell.

Amos backed off, holding his hand—his hands—close to his stomach, staring his eyes wide.

Taylor dove for the water hose, pointing Amos inside, to the garage. How there was a first aid kit there, and a fucking *man*ual for automobile safety precautions.

Amos turned, stumbled into the cool, dank air of the garage, and stood among the tools. His hand didn't hurt anymore, never had. Not really, not him. He became Indian again and slowly removed the Def Leppard shirt from the chain of the handcuffs and straightened it on the hood of a Cutlass. It was his favorite shirt, the one concert he'd ever been to.

The chain he set on a vise. The vise was welded to a three-inch pipe, the pipe set in concrete poured into an old seventeen-inch Ford wheel. There were probably bolt cutters here somewhere, a torch even, maybe a guillotine rigged from a cherry picker or something even more medieval, but the vise would work. He took a slag hammer by the very end of the handle, to make the most of the six inches of motion he had, then fixed the chain in the vise and tried to hit it with the hammer, missed; came down on the table instead, throwing sparks. Taylor heard, looked around, under the brim of his hat. He shouldn't have.

Right next to the vise was a bench grinder, with a foot pedal. Amos smiled. He wasn't White. He held the leading edge of the slag hammer under the grinder until it was shiny sharp, a flat point, then worked it between one of the links of the chain, started twisting, passing the handle of the hammer from one hand to the other. After three revolutions, the chain snapped; his hands fell free. And then he looked at the hammer, past it to Taylor, the Impala.

Kalvesta.

Maybe they wouldn't mind if he stayed here an hour or two.

7

30 MARCH 1999

GARDEN CITY, KANSAS

THREE hours after letting him into the Bronco, Jim Doe and the old man pulled into Garden City. It was back to the south, towards 156. The wrong way. There were already flyers of the longhair in the windows of some of the stores. The high school the old man directed them to was circled by probably eighty cars. They were Indian-issue. Hardly any of the fenders matched, and the only speed they had was leaning forward all the way, somebody's hands on the wheel at one and eleven, just wide enough for them to set their face, see. Jim Doe had heard some joke like that. People were always bringing them to him, Indian jokes, like he was supposed to laugh. He never could remember them until it was too late, though—until whoever'd brought it was leaned back, launching off into the punch line. Then he'd get it, Jim Doe, dread it, turn away because he'd always thought the side profile of his smile was less insincere than head-on.

Garden City. Like Eden.

Jim Doe trolled up one aisle of cars and down the other, and suddenly, impossibly, close enough that it had to have gotten there early, there it was: the Impala. Different plates, but the pattern of rips in the rotted vinyl top was burned into the back of Jim Doe's retinas. And there was a ragged dog nosing around the trunk, already slinking off.

The old man looked behind them and beside them when Jim Doe killed the truck right behind the Impala. He looked over to Jim Doe.

'You sure?' he asked.

Jim Doe nodded.

Jim Doe climbed down into the parking lot. He'd parked close enough to the Impala that he had to leave his door open for the old man to come out his side. He didn't wait for him.

The car.

He ran his hand over its lines, the tips of his fingers not even touching the snow enough to mark it. He wanted to call the DPS, the FBI. Agnes. But a white cop in an Indian place like this. Or, *cops*. All the men would fold themselves into lockers, spin the locks from the inside, stay there as long as they had to. And he wanted to bring him in himself, anyway, the longhair.

The rear door was still dented where Gentry had thrown him into it.

The steering wheel was rubbed shiny across the horn, right where your palms would rest if you were wearing handcuffs.

There was no rearview mirror.

Jim Doe looked up, remembering he wasn't alone here. Not quite. The old man was standing off. One car over, maybe.

'Thanks,' Jim Doe said.

'You could hear it, couldn't you?' the old man said, and when Jim Doe didn't get it, the old man dropped to one knee, dipping his ear to the ground, the tips of his grey hair brushing the snow.

Jim Doe left him like that. Turned back to the car. With one of the teeth of his truck key he hissed the air out of all four of the Impala's tires. The snow crunched as the radials settled down over it. They were all brand new, a matching set. At the front bumper, where the overflow hose ran, was a green-edged hole. Radiator fluid, very clean. At the rear bumper, the tailpipe was cold, the inside scorched black.

But the trunk. Jim Doe looked at it for a long time, the wind swirling around his legs, then turned his face up to the gym. The old man was already there, probably. That much farther from home, or, with all these Indians, the basketball, that much closer, maybe.

It didn't matter: he was here, the longhair.

Jim Doe palmed his wallet for a five—the seventeen hundred still bunched in the zipper part—and gave it to the mother sitting at her table at the door. She pulled hard on a cigarette, all the smoke rushing out of her mouth, into the haze inside.

'Who's playing?' Jim Doe asked, nodding towards the stands.

'Funny,' she said, and gave him three dollars change. One of the bills had a sharp blue goatee drawn on George Washington. Jim Doe folded it into his wallet with the rest, let her stamp his hand with a red wagon wheel, then stepped all the way in. The warm air stung his eyes and he blinked, blurring the crowd, smelling the dried saliva he always smelled at gyms, from people spitting on the floor, rubbing the soles of their shoes in it.

The longhair, though. That was all he was thinking, all he was trying to think.

He shook out a copy like the one he'd been taping up, but, as he was smoothing it, a group of four fifteen-year-olds slouched past, round-shouldered, their hands not so much buried in their pockets as thrust. Three of them had hair most of the way down their backs. The other was shaved bald, a tribal design tattooed into his scalp. He stared at Jim Doe, bared his teeth at the last possible instant, then passed. Jim Doe only flinched on the inside.

He turned back to the mother's table.

'Yeah?' she asked, looking at the flyer.

Jim Doe looked back to her, could see she was going to say it—see *him* there, on the flyer, instead of the longhair.

'Old man come through here?' he asked, finally. In defeat.

'Your grampa?' she asked back.

Jim Doe shrugged: sure. One big family. All my relations. Maybe you've seen my brother here, too. My mother, wherever she is. My sister.

The woman pointed at the two doors leading up into the stands. Jim Doe thanked her, walked across the cafeteria floor. For some reason he felt certain there was an institutional fork stuck in the ceiling tile thirty-four feet above him. Waiting for him. But if he looked it would fall into his eye, and then he'd have that to deal with.

He went back to the mother at the table again.

'There any other way out of here?' he asked.

'He's probably just getting nachos or something, think?'

Jim Doe stood, scanning for a side door. Because the longhair was going to see the sheriff jacket, the gun.

Jim Doe took the jacket off, folded it over his arm, on the side his gun was on.

'What if there's a fire?' he asked.

'I'll come tell you personal,' the mother said back, and blew a line of smoke between them. A signal to leave.

Jim Doe stepped aside for a man. The back of his hand looked like he'd just been shot. He was licking it like a wound, too, looking far ahead. Jim Doe followed him with his eyes, to a corner behind some folded tables. When he came back out, there were two more men with him. One of them was looking at the back of his hand, in appreciation. Jim Doe smiled: the fire door. That's where it was. Walking under the idea of the fork again, he touched the butt of his gun with the side of his forearm, just being sure.

He walked through the second set of doors and the noise of the crowd rushed up the hall all around him. He stepped up onto the first ramp there was, to the gym floor, then stood against the rail like he was here for the game, nothing else. In Nazareth he would have tipped his hat back to show he was just him, not a Deputy. If he had a hat.

The game was an Indian school and a white school. A replay of last year's regional finals. There was fry bread in the air. During a free throw, when everybody was on the edge of their seat, leaning forward for him, Jim Doe turned around to catalogue them but hadn't gotten anywhere before they exploded up, screaming. He turned back to the game, felt more than heard the scoreboard click another Indian point up, and then, from the corner of his eye, an old *Hysteria* shirt eased past.

It didn't even register for a full ten seconds—Def Leppard—but when it did he turned so fast he spilled a woman's coke. It slung all the way into the first row. He tried to catch her popcorn, but there were too many kernels, too much space between his fingers. Everyone for five people deep was looking at them. At him. And Jim Doe just didn't have time right now. He stuffed the three dollars from his wallet into her hand and took long steps back down the ramp, made the fire door at a run. It was closed. He ran his fingers along the rod that drove into the cylinder, to keep it from ever slamming. It was cold, frosted over a bit, even.

Good.

And he wouldn't have gone out the main door. There was a knot of white people there, all going the other way with their foam hands and plastic hats. One of them had a balloon feather tied to the back of his head, even, and lipstick under his eyes.

Jim Doe turned away, back to the hall, followed it into the lightless bowels of the high school. His heart was hammering in his shirt; the catch was off the hammer of his gun. Soon he was running across the low-pile carpet, rounding corners onto rows and rows of lockers. But always there was sound just ahead of him. And then it was all around.

He followed it to the practice gym.

The lights had been hit, but weren't warm yet, were still wriggling worms of heat far above.

Below them, at half court, was what looked like two people at first, but then it was just one. He was thrashing around on the floor like he was hurt. Or a seizure. He tried to stand but fell to his knees, tilted his head back, his hair touching his heels behind him, and screamed an animal scream, his voice ragged at the edges, booming over the hardwood.

Jim Doe held his hands over his ears, trying to make sense here, his mouth open too, like he was going to scream, or needed to. The only handle he could find on the situation was his gun.

He drew it when the lights finally came on, all at once, blinding him, and then held it loose before him, shielding his eyes with his other hand, angling the barrel of the gun in the general direction of half-court, and didn't realize what a mistake that was until the folded, metal chair came up to meet his face, and the last thing he knew was his gun, spinning on its side across the waxed floor, and then he didn't know anything anymore. Just what a soft place the world was. How little it hurt to fall.

8

31 MARCH 1999

QUANTICO, VIRGINIA

THE call came for Creed, but Creed wasn't there, so Cody took it.

It was nearly midnight.

Special Agent *Mingus*, as Creed called him—officially reassigned, now, a Wise Man for as long as the task force lasted—was in the office trying to catch up. Watts had told him now that he was on, he could just truck the box of files home, they had back-ups, but Cody had told her that the light was better up here. She had looked up to the long fluorescent bulbs, back down to him. Shrugged, left him to it.

And Creed, he was a ghost.

Instead of drinking coffee with him over a long conference table in an off-limits, soundproof room high above America, Cody was mostly just hearing about Creed. As in *he was just* here, *man*. Some of the rooms Cody walked into still had papers fluttering—Creed—or a lampshade still warm, but that was it.

Cody waited until five-thirty, carried the box into the room with the screen he'd drawn on. Unofficial headquarters—as official as a task force that didn't exist could have. There was a phone in it. He fanned the folders out on the round table, arranged them chronologically.

First, there were the crime scene photos, the black-and-white film really pushing the contrast. What the killer wanted, probably. Cody arranged the photos on a bare part of the carpet, on an East Coast he was imagining, then returned to the folders. He was looking for orientations—where the children who weren't children had been *looking*. Facing, anyway.

It took him all of two hours, a protractor (commandeered from Eggers, down the hall), and about forty little squares of masking tape, but he finally had pencil arrows drawn in the directions each male had been looking.

They didn't point to a common center—the killer's *Evil Dead* compound, like Cody had wanted—but out to sea. Each one of them. Europe? Some set of stars low down on the horizon?

Next, he started in drawing arrows for the females, but it was obvious: she was looking up to him, the boy. Meaning she was looking *away* from the Atlantic. To the west.

Cody sat in the middle of all the photos and tape with his chin cradled on his knees. He had no idea which way north was in here. *Up*. He smiled, shook his head.

'Go west, young man,' he said, deep.

It was late.

He looked at one of the photos again, at the girl. West. West west west.

He turned with her, to face it wherever it was, the west, and smiled: Manifest Destiny. From junior high.

He looked it up anyway, on the terminal by the door. Like his eyes weren't already fried.

It was the same boring history-class stuff, pretty much what he expected. But then he clicked on the image—Manifest Destiny the fifty-foot woman, striding bare-breasted above a ragged line of covered wagons. One breast, anyway. Milky white. None of the wagon drivers looking up her skirt.

Cody burrowed into the directory, pulled the jpeg, clicked her larger.

It was her neck that was getting him, her chin. Her head was tilted at the same angle as all the girls from the crime scene photos: looking west past the boy, the boy who was a man. The man who was painted white.

Cody buried the heels of his hands into his eyes, laughed with his shoulders. From behind, it would have looked like he was crying.

He wouldn't tell Creed about this, or Watts.

They'd just say he was trying to solve it all on his first day. After eight years. And he was.

But still.

He slid all the photos back into their sleeves, read about Manifest Destiny until his eyes hurt, until he realized he was distracting himself, then made himself read the small print of the files. Just in case Creed quizzed him, called him out on something. Then he'd have to decide whether to show him up on it or not, but at least he would get to decide.

It was all fibers and dust and crumbs.

The only thing that stuck with him from all of it was a note written in the margin of two of the tox-screens: that the Tuinol wasn't just in the blood. It was in the fatty deposits too. Which meant it had been a regimen, a daily thing—*Time for your morning hypnosis, children.* Or, too, and probably more accurate, it would make everything he said to his children 'right,' true, holy. But was it in the fatty deposits of all the bodies? There were no more notes about it. A different coroner's examiner, probably. Quincy would have found it, though.

Cody smiled.

Quincy would have figured this all out eight years ago. In fifty-two minutes.

And that was when the phone rang. Cody jerked away from it, closed his eyes, opened them back up.

He let it ring again.

Creed. It was probably Creed. Saying go home. Or Watts, with a weather report. Or Manifest Destiny, saying Go West.

Or the girl from the photo, reaching up to the boy, her voice unsteady, dead.

On the fourth ring, Cody picked it up.

It was the girl from the photo.

She was asking for Creed—crying, sobbing.

'I'm Agent Mingus,' Cody said, standing, holding his head down for the phone. 'Is there something I can do, miss? Ma'am, hey?'

There was loud music in the background, drowning her out almost.

'Help me,' she said, finally. 'He's . . . you wouldn't—'

'Ma'am?' Cody said when she cut off. *'Miss?'*

She was gone. The phone on that end changed hands. The song, the lyrics: *Look at the all the white men in the street*. And then, before Cody was ready, a voice: 'Creed.' Male, steady. In control.

'Sorry,' Cody said, then dropped into his answering-machine monotone just to steady his own voice: 'Office hours are Monday through—'

'. . . Cody *Wayne* Mingus,' the voice said, as if pleased.

Cody sat up.

'Who is this?' he asked. 'Who was that girl?'

There was no TRACE button to push, like in the movies, nobody in a booth to wave to. And the phone only reached to the end of the table, not to the door, where he could wave somebody down, in.

He repeated the question.

The voice laughed some.

'You know the irony of you having that middle name, don't you, Agent Mingus? John *Wayne* Gacy, Elmer *Wayne* Henley, Marion *Wayne* Isinger—'

'Who's the girl?' Cody interrupted. Again.

Beat, beat.

The sound of a shrug, maybe.

Was this being recorded? Maybe they recorded everything in this building, this room.

'A word of advice,' the voice said.

'Tell me that girl's okay,' Cody said back. 'Or I hang up.'

He was sitting again, his offhand holding his forehead up. It was almost one o'clock.

'Guess you better hang up, then,' the voice said.

In his background, the girl screamed, got cut off again.

'Now,' the voice said. 'I want you to listen, please.'

Cody just sat there.

'You going to tell me to shoot, at least?' the voice asked.

'Shoot,' Cody said, eyes closed for gunfire. One shot to her head.

The voice laughed again instead.

Contrived irony; misdirection. A situation he controlled, was controlling. The girl.

This had to be him.

'Tell your Mr. Creed something for me,' he said.

'Tell him yourself.'

This time, the man on the other end didn't laugh.

'Erzahlen Sie ihm ich *kenne*,' he said.

It was German. Cody couldn't kick-start it in his head fast enough, so he wrote it down phonetically, each syllable its own word.

'. . . what—what does it mean?' he said, his pencil still moving, transcribing.

Now the man did laugh.

'Not yet,' he said.

'Then when?'

The voice—the killer—laughed again, then, a real, accidental laugh. Like he was that easy.

'Thank you, Agent Mingus,' he said. 'Sometimes I . . . get all involved. Start taking all this Batman-Riddler stuff too seriously.'

'Thank *you,*' Cody said. 'That was forty-eight seconds.'

Beat, beat.

'So come dust this phone booth, Cody,' the voice said, much softer. A different person almost. 'Maybe I'll be watching. It's what we do, right? Can't even help ourselves . . .'

We. Cody was already trying hard to remember it, for Watts.

'Wait, wait,' the voice said then. 'I know. Say you traced me in those . . . what? Forty-eight seconds. But I wonder why you picked that number? What significance . . . the four doubles into the eight . . . even numbers—Is this from *Hawaii Five-O?* Nevermind. I'm sorry, Special Agent Mingus. Cody. Wayne from your father's side. I'll give you this. Since you, you know, *traced* me. Before I leave, I'll rig this phone to explode the next time the receiver's lifted. Got it? So even if it rings, FBI, don't get it. I know this won't hurt anybody because your bomb squad will get here long before dawn. . . .'

Cody wasn't saying anything now.

'And, Cody,' the voice said.

'Yes,' Cody said.

'April Fool's,' and then it was Dial Tone City. It was what Cody's girlfriend had called hanging up. In the eighth grade. Glory Ann Adams.

He looked up at the silhouette he'd traced on the screen that first day, closed his eyes, but it remained—them, them, *they* remained. The children, white and blank.

April Fool's.

His call got Watts out of bed and moving, but Creed slept harder. Cody let the phone ring and ring, waiting for it to explode.

9

1 APRIL 1999

KALVESTA, KANSAS

SHERIFF Debs toed over a shingle lying by the gas pumps. There was nothing under it. He was really just looking anywhere but at Taylor Mason, in the pit of the first bay. The slag hammer was buried in his forehead. There were no prints on the spring-handle, either. Of course. Taylor Mason's eyes were open, as if locked on the hammer, still not believing it.

Debs walked around the station again, looking for anything.

The cash register was out in the weeds, empty.

The radio in the garage was blaring. Debs hadn't been able to find the main control yet, so the cassette in the deck was just looping through itself over and over. Foghat or Steeler's Wheel or some hippie band like that.

Debs grinned displeasure. This wasn't even his county. He had just been taking the scenic route back to Garden City, after Tom Gentry's funeral, who shouldn't have died like that. Thinking maybe he'd luck onto the blue Impala on the way home. Because he owed Tom that, at least. Or Agnes. The badge, the office.

There were no surveillance cameras here, of course.

There were tire prints, but it was a garage.

There was Taylor Mason, dead.

The only witness who hadn't driven through to Colorado by now was a man across the road, who remembered going outside for a cigarette after dinner and seeing the garage lights still on. Like Taylor

Mason was working late, on his own car probably.

There were prints all over the hand tools. Debs could see them even without a kit. Some of them were already black. In the soaking tank at the back of the second bay—the only empty bay—was a spun-out water pump. It had been hidden in the oil. Soaking. Getting the gasket off, maybe. Except that it was shot, its race turned to steel wool. Debs had fished it out with a cat bar. The parts number on the side had been rubbed off with the grinder. The gouge was still raw, fresh. Meaning the local boys were going to have to get a mechanic in here, see if the pump was GM, Ford, or AMC, then work backwards from there. It would take days, though, and even then they'd have to check it against Taylor Mason's work orders, and whatever work he did for people *off* the book.

On the other side of the road from the station, Debs found the neighbor's cigarettes, rubbed into the gravel just where the asphalt quit. It was as far as he could get from his house, from his wife standing on the porch with her cigarettes. If they didn't see each other smoke, they didn't have to complain about it in bed, trying to go to sleep for one more night. Debs understood. He'd quit eight years ago, now.

He looked back to the station again.

The coroner's wagon was on the way.

Debs walked past the last island of pumps, stepping over the air hose, not wanting the bell to ding—for Taylor Mason to rise, hearing it—and was pulling away when he saw it, scrunched up in the tall grass just past the bathrooms.

It was a piece of paper, not as weathered as the rest. Eight by eleven. Crumpled up on purpose, then tossed aside.

Debs put on his gloves, uncrumpled it.

It was an Indian. Debs held the paper between his rubber hands and looked hard into the last few days, trying to place him, but couldn't. He'd seen him, though. Somewhere.

There was tape on the paper where it had been fixed to something. Probably the glass of the store.

73

'The Indian,' he said then, aloud. Of course.

From Gentry's funeral. The deputy. Just with long hair.

He gave the sheet of paper to one of the local officers, to bag. He'd already written the number down. The one under the face. He called it. The woman on the other end said 'Castro County Sheriff's Department.' Debs hung up softly.

Nazareth.

It was like it was following him.

10

1 APRIL 1999

GARDEN CITY, KANSAS

JIM Doe opened his eyes and nothing changed. The world was still black and painful, and then a bell rang. Of a high school. He tried the door but it was locked, leaned against it but it was solid, kicked it but it was tight. He thinned his lips into what felt like a smile, reached for his gun, finally found it nose-down in a gallon can of warm turpentine. He slung it dry, the gun, patted it down with his shirt, touched the end of the barrel to the doorknob that wouldn't turn, backed off two steps; fired. There was a half moon of students waiting for him on the other side. They were all wearing plastic safety goggles. From shop.

'Officer,' one of them said.

'Deputy,' Jim Doe said back.

He was still blinking.

The first exit he found opened onto a courtyard. There was a girl there, sitting in a windowsill, smoking. He still had the gun in his hand, at his thigh. He didn't know what his face looked like. Like it felt, maybe.

'Who won?' he asked her. The game. It was all he could think of that they might share, that would make her trust him, not scream.

She exhaled, watched the smoke. Looked to him finally. 'Who do you think?' she asked.

By the time he found the real exit, the law was there. Waiting for him. Because you're not supposed to fire weapons on school property, on a school day. You're not supposed to even have them. Or be there if you're not a student. Or at least a resident of the fucking state.

Jim Doe sat in the back of a black and white and watched the crowd disperse.

His truck was there, parked sideways to all the other cars. On the driver's side now, half across the gas cap cover, there was a red handprint. The longhair's, a coup, what it used to mean: touching the enemy while the enemy's still *alive*. Jim Doe could feel it. And more: in the supply closet, sometime during the night, his sister had called to him. He remembered looking up, following her.

A Sheriff Debs settled into the backseat with him.

'Hungry?' he said.

Jim Doe turned to him.

'I almost had him,' he said.

Debs narrowed his eyes, shook his head.

'Been a weird fucking day,' he said.

Jim Doe nodded. Weird fucking *state*, really, sir. So far.

Debs took him in his car to a diner at the west edge of town. He said it was his sister-in-law's place, and to eat what she served whether it was good, bad or poison. Those were his conditions. He let Jim Doe ride in front and clean his gun with an oiled rag, then a brush. The finish was coming off, like a clearcoat. Because of the turpentine. Jim Doe put all the soaked cartridges in his shirt pocket. They were warm, oily. He didn't know how they hadn't all gone off at once, when he shot the door. How he was still here, with two hands he could open and close.

'You were at the funeral,' he said to Debs.

Debs nodded.

At the diner, he ordered what Debs did.

'So you think you're a detective, Deputy?' Debs said. 'That right?'

Jim Doe shrugged, leaned back. They were the only ones there. Ever, it felt like.

'I almost had him,' he said again.

'Correction,' Debs said. 'You almost had *some*body.'

'You think he's in Oklahoma,' Jim Doe said. The resignation there in his voice.

'Until I hear otherwise,' Debs said. 'Listen. You're not like McKirkle and—and . . .'

'Maines,' Jim Doe said. The Rangers.

Debs nodded. 'Now those boys, son, they're what you might call *cops*. Compared to them, the rest of us are just security guards, hear?'

Jim Doe nodded. This was better than going to jail, at least. He wasn't this sheriff's son, though.

Their cheeseburgers got there, on a bed of soggy fries.

Debs nodded thanks to his sister-in-law. She blushed, scuttled away. She was the cook, waitress, and cashier.

Jim Doe asked her where the bathroom was, then peed forever and a day, studying his face in the tin mirror above the urinal. It was the same. His cheekbone was tender, raw on the backside if that made any sense, but other than that, you couldn't tell anything. That was why Debs hadn't insisted on a paramedic. And why he didn't believe him all the way, maybe.

When he came back to the booth, the two large bites he'd taken from his so-called cheeseburger had grown back. But there were two bites gone from Debs's, now.

Jim Doe closed his eyes, opened them. Sat down.

'He *is* up here,' he said.

'Even if he was,' Debs said. 'You don't have any jurisdiction, son—'

'*Deputy*,' Jim Doe said.

Debs paused, stared. "Deputy," he said, like it was an effeminate term. 'Your badge there ran out at the Sherman County li—'

'Agnes sent me,' Jim Doe said, cutting Debs off.

Debs stared at him. He knew her. You could tell by the way the bite of cheeseburger in his mouth was swelling into more than just ground beef and curdled milk and mayonnaise.

'Why here, then?' he said, the bite worked into his cheek for the moment. 'Why *my* county, out of all—'

Jim Doe interrupted again: 'I've been to sixteen towns already,

Sheriff. I didn't just pick Garden City off the map. But then I am only a deputy, right?'

Debs smiled, folded his napkin over his nearly-complete cheeseburger.

'I knew Tom,' he said. 'We went through together, back when it was still ball and powder.'

Jim Doe nodded.

'He was a good man,' Debs said.

Jim Doe nodded again, kept nodding.

Debs leaned close across the table. 'What were you doing with that high school girl though, son?'

Jim Doe stared at Debs.

'It's not like that,' he said. Finally.

Debs smiled. 'I saw her,' he said, cocking his head in appreciation. 'You tell me what it *was* like, then, how about? What were you really doing at *our* high school, Deputy? Looking for another girlfriend?'

Jim Doe stood, balling his napkin up.

'I'm free to go?' he asked.

Debs spread his fingers: Yes. Of course. Please.

Jim Doe's truck was already in the parking lot. Someone had delivered it. One of the officers from the high school. He was waiting in Debs's car now. So it was that kind of deal: here's your truck, there's the road.

Jim Doe smiled, looked over the sheriff's hat at the wall, the decorations. It was a series of black-and-white photographs—a town. It was destroyed, leveled.

Jim Doe stepped forward, touched it. It was like it was there just for him.

'Not Holcomb—?' he said, his voice barely there.

Debs didn't even look up. 'Lydia,' he said. 'Tornado hit it a few years ago. Maybe fifteen.' He smiled, eating a store-bought piece of pie, rewarmed for him in his sister-in-law's microwave. 'Came through the stockyards on the way into town, or a pig farm, something like that. Whatever, they say it was red all the way up. You can't see it in those photographs because they're black-and—*that's right.*' He clanged his fork on the plate, turned around. 'You were watching the clouds, right? Instead of backing Tom up? Watching the *storm?* Doing some sort of rain dance?'

Jim Doe shook his head, walked to the door. The cowbell above it shattered what was left of the silence. Jim Doe looked up to it, back through the open door and into the diner.

'He's not going to be there, either,' Debs said. 'Just because it got hit by a tornado too. That's nothing, son. Coincidence. Trust me.'

Jim Doe stood in the door, holding it open.

'My sister,' he called back, low and even, to Debs. 'She reminds me of my sister. That high school girl. Terra Donner. What my sister could have been. Anything else?'

Debs just kept forking the pie in.

Jim Doe got into his truck and drove. It was noon, maybe. He was thinking about a column of blood reaching down from the sky like the finger of God. And the flies that would have coated everything blue-black the next day. And his sister. Miles outside of town, on the way to Lydia, where the Impala had to be, he pulled over, put the radio to his mouth, and said her name. Just once. Like he used to after she died, when he thought she was still up there, that she could hear him.

11

2 APRIL 1999

QUANTICO, VIRGINIA

THE girl. Cody couldn't quit thinking about the girl on the phone. The way Watts explained it to him though, she wasn't really the one who made the call, even. Probably. Or their guy had let her *think* she was escaping, left her in a room with a phone, maybe, only it was rigged so that no matter what numbers were dialed, it rang *this* office. So she'd thought she was talking to the police, that they were about to come get her. That she was about to be saved. That she was going to live. But it was all part of their guy's authentication protocol: first he had to identify himself as *a* kidnapper—someone who had a hostage—then identify which kidnapper he *was*. Independent of what he said.

He satisfied the second part with the point of origin for the call: Bethel, Tennessee. Another form of Bethlehem.

The rest, they were still sifting. Everything Cody had written on the outside of all the manila folders over the thirty minutes it had taken Watts to get there, the forty-five it had taken Creed.

'Which Bethel?' Creed asked, when the trace came back.

Cody looked to him.

'There's two?' he asked.

Creed nodded.

One was down by Alabama, the other was just out of Knoxville. Theirs was the one out of Knoxville. Creed sat hard at the table. He looked up at Cody.

'Eight years,' he said. 'And then he just calls up. Out of the blue.'

'In German,' Cody said.

It had been broken, though, the German. Almost wrong but not quite: *tell him that I know*. Ich kenne. Watts smiled over it for them, traced the verb back to 'kin,' *related*. To Creed. One of his cases, maybe. But then none of them spoke German. Or, it hadn't been important enough to include in a case file.

Cody made himself quit thinking about it, bent over his handwriting again, still trying to fill in the pieces of the conversation he'd missed.

'He knew his middle name, Tim,' Watts was saying, above. About Cody. 'Did you?'

Creed cocked his head. 'Wayne, right?'

Cody didn't look up, heard his full name coming through the phone all over again, slamming into his limbic system.

'And this number, too,' he said. The obvious.

All the payphones in the Knoxville Bethel had a squad car guarding them. All of them they could find, anyway. The bomb squad was taking them apart one by one.

'Oh,' Cody said, stopping his pencil in the middle of the wing silhouette he found himself drawing. 'Batman,' he said. 'Batman, yeah. He said he was the Riddler.'

Watts nodded, filled in: '. . . brilliant criminal mind, compelled to leave clues. Insane, of course.' She smiled, in appreciation maybe. 'Try this. Did you ever wonder why the Riddler *left* all those riddles everywhere, either of you? I mean, he could have gotten away with all the crime he wanted. He was smart enough . . .'

Cody was watching her now. Afraid to interrupt.

'Like Moriarty,' she said, almost to herself now. 'Sherlock Holmes's guy. Arch-nemeses and all that, but . . .' She looked to Creed. 'He's calling you out,' she said, the tense muscles in her face relaxing with pleasure, realization. 'Like Moriarty. The Riddler. Because you're the only one who can catch him, the key somehow.' She smiled, at herself. 'Maybe that's the riddle, Tim? Your relationship to him. How you know each other.'

Creed shrugged.

'Or maybe it was a joke,' he said. 'April Fool's.'

'She called *me*, though,' Cody said. His voice weak.

'*Here*,' Watts corrected. 'He called here, Agent Mingus. If he wanted *you*, he could have called your apartment, right? Your cell?'

'You're thinking about her, aren't you?' Creed asked.

Watts set her eyes on Cody, waiting.

Cody shrugged.

'Don't,' Creed said.

Another thing Watts keyed into was his use of the word 'we,' near the end. If Cody was remembering it right. *We*, as in 'That's the kind of thing *we* do. We can't even help doing it, can we?' It was the second thing Cody had written, after the phonetic German.

Watts said it had two functions, the collective pronoun: the first was to diffuse blame, responsibility—put the burden of murder and all associated activities on the class of sociopaths, instead of the individual sociopath. Which was of course an indicator of guilt. An expression of it, maybe all he could manage. The second function—and, maybe their guy *didn't* mean this one—was that it revealed a knowledge of profiling that went a touch beyond the pop-stuff the movies feed.

But Marion Wayne Isinger?

Even Watts, their walking encyclopedia, didn't know who Isinger was, or was supposed to be. All they could think was that he was alphabetical—came after Gacy and Henry in the list of convicted serial killers with a Wayne middle name.

Creed said it was just a joke too, Marion being John Wayne's real name. That maybe he was the Joker, not the Riddler.

Watts shook her head. Said that making up a name like that on the spot just to fit an alphabetic progression showed both intelligence—verbal dexterity, at least, which younger siblings usually had—*and* a distinct need to control. More than need, though. Maybe, to him, Isinger was real. Because the list was incomplete without him.

'. . . messenger,' Cody said.

Watts looked to him.

'Like in chemistry,' he said. 'Coefficients. You cancel out what's the same on either side of the sign. Wayne. That's the same in all three names. Leaving Henry Gacy, Elmer Henry, and Marion Isinger. Now take it to initials. H. Gacy, E. Henry, M. Isinger. Then suck the periods out, and the spaces. Read it phonetically. *Mess*enger.'

'Or . . .' Watts said, eyes closed in thought, 'missing *her*. Like a question, see?'

Cody rubbed his eyes deeper into his head.

They were running the name through every database they had their fingers in, anyway. Which was all of them.

'How old did he sound?' Creed asked from his huge chair. It was the same size as the rest of them, but because of him, how he sat it, it loomed, somehow. His index finger was pressed up the side of his face, stopping at his temple, the thumb hooked under the square of his jaw.

Cody shrugged. 'He didn't give any indicators that—'

'How old did he *sound*, Agent?' Creed repeated. 'In your humble estimation?'

'Forty,' Cody said. 'Early fifties, maybe. Any older and he would have been—'

Creed waved the rest off though, and something in the way he moved his hand—orchestral, dismissive—cued the music playing behind the voice last night. Cody wrote it down: *Look at all the white men in the street,* then rotated the folder for Creed and Watts to see.

Watts said it aloud—' "Look at the all the white men in the street?" '—but Cody wasn't looking at her anymore. Just Creed: what little color he'd had in his face this deep in the a.m. was gone. Watts saw it too.

'. . . Tim?' she said.

Creed closed his eyes. Watts looked to Cody, then back to Creed.

' "Look at all the white men in the street," ' he said. 'It's a line from a song. "Kid Charlemagne," I think.'

Watts lowered her head in thought. '. . . and Charlemagne, he was, what? The first Christian—'

'Maybe he's saying he's not white,' Cody said, over her. 'Objectifying the Caucasian, establishing himself as other . . . ?

'Or it was just on the radio,' Watts said, picking it up. 'Tim?'

Creed was still staring at nothing. Or somewhere else.

' "Kid Charlemagne" came out in nineteen seventy-six,' he said. 'Bicentennial year.'

'Well then that's the joke,' Watts said. 'All the white men in America . . . ?'

Creed was shaking his head no, though.

He looked up to her.

'The album was *The Royal Scam*,' he said, and then Cody saw the water rush into Watts's eyes just before Creed said it out loud, made it real: 'Steely Dan.'

It took a moment for the name to click.

Steely Dan. 1978. One of Creed's old cases. Right after the Berkowitz show. The only one to ever get a bullet into Creed. A .38. But Creed got more into him, in places like the face and the sternum and the spine, and the face again, over and over. They had been in a motel room with two girls, then, one alive, one not. There was a trail of four more bodies behind them already, over four months, each found dead in the bathtub, with a note safety-pinned to her cheek.

'He's dead, though,' Cody said.

Creed didn't answer, just blinked slow.

'. . . so he knows your case history,' Watts was saying, her hand clenched on the table where it had been reaching across, for Creed's.

Cody nodded, and then the phone rang.

They all looked to it. It was hot now—traced and tapped—so they weren't supposed to talk to their girlfriends or boyfriends or pet gerbils on it. This was the first time for it to ring with an outside line.

On the third ring, Cody took it.

It was Bethel, Tennessee. The one by Alabama.

They'd never been told *not* to guard all the phone booths.

Cody breathed out, leaned back, palming the receiver to tell Creed and Watts.

'That other Bethel,' he said.

Watts nodded.

The officer he was talking to—Swanson—was being shuttled through Tennessee dispatch from a mobile unit, then through the boards downstairs, then half his signal split off for tape, the other half amped back up, to make up for what was lost. So there was a delay. But then their second line—the *new* one—rang, the phone by Creed. He looked at it, let it ring again, then picked it up. Cody was still waiting for whatever Swanson had said to filter through.

'What, Tim?' Watts said to Creed.

Cody looked closer. Creed was leaning forward, into the receiver, listening for the second time, it looked like. Just waking from 1978. When he looked up, it was to the television in the corner. He rose, crossed the room, pawed around for the power button, hit it.

Swanson came through, finally.

'. . . some kind of transmitter,' he was saying. 'Looks homemade to our guys, I don't know. It's rigged right into the . . . this little antenna. Can't be good for more than a couple of hundred feet.'

Then, nothing.

'They've found a device in Bethel,' Cody said to Watts.

'Device?' she said.

Cody nodded. 'Some sort of solid-state leapfrogger,' he said. 'Radio.'

'But he was in . . .' Watts said.

The news filtered in, whatever station the front desk had alerted Creed to.

It was Bethel, Tennessee. The one by Alabama.

There was a uniform leaning down into his car, to the dash mounted under the radio. Swanson.

'. . . *why are we on the news?*' Watts said, standing.

On-screen, Swanson had already stood up from his car, waiting for Cody to respond. Cody looked at the phone in his hand, waiting for Swanson to come through.

Watts said it again, stepping closer to the television: 'Why are we on the news?'

Beside her, Creed leaned back.

'Because he wants us to see,' he said. 'He phoned it in himself. Or left a tape, some kind of rig to call for him. Call us.'

They were all staring at the screen.

'*Officer Swanson*,' Cody said into the phone.

'—'re just going door to door right now . . . two-hundred-foot radius, checking to see if any of the residents noticed an unusual vehicle or—'

'*No,* Officer,' Cody said. 'This guy, you don't—it's a trap. He just made us *think* it was the other Bethel, I don't know how. But you need to get your guys . . .'

He trailed off, just watched the screen with Creed and Watts. There was nothing they could do. Swanson was standing in the open door of his car, his radio held up to his jaw waiting for Cody's response. He was watching something off-camera, across the street. Cody closed his eyes in pain, that it was taking so long.

'Tell him to say something to his wife,' Creed said, and then, on their nineteen-inch screen, the house just past Swanson's squad car bloomed orange, the blast tilting Swanson's car over on him, closing him in the door just as he had started to lift his handset to his ear, for Cody.

And then his voice came through, from the afterlife of radio lag: '. . . say again, Virginia, I think there must be a bird on the wire or some—'

Cody hung up.

He looked up to Watts, and then, behind her, someone was opening the door: Eggers. Their unofficial gofer.

He looked from Creed to Watts to Cody.

'Am I—?' he stammered.

In his hands was a sheet, still curled with heat from the printer.

'. . . you wanted me to—to . . .' he started, said again: 'Marion Wayne Isinger.'

He straightened his elbow, held the paper out.

Watts stood, took it.

Cody nodded to Eggers, watched him disappear. Go back to his hole.

'There's only one of him,' she said. 'In all of America.'

Creed looked up, his eyes intense, focused.

'Where?' he said.

'Gentry,' Watts said. 'Gentry, Tennessee.'

Cody closed his eyes—*Gentry*, *Gentry*, *Gentry*—and then it came to him.

'Gentry,' he said.

Watts looked over at him.

'Some Podunk sheriff in Texas who got, I don't know, killed or something.'

'Okay,' Watts said, doubtful.

Cody closed his eyes to remember better: 'I talked to their deputy. He called, I mean. VICAP. Because there were two bodies in the trunk of the shooter's car. Short bodies.'

'Texas,' Creed said. Like he was trying to remember it, place it.

'Like a week ago, maybe two,' Cody said. 'Not long.'

'Were they white, at least?' Watts said.

'I called back, that's the thing,' Cody said. 'And that deputy. He's gone AWOL or something.'

'How do you go AWOL in Texas?' Watts asked, sitting down finally.

'How do you not?' Cody asked back. To himself, it seemed.

'Where was he?' Creed asked.

'Nazareth,' Cody said, and Creed, from his chair, began to laugh, low and slow.

'Did this deputy have a name?' Watts said, leaning forward.

Cody thumbed through his notes, found it: 'Doe. Jim Doe.'

Watts churched her hands under her chin, looked up to Creed.

'You run his history?' she said, her eyes narrow, not expecting much.

Cody followed his index finger down the sheet anyway—Eggers's handwriting. That he hadn't had time for earlier. 'Shit,' he said, when he saw it, and told them: seventeen years ago a tornado had hit Nazareth, and taken Jim Doe's sister and a boy described as his sister's elementary school boyfriend, from the only other Indian family in town, then. A Jerry LeChapeau. It was all in a newspaper article. She had been ten, then, Jim Doe eight.

'What now?' Watts said.

'We find him,' Creed said. 'Jim Doe.'

12

2 APRIL 1999

DEERFIELD, KANSAS

FROM a payphone at the turn up to Lydia, Jim Doe called Castro County. Monica was working dispatch. He could see her in her wooden chair, one piece of chocolate lined up on the panel for each hour of her shift, Dimmit quiet all around her, waiting.

'Where are you?' she asked.

Her voice was hushed, like she was leaning down, talking into the keyboard. Hiding him.

Jim Doe looked around. 'Kansas,' he said.

'They're looking for you, y'know,' Monica said. 'Your shifts, I don't know how many . . .'

Jim Doe nodded.

'What about Oklahoma?' he asked.

'Nothing,' Monica said. 'You?'

'Nothing,' he lied. And hated to.

'You heard about that thing in . . . what was it? Kal—Kalver—'

'Kalvesta,' Jim Doe said. 'Wha—*when?*'

She waited, waited, looking it up probably.

Jim Doe hadn't seen a newspaper in days. Since Gentry.

'The thirtieth,' she said, finally. 'Station attendant got killed. They found part of a set of handcuffs there.' She paused. 'The serial number matches Tom's key, Jim.'

Jim Doe closed his eyes. What else had Debs not told him?

He told Monica thanks. She told him to be careful. He hung up, kept his hand on the phone long after she was gone. To the south there was an outflow boundary, a shelf cloud moving low across the land. In the parking lot, three of the six cars had feathers dangling from their mirrors. The thread wrapped around one of their spines was a military pattern, for Vietnam. Green and white and red. Jim Doe knew the colors from his father.

He got in the truck, lowered his face into his sunglasses, and closed his eyes for two seconds, woke to a man knocking on the window. He was Indian, tall.

Jim Doe cracked the window.

'Smells *hot*,' the man said, touching the hood to show what he meant.

Jim Doe looked at his gauge. Two-twenty. He'd fallen asleep with the engine idling, the doors unlocked. His hand not on his gun. Nothing hanging from his rearview.

'Yeah,' Jim Doe said. 'Thanks.'

'You okay?' the man asked. 'Not shot or anything?'

Jim Doe looked at his stomach, his chest.

He shook his head no.

In his rearview, the man's tall kid was placing his hand in the handprint on the back fender of the truck. It was more brown now than red. Like a scab. The kid's hand seemed to fit. Jim Doe watched him do this and watched him do this and then reached beside his seat for the nightstick he still carried, wedged it against the accelerator to cool the engine down. He stepped out into the late afternoon glare. The man towered over him. Kid too. Basketball. He had probably played in the game last night, even.

'Who won?' Jim Doe asked.

The man smiled. 'Who do you think?' he said.

The tall kid's hand did fit. He backed off with Jim Doe's approach. Jim Doe told him it was all right, though. He placed his own hand there. It fit too. The kid smiled. Jim Doe bent down to the print, took his sunglasses off one ear at a time, not wanting to mess anything up here.

There in the hand shape, where the longhair's hand had been, were four fingerprints and a thumb.

Jim Doe smiled.

The basketball-playing family was gone when he turned around, their car not receding down any of the roads in any of the directions. Jim Doe looked up—because this was Kansas, where people get lifted into the sky—but they weren't there either.

He backed inside, to the store, bought two cups of coffee, a disposable camera, and a newspaper, then shot the whole roll on the handprint—close, far, every angle, some lit with his Maglite, some not, one with a quarter by it, for size, another with the newspaper, for the date—then packed it into a padded envelope, addressed it to Sheriff Debs, Garden City. The clerk knew the zip. Jim Doe showed him the photocopy of the longhair. The clerk looked from it up to Jim Doe, and Jim Doe just smiled, looked away.

As he was walking out, though, suddenly aware that the emergency brake in his truck wasn't even set, the door unlocked, so that anybody could pop it into first, the clerk called after him.

'This is about the gas run, right?'

Jim Doe closed his eyes, didn't turn around. 'Yes,' he said.

'I never saw him,' the clerk said. 'Did they tell you I did?'

Jim Doe turned around.

'When did you not see him?' he asked.

'When he made the gas run,' the clerk said. He was all of sixteen.

'Yesterday?' Jim Doe said.

'I wish,' the clerk said. 'I was off then. Comes out of our check, you know? Ever since Arthur.'

'Arthur?' Jim Doe said.

He was still at the door. Holding his breath.

The clerk smiled. 'Arthur,' he said. 'He was selling premium to his cousins at regular price.'

Jim Doe faked a smile. It hurt.

He looked above the clerk to the security camera.

'But you've got *tape*,' he said.

The clerk nodded. 'Damn straight,' he said. 'I saved its ass, too.'

Jim Doe watched it in the supply room. His truck was still running, idling high with the nightstick, the plate glass at the front of the store pulsing with the exhaust. After the clerk left, he moved a stray brick over to the doorjamb of the supply closet, so it wouldn't close. So nobody could close it on him. And then he watched.

It was black-and-white and grainy and distant, but still, there it was, the Impala, the longhair keeping it between him and the camera. You could see his hair, though, whipping above the ragged top of the car. Behind him, low on the horizon, was a line of clouds, shaded like a mountain range. The same ones that were closer now. Developing.

Jim Doe smiled, stood, ejected the tape.

'Show this to Sheriff Debs,' he said.

'Is he coming here—?' the clerk started to ask, but Jim Doe just nodded.

'They all should be,' he said, and left the clerk standing there with the paperwork his manager would want filled out.

Standing by his truck again, his car beside him, was the tall Indian man. Like he'd been there all along. His tall son was dribbling a basketball beside the store, passing it to himself off the wall. The rain was almost on them now, already sweeping the trash into the air.

The man nodded down at Jim Doe's right hand.

'Gonna pay for that chocolate?' he asked.

Jim Doe looked down at his hand and there it was, a candy bar. One he couldn't explain. He offered it to the man but the man held his hands up, palms out. They were both red.

The last thing Monica had said to him on the phone was *come home*.

It was too late now, though. He was too far.

He got into his truck, moved the newspaper out of his seat, dislodged the nightstick, and pulled into Lydia three hours after sunset, one hour ahead of the rain. It already smelled like it, though. There were people stationed in the driveways of each house, watching it approach. Jim Doe slowed, like he was recognizing them, *this*, and then it came to him all at once, what he'd heard in the silence of the supply closet last night: the insurance man.

He was there to pay for Jim Doe's sister. Again.

Jim Doe was eight, his sister ten, forever. He was already calling her Dorothy, because the wind had taken her. Walking the stripped fields for her body.

But the insurance man, the one who came to pay for her.

Jim Doe never even saw him. He had still been hiding behind the one standing wall of his bedroom, then. Pretending. But then the car pulled up, its dust plume settling over the remains of Horace Doe's house, coating everything with a fine layer of caliche. Another fine layer of caliche. Jim Doe made himself smaller behind the partial wall, closed his eyes, and listened. It was the insurance man's voice he would remember. How he'd talked to his father, calling him *Mr. Doe* at first, then moving on to *Horace*, until that became something different too, more personal: *Horse*.

They were sitting on the couch his father had dug out. Or, his father was. He'd been there for days already. Just staring. Maybe the insurance man was standing, walking. Looking out the windows as he spoke. The whole house was a window.

The insurance man was saying how he was here as an extension of the company. To show how much they cared in this, Horse's time of loss, of grief, and grieving. That he knew Horse wasn't thinking about money yet, of course, but it was his job to.

'Just tell me what I owe,' Horace Doe said, his voice flat.

His wallet had blown away along with his daughter.

Jim Doe closed his eyes tighter.

The insurance man didn't say anything for a long while. It was just his feet on the broken glass of the floor. Then he said it: 'Nothing, Mr. Doe. Horse. We owe *you*.'

Jim Doe could hear his mother in the other room, sweeping. The walls around her were two feet tall, maybe. The broom was makeshift—rags and a stick; her real broom was stuck in a locustwood fencepost three acres away, like it had been shot there by a giant, inconceivable bow. Birds were already sitting on it, bobbing up and down, waiting for the straw to give so they could weave nests out if it.

The insurance man said it again: *Nothing*.

And then he extended the check to Horace Doe. Twenty-two hundred dollars.

Jim could hear him looking up, his father, hear the insurance man smiling, the check fluttering. The burial insurance that wasn't included in Horace's premiums was paid out on the check, listed on the stub. The amount was real. Horace looked from it to the insurance man. The insurance man said it must have been an oversight at the main office. That it happened all the time. That he understood what it was like to lose someone.

After that, silence. So long that Jim Doe put his hands over his ears, started humming to himself. It had been quiet like this right before the tornado. A roaring silence. And green. His hands at eight weren't thick enough, though. He could still hear the insurance man talking in low tones—private tones, like this wasn't for everybody. It was a joke. An Indian joke, one Jim Doe would never be able to remember, just that it made his father laugh, sitting there on the couch. Made him laugh for the first time in days. The sound of his laughter spilled through the house and out into the grass, and for a moment his wife stopped sweeping, and his son stood up, and the three of them looked at each other, and started getting better. To become three instead of four. The insurance man was already a car pulling away, back into Nazareth. Jim Doe waved, wanted more, please, more—make us laugh—but that was all.

Dorothy, he'd called out through the dust, *her name was Dorothy*, and then his father had him around the middle and was lifting him and his mother still wasn't sweeping, and he never told anybody this, because he held it too close, like a scab you keep pulling, all through junior high and high school and work, until one day you're sitting out in a truck with a girl named Terra, not saying anything, and it really starts to bleed, and you can't stop it.

When the tall Indian man at the store in Deerfield had asked Jim Doe if he was shot or anything, Jim Doe had had to look down, because he wasn't sure. He did have a hole in him, anyway.

He looked at the people of Lydia standing in their driveways watching the storm, and he wanted to tell them to run, to get inside, to hide under mattresses in their bathtubs, to hold each other close. That maybe it would pass. But then he saw that he was bringing it with him. In his rearview mirror. Headlights.

He pulled over and waited for them, but they turned off two streets short of his truck. Into residential.

Jim Doe looked at his foot, his boot. It was hard on the brake, everything behind him washed red. The color of warning. Like a stop sign.

He should have just clicked his lights off, coasted to a stop. Waited.

The headlights in his mirror had been dull, too. Like old bulbs. The kind the Impala would have.

He wasn't a detective. He said it to himself like that. He probably wasn't even a deputy anymore.

He held the steering wheel between his hands and pressed his forehead into it, counting the minutes, the *hour*, waiting for the car to ease back out of residential. It never did. And then the rain came, in great, winding sheets.

He rolled forward, to the dead end at the courthouse.

There in the lawn, by the sidewalk leading to the double doors, was the plaque. For the dead. Angled up for the sun to glint off of in the daytime, its base granite, and planted deep, so at least *this* wouldn't blow away. Jim Doe smiled. It was the only other one he'd ever seen outside Nazareth. He set the brake on the truck and stumbled through the rain to it. The names were all there. Thirty-seven of them. From a town of fifteen hundred. Their birth dates too.

Jim Doe ran his finger down the ridges of the letters, saying the names in his head because he had to, and then stopped near the bottom, at two. They were side by side: a Wallace Blue Kettle and a Dot Blue Kettle. Brother and sister. Ten and twelve years, the girl older. He closed his eyes, left his fingers there, and then someone was behind him, his shadow on the ground, his shape outlined by a sharp branch of lightning.

Jim Doe turned, leading with his gun.

It was a man wearing chrome sunglasses. At night.

And he had a gun too.

Jim Doe thumbed his hammer back. In the storm, no one would hear their shots.

The man was yelling already, for Jim Doe to drop it, *drop it.* His mouth was huge, full of harsh, white teeth. Jim Doe watched himself distorted in the twin lenses. He was crying, the water running down his face, his shirt.

'You first,' he said.

They stood like that, feet set, elbows locked, and then the sprinklers came on all around them, the crowns of water they usually made pressed down by the rain.

Jim Doe smiled.

'You're not him, are you?' he said. He had to say it loud to be heard.

The man thinned his lips in response. Jim Doe shook his head no for him. No. Because he'd already be dead if that was him, his long hair tucked up into his drooping hat.

'*What were you saying?*' the man screamed.

Jim Doe narrowed his eyes, looked at the man, the plaque, then back to the man.

'Dorothy,' he finally said.

The man cocked his head to the side.

Jim Doe nodded.

The man motioned for Jim Doe to lower his gun. Jim Doe did, all fingertips and slow motion.

Under the man's dark blue slicker was a uniform, a name tag. A *Lobichek.*

Jim Doe unfolded his own badge for him.

'I almost had to shoot you,' Lobichek said, lowering his gun.

'I almost had to shoot you back,' Jim Doe said.

'What are you doing here?' Lobichek asked. 'This isn't Oz, y'know.'

Jim Doe nodded, chewing his cheek. 'Just looking,' he said, shrugging, then two-fingered the photocopy out, still moving slow.

'For him,' he added.

Lobichek hooked his chin down the sidewalk. 'Saw your truck,' he said.

Jim Doe nodded back, that it was a hard truck to miss.

'What about *him?*' he asked, rustling the photocopy.

'What'd he do?' the officer asked.

Jim Doe looked away: everything.

'He's wanted in Texas,' he said. 'Here too, now. I think.'

Lobichek studied the photocopy through his fogged glasses, handed it back.

'It's not . . . *you?*' he said.

Jim Doe shook his head.

Lobichek looked around. 'Why would he come here?' he asked.

'I think it's the tornado,' Jim Doe said. 'I don't know, really.'

Lobichek smiled one side of his mouth.

'That was nearly twenty years ago already,' he said.

'Sixteen,' Jim Doe said.

Lobichek appraised Jim Doe. Jim Doe stood there, let him.

'He dangerous?' Lobichek finally asked.

Jim Doe nodded.

Lobichek folded the photocopy. 'I keep this?' he asked.

Jim Doe nodded again.

Lobichek shrugged. 'I'll keep an eye out,' he said. 'It's not a big town, here. As you can tell.' He looked back at Jim Doe's truck then. 'Got a place to stay?' he asked.

'I'm just here to get him,' Jim Doe said. 'That's all.'

Lobichek spit into the water they were standing in.

'Last time you slept?' Lobichek asked.

'I sleep,' Jim Doe said.

'Eat?'

Jim Doe thought of the candy bar, looked to his truck for it.

'Bad night all around,' Lobichek said.

It was. Lobichek left him alone with the memorial. To say *Dorothy* some more, and click his heels together. Jim Doe watched his cruiser pull behind the curtain of rain, disappear.

Lydia.

And Wallace, and Dot.

Jim Doe cruised the convenience store but didn't stay, didn't leave any photocopies on the glass. The clerk was sleeping on the counter by the hot dog ferris wheel. It rolled over and over in the same place. Jim Doe started shaking then. From the cold. From almost getting shot. From Wallace and Dot. He turned the heater on and his clothes steamed. His wipers couldn't keep up with the rain anymore, either. Or the defroster with his clothes. Soon the hail came, pinging off the roof, careening off the light bar. It was pea size. The Bronco's tires collected it in the tread, slung it up into the wheel well. It sounded like birdshot.

Jim Doe drove, in a trance.

If he didn't catch him here. He looked north. If he didn't catch him here, then it would be Nebraska. Which was just as big. He rubbed the heel of his hand into his right eye, drove.

On one pass through town, he pulled into each driveway, washing his headlights into the carports, for anything blue. It took two hours. Another thing he'd never told anybody, even Terra, was that part of him always knew his sister had just been set down in another town, in another state, after some other tornado. That she was out there.

At the cemetery, he shifted into neutral, coasted to a stop.

Her grave had been empty. That was the thing. The school counselor said it didn't mean anything, but it did. He had stood over it with Horace and his mom and they had sung like she was there. Like she could hear. But they should have been looking *up*.

He stepped down from the truck, into the wet, through the gates, and into another world. An older one. In it there were people gathered around a grave—a pair of graves. They all looked to him as one. He was saying to himself *Blue Kettle*, *Blue Kettle*. Looking for the name on the headstone, just to make that connection. And then he stopped.

They were Indian, the people looking at him.

An old man, an old woman. The longhair, one of his hands gauze-white.

Jim Doe smiled, reached for them, and they splashed into the night.

He ran after them, falling over headstones and over crosses and finally slamming into the tall iron fence. The pair of dim bulbs was already feeling away. Jim Doe stood there until the brake lights kissed each other goodbye, disappeared, then he fell to his knees, then he pulled himself up, went back to the two graves. One headstone said *Dot*. The other was just gone. Jim Doe touched the name *Dot* again with the side of his finger, where it was tender and could feel, and then looked down at his boot. It was sinking into the ground, into the dirt. He fell back, away from it, the *idea* of it, and in the next jagged line of lightning, saw it: his sister's plot again, empty.

He went to the groundskeeper's shed for a shovel.

It was Easter, and he was digging. In Lydia, Kansas. For two children who weren't going to be there, a funeral that couldn't have just happened.

He didn't stop until Lobichek made him.

13

4 APRIL 1999

GENTRY, TENNESSEE

IT was like cards falling, when it started: first, Eggers making his timid way down the hall, to shuffle in the doorway and tell Watts that that Jim Doe deputy was in custody, in Lydia, Kansas; next, the sheet on Marion Wayne Isinger. He had just been paroled two months ago, after doing eighteen years of a twenty-year sentence, for vehicular manslaughter. Before that, he'd done five for a 1975 armed robbery outside Baton Rouge. Before that, high school, the principal's office.

Because Tennessee was on the way to Kansas, the Wise Men set down in Nashville, floated back up into the sky on a helicopter, rode through their own contrail back to Gentry. Just to look at Isinger, ask him why his name would show up in an alphabetical list of child-killers. Why he lived in a town that shared a name with a dead sheriff.

They didn't have a warrant. Just questions.

In the rental car from the airport Watts folded the phone she'd had to her ear for the last twenty minutes, looked across the front seat to Creed.

'He has kids,' she said.

'Old as him, I'd guess,' Creed said, hooking his chin in the rearview, at Cody.

Cody looked out his window. At anything. The girl on the phone. Swanson.

'No,' Watts said. 'Conjugal visits, looks like.' She looked ahead, to the cones set up on the side of the road, directing them around the lineman, belted to the utility pole, his back to them. Cody watched him leaning back from the glass insulators, his fingers thick with leather and rubber, his face hidden under goggles.

'Nine,' Watts said. 'And ten.'

'Two,' Creed said. The holy number.

Watts nodded.

'Where are they?' Cody said.

Watts looked back, as if just remembering him.

'With the mother,' she said. 'Ohio, I think.'

'You've confirmed?' Creed said.

Watts unfolded her phone again.

Creed slowed for the patrol car they'd called ahead for, laid his badge out the open window, down the side of the white car. The patrolman looked from it up to him, then to Watts, Cody.

'Okay,' he said.

'Fifteen Mercantile Place,' Creed said. 'You know it?'

The patrolman nodded, hooked his chin over to a sign, the road they were on: MERCANTILE. It was the main road of Gentry.

'Been empty for about a year now,' he said. 'Somebody got it?'

Creed nodded. They followed him down the street to an A-frame overgrown with green. There was no car, no lights, no smoke.

The patrolman stepped out, came back.

'Want me to do the introductions?' he said.

Creed stood from the car, stretching. Cody came around.

'Marion Wayne Isinger,' Creed said. 'Ex-con. We just need to ask him a few questions.'

Behind them, another patrol car crunched into the ditch. Because the first patrolman had had to radio this in. The FBI being in town.

Cody looked down the road for another car, the whole force. All there was, though, was the lineman, small on his pole, his goggles glinting, throwing light all over the sky.

They walked up to the porch with the patrolman, Watts still in the car, talking into her phone, a phone ringing once inside the house, and then the third card fell: the patrolman knocked on the door with the short end of his nightstick, high up, almost even with the top hinge.

So it would sound more solid, maybe, have more authority. Make it seem like the patrolman were taller. Expose his ribs.

But the third card.

It was the door itself, exploding out against them, dusting splinters into the air. A stainless steel ball from a shotgun load passing through Cody's right ear, a line of sunlight suddenly piercing his shadow. Before he could even raise his hand to the warmth at the side of his head—or, *while* he was—the officer and Creed reacted, fell to either side of the door, rolled in in turns, shooting directly into the throat of the house.

Inside, in a clear path he had blasted open, was Marion Wayne Isinger, riddled now with holes, layers of duct tape across his lower face, his mouth. The tape was on his hands, too, making him hold the shotgun, and it was also on his legs and body, holding him to the chair. And the chair was nailed to the ground. And he wasn't dead yet, not quite.

Creed walked up to him in stages, knocked the shotgun clattering to the linoleum.

Marion Wayne Isinger smiled, red bubbling from his lips.

'. . . had to,' he said.

Creed took him by the chin.

'Why?' he said. 'Who?'

And Isinger died.

The blood from Cody's ear was running down his neck, under his collar. He was alive, but it still didn't feel like it. Suddenly his shadow merged with another: Watts, standing in the doorway, the butt of her gun exposed, undrawn. The phone in her hand more important.

She waited for Creed to look around.

'They're missing,' she said. The children.

Creed closed his eyes, lowered his head, and then Cody stumbled back suddenly, into the kitchen counter, sending a pile of pans into the sink.

On either side of the doorway, either side of Watts, were bodies. Duct-taped to the wall like grey angels. Child-sized. Straws embedded in the tape around the mouth, so they could breathe.

'Oh God,' Watts said.

That was why Isinger had had to focus Creed and the patrolman's fire on himself: so they wouldn't back up, shoot the house. The children.

They cut the first one down with a steak knife, tracing around the head first.

The patrolman's hands were shaking.

'. . . they're fucking cold,' he kept saying, until they peeled the tape off the face. It was stuck to an open eye. A painted-on eye. Department store mannequins.

Creed leaned down over the sink like he was going to throw up.

'That's how he got him here,' he said. 'He had his kids.'

They left the second mannequin up too, after cutting the tape away from a pale foot, to be sure.

Cody was shaking now, deep inside.

'Sit,' Watts told him, and handed him a paper towel for his ear.

'Disability,' Cody said.

'You never listened anyway,' Watts said, moving off with Creed and the patrolman to secure the rest of the house. Find the *real* kids, maybe.

Cody sat down on the counter by Marion Wayne Isinger, and didn't turn his back on him.

'Hey,' he called out, once, to Creed or anybody, but there was no answer.

He'd never even drawn his gun. Not even considered it.

And then Isinger moved, relaxing into his death some, under the tape, and the phone on the counter beside him moved too. It was off the hook still. Cody stood, felt his way over, to the monofilament line tied to the phone, taped to Isinger's gag. So he could answer, unhook it. Hear, at least.

Cody picked it up, held it to his bloody ear.

'Hello?' he said.

On the other end, somebody was breathing, waiting, and Cody flashed on what had been slowing down his thoughts now for minutes: the lineman's goggles glinting in the sunlight. His soft *plastic* goggles. Glinting like binoculars.

He pulled the phone to the doorway, to see down the road again.

'Boom,' a voice said into his ear. The same voice.

Creed appeared in the kitchen then, his gun alongside his thigh, his tie loose around his neck.

The *boom* was for the house that had exploded in Bethel. A whole family dead, plus Swanson and a man called Anderson. It had made the national news. Cody had watched it on every broadcast from his hotel room. It was punishment. He had even watched it in Spanish, and half-fallen in love with the anchorwoman, for making it all sound so beautiful, so lyrical, such a necessary part of this world.

The man on the other end of the phone laughed.

'Is she okay?' Cody said. The girl.

'Are you?' the voice asked.

Meaning he'd seen Cody's ear.

'Tell us where the children are,' he said.

The man on the pole laughed.

'In the basement, Agent. Where do you think?'

Cody handed the phone to Creed and stumbled out into the grown-over yard, out to their cars.

The lineman had had no truck, either. Just an armful of cones, spiked boots. An orange vest.

Behind him, Creed just said two words into the phone: 'Jessie Wiggs.'

Cody turned back to him, to make sure he'd heard right: Jessie Wiggs. Steely Dan's real name. Who was dead.

'He's gone,' Cody said, hooking his chin down the road.

Creed set the phone down—dead—then leaned into the patrol car, the radio, scrambled every car in Gentry, Tennessee.

Steely Dan. Four useless hours later, Sheila Watts couldn't stop thinking about it. What was He trying to tell them? tell *Creed*? that Creed wasn't telling *them*? She made herself go through it step by step in her head, the possibilities: steely dan. Before it was a band, it was a slang term for a marital aid, a vibrator, a dildo. Pointing to sex. Which fit—the control angle, at least: surgically altering the corpses, arranging them, manipulating the crime scene, making omniscient phone calls in a godlike voice. Sex was killing and killing was sex. It was all about power and domination and release.

But it could be simpler, too, more obvious—more of a *riddle*: if the vibrator used C batteries, was that their guy's initial? or, *Daniel* C.? C. Daniel? *see* Daniel, as in the Book of? had he found his mother's *steely dan* in the nightstand, understood in the way children will that *that* was his father, that *he* was an android, beyond all these messy human emotions? had he just had the radio on when he'd called, after all?

Watts closed her eyes, stepped into the bathroom and locked the door behind her. Her phone was ringing but she didn't answer it, had to think instead. She sat on the toilet lid, stretching her eyes open like her mother had always told her not to, and stared into the iron drain in the middle of the floor. She didn't realize someone was staring back at her for twenty seconds, and then she did.

Two hours later, they had the floorboards up.

It was the first body they would find—sheathed in plastic, doused with lime, so decomposed they couldn't even get a gender yet, without contaminating the scene. Young, though. Too young.

Creed sat on the edge of the claw-footed bathtub with his elbows on his knees, his hands clasped before him. In thought.

He looked across the body-length hole to Watts.

'It's old,' Creed said—the body. 'Early eighties, probably. And Marion John fucking Wayne here, you know. He'd been here, what, two days? I mean shit, Sheel. This could have even been done when he was inside for boosting that shit in Louisiana, you know. What then?'

Watts used to think Creed used profanity when he was unsure. To cover for his insecurity. Now she knew he just cussed. That they were just words to him; less.

'It doesn't matter,' she said, stepping forward, to the unstable lip. 'When this hits the news, God. He'll be a child-killer, Tim. Isinger. Whether he is or not. The media needs one. You know what this means, right?'

Creed stared, his wheels turning, then dropped his head, knew.

It meant that now, Isinger *would* fit on the list with Gacy and Henry. Who had been child-killers too.

'So it was that prior . . .' Creed said, searching. '—George Williams. From the lease. He our guy?'

Watts shrugged, turned to the window.

The ground under the first body was still fresh. Like it hadn't been lying there for long. Had been moved.

'It's not like the rest,' she said—the bones hadn't been shortened, and the dumpsite had been hidden this time, not put in some life-size diorama with glow-in-the-dark cardboard arrows labeling all the evidence.

Watts shook her head no. Not that George Williams wasn't their guy—all the thousands of *George Williams*es in the country—but that maybe their guy hadn't done *this*.

'How did he *know*, then?' Creed asked.

'How does he know *any*thing?' Watts asked back.

The tendons in the neck of the corpse had drawn the skull back years ago, leaving the lower jaw in place so that the mouth was open. Like a baby bird, waiting for food, or a person, screaming underground. For twenty years.

'Your phone's ringing,' Creed said.

Watts was still looking at the corpse. The skeleton.

'You know what he's telling us, right?' she asked.

Creed looked up to her.

'That's he not like them,' she said. 'That he doesn't have the middle name Wayne, like the rest of the serial killers in twentieth-century America. Specifically, that he doesn't kill children, like Gacy or Henry. That's he's *other* from them. That he's not like every other dime-store sociopath with a reasonably sharp knife, a repressed sex drive, and half an hour to kill. That his relationship to them is like ours to him—that he can *identify* them.' She swept her hand around at the A-frame. 'That he knows where they live. Or used to.' She paused, then. 'Maybe too that there's enough of them scattered around America that he could have directed us to one no matter what that Texas sheriff's name had been . . . or else he knew that sheriff's name, and studied this town. Which would suggest he knew that sheriff wasn't going to live, right?'

Creed spit into the sink, washed it down. The water was brown and gurgly, hadn't been on in days.

He nodded like he didn't want to be nodding. Something about the eyes: narrowed, averted.

'This because he interrupted your constitutional?' he said, nodding down the hole in the bathroom floor.

Watts made herself smile. 'There was a third option your understudy there didn't mention,' she said. 'About that initial phone conversation.'

Creed cocked his head, as if the words would drain into his ear better that way. As if she was that much higher up than him.

'That he talked to him instead of you as a way of insulting *you*, Tim. To taunt you. And you don't taunt people you don't know. By its nature it's a personal act—knowing the buttons to push, all that.'

Creed was looking right at her now. Like interrogation.

She didn't flinch.

'I don't have any open files,' he said.

Watts nodded; knew.

'Maybe a victim's family or something, Tim, I don't know. It's just that this—Gentry, Bethel, Isinger—is too elaborate to just be a distraction. If that's all he wanted, he could have let the air out of our tires or something. Every morning. No.'

Creed had his eyes closed now. To think.

Watts palmed her vibrating phone, started to open it. Didn't quite.

'He's been planning this for a long time,' she said. 'Waiting for Isinger to get out, and whatever else.'

'So what's Texas got to do with it?' Creed said.

'That deputy,' Watts said. 'The Texas one. His name's Doe, right?'

Creed nodded.

'Like he's related to all these bodies our guy's been leaving for the campers. They're *all* Does, Tim. To us.'

Creed sucked air. Maybe that was what he did when he wasn't sure.

'You're going to say it's coincidence, aren't you?' Watts said.

Creed shrugged.

'It's not,' Watts said. 'You know why the world's so holy to schizophrenics with religious delusions, don't you? It's because every last blade of grass means something to them. *Nothing* is accidental. It's all part of some bigger pattern, or plan. Design. Pattern.'

'Better get it,' Creed said—her phone.

Watts unfolded it, listened. Looked away when it was done.

'What?' Creed said.

In the yard, in the floodlights, Agent Mingus was getting his ear stitched by a medic. Past him was a wall of emergency vehicles. And the news vans.

'Lydia,' Watts said, just as one of the dogs alerted on something under the floor in the kitchen. Something dead. 'Lydia, Kansas. They just found two . . . bodies. Children, they think.' She couldn't look at him as she said it.

Creed held the door open for her and then they left Tennessee.

14

5 APRIL 1999

DEERFIELD, KANSAS

DEBS was sitting at the convenience store with the security tape balanced on its short end on the table before him. He'd been looking at it for almost an hour. Waiting for it to tell him what to do, who to call. Arthur Dance was watching him. The night clerk, taking a day shift. Debs could feel it, that the boy was nervous. And he should be: the Indian on the tape stealing gas was probably one of his fugitive relations. Debs turned the tape over on its other end. He hated Kansas, sometimes.

Another tape Arthur had given him should have been recorded over already. If Arthur hadn't forgotten to turn the camera on.

Debs had smiled.

'Forgot?' he said.

Arthur slid the tape across the counter, zero eye contact. Debs watched it in the supply closet. It was that deputy from Texas, palming a candy bar from the rack right by the register. Debs had looked him up. He was twenty-five, right about to be twenty-six. If he closed his eyes, Debs could still remember twenty-five. When he opened them, Arthur Dance was still watching him.

Debs stared back at him until he looked away.

The water pump in Kalvesta had come back. The only car it fit was a mid-eighties 305. Which had been stock on the Impala. Debs spread out his copy of the photocopy he'd found crumpled in Kalvesta. The deputy had left it. He knew that now. The phone number was Castro County. Not Gentry anymore, though. Not Tom. Debs had half-expected him to rise up out of the ground on Sunday, take care of all this. But no.

Jim Doe was in a fever state in the Lydia jail.

The charges were many.

Debs stood the tape on its other end again, considered it, then just got in his car and drove the hell on up there.

The deputy was sitting on one end of his cot in his cell, his feet up on the mattress, his knees under his chin. To stay warm. He looked to Debs like Indians he'd seen in the movies who just pined away to nothing, looking out the window of their jail. He looked like every other Indian after a night in the drunk tank.

He stood when he saw Debs.

'You came,' he said.

Debs nodded.

The deputy smiled.

'I saw him,' he said. 'He was—'

'—at the graveyard,' Debs said. 'Yeah.'

They stared at each other.

Debs said this was Kansas, you couldn't just go digging up bodies in the middle of the night.

'There weren't any bodies, though,' the deputy said.

He was still on his side of the cell. His lower lip was raw and split. From Officer Lobichek. Who'd had to buy a new pair of sunglasses. Debs had heard it all on the way in.

'Can you get me out?' the deputy said.

Debs looked around, at the jail. 'They don't care about the assault charges,' he said. 'And nobody needs to know about the graveyard . . . they were Indian, I mean.' He looked back at the deputy. 'But those are just the Kansas charges.'

The deputy closed his eyes.

Debs told him about the Texas charges—the grand theft auto. Taking a county vehicle without authorization. Abandoning his duties there, when they were already short-handed. The statutory rape that girl's father was trying to file.

The deputy sat back down on his cot, pulled his knees up. You could have put an eggshell around him; he was shaped like that.

'You should cut your hair,' Debs told him. 'Starting to look like a blanket Indian or something.'

The deputy just sat there.

'For court?' he finally asked. His hair.

Debs went back to the front.

Bill McKirkle and Walter Maines were supposed to be on the way up, to retrieve him, the deputy. As a kindness to the memory of Tom Gentry. Late tonight, probably.

Debs looked back to where the deputy's cell was, apologized through the concrete, and stepped back out, to his car. Another day wasted. He pulled around back, to the deputy's truck in the impound lot. Just to see it. He didn't know why. Then he pointed the car south again, a styrofoam cup of coffee sloshing on his dashboard, steaming up the blue of his shotgun.

Ten miles out, then, he heard it. It came over the radio.

Because Debs couldn't believe it, he slowed, turned wide in the ditch, and swung back north of town, where it was happening. The roads were all strange, unfamiliar—smaller and smaller—so he finally had to park on the shoulder, wait for an official car to pass him. It did; he followed, everything in his glove compartment crashing into everything else.

The patrol cars and rubberneckers were arranged in a loose half moon just short of a stand of cottonwoods. Past them was a rise, high enough that most of the snow had melted off. A bald place. And in it, there they were, like the radio had said: two scaffolds, made the old way, with lodge poles and leather ties.

The bodies were eight feet off the ground, wrapped in sleeping bags. One had cartoons on it, *Space Chase*; the other was just blue, with ragged tears trailing fibers of unnatural white. They were adult sleeping bags, but the feet were wrapped back under the bodies. Children. The poles had feathers tied to them at odd places, and pieces of cloth. Debs stopped breathing for a moment, trying to remember if it was Easter or not.

Officer Lobichek approached the car while Debs was thinking. The chrome lenses of his sunglasses were perfect, tiny little silver suns.

'Sheriff,' he said.

'What do you make, here?' Debs asked.

From the angle he had in the front seat, he could see that one of Lobichek's eyes was still swollen blue.

Lobichek shrugged.

'Indian shit,' he said.

Debs nodded. 'Who are they, though?' he said.

Lobichek spit into the grass, rubbed it in with the toe of his boot, and lifted his chin at the horizon. A black helicopter was taking shape.

'Buzzards,' he said.

Debs grinned displeasure, looked out the side window, to the east.

Buzzards, yes: the FBI. It wasn't feeling like Easter, anyway.

They hadn't known about the scaffolds. Watts looked at her phone like it was responsible, should have told them, warned them.

A uniform with mid-seventies mirror shades approached them through the wash of their rotors. He introduced himself as Lobichek, acted like he was taking tickets here. Creed introduced them as FBI. Just that. Lobichek shrugged. All the uniforms were milling around the copter now, except one in a sheriff's car.

'Jackie Gleason?' Creed asked Lobichek, nodding out to the sheriff's car, and Lobichek turned around, pushed his smile out with his tongue, to hide it.

They got the bodies down with little ceremony. No eagles attacked them or anything.

'Unwrap them,' Creed said, and Cody did.

The bodies were black with decay, but they were the same: shortened.

Lobichek held his hand over his mouth, squatted down.

There was a turtle shell rattle tied to the blue sleeping bag.

He touched it with a stick. It made a dry sound that lodged in

Cody's spine.

'Blue Kettle,' Lobichek said. 'The old woman used to carry it to church.' He looked up to another uniform. 'Right? When they lived here?'

The other uniform nodded, said how they used to think it was a real turtle that had bit onto her finger, never let go. Lobichek smirked.

Creed stood, into the clean air.

'It's not them,' he said, to Watts, Cody. 'Not Isinger's.'

Cody nodded. These had the turkey foot across their torsos, from an autopsy. From when they'd been found under their tree in Pennsylvania or North Carolina or wherever. Before they'd been stolen back.

'What's he doing out here?' Creed said, to Watts.

'Kansas,' she said, then, 'Lydia. Think the name means anything?'

Creed shrugged, turned to Lobichek. 'Where are these Blue Elk—Blue *Kettles?*' he said.

Lobichek nodded toward town, like it was no big deal.

'It's not their kids,' he said. 'Their kids have been gone for a long time now. Wallace. Wallace and . . .' He smiled, getting it, getting something: '*Dorothy*.'

Creed just looked at him. For a long time.

15

5 APRIL 1999

LYDIA, KANSAS

THERE was leftover plastic grass on the counter at the Property window of the Lydia holding unit. The window was a lot of other things, too. It looked like it had originally been to pass food from a kitchen to a staging area of sorts. Like a restaurant, a breakfast place maybe.

Jim Doe was standing at it.

He had little idea what was happening. His fever was one hundred and three, leaning over to one hundred and four. His shirt was a second, wet skin, peeling from his back. He threaded his bangs out of his eyes, looking at everything again. Trying to understand. One moment, the two patrol officers had been there for shift change, milling around at the desks, looking sidelong over at him like he was a zoo animal, Sheriff Debs saying his goodbyes all around, and the next they were gone, evaporated. He thought maybe he'd slept again, but done it standing up this time, with his eyes open.

The woman standing beside him was Martha Blue Kettle.

The man was just Blue Kettle. Like the bow and arrow days, from the movies. He was talking to the duty officer—the rookie left behind to catch the phones, sergeant the desks. He didn't want to be there, either. And he usually wasn't the person who checked overnighters out. Even when it had been three nights.

His name was Charlie.

Charlie was counting Blue Kettle's stack of ten-dollar bills and doing it slow, trying to raise somebody, *any*body, on the radio. To know what to do here.

Jim Doe smiled.

The Blue Kettles were breaking him out, just doing it through the front door.

He lurched into the counter, playing it up. Charlie looked at him.

'He's sick,' Martha Blue Kettle said.

It was an accusation. Charlie was twenty years old, maybe, to her sixty. A third the person, maybe less. He apologized, calling her *Mrs. Kettle*. Like he was responsible for Jim Doe driving for days, not eating, not sleeping, digging in the rain. Raising a shovel against the law.

Martha Blue Kettle just kept staring at him, into him.

He keyed his mike open, begged for somebody to pick up.

Finally, somebody did. It was Sheriff Debs. He was explaining how the Lydia PD were all butt-buddied up with the federal boys right now, how their shoulder rigs probably *were* working, yes, but the helicopter was probably drowning them out, too.

Jim Doe could see it in Charlie's eyes: *helicopter*.

'Ask *him*,' Jim Doe said. 'The sheriff.'

Charlie looked hard at Jim Doe.

Jim Doe smiled.

Charlie asked Debs if he was sure the chief was out of reach. Debs said back he was on his knees over what looked like two dead children. Martha Blue Kettle breathed in, the flat of her hand to the hollow of her chest, and turned away.

'Well?' Blue Kettle said.

The money was all there.

'*Ask* him,' Jim Doe said, nodding at the mike.

Charlie did. He asked Debs what he should do—if he should let this deputy guy out on bail, or what?

Jim Doe could see Debs in his car, thinking, thinking. Looking back at the tape from Deerfield, at the station attendant in Kalvesta. At Tom Gentry. Weighing it all out.

Finally he said it: 'Are there any Kansas charges, son?'

Charlie shook his head no, said it.

'Then it's none of our business now, is it?'

Martha Blue Kettle led Jim Doe out to their 1963 cat-eyed Chevrolet truck. He sat by the door, for the window. She sat in the middle, by her husband. Jim Doe didn't ask if those were their kids out there on the scaffolds. It would have been impolite. He knew that much, at least. Instead he just let the air from the window rush into him, and wasn't at all sure if the Blue Kettles were helping him escape, or if they'd just bought him.

The next three days felt like more. Jim Doe's chest was on fire. He was staying in Wallace Blue Kettle's old room, in a trailer that had just been moved, it looked like. Taped to the side of the dresser where he could see it from bed was a school photo of a blonde-haired girl, a fifth-grader maybe. She'd be thirty by now. Jim Doe fell in love with her, moved in and out of his fever until he thought maybe he *was* Wallace Blue Kettle.

Martha, his mother, brought him cups of water and pieces of ice and changed his sheets while he was still in bed somehow, and the Indian thing she did to make him better was give him Tylenol for his fever, TheraFlu for everything else. They read the directions together, trying to get the maximum dose. Jim Doe wasn't even sure if he'd been *able* to read before her, before this.

But then at night with his eyes closed he would see her and Blue Kettle again at the cemetery, the water stringing down through their grey hair, their eyes somewhere behind that hair, and he would almost wake screaming. Because the longhair was there with them, only the longhair was *him*, Jim Doe. They were both responsible for Gentry's death. It made them one person.

'Why are you doing this?' Jim Doe asked Martha on the third day, when he could.

She shrugged, chewing on her lip, and looked out the window.

Blue Kettle was in the door behind her, leaning on the jamb.

Later that day, he came back, stood in the far corner of the room.

'You shouldn't be here, should you?' he said.

'Here?' Jim Doe said, looking around.

Blue Kettle smiled. '*Alive*,' he said.

Jim Doe shook his head. No, he shouldn't be. He should be with his sister.

Blue Kettle nodded. Like he agreed. 'But he didn't take you, either,' he said.

'He?' Jim Doe said, half ready to laugh. Blue Kettle wasn't.

'You're Texas, right?' he asked.

Jim Doe nodded.

'Ever talk to any Pueblos down there?'

Jim Doe shook his head no.

Blue Kettle said maybe he should. They could tell him about Whirlwind Man. How he liked to take people away.

Jim Doe closed his eyes.

'Dorothy,' he said.

When he looked again, Blue Kettle was gone.

The following morning, he was at the window in his blanket when Martha walked in with oatmeal. She said it was a traditional Indian delicacy. The glass of water beside the bowl was the glass that had come in the oatmeal container.

'What are they doing out there?' Jim Doe asked her.

She stood beside him.

A boy of maybe fourteen was setting rocks down on the coals of a fire he'd started three hours ago. In a pit.

'You want to get better, don't you?' Martha said.

Jim Doe nodded.

Four hours later, Blue Kettle waved to him in the window, telling him to come down. Jim Doe did. Blue Kettle smiled. Jim Doe came up to his nose, maybe. They were standing in front of a lodge half-buried in the ground. It was covered in old sleeping bags and deerskins and something with more hair, even, under the rest. Something older. Blue Kettle slung Jim Doe's blanket off his shoulders, onto the lodge, then peeled his own shirt off, stepped out of his boots.

Looked to Jim Doe.

'You can take your pants off or not,' he said. 'Fuck if I care.'

He took his off, and stepped through the flap.

Jim Doe stood alone in the stomped-down grass for a few breaths, then, suddenly unsure where he was anymore—Lydia? Kansas? the twentieth century?—he stepped out of his jeans, into the lodge.

It was black in there like ink. And thick. And there were more people in there than just Blue Kettle and himself. The shapes of other old men glistened when the boy outside hooked the flap open, spooned another hot rock in. Blue Kettle had the water in a tall, plastic pitcher. There was a tin ladle in it. He used the ladle to drip water onto the rock. It hissed. One of the old men coughed and coughed. And then the tin ladle made the rounds, from right to left. Before the old men drank, they splashed some on the ground. Someone put a bundle of cedar or something on the hot rock. Jim Doe held his mouth close to the ground, just to breathe. Four times he thought he couldn't take it anymore, and four times, he did. On the fifth, though, he pushed open the flap, rolled out, into a pair of jeans. Maybe his own.

The boy was leaning on his forked stick.

'Pretty damn hot, yeah?' he said.

Jim Doe nodded.

The boy shrugged, said that this was when they stuck the thermometer up his ass, like a turkey in the oven. 'Indian Thanksgiving,' he said.

Jim Doe was looking at Martha in the window, though.

'You're leaving now, aren't you?' the boy said, behind him.

Jim Doe nodded.

The boy shrugged again. 'They said you were,' he said. 'That it was time.'

'I don't know—' Jim Doe started. 'How should I thank them?'

The boy smiled, straightened his arm into his loose pocket.

'Take this off their hands,' he said. 'They don't know what to do with it.'

It was a set of keys braided onto a piece of leather. Chevrolet, the *GM* stamped there on the head of each. The round one was broken off.

The boy hooked his chin at the barn up by the road, then wouldn't look at Jim Doe anymore. Just the rocks, the earth around them baked dry, cracking open.

Jim Doe walked to the barn.

In it, golden with hay dust, was the blue Impala.

The key fit.

Jim Doe started it.

In a steel thermos on the passenger seat was chicken soup. It was still hot. Another old Indian remedy. Off-center so it *was* a viewing obstruction now, in the driver's way, was a different rearview mirror. A wide one, from a truck probably. It was adjusted so Jim Doe could see his mouth. He made it look out the back window instead. There was a twist of tobacco hanging from it by a red string. Like an air freshener.

Jim Doe touched it, setting it spinning, then backed out, to the edge of the house almost. He leaned out the window to the boy.

'Which way was he going?' he said.

One of his arms was hanging down the outside of the door, patting the bottom part of the door panel. It was rough with tar.

'Who?' the boy said back, smiling with his eyes, and Jim Doe smiled too, with his mouth, his tongue bit between his teeth, and pulled away, into Kansas, or wherever he was. He needed a shower, after the sweat. But it felt good, too. Clean. He thumbed through his wallet as he drove. All that was missing was three-ninety from the seventeen hundred. For bail. Which he was now jumping. He hesitated at the blacktop—north, or south—and then turned right. North. Into the clouds.

16

6 APRIL 1999

GENTRY, TENNESSEE

TENNESSEE was awash with bodies when they got back, each of them laid out in black bags on the lawn. Five. A whole family. And the house, it was crawling with forensic techs. Because their guy had been close, maybe here. On the utility pole up the road anyway. There was a crew down there already, pulling fibers from the wood, canvassing the houses in the area. Asking questions of the birds and the squirrels. Serious questions.

And the name on the lease, George Williams. Nobody. Invisible.

Cody smiled. Like this all hurt. Watts said they were the three blind mice here. Definitely not the cat, anyway. Cody touched his ear; it was still tender, some from the pellet, some from Creed, when Jim Doe had been gone from the Lydia jail, minutes ahead of them. Creed had asked in his calmest voice if the flying *monkeys* took him away, maybe? Lobichek hadn't laughed. Neither had Officer Charles Hawkins. And then when they got to the Blue Kettles' place, it was just a pad of dirt, their trailer gone for at least a year already.

The only thing they'd come out of Lydia with that had been any good was a set of fingerprints that the Garden City sheriff's office had faxed. He said they'd been waiting in his mail for him when he pulled back into town. Creed had rushed them through the field office in Nashville, and then sat looking at the wall a long time with Isinger's phone still off the hook before he said anything.

'Well?' Watts finally said.

Creed looked to her, to Cody.

'The prints are logged with Missing Persons,' he said. 'Some kid.' He looked to Watts. 'He's been missing almost twelve years now.'

Amos Pease.

But Creed wasn't finished.

Amos Pease's file was indexed with another. An *Amanda* Pease. They'd been eleven and . . . eleven. Brother and sister.

'Like Nazareth,' Creed said. 'Like Isinger.'

'We need an ID on those dead kids,' Watts said. Again.

'Blue Kettle,' Cody said. Like this was the first time they'd talked about it since Kansas. Like they'd been able to sleep on the plane.

Watts looked to Creed. 'There weren't any bodies in the graves, were there?' she asked, confirming.

Creed shook his head no.

The two graves the Texas deputy had opened.

'I don't know,' Creed said, standing from the chair, sending it skittering back into the wall.

'We'll find them, Tim,' Watts said. The Isinger children.

'Like we found the others . . .' Creed said.

Under a tree. Preserved.

Just outside the window was the dead family. The family of one Robert 'Rock' Bingham, according to the wallet on the tallest body. A shady parole officer, gone missing fourteen years ago. Marion Wayne *Isinger*'s one-time parole officer, from his first stint inside.

Killing his parole officer probably made some sort of sense at the time. But his *family* too? What had he *done* to Isinger? Or, how could the parole officer have done anything to their guy, to set him off this bad?

By three in the morning, the news vans were just idling in the street, the camera men slouching off towards the vague idea of coffee, the reporters walking the aisles of the convenience store for beauty supplies, the local PD taking discreet pictures with disposable cameras, of each other, here, now. They held the cameras low and casual, and then coughed when they wound them.

Creed stood at the window and watched.

'He was inside too,' he finally said—'locked up with Isinger'—then waited for Watts to respond.

'Maybe,' she said. 'We need to find out who he . . . vehicularly manslaughtered,' she said. Because maybe it was some dead girl's brother. Maybe it would all be easy like that. Easier than sifting through every inmate who did time with Marion Wayne Isinger, in two states, across twenty-five years.

'Amos Pease,' Cody said, then.

Creed turned to him.

'He killed that Texas sheriff,' Cody said. '*Gentry*. Two months after this house was leased. In *Gentry*.'

He was a data analyst.

Creed nodded.

'But he's not our guy,' Creed said, 'right?'

'Doesn't mean he doesn't work for him,' Cody said. Creed turned, looked at him until he looked away, the kid.

Maybe.

17

9 APRIL 1999

BETHLEHEM, PENNSYLVANIA

HE got a new car in Missouri, from another garage. Honest Injun's. In the daytime, Mr. Honest Injun in his Honest Injun coveralls bleeding out behind the Honest Injun tire-balancing rig, an Honest Injun fan belt wound tight around his throat. It left little grooves for the blood to run around his neck in. In trade, Amos left the car he'd driven out of Kansas. The new car was a 1981 LeMans.

At the first truck stop, nervous without any music, the road too full of sound, he found a plastic-wrapped *Royal Scam*, thumbed it in, turned it up. Drove. The states melted away behind him. This was his third run already. He was fixing the world. Making up for everything. All it had taken was one ambulance left parked on the street, two bottles of Dilantin in the cage. He mixed it with some Percocet and Xanax.

He tied his hair back, high up on his head, and became a woman he'd seen at the last gas station. He could feel the truckers looking at him from their high seats. He waved his fingertips at them.

In Ohio, a clerk asked what his name was. He recited from the paper in Kansas: Jim. Jim Doe. He stood around then, letting the camera get him from all angles but making it look accidental too.

No cops pulled him over. Because they'd heard about Texas. And there were no fireman anywhere, anymore.

The back of the LeMans was squatted down on the springs, so sitting behind the wheel was like sitting in the water, on a boat.

From a payphone he found himself at in West Virginia—detouring the long way around a weigh station at the Pennsylvania state border that was thick with highway patrol for some reason—he placed a call. His fingers knew the number without him, had been dialing on the dashboard for miles already, until he had to pull over.

The phone on the other end rang fourteen times before somebody lifted it. Amos could almost hear the cardigan, sweeping across the room.

'Mr. Rogers's house,' the man on the other end said, the voice cheerful, false, perfectly medicated. The kind that can only last for ten minutes, maybe, twenty in a perfect world.

'Um, yeah,' Amos heard himself saying.

While part of him talked, the other part did the necessary things. Like become aware again of the eight-ounce lighter in his front pocket, making Amos into a trucker, leaned into the booth, calling his wife, praying she was alone this time. But then it started pulling him down, too, the lighter. Pulling him away from the phone, trying to light itself, set the place on fire, bring all the firemen for three counties here like moths.

And then he would die.

He focused on his hand, the voice on the other end. He knew it from somewhere. Television?

On the screen in his mind, Mr. Rogers walked to the closet, hung his cardigan up in it, then turned around, but it wasn't him. His *face*—

Amos made his hand hang the phone up, went back to wipe it down, look along the wires, the strings. His. The puppet. But no.

He drove up into Pennsylvania, into Bethlehem.

He was very focused.

He sat in the LeMans cleaning his teeth until dark, then rolled the headlights on, eased through the outskirts of town, to the cemetery. They were all the same: unguarded. Like the dead didn't matter. But they did.

He didn't have to look at a list for the two names. He'd known them, could still see their faces in the darkness of the basement, even, when he didn't want to.

The ground above them was soft.

And the names on their headstones weren't theirs, anyway. They were fawns: LITTLE BOY DOE and LITTLE GIRL DOE. Because only adults were *John* and *Jane*. But Jane was supposed to be married to Tarzan. And Tarzan was a town in Texas, near Nazareth, where Jesus wasn't born. It didn't matter. The ground was soft, like the east. And fertile. Not the hardscrabble Amos knew from Nebraska.

But he couldn't think about that either.

Ever. Again.

He grubbed for pills, crushed them on a headstone, inhaled them from the crook of his thumb.

It made him dig faster, not thinking about it, not *letting* himself think about it. And then there they were, staring up at him, grown small again. One of them—the girl, always the girl—raised her arms for his neck, and he bent down, pressed his face into her shoulder as he lifted her from the ground.

The LeMans had a spacious trunk too. Like the Impala. *Spacious* was what they would say in the brochure. And *luxurious*. Amos smiled. His hair had grave dirt in it. He laid tobacco ties on each of the children's chests, at the point where the turkey foot carved into their torsos branched out into toes. Like the turkey had been what pressed them down into the ground. They put their hands over the tobacco in thanks. Because it was right, proper. And things had to be proper.

Amos closed the trunk, looked back across Pennsylvania, and turned the great car around, for South Dakota. He was fixing the world, body by body. It was a beautiful day in the neighborhood.

18

6 APRIL 1999

PAWNEE CITY, NEBRASKA

JIM Doe woke to the sound of a door shutting. He was on the side of the road, close enough that the big trucks still rattled his dash. He had been making himself sleep, making himself wait. There was a woman at his window, looking in, her hair dark around her narrow face, grey at the edges.

He blinked, she remained, and he said it before he could stop himself, in his head: *Mother? Mom?*

Behind her, strung out on the road, was her caravan. Ragged trucks with antennae sprouting out at odd angles, compact cars thick with laundry. A twenty-six foot Airstream camper with TAMBOURINE SKY stenciled on it in vivid blue, propane tanks clustered at the nose. Stormchasers.

Jim Doe stood, pulling himself up with the roof of the Impala. It left dry crumbs of vinyl on his hand. He held his palm open and they lifted away.

The woman was looking at him like she was trying to recognize him, remember him. She was hard, angular. Forty, fifty.

'Just wanted to see if you were alive,' she said, finally.

Jim Doe looked at his car, sitting at a slant in the ditch like it had just thawed out of some big drift.

'I am,' he said.

She stared at him, studying him. There was still sleep in her eyes, in her breath. She shrugged, started to say something, didn't, then just looked past him at the Impala. Turned; left. The people in her gypsy train were ragged and roped with veins.

Jim Doe watched them pass, then turned around and peed into the tall grass of the ditch. It steamed. He closed his eyes. A horse was watching him.

'I *am* alive,' he told it.

Under the front seat of the Impala was a bulky .44. Because he felt naked without a gun up here. He'd had to pay extra for it, because he didn't want the man behind the glass counter at the pawnshop to run his license. Or ask any questions. So they'd done it person to person, instead of shop to customer. There was no tax. Four hundred dollars. That was South Dakota. Rapid City. He talked to Monica almost every day now. She was all he had left of Nazareth.

He sat back down behind the wheel and pulled his new hat on, closed his eyes. He was still waiting. It would be suspicious to pull into Pawnee City before working hours. Or after. So last night he'd slept in the ditch, the horse's eyes glowing green at the fence, watching him. Until his windows had steamed over with breath. The long, clear lines in them were from hair that had been there two weeks ago. Long hair. At night they were black. Jim Doe looked through them sometimes, out.

Pawnee City was ninth on a list of nineteen towns.

The list was in one pocket of his shirt. In the other was a list of children's names, rubbed from plaques in town squares; from cemeteries. Monica had looked the towns up for him. It hadn't been hard. They had all been hit by tornadoes in the last twenty years. Since Nazareth.

Jim Doe closed his eyes again.

His hat was black. Seventy more dollars, but worth it. To be able to dip his head in a crowd and disappear again. He'd creased it in the steam rising up out of a motel bathtub mottled with stains. It had taken two hours to get it right—low in front and back, rising up the same on both sides. Motels were best for it. Because they had bigger water heaters, and kept them turned up, and there was nobody to yell at you from the kitchen.

The horse blew on his side of the fence.

Jim Doe threw him a frito.

It was why he'd stayed there all night, the horse: for more. It was the salt. He needed it after whatever winter had done to him. Maybe he was the last of his herd, even, the rest dying on their feet in the cold, the birds picking the meat from their backs first, and their eyes. Jim Doe hooked the bag on an old staple in one of the fence posts, let the horse have the rest. He wouldn't come near while Jim Doe was standing there, though. Jim Doe understood.

Two of the first four towns Monica had given him had had pairs of children missing, presumed dead. Each older than eight, younger than twelve. All Indian. Always a brother and a sister. Jim Doe's hand trembled near the bone when he copied their names down, and then he left. The longhair had to be doing something similar—why else would he have been in Lydia? He was following the storm, like Jim Doe. The storm that could select children by age, relation, race. Only he was carrying dead children around. Burying them the old way, in the air. Killing people who didn't need to be killed.

A truck blasted by, rocking the Impala on its tired springs. It had a mural on its forty-foot trailer—a stagecoach. The Old West. Jim Doe almost smiled: maybe when the trucker made it up to South Dakota, there'd be some Indian-muraled trucks waiting for him in ambush, the feathers outlined in chrome on their grills.

The truck pushed seven white birds up into the air before it. They had been in the ditch too. Probably something dead there. To sleep in. The birds rode the truck's air up into the grey sky, the sunlight blazing into their delicate bodies, ahead of the sun.

Working hours.

Jim Doe pulled up onto the blacktop. The plates he had now were still Kansas. Monica had run them. They were Taylor Mason's. Out of Kalvesta. Nobody had thought to declare them lost yet. His car was probably still in the garage, even, the yellow tape around the second bay fluttering and torn, plastic bags taped over the handles of the gas pumps.

She still told him to come home, Monica. Leaning low into the headset.

Bill McKirkle and Walter Maines were after him now, officially. After driving to Lydia. Jim Doe could feel them behind him, almost see them in his wide rearview, their legs long in their riding boots, their arms longer, with their guns.

He'd called Debs once, but not said anything.

Debs had laughed a little, then just said *run, boy, run*.

Because the Texas Rangers do not fuck around.

The tobacco wasn't hanging from the rearview mirror anymore, either. Because he couldn't get pulled over, Jim Doe. And he didn't speed. And he kept both hands on the wheel. And he did all the other things an Indian does not to get stopped, caught. Judged and sentenced on the side of the road. Sometimes he still half-expected Gentry to rise up over the trunk, call him home.

Jim Doe smoothed all his hair into a nervous ducktail, ran it under his collar.

It was too late to go home now. He'd gone too far. Pulling out of the Blue Kettles' a week ago, he maybe could have—turned back to Nazareth, rolled into town with his trophy Impala—but there had been another option too: stay out here in the badlands, letting his hair grow out, get long enough that he could just turn himself in. Because they were both the same person, now. They'd both killed Tom Gentry.

He drove.

Pawnee City rose up out of the haze to meet him.

At the plaque set into the ground by the tree they'd planted for them were the names, the children. Jim Doe ran his finger over the ridges of their raised letters, then did it again at the cemetery, where the letters were carved in granite. They both felt sharp—the brass, the stone—but different. He stood still and listened for the sound of decay beneath him. It wasn't there. Like his sister.

They had been eleven this time. Same birth dates.

The only breakfast place in town was the Red Burrito. Jim Doe sat there until noon, trying to write Amos and Amanda Pease into his notebook without saying *Dorothy*. Or the name under Dorothy. But then the highway patrol leaned into the glass door for the lunch he would insist he pay for this time, and Jim Doe lowered his head, his hat, and walked back to the Impala. It was at the edge of town, in the electric company parking lot. Those always seemed to be the best. Before five, anyway. And sometimes he could talk to the linemen, their gloves so thick they could catch lightning probably. And some of them did, just in places like the head.

At the intersection on the way out of town, there was a banner lolling from the blinking yellow light to a rain gutter on the second story of the beauty salon. The second story was boarded up. The banner was for a two-year high school reunion. Jim Doe smiled. What would they have to catch up on so soon? Who had moved out of their parents' garage? Who had moved back in?

He drove.

The longhair's tape was stuck in the player, looping through itself over and over. Jim Doe listened to it or to nothing, nodding with either, and then, ten miles out and on accident, he did the math: Amos and Amanda Pease had been eleven when they had been taken. Twelve years ago. Making them twenty-two now. A grade or two ahead of all the twenty-year-olds at the reunion tonight. Walking the same elementary halls. Sharing gum.

He sagged off the accelerator, let a grain truck hurtle past him.

He was shaking his head no, but then he was back again, at the beauty salon. The flyer taped in the window had more details. It was tonight, at the park, the NO ALCOHOL crossed out from every angle, a large bottle finally traced around the words like they were a model ship. Jim Doe tried to remember which liquor had a clipper on front like that. All the sails. He leaned into the beauty salon. Three old women peered up at him out of their hair dryers. It looked like they were subjects in a science experiment, their brains moving from one node to the next. Jim Doe thought of their husbands.

'Yes?' the stylist said to him. She was twenty maybe, and looking at his hair, a pink comb poised over a blue head.

The flyer. She'd probably put it up, and the banner too—would have a key to upstairs, anyway. Where they kept their beauty supplies.

'Which park?' he said.

The stylist let the hair she'd combed up sag down onto the old woman's head. The old woman had her eyes closed. Waiting for the magic.

'When did you go here?' the stylist asked.

Jim Doe stared at her. In his *other* other pocket was the picture of the girl Wallace Blue Kettle had been in love with in the fifth grade.

'Twelve years ago,' he said, letting her do the math later.

She turned her head to the side, catching him from another angle.

'*Chief?*' she said.

Her voice, not Gentry's.

'The park with the rocket ship,' one of the brain-transplant ladies finally said, impatient, her voice flat with it. Like Jim Doe didn't belong here. And he didn't. He nodded thanks, lowered his hat, and disappeared, found himself at the only payphone on the street. There was a thin directory dangling from it. More like a brochure, or a pamphlet.

He looked at the phone and told himself no. Because he knew he shouldn't. That it would be wrong.

The reunion wasn't until seven, though. At the rocket.

There was only one Pease in the book.

He dropped his quarter in, then the dime, and dialed, but couldn't say anything.

The person on the other end held on, though. With both hands.

'Amos?' she finally said, then, her voice quieter because there was more hope in it: '*Amanda?*'

Jim Doe hung up softly.

He could feel the stylist watching him from the second floor of the beauty salon.

At the convenience store, he bought Mrs. Pease a satin rose from the five-gallon bucket under the register, and then threw it out the window twenty times on the way out to her house, but never quite let go.

Mrs. Pease was wearing a Mexican sundress on the porch. She fainted from view when Jim Doe pulled up. When she saw his face. He arranged her on the couch. All ninety pounds of her. She fanned herself back to consciousness with the wing of some bird. Eagle? Goose? Jim Doe wondered where the other wing was. The rest of the bird.

She put her hand around his forearm. Hard.

'Amos,' she said.

Jim Doe showed her his badge, shook his head no. Apologized.

She looked away.

Mr. Pease was gone. Who knew where. Not at the cemetery anyway.

Jim Doe said he had some questions about twelve years ago. The storm.

Mrs. Pease brought him the album. In it were pages of milk cartons, all flayed open, the picture on the back split—one side for Amos, one for Amanda.

'They're still alive,' Mrs. Pease said, her voice hushed.

Jim Doe looked up at her, at his sister in some room she didn't know. At Jerry the Hat, having to pretend to be her brother.

'That's why we did the missing people paperwork,' Mrs. Pease was saying. She pulled one glass out of a small box, then another. The glasses had been dusted. For prints. They were the children's juice glasses, the morning they were stolen. The wind had left them for her out in the field. The prints had been good, set in orange juice. And the children. They were in pictures all over the house. Amos and Amanda. Jim Doe understood Mr. Pease a little. Being gone. The children watched you here.

He made himself look at the table again, became aware of the glass he was holding, the oily fingerprints he was leaving on it. How long they would be there.

Mrs. Pease was standing at the kitchen window, looking out at the Impala.

'Amos always liked blue,' she said.

Jim Doe nodded. He hadn't thought about blue as a color for a long time now.

'Who took them?' he said, closing his eyes for the answer.

He heard Mrs. Pease turn to him.

She sat a plate of food on the table by his glass.

'Eat,' she said, and he did, and as he did she turned the radio on for cover and explained to him how the government had taken Amos and Amanda. Because they wanted twins for their experiments. Everybody knew it, that twins were best. Just put them in separate rooms and see how they're the same as their brother or sister, how they're different. And her twins were special, *Indian*. She smiled. Jim Doe was still eating.

'I understand why they took them,' she said, finally. 'Just not why they haven't given them back yet.'

Jim Doe swallowed in a big lump that bruised his throat all the way down.

'They wouldn't—*won't* be . . . eleven anymore,' he said.

Mrs. Pease nodded. Lowered her eyebrows. Like of course they would.

But he could still see how she'd looked at him when he pulled up.

Two miles from her house, back towards Pawnee City, Jim Doe opened the door, threw up everything he had in him and cried, for his own mother, wherever she'd gotten herself by now. After Nazareth, after waiting for him to graduate. Counting the days until she could leave, helping him with his algebra so he wouldn't fail, slow her down.

Jim Doe took the .44 out from its place.

There was a system building to the east. He'd watched it two nights ago on a motel television, under a different name. He couldn't see it yet, but it was there. The small animals knew already. Jim Doe could picture them, even, the children pack rats in their rag-and-stick school, their teacher showing them how to lace their fingers over the backs of their heads and hide under their desks from the wind, one small student in back sneaking peeks at the wall, where there was something shiny buried, a bottle top or chip wrapper turned foil-side out, he couldn't tell. If he could only get his mouth on it, taste it, take it back to his room and bury it, keep it for himself.

Jim Doe still had his mother's wedding ring. She'd left it on Horace's remote control the day she left. It was another thing nobody knew about. Like the .44. Jim Doe lifted it to the sky, brought the back of it back down to his forehead. Didn't know what to do anymore. He hadn't even given Mrs. Pease the rose. He laughed. It was funny. Everything. Nebraska, Kansas, Texas, all of it.

The stylist was still calling him Chief at the reunion. Jim Doe had sat in the nose of the metal rocket, waiting for it to start, then descended when the whole class was there. Or everybody that was coming. There were twenty-two people.

'You used to have a sister, right?' the stylist asked him, and Jim Doe pretended to just look through her, to the punch bowl. It was transparent with vodka. No flies.

One of the stylist's cheerleader friends made eyes at her, pulled her away, holding her hand out to Jim Doe, palm up, in apology.

'Yes,' he said. I had a sister.

He slammed the punch, threw it up in the street—his throat swollen now—and came back, filled his cup halfway, just so nobody would bring him any more.

Pawnee City. These were the people that had known them, Amos and Amanda. They were all clumped into groups of two or three, except one guy. He was standing off with the beer he'd brought. The cans glinted. He was short and rangy, his hair like a surfer's. A thick line of scar tissue across his chin. He lifted his can to Jim Doe. Jim Doe lowered his hat. He didn't know why he was here. What he was doing.

The next time he looked up, the guy was there.

'You're not dead,' he said.

Jim Doe shook his head.

'Lindsey thought maybe you were,' the guy said.

Jim Doe looked to him.

'In the ditch?' the guy said. 'This morning? You must have been gone, hoss. Shit.'

Hoss. It was another of his father's names. Right after *Horse*.

Jim Doe smiled, pretended.

'Tambourine Sky,' he said.

The guy nodded, said his name was Sandy. It matched his hair. His classmates were all pretending he wasn't there.

'Jim Doe,' Jim Doe said.

Sandy shrugged. 'Fine with me, man,' he said. 'Whatever.'

Jim Doe shook his head, wanted to say no, *really*. It wasn't a fake name.

Sandy told him how they'd found a dead guy last week, was the thing. Just pulled over, not breathing. It happened. But now they were looking in all the cars. Like they *wanted* to find more. Like Lindsey did.

'I thought she was my mother at first,' Jim Doe said.

Sandy looked at him all over again.

'She supposed to be up here?'

Jim Doe shrugged: yes. Maybe.

'What do you do?' Jim Doe asked.

Sandy offered him a beer. Jim Doe cracked it open, didn't drink. Couldn't.

'Tambourine Sky,' he said, shrugging. 'The noise in the sky right before a tornado, yeah?'

Jim Doe tried to remember. *Tambourine* wasn't a word he would have used, though. It didn't have any blood in it.

'You know you're freaking these people out here,' Sandy said, his index finger pointed past his beer, the rest of his fingers holding on.

Jim Doe looked at them, the people.

'They think I'm Amos,' he said.

Sandy nodded.

He had a joint in the picture part of his wallet. Jim Doe shook his head no, thanks. As if he were still on duty. Sandy shrugged again, sloped off to the road. Jim Doe followed. They stood on the other side of an old Dodge van.

'Why are you here?' Sandy asked, voice strained, lungs compressed, holding the smoke in.

'I don't know,' Jim Doe said. 'My sister—'

That was all he could manage.

Sandy nodded, his eyes watering.

'The storm took her,' Sandy said, breathing out smoke. Not looking away.

Jim Doe made his hand into a fist by his leg.

Sandy smiled. 'Not an uncommon story, around here.'

'Here?'

'Tornado Alley, man.'

Jim Doe nodded.

'You should talk to Lindsey, you know?' Sandy said.

Jim Doe was watching the shapes of Sandy's classmates move in the dim glow of the barbecue pits. 'I already talked to their mother,' he said, finally. 'Mrs. Pease.'

'Rita,' Sandy said, tossing the roach. It sparked across the asphalt.

'Rita,' Jim Doe said. He hadn't known what the *R* was for in the phonebook. Didn't ever expect to.

Sandy laughed. To himself. 'I should have told her,' he said, then lowered his face, like he was looking away from Jim Doe. But he wasn't. 'Of all the people you could have talked to here . . .' he said.

'You picked me,' Jim Doe said.

Sandy shrugged.

Jim Doe didn't say anything, and while he didn't, Sandy explained it, what got him started. It was back in elementary, when Rita and William and Amos and Amanda still lived in town. When the storm came through. It had pulled the wall of their house away brick by brick. Sandy standing there, no longer hiding. The insulation had floated up slow before him, to a certain point, then slipped away. Amos had been behind him, watching him watch, but then Amos pulled him into the fireplace with him and Amanda. Amanda was already black with soot. They balled up as deep as they could, held the andirons in front of them, and then the roof was gone too, the wind screaming down the chimney at them, the damper slamming open and closed inches from their heads.

Sandy lifted his chin, touched the scar.

'This is what you get for looking up in a tornado,' he said.

Jim Doe nodded. Sandy went on.

After the wind was gone, a man was there with them. They hadn't even heard him walk up, even though everything was glass and wire and broken stuff. Jim Doe nodded. The man had been a fireman, Sandy said, his facemask pulled down tight. He looked around, then into the fireplace.

'Your father,' he said, 'he's waiting.'

His held his gloved hand out, down.

In his other hand was a six-foot pry bar. Sandy said that's what he had been watching, the pry bar. Because it was like a great iron spear.

'Who are you?' Amos had said, not taking the hand yet.

The fireman had laughed. 'Amos?' he said. 'That you?'

Amos had looked over to Amanda, and then, before he could stop her, she'd taken the fireman's hand. He pulled her out, set her down.

'Amanda,' Amos said, hissing it.

She turned back to him, still holding the fireman's hand.

'C'mon,' she said. '*Daddy*.'

Amos breathed out through his teeth, looked back to Sandy, then stepped down, and then they were gone. Just like that.

Jim Doe watched Sandy as he said it: Gone. Poof.

He leaned his surfer head back against the stars, his Adam's apple distinct against the white brick of the house across the road.

The fireman had never seen him.

He had been black from the flue, from the soot. Blood dripping off his chin.

'Why didn't you tell her?' Jim Doe asked. 'Mrs. Pease?'

Sandy shrugged. 'I tried, hoss. Honest. But that next Sunday—you know how everybody goes to church, if it's still standing?'

Jim Doe nodded. They did, yes. To raise their voices to God, in thanks, in anger, in something.

Sandy smiled. 'Well, our preacher then. Brother Moss. Mossman. Like the shotgun. I wanted *him* to tell her for me. Because she was crazy back then, man. Rita. Serious. Losing both her kids like that.' Sandy laughed then, to himself almost. 'You know what, though? Mossman, that motherf—that *preacher*. He told me what I'd seen. That it was the angel of death, taken human form. To ferry Amos and Amanda up to heaven. I wasn't supposed to have seen it, even. You don't know how it scared me, dude. To have a secret with *God?* I mean Holy . . .'

Jim Doe had his eyes closed.

But there was more.

'He was wrong, though,' Sandy said. 'You know how I know? When they drained the pond in high school, man. Goddammit. I don't know if you can understand what it's like, but . . .' He stopped, pinching his nose between his thumb and forefinger. 'That fucking pry bar,' he said. 'It was in the pond. That six-foot pry bar. And you don't just throw those away, even if you're an angel, y'know? I mean, they cost like seventy dollars . . .'

His words were slurring together.

Jim Doe wanted to touch him on the shoulder, couldn't.

Sandy raised his right knee once, then his left, ran in place a bit. 'I can't believe I'm even telling you this,' he said. 'But, hey. You want to hear some real tornado bullshit, you should truck it out and talk to Lindsey, man. The woman's mad.'

Tambourine Sky.

Jim Doe asked where it was, the camper, and the last thing he saw walking away from the park was the rocket, nosing up into the sky. He walked backwards until he couldn't see it anymore, and then he walked forward, his hands in his pockets, his breath white in front of him.

The Airstream was parked at an angle in the ditch, the propane rack pushing up against the city limits sign, the tongue of the trailer sticking out over the line. There was laundry drying on the sign already, music rolling out the small windows.

Jim Doe knocked on the door everyone looked at when he walked up, as if telling him where to touch.

Lindsey opened it, stood in it.

'Sandy said to talk to you about . . . my sister,' he said.

Lindsey smiled.

'I'm the old woman in the cave,' she said.

Jim Doe stepped up when she stepped aside.

In the camper you had to stand with all your weight on your downhill foot, hold your drinks at a permanent tilt.

'You're the one they're looking for,' she said, touching his face without quite touching it, with the palm of her hand. Like she did have children, who slept in beds, that she could come look at whenever she wanted. 'That's where I know you from. Every store in Kansas. I can't buy cigarettes without seeing you.'

Jim Doe shrugged.

He'd probably put some of those flyers up himself. And some he hadn't.

'So what's the occasion?' Lindsey said. 'You just trying to bring the law down on us?'

'I am the law,' Jim Doe said. 'Used to be.'

Lindsey looked at him again, still studying him, gauging him.

'Sandy told me about Amos Pease,' Jim Doe said.

Lindsey shrugged, straightening things on the counter.

'I never knew him,' she said.

Maybe five feet from where she was sitting, a jeep roared by. No pipes, just straight headers. One of the caravan. Lindsey turned to the sound.

'You should see,' she said, and led him outside.

On the road, some of the Tambourine Sky people had a parachute tied to the roll bar of an orange jeep. They were running the jeep up and down the road, jumping into the air for long minutes. When they landed it was on knee-pads, loud.

'Wanna try?' Lindsey asked.

The parachutes looked like kites. Jim Doe shook his head no.

'Sandy says you've heard stuff,' he said.

Lindsey was watching the jeep.

She nodded.

'Travel in chemistry circles, you hear about formulas,' she said, then turned to him. 'I run with the stormchasers, mostly.'

Jim Doe nodded.

They sat in the gravel inches from the road—close enough to still get the heat it had soaked up during the day—and she told him about being a little girl with the measles. About running for the cellar, the hail raising red welts on her back, through her muslin nightgown. About how her aunt was already there, her pregnant aunt, and their grandfather had to look down at the two of them like Solomon, make the decision. Who got to hide from the wind in the cellar. Because the measles can't be with the pregnant people.

Lindsey turned to Jim Doe, her hair strung all across her face. She shrugged. 'That was my first time,' she said. 'In the storm, I mean. Kind of ruined me for normal life, I guess.'

'What about the Whirlwind Man,' Jim Doe said.

Lindsey closed her eyes hard, then let it out in a laugh, through her nose.

'I'm sorry,' she said. 'You're not the first one to figure it out, y'know. If that helps.'

'Figure what out?'

'It's nothing,' she was saying. 'Urban legends and all. Like the Candyman.' She stopped. 'But not, I know.'

'*What?*' Jim Doe said.

She stood. Out past them, someone was floating down out of the sky, steering onto the road, their lead lines trailing, the jeep driving underneath, trying to get them again. Flashlights cutting the night into pieces.

'That he comes during the storm,' Lindsey said, all at once. 'That he takes . . . that he takes the people the wind missed somehow.

Because it should have got them. It's about balance. I think it's Indian, a long time ago, maybe. Making the world right and all. Balancing it.' She looked to him. 'It's just not . . . easy,' she said. 'Right?'

Jim Doe nodded.

He'd driven two thousand miles to hear somebody say that. A mom.

'Where does he—*it*—take them?' he asked.

Lindsey just looked at him, then.

'You won't find her,' she said.

Jim Doe didn't let himself look back at her.

'I'm looking for somebody who . . .' he said, unable to make it into words—Gentry. 'I need to find somebody else.'

'The one in the flyers.'

Jim Doe nodded.

'Not yourself,' Lindsey said. Not a question.

After a few minutes, Jim Doe was alone again, leaning against a post, watching the parachutes glide down. At some point he slept, woke to a jeep, twenty inches from his face, then gone, then he slept again. In the morning, Lindsey offered to trade cars with him. That he might make it a little longer like that. A little farther. He looked to the Impala. The trunk was still tied down, from being pried open in Lydia. It was the first place he'd looked for the longhair, balled up in there like an embryo. It still had a smell to it. Maybe that was why the horse wouldn't come close.

Jim Doe nodded, handed the key to her, worked the pistol into his jeans.

'It's a gift,' she said, underhanding the keys to Sandy. 'You're Indian, right?'

Jim Doe nodded.

She told him he couldn't say no, then.

The car they were trading him was an old Monte Carlo, late seventies. It was supposed to run good, or, good enough.

Jim Doe stood against it as the caravan pulled away, then the brake lights of the Impala flared. Sandy reversed back to him.

'Hey, hoss,' he said. 'I can't be driving around with this, man. Shit. Bad luck.'

It was a newspaper clipping. From mid-May 1991, a North Carolina paper.

The bead of his pistol must have pulled it out from under the seat.

It was an artist's recreation of two children, a boy and girl, found in the woods, dead. In a holy little place called Bethlehem.

Jim Doe looked up, over the paper, to the east, the Atlantic, and waited for it to rise up, crash over him.

19

19 MAY 1982

NAZARETH, TEXAS

THE fireman. He was moving along the edge of town in the boots. The boots were too big for him. His heart was slapping the inside of his chest. He wasn't even sure he was going to do it, yet. Maybe he would just look at them. Or maybe they'd be already dead. Everywhere there was rain, and water. Power lines waved in the sky like tree branches, and trees lay on their sides like fallen people, still reaching up for something. The roots were gnarled and black and terrible. He held the back of his hand over his mouth, to not have to smell them.

The fireman he'd taken the jacket and boots and helmet from had been stuck in a barbed wire fence. He'd looked up at the rock coming down for him, then just taken it, as he had to. The human skull was like a dried gourd. He'd half-expected flies to mass up out of it, each one with a fraction of intelligence, emotion. Scattering. He would have chased them and eaten them and saved them inside.

But it was just the usual grey, the usual red.

He put the boots on, and the jacket, and the gloves, over the cotton ones he was already wearing. His fingers were thick and protected now. He flexed them as he moved from tilted cornice to tilted cornice, telephone pole to telephone pole. Nazareth was gone. Things were still falling from the sky, even. The first dead people he'd found had been three women in an upside-down car. They still had their seat belts on, were staring straight ahead, their ponytails hanging down, brushing the roof liner.

He'd wanted to take a picture, but the gloves were so thick, and the flash: somebody would see it.

He was supposed to be *helping*.

He laughed, ran.

He wasn't going to do it. He knew now. Because it could never work. How would he get them back, even? No. The thing to do was walk back to that fireman in the fence, dress him, maybe leaving the jacket inside out or something, just because it would get blamed on the tornado. Everything would get blamed on the tornado, even him, maybe, if he got caught.

He ran, and laughed, and the cotton in his ears made the laughter sound foreign.

The fireproof jacket billowed around him, the air still charged blue.

People weren't even emerging from their homes yet, or their fallout shelters, or the mattresses they'd pulled over their bathtubs, the down jackets they'd wrapped themselves in, in the cedar closet, their grandmother's scent all around them.

After a few hundred feet, he just stood, listening, and finally a female cat broke from a tumbled wall, raced across what was left of the street. He knew she was female because they were all female. He'd heard it like that in a joke once. He looked behind an untouched car, for the idea of a dog, because dogs and cats went together. He had an axe in his hand, though, while he was looking. Which made it different. He looked down at the head as if just realizing it was there. Yes. He looked to the cat, nodded, smiling, and said it: 'Here kitty kitty kitty.'

The cat just watched him, its ears slicked back.

They stared at each other like that until the woman stood from under her couch. She was bleeding. She stumbled through her open-air living room, leaned in the doorframe. It was the only thing left.

The fireman with the axe waved at her.

She lolled her head to the side.

'You okay?' he called out, cupping his mouth with his thick glove.

She looked around, maybe laughed.

He walked to her at right angles. Because that felt like the right angle, right then.

'Are you hurt, ma'am?' he asked.

His facemask was down now, already, but it didn't matter. She was looking at his axe.

He looked at it too.

There were still pieces of the other fireman on it.

'It's not what you think,' he told her.

'What?' she said.

Her pupils were blown wide. There was blood trailing down from her right ear. He traced it with a numb finger and she shivered, hugged herself.

'Are you going to save me?' she said.

He smiled, touched her shoulder.

'Not all of you,' he said, and she turned to him slow.

This was like the old days, God.

But no. Not anymore. Just this once.

After her, he found a dog, maybe the dog the cat had been remembering, even, and he let it go with a broken pelvis, and then, for long, boring minutes, nothing. He was shrugging out of the yellow jacket—the *game*—when the girl stood from the broken boards and gritty shingles. The children, yes. He'd nearly forgotten about them somehow. And she was so dark.

'Where's your brother?' the nice fireman asked.

A boy stood up beside her then, as dark as her and almost as tall.

Yes.

The fireman put the middle finger of his glove into his mouth, bit the empty part at the tip, pulled his hand away, then did it again with the cotton underneath, until it was just bare skin—*him*.

He held his hand out to the girl.

Later he would learn that it was always the girl who reached up first. Because he was the perfect father—the hero, saving her.

'Hello,' he said to her.

She had wet sheetrock dust over one side of her face.

She told him her name. He told her yes, he knew, it was a beautiful name too, and then she took her brother's hand and they picked their way out through the rubble, and he had no idea then where he was going to take them, what he was going to do. Just that they were holding his hand, that they were alive, warm, and that they would be enough.

PART TWO

20

27 APRIL 1999

QUANTICO, VIRGINIA

SPECIAL Agent Cody Wayne Mingus took the call. This time it was really for him. A Texas Ranger. *McKirkle*. He didn't ask questions, just talked. Cody held the phone to his ear and listened. The trace was already coming back on the new rig by the phone: Ypsilanti, Missouri. There was no attempt to mask it.

McKirkle didn't want to be calling, either.

It was about Jim Deer. He corrected himself: *Doe*. Like Jim Doe was there, having to listen.

McKirkle said something off-phone, then came back. What he wanted to know was why their girl in Castro County thought the FBI had this former deputy's file flagged.

'Because we need to talk to him,' Cody said.

McKirkle spit. That's what it sounded like.

He said they'd *already* talked to him. That he didn't have much to say anymore, really. His voice was gravel.

The address that matched his phone came up. It was a motel.

'What's he doing now?' Cody asked.

McKirkle laughed.

'Think Deer Boy here's watching himself a little John Wayne,' he said.

Cody hated Texas. Even the shape of it.

'Well,' McKirkle said. 'You can take your flag off now, I guess.

We're taking him back. Nothing to worry about.'

'I don't think you understand,' Cody said.

'No,' McKirkle said. 'Think it's maybe the other way around, FBI.'

'I'm asking you as a federal officer to surrender your prisoner, *Officer*.'

'And I'm telling you back as the man who caught his ass, Agent. *No*.'

Cody leaned his head back, eyes closed.

'You know you can give this one up,' he said. 'It's not like he's the Alamo or anything.'

Then he had to call back.

This time a Maines answered. He leaned forward, into the phone, documenting for Special Agent Cody Wayne Mingus just how many states they'd chased this Indian through. What the room they'd finally caught him in looked like now.

'And anyway,' he said. 'We like to kill our own rats, Agent.'

Cody said he was sure they did. But James Alan Doe wasn't one of those rats.

'He has to answer in Texas,' Maines said.

'He can do that when we're done with him,' Cody said, just as low.

'What do you want with him?' Maines asked.

'That's federal,' Cody said.

Maines laughed. Texas was the only state in the union that could raise its flag as high as the American flag. Cody had seen that somewhere. He could hear it in Maines's voice, now.

'I can make you give him up,' Cody said.

Maines didn't even bother to cover the receiver when he repeated it to McKirkle. Their laughter boomed up out of Missouri.

'Repeat,' Cody said, leaning forward now himself, 'I can goddamn well *make* you surrender him.'

Maines was drinking something. He swallowed, exhaled.

'Want us to deliver him to your *door*, Agent, or should we just leave him with a Marshal?'

'Local will be fine,' Cody said.

Maines snorted.

'Hope you never need us for anything,' he said.

'If we decide to chip a piece of Mexico off again,' Cody said, 'we'll give you a call. How's that?'

McKirkle said something in the background but Maines was already hanging up, pushing the phone down deeper than the manufacturer would recommend, it sounded like.

Three states, two planes, and one rental car later, Special Agent Cody Wayne Mingus was standing outside Jim Doe's cell. Jim Doe was battered around the head, probably blue on the inside.

'You fought them,' Cody said.

'Just a little Cowboys and Indians,' Jim Doe said, standing. 'You're here to take custody of me?'

'I'm here to take custody of you,' Cody said.

Jim Doe nodded, chewed his cheek. 'It's not me, you know,' he said.

'We know,' Cody said.

Jim Doe smiled. 'You ran my duty roster anyway, right?'

'And your bank records, and your taxes, and all your quarterly evals.' He smiled a bit. 'Even that D you got in geography in the sixth grade.'

Jim Doe smiled. 'I should have known Missouri was here, right?'

Cody shrugged. Jim Doe was still looking at him.

'So it wasn't me?' he said.

'It wasn't you.'

Jim Doe pursed his lips, still unsure.

'What do you want from me, then?' he asked.

'Just to come in from the cold for a bit,' Cody said. 'Maybe talk.'

Jim Doe smiled. 'Talk,' he said. He was watching the sky on the television on the duty officer's desk. Cody looked too. It was time-capture weather—clouds roiling across the face of the earth.

Cody nodded, said it again: 'Talk.'

Jim Doe adjusted his jumpsuit. It was tight across the shoulders, orange everywhere else.

'You haven't said anything about my name,' he said.

'It's an hour to the airport we're using,' Cody said.

The paperwork was already waiting for them at the front desk.

Cody nodded to the uniforms as he left. They stared back. Missouri.

'So what can you tell us about Amos Pease?' Cody said, in the parking lot.

Jim Doe looked to him.

'The one who shot your sheriff,' Cody said.

Jim Doe smiled, looked away.

'I just talked to his mother,' he said, in wonder.

'You're after him,' Cody said. 'All that vigilante Texas crap, right?'

'Something like that.'

'And he was in Missouri?'

'Was, yeah,' Jim Doe said. 'Maybe.'

They settled into the car, Cody opening and closing Jim Doe's door, Jim Doe stepping small, around the shackles holding him at wrist, waist, feet.

'So you want him too,' he said. 'Amos Pease. The FBI wants him.'

Cody pulled onto the empty road. Any lane, just east.

'We could ask him a few questions, yeah,' Cody said, then looked over at Jim Doe. 'Like who took his sister. Who took yours.'

Jim Doe looked back across the seat, locked eyes.

'You know?' he said.

'Some,' Cody said, and filled Jim Doe in on the White Chapel case, nevermind clearance.

'White Chapel,' Jim Doe said. 'Like London. Jack the Ripper.'

Cody nodded. 'You've got the Discovery Channel,' he said.

Jim Doe nodded. 'He didn't kill . . . sixteen?'

Cody nodded.

'He didn't kill sixteen, though,' Jim Doe said.

'That we know about,' Cody said.

Missouri fell away behind them. Ten miles from the airport, they nosed into a truck stop just as the clerk was flipping the neon on. It changed everything.

'Can I trust you?' Cody said, his hand still on the shifter.

Jim Doe thinned his lips out. 'Buffalo Bill wants to know if he can trust me,' he said.

Cody looked over at him 'You're what?' he said back. 'Crazy Horse?'

'Do you even know any more Indian names?' Jim Doe said.

'Like Buffalo Bill's so original?'

Jim Doe shrugged, smiled the other direction.

Cody left the leg-irons on. Jim Doe's Levi's almost covered them, except for the chain. The rest of his personal effects were in a cardboard box in the trunk of the rental car: one Smith & Wesson .44, nickel-plated, pearl grips; one pair Tony Lama boots, 11D, the uppers fitted with mule ears that wouldn't go past the shackles; one men's wallet, leather, with a check in it from the City of Ypsilanti for $411.35. The cylinder to the pistol was in the glove compartment, the chambers stuffed with plugs of cloth from a motel bedspread. The box of shells was in Ypsilanti, along with the Monte Carlo. It had been in somebody in North Dakota's name. They didn't have a phone.

Bill McKirkle and Walter Maines had left the bill for the motel room for Cody, too. For the FBI. It included damages, possibly a lawsuit.

Jim Doe's badge was clipped to his wallet. It wasn't good anymore. Earlier, Cody had called him *Deputy*, and Jim Doe had repeated it, tasted it in his own mouth again.

Cody held him by the elbow, guided him around the front of the car to the truck stop. They hadn't been able to find anything decent on the radio for all of Ypsilanti.

'Isn't there some famous killer from here?' Jim Doe said.

Cody looked around, shut the door behind them.

The government bought them forty-four-ounce drinks. The sign in the window said twelve of those ounces were free. The chain of Jim Doe's leg irons rattled across the tile. In the convex mirror back by the cooler, everyone was watching them, the law officer and his prisoner, each trying to decide which plastic-wrapped hamburger to get, which to leave.

Finally, Jim Doe shuffled through the line, Cody right behind him, between him and the door. Their burgers were still in the microwave, their clear shells swelling. Jim Doe told Cody to be sure to get lots of ketchup, said it while Cody was already getting the ketchup. Meaning if he kept getting it, it was because Jim Doe had told him to. Cody countered by just getting more ketchup than two people could possibly ever eat.

'Ever carried a prisoner across state lines before?' Jim Doe asked him.

'You?' Cody asked back.

Jim Doe set something else down on the counter by their drinks: a cassette tape.

Cody looked up at him.

'Had to leave my other one in impound,' he said. 'It was stuck in the player.'

'What is it?' Cody said.

'It's good,' Jim Doe said.

Cody looked at the tape rack. Had they even walked close enough to it to get one?

He nodded to the clerk, bought it, bought it all, then let Jim Doe thumb it in while their cellophane hamburgers were cooling on the dash, in the sunlight. The music rolled out syrupy and stoned through the rental car speakers, and Cody felt like Creed, maybe, when Cody had said it, about all the white men in the street.

The music washed over him. The song, the album.

He groped for the plastic case: Steely Dan, *The Royal Scam.*

'Where'd you get this?' he managed to say to Jim Doe.

'At the store, Sherlock,' Jim Doe said. 'Remember?'

That wasn't what he meant, though.

Thirty minutes later they were at the airport, Cody leaned into a booth, for Creed. The Isinger children's faces were on all the monitors in the terminal. Jim Doe kept looking at them.

'What does he want with them?' he said to Cody. 'They're not Indian . . . ?'

Cody shrugged.

Creed was telling him they weren't coming to Virginia, not yet.

'Where, then?' he said.

'Pennsylvania,' Creed said. Like an apology. 'Since you're already in the air and all. We've got other agents checking the rest.'

'Why?' Cody interrupted, watching Jim Doe. Because he never had transported a prisoner across state lines, didn't know how fast they could run.

'Those bodies in Lydia,' Creed said. 'The X rays came back positive. They're definitely ours, we're just not sure which ones.'

'You've got a radiologist looking at it, right?' Cody said.

Creed smiled. Cody could hear it.

'Just make sure they're still there,' Creed said.

'Why is he taking them?' Cody said, quieter.

'Who?' Creed said.

Cody nodded. Which one: Amos Pease, or the one behind Amos Pease.

Because of Jim Doe's shackles, they got their own row on the plane.

'So'd they find them?' Jim Doe asked.

Cody shook his head no.

Jim Doe looked out the window.

'We think—somebody's taking back all the bodies we've been finding. Your longhair, maybe.'

Jim Doe kept looking at the blur the ground had to be.

'My sister had a . . . she broke her arm up here'—he cuffed his left hand around his right bicep—'when she was young. Younger.'

Cody nodded. 'I don't have the films with me,' he said.

'I never thought she was really dead,' Jim Doe said.

'Seventeen years?' Cody said.

Jim Doe shrugged.

The flight attendant asked if he was Indian.

Jim Doe said he just tanned well.

On the downslant into Pennsylvania Jim Doe asked what Cody would get a widow for her twenty-fifth anniversary present?

Cody watched the armrest between them, the relict ashtray.

'What's her name?' he asked.

'Agnes,' Jim Doe said.

"The lamb of God," Cody said after thinking about it, then, 'I don't know. What'd you try?'

'It's the silver one, right?' Jim Doe asked.

Cody nodded. Sure, probably.

'A doorknob,' Jim Doe said, finally. 'It was brass, though. Maybe copper.'

Cody stared at him, then the waitress.

'A doorknob,' he said.

'It used to go to our house,' Jim Doe said, 'our first house. I couldn't think of anything.'

The rental car was waiting for them in the parking lot of the airport. They drove to Bethlehem, an all-night diner—Jim Doe's shackles on the backseat, now, time off for good behavior—then followed cemetery directions the cook had traced onto a napkin for them.

'You sure you want to do this?' Cody asked, the rental car's headlights up against the gate, throwing bars of darkness across the headstones, row after row. Because it could be his sister.

'Yes,' Jim Doe said.

Cody left the headlights on, so that each step they took was into their long shadows.

'You don't say her name,' Cody said.

They were going to the far side of the cemetery, the newer graves.

'Dorothy,' Jim Doe said.

Cody looked at him, shook his head no, slightly.

The east side of the cemetery trailed out into a field of some kind, the even rows curving away back to the road. While he'd drawn the directions, the cook had told them about the guy who farmed that land back when—about how he'd woke one night in the seat of his tractor, the spotlight on his cab pointed across the west side of the cemetery, the side he hadn't just pulled a cultivator through. He'd asked Cody and Jim Doe if they were the farmer, would they have looked back at the rig, to see what it had pulled up? What was caught in the blades, holding on?

The directions he'd given them were obtuse and winding, like the grave they were looking for would be at the end of some labyrinth. Like there was a ritual of movement they'd have to follow to get there, a dance.

'No,' Jim Doe had said to the cook. About the tractor, the plow.

Cody couldn't help it though, the idea of looking back. Having to know.

He pressed his left arm into his ribs, for the warm shape of his gun. He'd reloaded it after the airport had given it back to him.

Jim Doe was eight steps ahead of him, maybe. Two body lengths. Enough to run if he wanted, his Amos Pease out there somewhere, and the other one. But he didn't.

'What do you call him?' Jim Doe said, touching each headstone he passed. Two fingers, like a kiss.

'We don't really know him well enough,' Cody said.

'All the kids are Indian, though,' Jim Doe said. Like it was obvious, should be part of the name somehow.

Cody stopped walking.

'Say that again,' he said.

Jim Doe turned around.

'I've got the list,' he said, 'the names. He only takes Indian children.'

Cody's head was white with thought, possibility: the *victimology*. The *pool*.

He was smiling. Standing among the dead and about to cry with relief.

First Steely Dan, linking Amos Pease to their guy, then the victims. It gave them *geography*—gave Watts everything, probably. Enough, anyway.

'. . . what?' Cody said, Jim Doe three plots ahead now.

Jim Doe shook his head no, nothing.

Dorothy, though. That's what he'd been saying.

'What do you want to call him?' Cody said, catching up, stepping wherever now.

Jim Doe shrugged.

'Tin Man,' he said, finally. 'I don't know.'

'Why not just the Wizard or something?' Cody said back.

'Because the Wizard had a heart,' Jim Doe said. 'This one doesn't.'

Cody nodded.

'So you the scarecrow then, or the lion?' he said, using a headstone to push off.

Jim Doe smiled, maybe. Not a good one. 'Neither,' he said. 'He didn't take me, remember?'

Cody shrugged.

'And you don't know why?' he said. 'Why he didn't take you?'

'Because I wasn't there,' Jim Doe said, his voice too full, too dry—*consciously* dry—and then he nodded down to one headstone with two names.

John and Jane Doe, cherubs carved into the granite.

Cody stepped forward to see the dates better, make sure, but Jim Doe raised his hand, shook his head no, not to step.

The ground was fresh, caved in.

Cody's federal ID got the backhoe started at dawn. The groundskeeper's lips were cracked from alcohol. He smoked and dug, smoked and dug, and then used the shovel when he got close enough.

Both caskets were empty, broken.

The groundskeeper looked to Cody, to Jim Doe.

'He knows we're after him,' Cody said, 'your *Tin* Man. He's collecting them again. Because they're still evidence. They can still point to him somehow . . .'

Jim Doe just stared into the twin holes.

'A doorknob,' he was saying.

'Are you listening?' Cody said.

Jim Doe looked up.

'The last two you found,' he said.

'Virginia,' Cody said. 'Yeah.'

'They buried yet?'

21

1 MAY 1999

ARARAT, VIRGINIA

HE would be on the monitors for four minutes and thirty-three seconds. The tape was recording at extended play. After he left there would be Amos Pease fingerprints everywhere. The morgue was stainless steel, made for capturing prints. A funhouse. The cameras were new. This was their test.

The one over the door looked out onto the parking lot.

It caught the 1981 LeMans rolling in, headlights off, driver's side door already open, the sole of a shoe skimming the gravel top of the asphalt. And then he stood up on the other side of it, Amos Pease, letting his eyes adjust. It was military almost: using the car's body to shield him. But then he walked around it, with purpose. In his hand was a bat. His face was painted. His shirt read HYSTERIA.

He looked up to the camera and smiled, then the round end of the bat was at the lens. It just nudged it—the camera—over, to the trees. It was on an actuator, though, had only been still because he'd been moving. When he was inside and there was no more movement, it continued its cycle, sweeping from one side of the parking lot to the other.

And then it was the Reception Area.

The camera here was behind the bulletproof glass.

The station was empty, the graveyard shift mopping up in back.

Amos Pease hitched the narrow handle of the bat through the long handle of the door, reached through the reception window, buzzed himself in.

He was smiling. A real wolf grin.

At the edge of the first hall camera's frame, he met the first attendant. A Ronald Sepps. Ronald Sepps dropped the clipboard he'd been leading with, and flattened himself against the wall. For a moment it looked like that was going to do it—that all Amos Pease wanted was to get by—but then, a half-step past Ronald Sepps, he spun on his heel and drove the butt of the bat handle into the attendant's midsection. Ronald Sepps folded around it, his glasses arcing out across the tile. It was slick and shiny, the tile. The bat was wooden.

When Ronald Sepps was down, Amos Pease hit him again.

For eight blind seconds, then, he was moving along the hall, from Entry Hall Cam 1a to Entry Hall Cam 2a. It was what the security company had labeled them with masking tape. The monitors had cost too much, though. All the cameras just fed into the video recording unit in the ceiling. It wasn't real-time protection, wasn't really for intruders at all, but for the morgue attendants. Because of alleged impropriety with the dead.

Amos Pease pulled Attendant Marcy Stonecipher into Entry Hall Cam 2a's field of view by the hair. She was bleeding from the face. Later it would be a skull fracture, reconstructive surgery, therapy.

'Impropriety with the *living*,' one of the detectives watching the tape would say, sitting in a jagged half moon with the rest, around their television unit.

All the doors in the hall of the morgue were steel, with glass windows, wire buried in the glass like circuitry. Amos Pease passed each—going to cameras 3a and 1b—and shattered them inward as he passed. In slow motion, the arc the tip of his wooden bat left was traced perfectly by his hair, following the motion. He was going to get the children who weren't children anymore, just dead.

There were no more attendants until the last room. And then it was all of them. This was the one room without a smoke detector. Iris Caine, Buddy Colbert, and T. Elliot Mase were all mopping in there, over and over. The floor was like ice. They called it the Cooler. On the wall behind them was a bank of body-sized drawers. Buddy 'Bud' Colbert's cigarette hissed to the floor. The cameras didn't get sound, but still, the detectives could tell it hissed, with Amos Pease standing in the door, his bat held low and bloody.

Iris Caine said something then, and Amos Pease slung his hair over his left shoulder, looked at her. They were at opposite sides of the Cool Cam 3.

Maybe she asked why his face was painted, or what he was doing here, or that now somebody was going to watch this tape, see them smoking around all these people who couldn't get cancer anymore. Or maybe she explained why they all smoked: the smell, the idea of the smell, of particles rising off the dead, invading your body through the tympanum mucosa high up in the nostril. Or maybe she just said her first please. To get it over with.

Amos Pease held his bat out and she stepped forward, and he tapped her once on the head, getting the spacing down, then put his shoulder into it.

Buddy Colbert leaned on his mop and watched her fall.

T. Elliot Mase slammed himself back into the drawers, scrabbled on the countertop for something, anything: a saw that glinted in the fluorescents.

He used it like a hay hook in a slasher movie, windmilling high over his shoulder, the tip trailing the ceiling, bringing flakes of white down after it. Amos Pease caught the blade on his bat. It hardly bit. He flung it away, used the handle end of the bat like the flat cap of a bo stick, right to T. Elliot Mase's chin. He crashed back. Buddy Colbert was running by now, pushing his mop bucket over behind him. Amos Pease nodded, let him run, let the water wash over his feet, and then he closed the door, wedged a chair under it, and started opening drawers.

The children were in the third and fourth up, on the end.

The camera was right on Amos Pease. He closed his eyes, his lips moving in apology, in song, then cradled them out, set them on the floor. Applied the bundle of sage or marijuana or jimsonweed or whatever it was. He moved like they were moving with him, too, or like he thought they were. The detectives could only tell after watching it four or five times, but once you saw, it was unmistakable.

When Amos Pease looked up to the camera again, his tears were black.

He lifted the girl onto a gurney, the boy onto a coffin trolley, then rolled them back down the cameras, to the front desk, and buzzed himself out. The LeMans was parked angled slightly away from the outside camera, but, frozen and enhanced, the trunk Amos Pease set John and Jane Doe into already had a John and Jane Doe. They were black and staring.

'God,' the last detective to get there said.

The first detective shook his head no, not God, not this, and then the LeMans pulled away, still no lights, and in its wake Buddy Colbert rose, still holding his mop, and looked up to the camera, and the only statement he had for the responding officer was that Indians were mad again, it looked like. And that the city morgue needed better security.

22

1 MAY 1999

ROANOKE, VIRGINIA

THEY were in a basement. He kept coming down to look at them through the chain link, and say things that they couldn't quite hear, and then sit in his corner with his headphones on. There were other children too; Jana Marx-Isinger could hear their feet upstairs sometimes. The back of her neck was sore from craning up.

'They're ghosts,' her brother said, when he saw her looking. Jameson.

She turned to him. He was older, ten already. But he didn't know.

'They're real,' she said.

'Real ghosts,' Jameson said. 'That's what he's turning us into.'

He'd heard it on one of his shows, probably.

On the ride in the van to here, the basement, the man had asked them about their father, if they were excited about seeing him, now that he was out. His voice had been soft and even, the smile there on his face. Jana and Jameson had been wearing their Easter clothes still, then. It was Sunday. Now their clothes were folded on a chair by the door that went up to the rest of the house.

He brought them their favorite foods—hamburgers and tacos and pizza, and then watched them eat it, in wonder.

Once Jana offered him some through the chain link and he took it and held it and held it.

'Thank you,' he said.

He was crying.

'I'm sorry,' he said.

It made Jana cry too, then Jameson.

Upstairs, the ghosts were still walking.

'Is Daddy going to come get us?' Jana asked.

The man narrowed his eyes at them, made his mouth to say something, didn't.

The second week, he took them to the water. It took years to get there, riding in the back of the van again. He said it was the ocean, but Jameson knew, said it was just a lake. The man shrugged, tousled Jameson's hair. It was what Jana's mom had always made him do when they were visiting jail: *stand still, let your father tousle your hair.* After the guards had combed through it for files and saws and drugs.

The man didn't get in with them, just watched. Their swimsuits still had tags on them. A thin fish darted in and out from their legs, doing things with the sun. Jana laughed on accident and Jameson heard her.

'A few years ago,' the man said, looking out across the water. 'They found two children here. Drowned.' He looked down to them, in knee-deep water. 'Be careful, I mean,' he said, and all at once Jana understood: he was getting them *used* to this place.

The fish was gone.

He made them play for six hours, then sat in the van with them in the parking lot, patting Jameson's sunburned shoulders with a cold wet tea bag, to draw the heat out. They were eating all the hamburgers they wanted. Jameson started crying, then. The man slowed with the tea bag.

'Jameson?' he said, looking to Jana for help.

Jameson couldn't stop, and all Jana could watch anymore was his feet on the floor of the van, moving, and then she understood: to any children under the van, *Jameson* was a ghost now. And she was too.

23

3 MAY 1999

GARDEN CITY, KANSAS

THEY'D brought the two bodies down to him, Debs. From Lydia. Garden City was on the dogleg to the FBI field office in Wichita. But no black vans had shown up for them yet, and then, on May first—May Day—the two old Indians had shown up, the woman in an intricate shawl, the man in a cowboy hat. What they had was a yellowed piece of hospital paper. There were two neat little prints there. Plantars.

Debs had taken his hat off and looked out across the parking lot and shook his head no. He was sorry, but no.

'But they're ours,' the old man had said.

They were fifteen years too late. Debs didn't say that. 'They're evidence now,' he said instead.

'We'll bury them Christian, if you want,' the man said.

This time, he wasn't saying.

The woman just watched. He was glad she couldn't talk, not if her words matched her eyes.

Debs took their piece of paper. It was a reservation hospital.

'They don't have . . .' Debs started. 'Their feet, the bottoms of them. They've been—there's no *prints*. Anymore. Years.'

The woman's eyes changed.

Debs put his hat back on.

May Day.

'Do you have reason to believe there are plantar prints on them?' he said.

Yes. No. They couldn't, not without admitting to an illegal burial. Not without being Indians admitting to an illegal burial. To having corpses they weren't supposed to have had. The photographs of the scaffolds had made the AP wire. Debs didn't know why he'd let the Texas deputy go, still. Maines and McKirkle had just stared at him in the space after his shrug. They'd been on the side of the road, in the shade of a billboard.

'This could have been easy,' McKirkle said.

Debs nodded. It wasn't, though.

And now the Indians, these Blue Kettles.

'Do you remember the storm?' he asked the man.

The man smiled, his face creasing into a thousand wrinkles. He nodded. 'Should have heard the pigs screaming,' he said, then held his forearms up, like waiting for rain, but spread his fingers for the sound. Like it had been all around, red everywhere. His children part of it.

Debs blinked, spit, and told them they were going to Wichita, the bod—the *evidence*—and that maybe they could see them there. That he didn't have the equipment to compare the footprints, anyway, and how they'd changed since the hospital.

'They don't,' the woman said.

The man put his hand on his wife's shoulders.

'I'm sorry,' Debs said.

'Wichita,' the man said.

Debs nodded.

They were gone.

He stood there and watched the cars pass and pass.

The next day, the phone rang for him. It was long distance, that deputy. He was in Virginia, with the FBI.

'When are they coming to get these bodies?' Debs asked.

The deputy said that was what this was about. That agents were on the way to the graves of *all* the children taken by the storm. By the Tin Man.

'That's right,' Debs said. 'You think this is Oz.'

The deputy said look again, that there were federal men in blue jumpsuits falling out of the sky into cemeteries all over the state, to guard the headstones, apprehend anybody with long hair who approached the graves—anybody who approached them at *all*, really.

'Amos Pease,' Debs said.

The deputy said they were going to his grave too, whichever one it was.

'So what do want me to do?' Debs said.

'What you're already doing,' the deputy said: watch over the bodies. Because Amos Pease may have meant for them to stay on their scaffolds.

'Why are you telling me this?' Debs said.

The deputy breathed—a laugh, maybe—and said Debs knew why. And that now they were even.

Instead of goodbye, then, the deputy said to be careful. That Amos Pease was violent, now; worse. That something was building.

'What?' Debs asked.

A cowbird was sitting in his window, watching him with one eye.

The deputy said they didn't know yet, and then he was gone too.

It took Debs twenty-four hours to make it back to Garden City's Paddyshack. They called it that because it used to be the meatbox on a bobtail truck, still had the refrigerating unit at the back end, up high. It was from 1962; it still worked. The *Paddy* was from the four padlocks on the door. Before Debs's term, someone had built a shed around the box, then angled a building off it, which had been remodeled into usable county offices. But it had started with that cooler, its truck broken down, parted out. Debs made small talk with the tax assessor secretaries, then got the keys from the back office, walked around to the carport. That was what the Assessment people called it. Not something that could hold bodies.

The locks were shiny where they'd been touched three days ago.

Debs opened all four, starting at the bottom, then chocked the door open behind him.

They were the only two bodies in there, on the same shelf at the back.

He followed his flashlight to them, placed his hand on a shin—male, female, he couldn't tell—then made himself breathe, breathe. Because he didn't have to do this. He could be choking down one of Rhonda's Messy Burgers out at the edge of town. He would eat it all, too.

But he wasn't there.

A cold leg was under his hand.

He followed it down to the foot, out of the glow of the flashlight, and let his fingers feel over the ridges and whorls there, and if either of the children had laughed, then, Sheriff Debs would have had to laugh with them, until his face was wet with it.

24

4 MAY 1999

JERUSALEM, RHODE ISLAND

WATTS had to button her blazer up the neck, over her shirt. Because her shirt was white. Because she couldn't get to her gun in her shoulder holster, then, she already had it out, one in the chamber, pointing at the ground beside her as she moved.

Creed crouched into the cypress trees ten feet ahead of her, and disappeared. Watts's heart was pushing more blood than she thought she even had.

The steeple of the church was a long shadow across the cemetery.

There was a car coming. A plainclothes two miles up the road had radioed it in. They were supposed to be running the partial plates he'd pulled. Maybe it had been a LeMans, maybe it hadn't, he wasn't sure. He sounded too young to even know a LeMans, Watts thought. Probably thought it was French, a beret tossed up on the dash, an Eiffel Tower hanging from the rearview.

There weren't any headlights yet, anyway.

Watts backed up to a headstone, keeping it between her and the road. This was one of two places that still had a hard shell of dirt over the two graves. The other was Connecticut. So, if he was getting them *all* this time—Amos Pease, their only link besides Jim Doe—he'd have to come to one of the two.

To calm herself, Watts recited the names she could remember from the list they'd had faxed, of every hotel occupant around Gentry, across six days. The list was unrolled on a pew now, the thermal paper remembering its cardboard core. On the pew directly in front of the list—closer to God—was the other list she'd requested: every inmate who'd shared time with Marion Wayne Isinger. Thousands. Some had just ridden in a van with him from the courthouse, but they were there. The only way she had to thin the crowd, even, was Isinger's file, how, starting in 1990—the week of his first tentative parole hearing—he'd started instigating trouble, messing up his hearing. *Trying* to stay inside. To hide. So it was somebody he'd come into contact with before then, someone who was out himself by May 1991, when they found the first pair of bodies in North Carolina.

But still, there were hundreds upon hundreds.

Over microwave burritos in the spacious church kitchen, she had read all the Tennessee hotel-men slowly to Creed, while he scanned for matches on the pre-1988 inmate lists: Washington Correction Institute in Angie, Louisiana and Brushy Mountain Correctional, the Brushy Site in Petros, Tennessee, then his last five years at Middleton in Nashville. There were no matches. Not even a John Smith. Or a George Williams.

That name kept sticking in her head, though: George Williams, George Williams, George Williams. But it was too basic to run any kind of search on, unless there was some other delimiter.

Of the hundred and twenty-two names from the hotels, eighteen had come back hot, with priors. Two were registered sex offenders. Watts crossed them off first. She'd put dots by the sixteen who had history. It was just the usual stuff: parole violations, traffic disputes, welfare fraud. No Tin Men, anyway.

Of the sixteen, too, she could only remember six names: Byron Rawls and Bryan Edwards—because she kept getting them confused; Samuel McKay, one of the sex offenders; Glenn Turner, a boy she'd met at a dance, once, but hopefully not the same one; and Mitchell Saginaw and Dwayne Laramie. She had no idea why she could recall the last two names. She said them to herself over and over, not looking at the moon because she wanted her eyes to be ready. For Creed, this was probably 1972 all over—the Mekong Delta or some other

Magnum P.I. place—but 1972 for Sheila Watts had been her junior year of high school. She had been voted least likely to find herself in a cemetery at night, with a gun she'd never had to fire in eighteen years of service.

Mitchell Saginaw. Dwayne Laramie. George Williams.

Just as the headlights washed across the cemetery, blazing past her on all sides, she got it: George *Williams*. It was one of Harvey Glatman's aliases. From when he was pretending to be a photographer in California, luring girls out into the desert. George fucking *Williams*. The Lonely Hearts Killer. And that Steely Dan album—'Steely Dan' was Jessie Wiggs, one of Creed's media events. They'd called him that because he'd signed some of his letters *Just Another Scurvy Brother*. Creed hadn't even recognized the line. That had been some reporter in Minneapolis. God. But the names, one fake, one slightly more real, it was a pattern. Him telling them something.

She wanted to call out to Creed, tell him all of it. Figure out Saginaw and Laramie, go over the list again.

He didn't think they'd be smart enough to see it this soon. Their guy—the Tin Man now, according to Cody's last check-in.

That was the rush. That he didn't know they knew.

But the car.

It stopped at the low wall to the cemetery, and Sheila Watts stood into its headlights, leading with her gun, but Tim Creed was already there, at the passenger side window, and Watts felt all the blood leave her fingertips, her lips: outlined like that—his shooting arm one continuous line of anger—he was Berkowitz all over again, about to shatter another window.

But it wasn't Berkowitz's stance all alone, either.

He'd gotten it from San Francisco. The Zodiac Killer, the *idea* of the Zodiac Killer. The one they'd never caught, really.

'*Creed!*' Watts yelled, the car's headlights hot on the back of her throat. Things were going that slow for her.

Creed was yelling too, at the people in the car. The seventeen-year-old and his date. Creed was telling them to get out, *get out*, and when the boy did, his foot came off the brake and the car—a tan, un-LeMans-like Caprice—eased forward, still in gear, until the bumper crunched into the low wall. It didn't give, the wall, but the ground beneath it groaned.

Watts approached, leading with her gun, her right leg.

She unbuttoned her blazer as she came, her shirt glowing.

'It's not him!' she said to Creed, and he nodded.

The girl was crying on her knees, her head leaned forward to take the shot.

In the distance, a helicopter was coming.

'I just used up three years,' Creed said, lowering his gun.

Watts nodded.

'Tim,' she was trying to say. 'Tim.'

They cleared the car, put it in Park, and took the kids' IDs. The girl sobbed that this was their place.

Creed looked to Watts: their *place*.

He radioed their numbers in anyway, and the car's numbers, but it all came back clear. Their trunk was empty too. Virgin. Creed told them to maybe find another place this week, then slipped the boy thirty dollars for a motel, in apology.

'Wonder if he'll still be able to get it up,' Creed said, holstering his gun.

Watts didn't care.

'*Tim*,' she was saying. 'What do you remember about that Zodiac guy out in California?'

Creed shrugged.

'Wasn't mine,' he said. 'Any particular reason?'

Watts closed her eyes, hard, then went to the radio, got patched through to somebody she knew at the Academy, and they looked it all up for her.

'*Victims*, then,' she said, interrupting.

Two of them were Mitchell Saginaw and Dwayne Laramie. A third was Byron Calle. He was on Agent Mingus's list too. They'd been at three different motels on three consecutive nights. In the order they'd been killed.

'He's telling us something,' Watts said. Again.

Creed leaned back against a pew, looked up at the cross. 'That we won't be able to catch him?' he said, finally. 'Like Zodiac?'

'To look for names,' Watts said. 'That he's under layers and layers of names, names that have meaning for him . . .'

There were already agents en route to the three motels, for descriptions. He wouldn't be that easy, though. Not after *telling* them that's where he'd been. And they could wipe the rooms until the walls were transparent.

'We were close,' Watts said. 'God. We might have even passed in the aisle of the store or something.'

'On purpose,' Creed said. 'His, I mean.'

Watts nodded. The adrenalin had left her muscles stiff, her eyes dull.

'That deputy from Texas,' Creed said. 'What do you think?'

Watts opened her eyes, focused.

'You think he's inserting himself here?' she said. 'Or that he's a . . . a plant?'

Creed shrugged. 'It doesn't make sense,' he said.

'. . . or a victim,' Watts said, just aloud, then, to Creed: 'I thought that was him tonight. Pease.'

'Maybe it still will be,' Creed said.

In the rafters above them, a bird shifted. Or a bat.

'Tell me a story,' Watts said, sloughing down the wall. 'A case.'

Creed blew air through his nose.

'Which one?' he said.

'Steely Dan.'

Creed rubbed his shoulder where the hole still was, caught himself doing it; stopped. Sheila Watts was just watching him. Waiting.

'Just your everyday garden variety fuck-up,' he told her, finally. 'Jessie the dumb-ass Wiggs. It wasn't even about getting the psychological make-up with this one. It was just about following him. You know he did six people in two weeks?'

Watts nodded.

Had he told her this before?

It wasn't him, though—Jessie Wiggs wasn't their Tin Man. Couldn't be. Creed knew. He still had the shell casing of the one he'd put into Wiggs's eye. You don't come back from that to keep killing.

He didn't just have it; he'd reloaded it. For whoever shot him next.

He didn't tell Watts about that. It probably wasn't healthy.

But Wiggs. He told her all about Wiggs—again, maybe, but what the hell. They were two federal agents sitting in the nave of a church and weren't even sure what denomination it was. When they'd pulled up, Watts had pointed out how *denomination* was for both religion and money. Creed had thought about Jesus throwing the money changers out of the temple. How what Watts was saying changed that. He told her about Wiggs.

It had started in Pueblo, Colorado, in August. Creed didn't even see that one, except in black and white. He hardly ever did: they only called him when the bodies started stacking up. The idea of course would be that they were stacking up *behind* someone. That Creed could climb up onto them, see the perp.

Yeah.

Pueblo PD should have known, though. Even if it was '78. There was a damn page out of a spiral *notebook* safety-pinned to the woman's *cheek*, for Chrissake. Just one line on it, in pencil. The number one. Until number two, the line was just a line, and even then, the *2* was a *Z*, a *5*, upside down, an *N* on its side. But number three stood it up on the right end. That was when Creed got onto Wiggs. He didn't know he was Wiggs then, of course. He hadn't even been Steely Dan, yet.

The woman with the note—number one—had been a third-shift waitress. The bathtub she was found in was in the motel next door to her all-night diner. The staff and regulars all remembered Wiggs, ordering plate after plate of food from her just to watch her walk away. The ones that lasted were smarter than that. The late crowd had even seen Wiggs's car parked in handicap: a ruby-red Trans-Am, with a mannequin in the passenger seat.

'A *mannequin?*' Creed had said to a Chief Investigator Rodriguez.

Rodriguez said it again for Watts: a mannequin.

That was one of the things they never found. Another was the red stovepipe hat Wiggs had worn in a photo booth. He left the strip of pictures tucked in the corner of the mirror of number four, another waitress. Like she loved him. She was the first one on Creed's watch. This time, there was a letter to the editor showing up days later, with the *You Zombies* envoy, and the signature signature. And of course Bozeman police leaked the note to the press, and of course it got high-profile, then. An all-American 'rampage.'

Creed pressed the back of his head against the wood paneling of the nave.

1977 was when *Smokey & the Bandit* came out.

Watts cocked her head.

'Burt Reynolds?' she said.

'The car,' Creed said. 'That was the only fucking reason he went so long. Because every cokehead in America had himself a lookalike Trans-Am that year. Just to do lines off the sparkly-ass dash.'

Creed chewed his cheek, wanted to spit, swallowed instead. Not because it was a church, but because Watts was there.

'I wish they were all as stupid as him,' Creed said.

'He got six,' Watts said. 'In the same age group, occupation, ethnicity—'

'You think I don't know their names?' Creed said.

Then it was quiet for a while.

'Jessie Wayne Wiggs,' he finally said, bringing his hands together. 'You know how we got him, don't you?'

'Maybe.'

She did. It was standard procedure, almost: when the perp isn't leaving any prints, or secreting any saliva, or getting identified with the victims in some place other than, say, their diner, all that's left is to bait them in. Wiggs had been the test case; Creed had had to stay up thirty-six hours talking to even get his section chief to sign the requisition. But he had, finally. And it was for airtime, because *Royal*

Scam was still new then, meaning their guy was tuning in. They broadcast on all the channels he might be listening to, whoever he was (white, single, probably not older than his oldest victim—twenty-six—etc.). And it worked. Like luring a six-year-old in. Except Wiggs killed another woman on the way. She was in a straight line for Bismarck, though. Where Burt Reynolds was supposed to be, with his *Hooper* car. It was all over the FM.

'I would have never caught him,' Watts said, explained: '. . . movies.'

'You'd have found a way,' Creed said. 'He'd have *given* you a way.'

Watts shrugged.

Creed went on.

They'd had agents at every truck stop and diner around Bismarck for two days, then the red Trans-Am rumbled up out of the Great Plains. Jessie Wiggs didn't even use the door, just stepped up out of the t-tops. He was tall, his hair disco. Because there was a bulge in the waist of his pants, the agents across the crowded room from him just ate their hamburgers and watched him in the chrome reflection of their napkin holders and lifted the third drink on their table, for the first time. It was the signal for the recruit in the car. The recruit called, Creed came, night fell, and then it was the motel Wiggs had talked Mariah Curry into. Which was the part that Creed said hurt.

The motel was a shotgun affair—two buildings, one roof. You could shoot a load of birdshot straight down the middle alley and not pit either wall. That's where Wiggs's room was, somewhere in the middle, upstairs or down. Creed hadn't been able to keep a line of sight on him because Wiggs had parked on the grass when there was nowhere else, then watched Creed ease by, looking for a place of his own. He'd had to keep easing for as long as he thought Wiggs was watching.

By the time Wiggs would have made the lobby to check in, there were already agents there, badges out, sunglasses on, the night clerk stammering about something that wasn't his in the refrigerator.

He *didn't* check in, though. Wiggs.

After the fact, they figured that was part of his m.o.: getting the room earlier in the day, so he was just one gentleman, not a tall man with an unlucky, name-tagged woman. And he never used the same name twice, so the agents couldn't scan the register, radio it out to Creed.

In the space of a football field, they lost him. Poof.

Creed had three other agents in the car with him—maximum capacity. He left one of them at the Trans-Am with explicit orders *not* to tamper with it, not to even lean in. The other two he took with him to the alley between building A of the motel and building B. Which was when he recognized that it was a shotgun shack. A *dog run* his father would have called it, because he hadn't been a violent man, preferred animals to guns, Canada to Vietnam.

Watts canted her head over a bit, with this. Why Creed had enlisted.

He looked away. He knew it was the first he'd ever mentioned of his father. And, now, the last.

He took her back to the Motor Arms Motor Lodge.

Counting the second story of the motel, that made for four levels between three agents: 1A, 2A, 1B, and 2B. They did it at a run, slamming their shoulders into the doors, trying to save Mariah Curry's life.

Creed wasn't the one who found him, either.

It was Mikelson, the fish. He was closest when the screaming started. When Mariah Curry started screaming. Later she would say that when Wiggs turned the light on, he'd just stood there blinking. Mariah'd tried to run, but his hand was locked on hers. Wiggs was shaking his head no, making a sound in his throat that wasn't going to be words.

Getting himself ready for it, the shrink they'd called in said.

And then Mikelson had interrupted him.

Mariah Curry said it took him two times to come through the door—the deadbolt, then the chain. It cost him his life.

In that space between the first and second attempt, Wiggs crossed the room, took the silver gun off the bed, looked at both sides of it, or his hand around it, maybe, then raised it to head level, holding it horizontal to the ground like this was a liquor store and he was having to reach through a window.

Mikelson was tall; he took the slug in the throat instead of the face. It came out at the base of his skull, the white powder settling onto Creed's lips. He didn't tell Watts what it tasted like, what it didn't. He didn't look at her, either. Or Mikelson. Just swung past him, framing himself in the door for an instant, testing the waters of Room 23a: nothing.

Had Mikelson got him? Was the waitress alive?

Creed had his back pressed into the narrow section of wall between the door and the one window. And he didn't know if there was a back way out of these units, a fire escape or laundry chute for the sheets or whatever. He counted to three in his head, apologized to his then-wife Marcia, then counted again, then stepped away from the wall, kicked the air conditioner in like he was coming that way but spun through the door instead.

Jessie Wiggs was waiting for him.

'*You*,' Wiggs said, stepping back to fire. His eyes were flared white.

Beside him, Mariah Curry was falling away, into the dead girl, the note fluttering from her right cheek, right below the eye. 6. Just to the left of Wiggs's pistol was his shirt pocket, a slick silver pen tabbed there. The other pocket was cigarettes. And the picture behind him, it was a seascape, the painter some *Raymond Ocat*—

Creed never even heard the shot.

It spun him back into the doorframe, the fingers of his gun hand drawn back, their tendons spooling up the inside of his arm, back to his chest, where they'd been cut. The gun, suddenly made of paper, floated into the room and Creed did the only thing he could: fell. Onto Mikelson. Who'd already had his gun out, like he'd been trained.

Creed palmed it against his stomach, let himself sag half out into the walkway, and the last thing to roll over was his hand, the gun in it slick with blood.

Jessie Wiggs only had time to see it, then he was dead. Over and over, dead, the tobacco flakes from his cigarette drifting above him, blue ink spreading across his shirt, into it, red welling up underneath.

'The safety pins were brass,' Watts said, pulling Creed out of it. Thankfully. 'His sister's, right?'

Creed nodded. He was breathing hard. Hating that it still made him breathe hard.

Wiggs's sister had worn safety pins in the slack parts of her face, when punk was still young and British. And that was it. No childhood molestations, no family dementia, no trauma. Not even a good old-fashioned divorce. Just seeing his sister like that, maybe, and then touching his own face.

'Why did he number them, though?' Watts asked. 'The victims?'

Creed laughed through his nose again, just with nerves this time.

A slow pitch. From her.

'He wanted what they all want,' he said. 'For everyone to know his name. He couldn't be Burt Reynolds, but he could be in the news at least, right?'

Watts shrugged, rubbed one of her temples with one of her hands.

'And he was,' she said, finally. 'And here we are still talking about him.'

Creed shrugged.

'They ever find his sister?' Watts asked, quiet. Like this was where she'd been going the whole time.

No.

'Maybe that's it, then,' she said. 'The connection.'

Maybe. Creed said it in his head to himself, for her, and then they just sat there waiting for morning to leach through the stained glass with their replacements, or for the radio to light up with Amos Pease, or for Connecticut to call for back-up, and Creed only had to close his eyes once, with Watts, and then he was asleep on duty for the first time in thirty-two years.

25

5 MAY 1999

NINETY SIX, SOUTH CAROLINA

THE reason Billy Sparks didn't call her in right away was that he had a coke machine in the bed of his truck, from Greenwood, where nobody would miss it. His refrigerator had burned out four days ago, and his next paycheck was still a week and a half away, the fifteenth. And it wouldn't cover a fridge anyway. The plan was to run an extension cord out to the smokehouse, tuck the machine out there, then hollow out some beer cans, pack them with meat and sausage, slide them into their slots then re-label the buttons so they were a menu. That was the plan. But then he saw the blanketed figure moving behind the counter at the Texaco he used to sweep for. All the lights were off except the big red star above. Her hair was a shroud.

Billy passed once, and then again in his memory. And again.

The thing was, King Thompson ran that Texaco. And Billy knew him, had been to supper at his house, even, when there was nowhere else.

He shifted the truck into neutral, coasted to a stop with the lights off and stared at the line of reflectors running down the center of the road.

He was home free. But King.

Billy turned around deep in the ditch, stopped the truck a half block down from the Texaco to recheck the tarp stretched over the coke machine. He could make an anonymous call, he supposed, except that Sherry, who worked the boards from her utility room, lived next door to him. The conversation would run like this:

—Sherry?

—Yeah?

—I mean, I just want to report a suspicious character down at King's.

—Billy?

—Billy's at home.

—Why don't you just come over?

—I don't know what you're talking about, whoever you are.

—Your kitchen light isn't even on, heart. How'd you dial the phone?

Which is why he just decided to figure it out himself.

He left the truck running beside the store, reached behind his seat for a proper lug wrench, settled for a four-way, then stood by the open bathrooms trying to figure how best to hold it. By the center, like a flea market throwing star? By the 7/8ths end? 13/16ths?

He walked around the corner holding it both ways, then settled on the center, because then it was a shield, too. Against pipes, at least. Not bullets.

The plate glass above the Quaker State display was crashed in.

Billy Sparks reached through it, unlocked the door, held it open with his foot as he stepped in.

'Hello?' he said. 'King, that you?'

Nothing.

He reached around to the register. It wasn't sprung. But the cooler, and the candy rack. It was like raccoons had gotten in. Or one big raccoon.

Billy looked around, back to the door.

It was a girl, half a head shorter than him. Her hair was matted and she was wearing a blanket, and under that an old Night Ranger T-shirt. And she was dark.

'. . . Sister Christian,' Billy said, the only Night Ranger song he knew anymore, but then the blanket shifted, a blade flashed, and Billy Sparks was down, watching his truck lurch out into the road, the tarp catching on some of the hogwire King used to keep the junior high kids from painting on the gravity tanks. The girl was driving, for the first time, maybe. At twenty-whatever-she-was. And the coke machine. It was a beacon in the bed of his truck, lying on its back like that. It was the first real crime Billy'd ever committed as an adult. He looked down at his large intestines. Just like a hog, he thought, and then turned all the lights on at the Texaco station and sat on the toilet bleeding until the law got the other bathroom key from behind the register to let him out. It was tied to a cinder block. The state patrolman held it easy with one hand.

'. . . she went that way,' Billy said, hooking his finger towards Georgia. 'She was saying something about a coke machine, I think.'

When Sherry got there she just stood in the door, looking at him.

'What have you gotten yourself into, Billy Sparks?' she finally said.

Her cigarette was a mile long. Billy flinched from it, sure it was going to burn the white of his left eye out.

'I don't know,' he said, just barely, like an apology, then asked if he could go home now. He still had to pull the curtain closed over the window above his sink, because that's where he'd iced down the meat. By noon it would be too late—the flies would be a curtain, then, just on the outside of the glass. Billy looked down at his large intestines again.

Not like a hog, he thought. Like a person. Like me. And then he slumped off the toilet and rested his head against the toilet paper dispenser and watched the red star flicker above him like the Bible, telling everyone here, come here, look at this. Look what I found.

26

5 MAY 1999

BETHLEHEM, PENNSYLVANIA

JIM Doe heard about it first, before the FBI, even. Before it was official: he was in the hotel room with Cody, killing six hours until their flight to D.C., which was just a dogleg up from Quantico. Where they were supposed to *talk*.

Cody was asleep in the chair he'd pulled up against the door, dreaming federal dreams.

Jim Doe sat on the edge of the bed facing the wall opposite the window.

In Kansas, he could have found the longhair, maybe. Given enough time. Because it was flat, you could see for miles. But here. The trees made it claustrophobic, the sun in the sky just for a short arc. A useless wedge of time. It hardly even made any heat.

The way Jim Doe heard about it was calling Castro County. Nazareth. Monica at home. The area code was almost foreign.

'Jim?' she said.

She was alone. You don't say another man's name in bed if you aren't.

Jim Doe stood, pulled the phone as far as he could from the door, from Cody.

'Just, y'know, checking in,' he said.

A light clicked on in Texas.

Jim Doe pressed the phone to his ear with his right hand and pushed his left wrist into his hip, for the gun that wasn't there.

'Walter and Bill bring my truck back?' he asked.

No. She told him: when they'd left Lydia, they'd been heading north, after him, into Missouri finally, the rawhide straps of their hats digging into their leathery jaws.

Monica waited then, like she was counting to herself before she said it, then asked where he was this time.

Jim Doe looked around.

'With Buffalo Bill,' he said, smiling at himself in the mirror. 'I'm still after him, Mon.'

'You shouldn't come back to Texas,' she said.

Jim Doe smiled. 'Gas prices up again?' he asked.

'You are,' Monica said.

They left it at that, and she filled him in on the news, on Garza taking Gentry's office for the time being, hiring his brother Sonny in Jim Doe's place, as temporary deputy. On how it hadn't rained since Sheriff's accident, like Gentry'd taken all the good luck into the ground with him. On how she'd already been talking to the FBI today.

Jim Doe stopped, turned back to the bathroom mirror.

In the reflection, Cody was still slumped in his chair.

'Already *when?*' he said.

They'd called Castro County about two hours ago, the end of her shift.

'Why?' Jim Doe asked.

Monica didn't answer.

'I thought you knew,' she said instead. 'I'm sorry.'

Jim Doe shook his head no.

'*Monica.*'

'They wanted . . . they wanted your sister's prints, if we had them. Or anything distinguishing.'

Jim Doe's head was swimming.

'We don't—' he started to say.

Monica finished: 'I told them that.'

But there was more. Jim Doe waited.

Monica *had* told them about his sister's arm, broken high up from being closed in the door of a truck when she'd been reaching for something behind the seat. When she was short enough to stand up and do that. Social Services had come to the house, even, their clipboards tilted up to their unsmiling faces. Because the Does were Indian.

Horace had opened the screen door with a beer in his hand, offered the woman in the pantsuit one herself.

Jim Doe closed his eyes.

'Why do they want to know?' he finally asked.

Monica didn't answer, and didn't answer.

Finally Jim Doe did: 'They found her?'

'They found somebody,' Monica said. 'Indian. In her twenties. I think they're taking her to the hospital to get an X ray for her arm so—'

Jim Doe lowered the phone.

The *hospital*. Not the coroner's office.

'She's alive,' he said into the phone, afraid to even give the words shape this time.

'Calhoun Falls,' Monica said. 'South Carolina. It's right on the border, Jim. At least that's the number I faxed the—'

Jim Doe nodded, thanked her, set the phone down.

Calhoun, South Carolina.

'What?' Cody said, awake now. Listening.

Jim Doe looked up to him.

'She's alive,' he said. 'They found her.'

27

5 MAY 1999

BETHLEHEM, CONNECTICUT

IT was a beautiful day in the neighborhood. Or close enough. Amos walked through it, left the bat in the old baseball dugout it had been in in the first place, where he found it, leaning in the same corner. Because he didn't want to mess anything up any more than it already was. Walking out onto the diamond, though, all his pills gone for days, he flashed on elementary school, parents sitting up in the wooden bleachers like metal ducks at the county fair, all their smiles painted on. He was looking at one of them in particular, a man, a father, when the girl in the outfield started screaming.

Jennifer. Her name was Jennifer. Jessica.

One of the high school boys vaulted over the fence, never spilling his coke, and trotted out ahead of everybody, then stepped back himself.

There was something on the ground.

It filled his head. Then, now. It was a turtle, with no shell. Not one that had been cracked open on the road by a car and had the bad luck to live, but one that had been born naked. And now it was turning itself in to the proper authorities. Nobody threw any firecrackers on it—at first—and Amos didn't run away, but inside he was on his knees still, wanting to cover the turtle.

It took him forty-two minutes to slog through the memory to the gap in the chain link. He knew it was forty-two because Father had taught him to count in his head, separate from the world. Father in the stands.

Amos cried standing up and then shifted from foot to foot until it was better, until he could drive.

He had to get out of Virginia.

In a convenience store buying jerky and peanuts, he saw himself on two screens—the closed circuit black-and-white angled behind the clerk, and the small color unit opposite the register, tuned to the news. To the footage of *him*. He walked out on stilts.

Two blocks down, he eased the LeMans into long-term parking, eased out in a low-slung Bonneville Brougham. It wasn't in the news like the LeMans was, and wouldn't be: the booth attendant was locked in the trunk of a compact, and the plates the camera recorded on the Brougham belonged to a Pontiac, and the Pontiac had different plates now too. Three out of every five cars in the garage did, and six of the plates were ones he'd had under the seat of the LeMans already.

The children nestled into each other in the trunk and understood, told him to buy some speed for Maryland, because it was too late for barbiturates now, and he did, with money he invented for a trucker, and he crushed the pills and breathed them in like snuff and bled from the nose as he drove and let it dry on his neck, to keep his head up.

Maryland took maybe ten minutes to cross, Pennsylvania eighteen days, two of them spent looking for that church again, just to be sure, but then it was Connecticut.

Nobody stopped him at the borders because he was a woman now, again. His eyelashes were barbed on the end, too, and long enough to catch into the undersides of his brows. The children raised their voices, telling him right, right, left, here.

Another church, another cemetery.

But something was different.

Amos parked in the ditch when everything was telling him to drive, rubbed the paint into his face, smoothed his hair back with bear fat he'd fingered from a pork 'n' beans can, and let himself drift into the near trees, move from shadow to shadow to the low retaining wall. It was the darkest it had been for him now, this time, and then he understood: the sky was velvet, no stars. He couldn't tell how far the clouds were, either, so he ducked, went on fingertips and toes, and when the first heavy drop of rain hit his back he remembered the turtle and rose up as high as he could, just let it come.

As he drew closer to the graves, he stuttered, stumbled, stopped: the dead were already rising—a man and woman, in black suits, each shot once in the face. He looked to the rain again, and for stands to be set up all around. For somebody sitting in them, watching. Father.

The first time he'd seen him his face had been glass, a nothing face, but then he'd taken his glove off, then the glove under that, for his real skin, and Amos had pulled back, deeper into the chimney. But not his sister.

Father.

Amos Pease saw it happen from the corner of his eye—the FBI man, rising—and tried not to see. That if he just didn't look. But he had to.

Father.

Somebody laughed.

Father.

The real FBI man's naked arm was trailing down out of a tree.

Amos Pease shook his head no—no, *please*—but that was never enough. He'd brought the rain. Now it was all clear.

'*No!*' Amos Pease said, iron in his throat, and then he was running, his bare feet pounding the hard-packed dirt. If he could just make it to the dead FBI woman, grub for her gun, get it up in time.

Father stepped neatly away in his suit, rubbing the fingerpoint of blood from his forehead.

Amos Pease came up with it, the gun, stood again, behind it.

'I'm *White*,' he said, way back in his throat, and pulled the trigger.

The hammer fell on air. Like Nazareth. He slid the action back and more nothing came up into the chamber, too. Just a sick sense. Invisible bullets.

This was what he was *supposed* to do, though. What his training *said*. What Father had been expecting.

He was crying, now, Amos. For the children, for the child he had tried to be, once.

And now, Father was gone.

Amos back-pedaled into the cemetery, turned a birdbath over, and just ran, ran, until he was in a corner by the church and the nice fireman was standing twenty feet away.

He'd brought it with him, the slick jacket, the helmet. For Amos, for this.

'I'm sorry,' the face behind the glass mask said, not Mr. Rogers anymore, not even close, and Amos Pease collapsed, understood, then thought of the children again, locked in the trunk. And he started shaking his head no, *no*. Had maybe been shaking it all along.

The nice fireman saw this, cocked his head to understand better, and Amos nodded now, smiled, knew his teeth were a harsh, beautiful white crescent against his face, the black paint running down it, down his chest, his legs, making him one with the night, invisible. Again.

He crawled backwards up the wall, to the steeple, so that all the graves were long squares below him, a grid, a chessboard. His neck was moving fast now, jerking his head to each drop of rain, counting them, saving the numbers so that when he opened his mouth they would mass out like flakes of ash.

Father was watching him too, the reflective stripes on his jacket not as wet as the rest of it.

He was holding his hand out again, up. Like *come home*. Like he was here to help. Like he had never let Amos, his favorite, go in the first place. Never sent him out.

But Amos knew, this time. And he wasn't going back, not again.

'No!' he said, and then before he could talk himself into anything else he pushed off the clapboard siding hard, streaking across the twenty yards to the hand, past the hand, to the neck, the only piece of real skin showing.

'You should have taken your glove off, old man,' he meant to say. It just came out as *no*, again. It was enough.

The nice fireman didn't say anything, couldn't.

The backside of his glass mask was fogged, fogging.

Amos Pease set his knee into the yellow plastic chest, locked his elbows, and started singing then, harder than he ever had, his father's hands driving into his ribs again and again, the dead FBI woman watching him through the holes in her face, shaking her head too that *no*, he *shouldn't* have to go back. That what he was doing here was *good*. That he could win. That if he could just roll this man in this fireman jacket over to Eddie and Rachel's graves, they would remember too, reach up through the earth and grab him, pull him into the ground with them. Please.

28

5 MAY 1999

CALHOUN FALLS, SOUTH CAROLINA

IT had been the Tuinol in her blood that rang the federal bells. In Jane Doe's blood. In the parking lot Jim Doe listened to Cody explain how it was probably just a dead end, that most investigative work was. And then it was silent in the car, their third rental in three days.

'You finished?' Jim Doe said.

'I'm just saying,' Cody said.

The Emergency doors of the clinic parted for them long before they got there.

The chief of Calhoun police was waiting for them. To brief them on the charges against Jane Doe. He offered them donut sticks. They were sitting in the glow of the lone television set, angled up in the corner. KRCL, the Oracle. Instead of listening to the chief, they listened to it, the news: two federal agents had been killed last night. A man and a woman. And the reporter somehow had all the dumpsites for the past eight years, too—where all the agents had been stationed, waiting for Jim Thorpe. That was what one of the papers had called Amos Pease. Because of the bat. Jim Thorpe the football player.

Each of the Bethlehems and Jerusalems had a star—five points, not six—except in Pennsylvania and Connecticut. There the two cemeteries were close enough that the star and the skull overlapped.

Cody stood to see better.

Maybe it was all skulls.

Jim Doe knew what it meant, anyway: the Tin Man had been born into the media. The reporter even said his name, but just as an aside. Like she'd heard it or seen it, not been able to attach it to anything, anyone. And Jim Thorpe was the real focus, anyway, moving stoop-shouldered through the silver morgue over and over like it was a house of mirrors, and he couldn't find his way out.

The names of the two dead agents were being held, pending family notification.

'Can I see her?' Jim Doe said.

It felt like he'd been saying it for days.

'She's related to this Tin Man shit, isn't she?' the chief asked. 'A real, live Dorothy?'

He didn't even say it right, *Dorothy*.

'Can I see her?' Jim Doe said again.

The chief shrugged, finished his sixth donut stick, crumbled his cup into the trashcan, flicking the white off his fingertips, and said that once they walked into that room, then, she wasn't his responsibility. That he didn't want her—no name, no history, just a knife. And a truck. And a coke machine.

Jim Doe nodded.

'I just want to see her,' he said. 'Please.'

He stood, then the chief, then Cody.

They left the waiting room chairs at odd angles, the television looking down on them at a severe angle. The coins in Jim Doe's pants jingled as they walked. The hall was seventeen years long. It was all he could do not to run.

The room was 183. The light outside it flickered yellow—a late moth, or early June bug—and the carpet on the wall smelled of urine. Jim Doe pressed his forehead into it.

'What if it's not her?' he said, to Cody, his voice muffled.

Cody looked over at him.

'How will you know?' he asked.

Jim Doe stared at him.

Maybe she'd look like her mother, *their* mother. Gone. Sweeping.

'She was older than me,' Jim Doe said, to Cody. 'There was nothing I . . . nothing I could have—'

Cody nodded, didn't make him finish.

'Just go in there,' he said, then was asking the chief if he needed them for anything else.

Jim Doe looked around at *chief*. It wasn't for him, though.

He was saying *Dorothy* in his head. And her real name, much quieter. And that it had all been worth it, if it was her. Please.

Behind him, papers and pleasantries rustled between Cody and the chief of police, and then the chief was saying something about a key at the nurses' station, a bag of evidence and possessions, a charge that might turn out to be murder, and then he was gone, no longer a presence.

'Well?' Cody said.

Jim Doe looked back at him, faced the door, placed his fingertips on it, and went through.

She was on the bed, her back to the door, her hair spilled out behind her.

She was rolled over as far the handcuff chain on her left wrist would let her roll.

Jim Doe felt the indentation his cuffs had left in his wrist, and in that way touched hers. Her.

There was blood dried just under her elbow, too, and a hundred other details—the hospital gown, the sun, the way one of her bare feet laid on top of the other. The lights, dimmed.

Jim Doe placed his hand on Cody's chest, holding him back.

Room 183 was the only room that existed anymore.

Jim Doe put his foot down on the floor, crossed it, and she said his name before she even looked around: *Jim*.

It was the name he'd grown up into.

It meant she'd thought about him.

His knee faltered; he grabbed for the bed railing, got it.

Behind him, Cody rolled the light brighter, and the girl on the bed shrank.

Cody dimmed it back down.

Jim.

Her hair.

Jim Doe touched it as lightly as he could and she let him, and then he knelt by her bed like a fairy tale book. Like he was penitent.

'Is it her?' Cody asked, the sound of his voice profane.

Jim Doe didn't answer. Her hair.

It slid from between his fingers.

She was rolling over.

'Jim,' she said again, then, flatter: 'James Alan Doe.'

Jim Doe's hand was empty now. Again.

'He told us about you,' she said, studying his face, reaching for it.

Jim Doe caught her wrist, his thumb to her pulse.

'He?' he said.

She smiled a sedate smile.

'Father,' she said.

A psychiatrist came over from Greenwood to help them talk to her. It counted as his community service. It took him until one to get there. His eyes were red around the edges, like he'd just put them in over lunch. Sterilized them with gin.

Jim Doe stared at him, and Cody stared at him.

He smiled, asked who was the good cop here?

Cody recounted what they knew: that an individual had kept this girl prisoner for between six and ten years now. Maybe more. That she'd been kidnapped from her home in the lull after a storm, when the worst was supposed to be over. That she called this individual 'Father.' That this 'Father' mixed and administered his own Tuinol, for purposes unknown.

The psychiatrist had to look into the pattern of the tile floor to remember *Tuinol.*

His name was Lucas.

'So she's, um . . .' he said, loosening his tie for the job, '*open* for suggestion, as it were?'

Cody nodded: hypnosis. There'd likely been a regimen of it, suppressing her own personality, replacing it with one the kidnapper wanted.

'And him?' Lucas asked.

Jim Doe looked up.

He hadn't said anything since walking out of 183. The room number itself didn't even make sense: there were only four, for patients—180, 181, 182, and 183. With afternoon, now, too, they were stacking up, the waiting room milling with feet, filled with the coughing and underinsured.

He'd wanted to show her the boots he had on, see if she remembered them, Horace coming home with them from Muleshoe. Mule-ears from Muleshoe.

She wasn't Dorothy, though.

She couldn't be.

He'd spent the lunch hour watching the news, anxious for her to just tell it all to them right then. But the FBI: Cody needed a cassette recorder. And the girl, the charges. They had to do it all by the book, more or less. Representation, evaluation, all of it. The attending physician was supposed to be driving in from his golf tournament even, to sign whatever he'd forgotten to sign last night, when the ambulance had delivered her.

God.

And the news in the waiting room, the Oracle anchorwoman filtering the national headlines for South Carolina. Four graves had been plundered in the night now, not just two. It was her word, *plundered*. And there were two more dead agents, found head to head in the pews of the church they'd been watching. Pennsylvania and Connecticut both had skulls over them now. Pennsylvania. Where they'd just been, Jim Doe and Cody. Where they could have waited.

'He likes that graphic, I bet,' Cody had said, nodding to the twinned skulls.

The Tin Man.

Jim Doe shrugged, tried not to breathe in any germs.

They sat down with her in 183 twelve minutes after Lucas got there. He didn't have a last name, said he wasn't that kind of doctor. He rolled the window open to smoke. Jim Doe saw the chief of police's blazer roll past, then looked back to her. She was sitting up now, her knees under her chin, the blanket over her knees, the chain of her cuffs lost in the synthetic wool, emerging on the other side as an IV line, the drips falling from the bag without any sound.

She was looking at him, at Jim Doe. Like she wanted to touch him again. Jim Doe turned away.

Lucas introduced himself as *Lucas*, asked what her name was.

She just stared at him.

'Jane,' Cody said, confirming with Jim Doe. 'For now.'

Jane. Jane Doe. Like a sister.

'Tell us about last night, Jane,' Lucas said. 'If you want to, I mean.'

She looked over to him.

'You're not him,' she said.

'Not to you,' Lucas said. 'No. To my little girls, though, yes.'

She faced the window. 'What do you want to know?'

'Whatever you know,' Lucas said.

She laughed. They couldn't see her face, but they could hear her.

'No you don't,' she said. 'Trust me, Doc.'

'Lucas.'

She looked up again, pinning Jim Doe to his chair. 'He wasn't always that way about you, y'know. He just started that . . . I don't know. *Time*.' She smiled at the concept. 'Years, months, yesterday.'

'Your voice,' Cody said, like he knew it, suddenly and all at once, and Lucas's eyes flashed over. Because they'd talked about this—there being only one person talking for all of them. Lucas didn't want to disorient her, put her on the defensive. Because this *wasn't* an interrogation.

She smiled at him. Cody.

'Middle name Wayne,' she said. 'Last nammme . . . *Ding—*'

'*Mingus*,' Cody filled in.

For this, Lucas did look over. At whatever she'd uncovered from Cody's elementary days. You could see it in the hard, new lines of his jaw.

She shrugged, then falsettoed her voice, said it: 'Help me,' beat, beat, beat. 'He's . . . you wouldn't—'

She handed the phone over her shoulder to the imaginary Tin Man, bored with the act already. The reenactment.

'What was their name?' she asked. 'I've been wondering that lately. Those people in Tennessee?'

'Coleson,' Cody said. 'And Swanson. Anderson.'

She nodded, pointed her finger at him like a game show host, her eyes half-closed in appreciation. 'He said you'd know,' she said.

'He,' Lucas said, fighting.

'Father,' she said again.

'Tell me about him,' Lucas said, leaning forward, fingers churched together, his cigarette the steeple, trailing smoke.

'He's . . .' she said, searching, 'he's . . . got three houses. Does the FBI know that, Dingus? They're all the same, though. I never knew it until, well. A little while ago.'

'How are they the same?' Lucas.

'They all have basements, I think,' she said. 'Basements full of us. He lets us out sometimes, though. For field trips, socialization. The occasional concert. Oh, and you know the kachina dolls he makes?' Jim Doe closed his eyes. She went on. 'He has this big oak table—three of them, I guess. I don't know. But that's where he does the . . . first parts. With the legs. And arms. It's like sex with him, reaching his hand in . . .'

Jim Doe could hear it, the saw on the bone. The children watching.

'It's like school,' she was saying. 'He's always . . . *teaching* us stuff. Indian stuff, I mean. About who we are. Like the trees.'

'Trees?' Lucas said.

She pointed to Cody to answer. He did. 'The trees he leaves the childr—the trees he *uses*. For these "dolls." They're all bent over, from the top. Like the Indians used to do.' He paused, looked over to Jim Doe for a moment. 'It's not in any of the reports,' he said.

Jim Doe looked back to her.

'But you lived,' Jim Doe said.

She smiled at him with her eyes.

'I was a good student,' she said. 'Daddy's little girl. Pocahontas.'

'Pocahontas wasn't a good girl,' Jim Doe said. 'She ran away.'

Jane Doe shrugged, turned to the window again, inhabiting the young girl persona for a moment, a pose, her elbows locked, wrists together.

'. . . like *you* did,' Lucas picked up.

'He has a van,' she said, her voice small now. 'A big one, no windows.' She turned back to Cody, the FBI. 'Standard serial killer issue, right?'

Cody just stared.

She shrugged, went on. 'He thinks I don't know how the vent in top unscrews.' She smiled, pulled her head into her shoulders, flaring her eyes. 'But I do.'

'He needs the vent for transporting the . . . kachina,' Jim Doe said. 'The dolls.'

She nodded.

'He said you'd know,' she said. 'That you'd understand. Like him.' She tapped her temple to show.

'Not like him,' Jim Doe said.

'Think what you want,' she said.

'Why did you run away, Jane?' Lucas asked, asserting himself. 'This . . . your *father*. He sounds like a good man.'

She laughed through her nose.

'I like being tall,' she said. 'And I never said he was a good man, *Lucas*. But he is good at what he does.'

'Which is . . ?' Lucas, again.

She held her hand up to the dormant television in reply. 'He kills people.' She looked at Jim Doe for the last part: 'And he shows us how to do it when he's gone. Because nobody lasts forever. And it's too much for one person, anyway. Unless you're Hitler, or Andrew Jackson. And Father's not that, um, *political*. More the stalking horse kind, y'know? Or dark horse, or whatever the right thing is to say.'

Jim Doe could hear the wheels of Cody's borrowed recorder straining to turn, to get all this down on tape, the words she wasn't speaking, the words underneath.

'Who are you?' he said, finally. Jim Doe.

'Who do you think I am, *Jim?*' she asked back. 'Who do you want me to be?'

She was kneeling on the bed now, as high as she could get, her back straight.

Jim Doe stood, his chair scratching forward, away from him.

'Nobody,' he said, and walked out, made it down to 181 before closing his eyes, leaning his back into the wall, sliding down, his hands over his face. Dorothy. The X-ray film the tech had slapped onto the wall earlier was still there, and the fine line of shadow across the humerus, high up, just like Monica had said it would be.

When he looked up again—hours, minutes, *time*—someone was staring at him from the waiting room.

It was Creed. He walked up, shrugging off the admitting nurse.

'Where is she?' he said.

'You're alive,' Jim Doe said.

Creed looked down at him a moment longer, not getting it, then pulled the chart on the door of 181, read the name, and started moving down the hall like that, reaping the folders, letting them fall behind like chaff. Jim Doe stood into the antiseptic smell of rubbing alcohol and pain, shook his head to clear it, to think, but finally just followed Creed back down to 183. Because that was the only place.

'*Tim!*' Watts called from Admitting suddenly, the leash between them snapping, and Creed turned back to her with his eyes, Jim Doe too, but something was wrong. On the floor. It was wet, from under the door. Something clear, with an iridescent film, the fluorescents pooling in its surface. Not water. Creed was looking now too, his hand shading into his jacket, his holster, his rear foot setting itself. And then Jim Doe understood, saw: it was the contents of an IV bag, sugar and water and antibiotic. The beginning of another end.

29

5 MAY 1999

ROANOKE, VIRGINIA

BLUE monkeys. He could understand them calling him the Tin Man if he had some blue monkeys, *maybe*.

He'd had his thumb on the remote all morning, watching the news. It was like looking in the mirror.

Maybe it was the axe.

He'd already called the video store, reserved *Oz*, to see how he was supposed to act, now. Whether he had a big dance number in the next scene or not.

It didn't matter.

They could call him whatever they wanted. Creed, *Creed* could call him whatever he wanted.

Downstairs, one of the children had a broomstick, was poling it up into the floor, using sound to locate the weak points, like he or she'd been taught. Or was it Morse, or something deeper, that they could program him with?

Nevermind.

The Tin Man.

He pulled the lever, leaning his chair back to full tilt.

The van he used was in a storage facility on the other side of town, in yet another name than the one this house was in. But *Tin Man*. He could work with that: *T*om *M*atheson; *T*heodore *M*iur; *T*rade*m*ark.

He dug two of his pills from his pocket. They were in a waterproof match container. Because now he knew about rain. In the old days—

Nazareth, Pawnee City, Lydia—he'd just used an old Bayer tin, but then, driving out, he'd gone under the storm again, and it had been angry, left him leading an eight-year-old and her ten-year-old brother across the landscaped prettiness of a rest stop and falling to his knees on the green green grass, Kentucky wavering before him, his vision reduced to a tunnel. At the end of it there had been a horse, a white fence. And the horse had *known*, had its ears pricked forward two days, to the motel room where he had the children tied. Where he'd been convulsing on the bed, the television up to drown out his moans. When he woke the following morning, they were gone, and that had been the worst four months of his life, almost. Waiting for Creed to knock on his door with a notebook full of questions.

But Creed hadn't even been on it yet.

Nobody even knew about him, then. About the Tin Man.

And the children that time, they were just gone. The Tin Man hoped nobody like him had found them, walking hand in hand down the road.

On a return trip, he tranquilized the horse, removed its tongue.

In the tabloids, he was an alien.

That was about right.

The tongue he'd cooked like it said in a coffee table book he'd inherited about the Plains Indians. He'd just looked at it on his plate, though, unable to eat it. Not because it was a tongue—not *all* because it was tongue—but because he could only eat certain things: black radish, artichoke leaf, boldo, milk thistle. He pictured his liver like a bloated, black bean inside him. Made of glass.

For a while, he'd considered a transplant—having a *coolerful* of livers delivered to the hospital he was checked in to, from men and women of all ages and blood types—but in the end couldn't do it. Submit to another person like that. Someone with a knife, a mask.

Maybe a surgeon had found the two lost kids.

Someone like him. Someone without fear.

The children had eaten the tongue for him, anyway. It was in their genes.

He'd listened to them sleep afterwards, too. For the horse to talk.

It never did.

The year after that—no storms, the Great Plains baking in the sun, curling up in pain at the edges—he spent in terror that a psychic was watching him, documenting him for VICAP. Using his own *eyes* to watch him.

That was the year he looked at no newspapers, no mail, in no mirrors. That year it was all about the children, giving VICAP long views of them sleeping. And then he learned to sew. Not with thread, but sinew, the old way. A bone awl, even.

He made the first two in the image of Donny and Dawn. And all the rest.

He could eat whatever he wanted, he decided. But he didn't. Because to instill discipline in others, you first have to have it yourself.

Creed, though.

Nevermind Creed.

Below him, under the wood runners of the chair, the tapping in the floor stopped. Meaning now they had an acoustic map of the ceiling above them. And he'd left them tools in the room, too—wire, string, a ruler they could fashion into a shiv. This month it was Confinement. Last month it had been Anatomy. He'd needed live specimens for that.

The children had watched from their beds, their eyes soaked with knowledge, their floors coated with plastic. First they'd eaten dinner with the specimen, though.

They'd eaten more than usual, of course, trying to delay the inevitable.

They kept it down, though. He made them.

And Amos. God. He'd been so proud to see Amos on the news, moving through that morgue with the hair they'd taken such good care of, securing the perimeter calmly, deliberately. Not that he could endorse such public behavior, of course, not without *reason*, but it was to be expected: if you taught them enough, they soon used it against you, as any adolescent would. Show them Confinement, and they might unconfine themselves. During Transport, say. If you wanted them to.

Children.

He smiled, shook his head, thumbed the channel up to himself, again, and Marion's kids, locked in the bedroom today. But him. Now he was looming over the anchorwoman's shoulder, his face a mask of metal taken from the movie. Or, rather, *tin*.

He touched his right fingertips to his right cheek. It was dry. He knew it would be.

After the news, it was the weather station, the television on mute, the tape in the intercom, so that it filled the house.

It was Jim Doe, the one he'd missed.

He was talking to Nazareth.

The *Tin Man*—he smiled: the name—had found it on his receiver just after lunch, after Connecticut. A surprise. His ears had still been wrong from the flight, then. It was worth it, though. Just to see Amos again. And Eddie, and Rachel.

He took another pill, ate a carrot.

The silence downstairs was good.

The specimens he would collect for them later would be silent as well. The children would learn soon that that was worse than the screaming they would do at first, and, more importantly, they would see *themselves* in the specimens, for the first few months after being rescued. How they'd fought too, and cried, and screamed, and not eaten, not *understood*.

Now it was better, though.

They just needed the proper discipline. To hold the knife in their hands.

The Tin Man swallowed his pill. Maybe he would call it *oil*, now. As in, *I'd better get my* oil, *don't want to get stuck out here again*. In Kenfuckingtucky.

He raced through the channels until they blurred together, starting to resolve into something else, an image greater than themselves—a low pressure system moving across the Midwest, up out of the Gulf—and then a shadow moved on the high gloss wall opposite the basement stairs.

He'd put the 150-watt bulb by the door down there for just that reason.

Paul's head crested the stairs. He was leading his sister. The broom had been a distraction, cover noise.

The Tin Man took his hand out of his pants, raised it, clapped quietly. Like an aristocrat would.

Paul's sister was Gina. They stood on the landing waiting.

'Good,' their father said, then to Paul: 'Almost done.'

Paul just stared.

The Tin Man nodded to him, his head moving just once.

Paul's hand slipped from his sister's, she looked over to him, and then he grabbed her again, higher up. By the wrist. His technique was without flaw, without hesitation.

Paul ratcheted his sister's arm up behind her, pushed her across the living room carpet, pausing only to see if he could walk in front of the weather. Had it been on that station all along?

The Tin Man nodded, rolled his hand out to let the boy pass. Give him the red carpet.

Paul was fourteen, Gina thirteen. Nakota by birth. It had been dormant in their blood, though, until him. Until the Tin Man. Now they knew all the battles and warriors and injustices, could recite them alphabetically or by date. At least Gina could. Paul had been older when the Tin Man had found him. But he was learning.

Paul set his sister down in one of the kitchen chairs, then dragged the chair across the tile to the junk drawer. Because you can't trust them for an instant.

In the drawer was duct tape, twine, twist ties from all the bread that had passed through this house and select others, and half a roll of saran wrap. The saran wrap was really for Anatomy. And Storage.

Paul raised each object out of the drawer until his father nodded.

The twist ties.

Paul looked at them.

Sometimes you would have even less.

Amos was the one who had figured it out first, how to use them, how there was no way to tie them together where they could actually *hold* a struggling specimen, but not all restraints are physical, either. Some are just *felt*.

On his second try, after first stripping the paper from a handful of ties and fastening them around the ankles and wrists and pulling them deep, he'd used the remainder—the ones with the paper still on—to fashion an elaborate crown. The Tin Man had leaned his recliner up, sat on the edge of the seat, fascinated.

The crown Amos Pease had built was simple but brilliant: it ran one set of ties down to the eyes, the metal tips resting on the whites, and had another pair running far into the ears. It took nearly all of them. But he'd remembered: not all restraints are physical.

The remaining two he'd tied from the back of the crown to the back of the chair, then whispered into the girl's ear—his *twin's* ear, which was like his own—that if she moved the slightest bit, if she even fell asleep on accident, then the delicate line of ties she could feel on her neck, running down to her wrists, would tighten, and she would be blinded, and deafened. And then he wouldn't need the ties anymore.

She'd stayed awake for twenty-two hours, never knowing that there was no pulley system of twist ties on her head, to properly retract the metal into her eyes, her ears. But she couldn't *see* up there. That was the thing.

Some restraints are psychological.

That had been years before Amos had slipped away.

He was a natural, might have even started doing it on his own, with pets, livestock, the stray drunk, alone behind the bar.

But the girl, Amanda.

The Tin Man had sewn up her imperfections in the basement then painted her white, as an insult, but then felt bad about it, held her close to him, cried as he drove, barely been able to breathe as he arranged her under the tree with the other one, lifting her chin to just that perfect angle. Like nothing could ever happen to her.

'Father?'

It was Paul.

He had his sister's mouth stuffed with saran wrap, her hands tied behind her with the ties. Which she could stand up out of. Not that she would. Because she loved him, Paul, wanted Father to think her brother was doing this right.

'Father?'

Paul, again.

The Tin Man lowered his head, allowing Paul to speak.

'Someone's at the door.'

The Tin Man turned to it.

It was open, just the storm door still in place.

Standing at the bell were two children, just slightly younger than Paul and Gina. But close enough to play.

The Tin Man rose, crossed the room to the foyer, reached out of it for the door.

'Derek,' he said, to the boy.

The girl was Megan, *Brehneman* like her absent father, but he pretended not to remember.

'Can they play today?' Derek said.

Paul. Gina.

Jana, Jameson.

The Tin Man smiled, took an umbrella from the stand. Opened it. Closed it. Looked down the length of it.

'Have you been watching the news, Derek?' he said.

Derek shook his head no.

The Tin Man leaned against his wall in thought, his body blocking Gina, in her restraints, the open umbrella blocking the rest. He was rotating it slowly.

'You should,' he said, finally. 'The world's getting more dangerous every minute.'

'We're all right,' Megan said.

The Tin Man smiled.

'I'm sure you are,' he said, closing the umbrella in a rush. 'But Paul and Gina, I'm sorry. They're busy today.'

'Home school?' Derek said, in anticipation.

The Tin Man nodded, reached for Derek, touching him on the head, the hair. It took all the control he had—the boy was so *white*, so pale. And his sister. Sheep.

'Maybe tomorrow,' he said.

Derek stared at him.

'That's what you always say,' he said.

The Tin Man nodded, caught.

'Maybe I'll tell him to . . . to look you up later, Derek,' he said. 'That good enough?'

Derek shrugged. 'Whatever,' he said, and turned to leave, his sister staring for a moment longer. Into the living room, the kitchen.

'Megan?' the Tin Man said. 'Have you ever seen *The Wizard of Oz*?'

Megan looked up to him.

'What happened to your neck?' she said.

The Tin Man touched the tender, uneven blue line at his windpipe. It had risen on the plane. Like he'd swallowed a turquoise necklace. One Amos had made, just before his own sixth rib punctured his own lung, frothing blood from his nose.

He leaned down to Megan, using the umbrella as a cane.

'It's from my mask,' he said at a whisper, raising his chin so she could see what it had done. 'I'm the Tin Man, see?'

Megan shook her head no.

'Scarecrow maybe,' she said.

The Tin Man shrugged. Lions and tigers and bears.

'I can see Paul,' Megan said. Like she was just telling him. Like he wasn't playing right.

The Tin Man nodded, settled his eyes on her.

She backed up, but he hooked the handle of the umbrella into the pocket of her jeans, holding her there.

'Megan,' he said, tasting each letter. 'Middle name Gay. It means *happy*, right?'

Megan breathed once, deep, like she was going to cry, then turned, left after Derek, her legs stiff, the bones in them long and slender.

The Tin Man stood, opened the umbrella halfway, limp, then ran his hand along it, tying it down.

Mrs. Brehneman across the street was watching. Pretending to pull weeds and watching.

The Tin Man stood in his door and raised his hand to her, giving her Megan, and she waved back, flustered to have been caught spying on a such a *normal*, gentle man. Right down to the haircut, the thread-worn robe. The name. The Tin Man could practically hear her thoughts. He stood there long enough for Megan to safely cross the street, straightened the welcome mat with the point of the umbrella—just another home owner—then stepped back inside, to check on Mr. Brehneman. He was Decomposition, in the basement. It was an important lesson.

30

5 MAY 1999

CALHOUN FALLS, SOUTH CAROLINA

LATER that night, at the motel, the four of them—Creed, Watts, Cody, and Doe—would sit listening to Cody's recording of the session in 183. That would be the subtitle of the tape: *183*. The numbers were right after *Jane Doe*. And it wasn't an interview anymore, after Jim Doe left. Lucas had rolled the lights down just enough to foreground himself, leaning forward out of his chair, to her bed. Cody didn't need the recording to hear Lucas's monotone again. It was in the base of his spine now, forever. And *her* voice, in lockstep with his after counting up to twenty, back down again.

She was highly suggestible.

It was like a second pair of eyelids rose up out of sheathes in her upper cheek—clear, reptilian. That was the part of the brain Lucas was talking to now.

'Jane,' he said.

His voice was all fathers in one octave. *You can trust me*.

She looked up to him, over his shoulder at first, then tracking over to his face, zeroing in on the sound, the words, the tone.

She had the blanket up to her shoulders now. For security.

Cody leaned forward to the back of Lucas's head. It smelled stale, like the air at a bar. 'This isn't right,' he said.

Lucas held his index finger up to Jane, amended what he'd said during induction: that not only would she only respond to his voice, now, but, too, she would only respond when *Jane* was spoken.

She just stared at him. A somnambulist.

'Jane,' she said. 'Jane Doe, right?'

Lucas looked at her for long moments, moved his left hand in what would have been her peripheral vision were she not under, and then nodded, said it aloud: 'Okay. Jane, Jane Doe.' Then he turned to Cody.

'Do they usually do that?' Cody asked.

'No,' Lucas said, keeping the baritone out of his voice for now. 'That's why we *adjust*, Agent Mingus. Each session is different. Each patient.'

Which was when it became a session.

'Her legal counsel's going to butcher us,' Cody said, '*this*.'

'Donna?' Lucas said.

Cody shrugged.

Lucas smiled, said he'd had lunch with her, Donna. Then on her.

Cody saw the words lodging in Jane Doe's subconscious to rise from a dream later. He wondered what kind of minstrel or demon he would be in his almost-black suit, whispering just below her hearing.

He sat back as far as he could into the darkness.

Lucas looked to him to see if he could continue, and Cody shrugged.

'Now, *Jane*,' Lucas said. 'You've done this before?'

'It facilitates the absorption of knowledge,' she said. 'Embeds it at an instinctual level, so your mind doesn't get in the way when you have to respond.' She was reciting, reading off a blackboard. '. . . thought impedes action, enables the conscience to assert itself, which is just the temporary society of today trying to make you fit into its system, to make you like the rest.'

Lucas smiled, the side of his face crinkling around the eyes. Cody could see a book contract in there, Jane Doe as Bridey Murphy.

He put his hand on Lucas's shoulder.

'Ask her why she ran,' he said.

Lucas did, bringing her around to him again with another *Jane*.

She looked over his shoulder again, relaxed her neck on her shoulders.

'It was Amos,' she said, like it all made perfect sense. 'After Amos, I don't know. I just wanted to be like him.'

'Amos, Jane?' Lucas said.

You weren't supposed to invert interrogatives. Cody knew that much at least. Saving the meaning, the intent, her *cue*, for the end of the sentence was a dramatic trick, for the stage, or the cocktail party. Not the kind of thing to establish trust.

'Amos Pease,' he said.

Jane Doe's eyes didn't even twitch his direction. He was invisible, a disembodied voice, each syllable repressed as it was spoken. It felt as if just his lips were moving, even.

Lucas looked back to him. Amos Pease?

'Jim Thorpe,' Cody said.

Lucas nodded.

'And, *Jane*,' Lucas said, 'your father. He loved Amos the most, right?'

Leading questions, now.

Cody crossed his arms.

This wouldn't be admissible in a UFO-abductee chat room. It was like Lucas was building it to crumble under inspection. For Donna.

Jane Doe nodded her head. Yes, father loved him the most.

'The Tin Man,' Lucas said. 'The Tin Man loved him the most.'

She nodded again, hadn't been directed to speak into the recorder.

How could she know, though? The name?

Cody touched Lucas, told him to ask her.

Lucas made a show of turning around in his seat.

'Do you just want to talk to her?' he asked.

Cody shook his head no.

Lucas shrugged, as if his shoulders were on strings, maybe, Cody the puppet master, and turned back to her, asked how she knew her father was the Tin Man.

She just stared at him.

'Is that what he calls himself, Jane?' Lucas asked.

Still, just staring.

'A blind alley,' Lucas said. To Cody.

It had just broken on the news this morning. That was the thing.

Cody craned his head up to the television, touched it for warmth. Maybe that was how. It had to be.

'Jane,' Lucas said, going his own direction now. 'Tell us about the basement.'

She focused on him again.

'You can see his legs on the stairs,' she said. 'And then you know.'

'What, Jane? What do you know?'

'That it's time again.'

'For what?'

No answer; bad question.

'For what, Jane?' Lucas said.

'To do another one.'

'What do you mean when you say that, Jane?'

The question bogged her down, her eyes narrowing with it. But then she looked up, like it was obvious: 'To kill again, Doctor.'

Doctor.

Now, in the motel room, Cody knew he should have heard her say that. That Lucas should have. But they'd been in the basement with her then, their breath close, no echo behind the walls, the Tin Man descending, leading another victim down the stairs to what would be hell to them. Or the gate, anyway.

Lucas clasped his hands together at his knees, leaned even closer to Jane Doe's bed somehow.

'How many have you yourself . . . *done*, Jane?' he asked.

It was a thrill-question. It would look good in the book, when he changed it to *kill*, how many have you *killed?*

Cody looked up to hear the answer all the same. Saw her smile as she said it: 'Ask me again in a *minute*, Lucas.'

The second set of eyelids orbited back down into the bottom of her eyes.

Cody started to stand, to do *something*, but she was fast, trained, efficient.

Her hand rose from the sheets with her IV needle, the cuff that had been around her other wrist slipping out through the rails. Its keyhole was bloody from the needle. It never hit the ground, just reached the end of its chain, swung, a pendulum, three-quarters of its arc still to go.

'*What—?*' Lucas started to say, the last clear thing on the recording, and then she was driving the needle into his eye, through the tear duct. It pulled her IV rig forward, the wheels catching on the cord that fed her bed, the bag spilling over onto the tile. In moments—three heartbeats, maybe—Lucas's blood was pumping from the disconnected end of the IV line, where the bag had been. Cody didn't know there was that much blood in the human head, even.

She had given him a lobotomy, like they used to do it. Had probably seen books explaining how they used to do it, with a line of hyphens tracing the procedure, the instruments moving through time, frame by frame.

Lucas was a sack of organs. Meat.

And then she looked up to Cody.

'*Agent*,' she said.

Cody crossed himself with his right arm, reaching for the gun that was checked into the nurse's station down the hall. It was standard procedure for anything where a confession even *might* be involved.

He should have known, though. Remembered that guy over in Ninety-Six, trying to pick himself up off the ground, reel his digestive tract back in.

But it had all been so fast.

She was on him before he could even get his hand in front of him again, and it didn't matter that he outweighed her by ninety pounds, knew all the legal and not-so-legal ways to subdue a perp, had prepared for this moment for years. She'd prepared longer.

He slipped back on the IV fluid into the wall, her weight driving them into it, then they fell together, her toes grasping the legs of his slacks, her index finger and thumb set into the flesh between his nose and upper lip, her whole upper body twisting it.

Cody tried to scream, but he was struggling through the event horizon of consciousness: his voice elongated before him, swirled back into his throat, and then the world exploded and became silent all at once, the bundle of nerves she'd found driving him into some set of defensive convulsions programmed into his basal ganglia before *fire*, even, and, in whatever time-lag his vision was cycling through, when he saw her standing over him in her hospital gown, the IV needle bloody between her fingers, he knew he was dead.

Creed floating in just confirmed it.

They were in limbo together, here to atone for all the killers they hadn't caught, all the people they'd let die.

But then Creed pulled his real, physical gun.

And Jane, Jane *Doe*, turned to him, Creed, her hair slinging around, oily and black.

'*You*,' she said, and Creed paused, like he'd heard that before, like this was a replay of another crime—the reason he was *here*, in limbo—but then he lowered his weapon, shot through it, the barrel leveled to what would be her sternum a muzzle flash later.

It was impossible, but, just before the recoil, Cody saw the slug, pushing through its white donut of sound for her.

The only reason she lived was Jim Doe, risen beneath Creed's arm.

For Jane Doe.

She was falling now.

I wanted to save you, Cody tried to say, to the girl on the phone in Tennessee, as she wheeled back across the room in a spray of shoulder blood and clavicle matter, Creed's slug taking the window out behind her, ahead of her.

She was out of the room now.

The interview was over. The session.

Agent Cody Mingus had barely lived through it.

Watts worked it from all angles. Him, the Tin Man. You had to. But it wasn't all analytical. Part of knowing someone as well as she wanted to know him was desire, she knew. For intimacy. A longing. It could feel like love, if you let it. Infatuation. It was documented everywhere, the cop becoming the criminal to catch him, the criminal becoming the cop to know how to get away, but there were branches between the two, veins. Alternate models: Creed and Watts doddering their old age away together on the couch. Watching game shows, then slowly becoming aware of something moving on the porch. Something dying with its mouth open. They'd make their way to the door, pull it back, look through the screen at the mole or rat or bird that had been left for them, then try to judge from the way the neck was torn open, the entrails trailing, what kind of cat could have done this. Whether it did it with its mouth or its claws. Why it left the body there, like it wanted them to see, needed their approval, like they were part of it. And its grin, an afterimage against the faded porch furniture.

Agent Mingus had almost died in there, though, today.

And the psychiatrist, he didn't even have the faculties to know what death was anymore.

And the girl. Had she even known what she was doing, or was she another Amos Pease, moving on automatic? If he even was. Watts pushed her mouth into a smile with her fingers.

Creed had been the first one to see it, anyway—*her*. From Connecticut he'd seen. Standing above the four sets of footprints in the cemetery that should have been them.

He'd ripped the photograph of her from the fax while the paper was still warm, then fed it back, with a note to circulate it around Calhoun Falls—around that Ninety-Six-Sixty-Nine place—for a radius of two hundred miles. Every gas jockey, every motor lodge desk clerk, every waitress.

One hour past dawn, they'd gotten a hit.

That same hour, they were heading south at two hundred miles per hour, the birds parting to make way for them.

A night manager at a tourist trap near the national park or whatever it was had recognized her, or her little sister.

'Sister?' Creed had said.

The flyer gave her approximate age as twenty-seven. The clerk said his girl was more like twenty, on a bad day. And that she'd been in his 308 cabin for five nights, still had two days paid for.

'By *whom?*' Creed had asked into the phone.

Watts appreciated the proper grammar.

The clerk hadn't known. The money had just been in an envelope, the envelope in the trash already, the trash picked up that same day, the money long spent.

Creed had dug his fingers into the armrest of the plane.

He'd known because the Tin Man couldn't have been in two places at once: the cemetery in Bethlehem *and* in a van in South Carolina. But they hadn't known about the van, then, just guessed it. That was their job. And they were good. It felt good to be good, to walk onto a scene suddenly holy because you're there.

Behind them, in Connecticut, casts were being made of the footprints, matched against the dead agents' shoes, the first state trooper to respond, and Denny from Latents was doing the reconstruction himself: what had *happened* there. It had been different than Pennsylvania, anyway.

There, then—*last night*—Creed had nudged Watts awake with the toe of his shoe.

They were being watched.

It was their replacements, standing in the door.

Watts died, made herself live. Walked out, into the car, for the news of the girl Calhoun Falls PD had picked up for unlawful possession of a vending machine, suspicion of transporting it over state lines. The spatter of blood on her face, though. It wasn't hers.

Think, Watts, she told herself.

Not about the girl, in Critical, in 181 now—not twenty-seven by a longshot, like the highway patrol*man* had written up— but the girl's *father*. She held the tape of the session close to her ear, so he could whisper into it, through her, the ball of her thumb brushing the peach fuzz at the back of her neck.

Creed's and her replacements in Pennsylvania had been shot with one of the Connecticut agents' own weapons.

At least the news hadn't picked that up.

Execution style; no defensive wounds. Their forearms clean, virgin, their heads simply open.

Watts shook near the bone, because it could have been her. Because she'd been asleep and it should have been her.

She made herself think about him, thumbnailed him onto a napkin:

(1) Lost two children who were important to him. A boy, a girl
(2) Has means. Has acquired means
(3) Has opportunity
(4) Identifies with the storm
(5) Lives in the east
(6) Is training these children he takes to be killers. To be like him
(7) Avoids Oklahoma. From there?
(8) Older
(9) Unafraid. Brazen
(10) Knows the history of murder in America. Pop-knowledge. Schechter?
(11) Something about J Doe. Texas. M Isinger. Missing her. Messenger
(12) Has been saving these children for now. For eight years now. More than eight.
(13) Indian children
(14) Physically incapable, or unsightly? No
(15) Strong. Emotionally. Physically. Yes
(16) Has a plan, is executing it. Carrying it out. To fruition
(17) Copycat?
(18) James Doe. Amos Pease. This girl: Indian.
(19) Nazareth, Bethlehem, etc.
(20) Creed. Wayne.
(21) Steely Dan. That lump in his belt, J Wiggs.
(22) Tuinol. Education
(23) He's a father. Not a husband

Before she could get to *24*, then, it came to her, all at once: why serial rapists often started stabbing their victims. Because they couldn't maintain an erection. Because the knife could, again and again. Penetrate.

He was a *father*, not a husband.

This was not the usual order.

Watts realized she wasn't breathing; breathed.

Number 14. She crossed out the No, followed it with Yes: he was impotent. Maybe not sexually, but *biologically*: infertile. It was why he was taking children over and over, and going to such extreme measures to make them like him. Because that was the only way he could do it. It was the fundamental human drive. Before sex, even—the reason *for* sex.

And those first two children.

She closed her eyes, said it aloud: 'Of course.'

They were Indian. Adopted out of some bad situation on some reservation. Saved. But then something happened. To the wife, too. Because a single man can't adopt, not in the late 1970s, or very early '80s. Before Nazareth, anyway. 1982. Before he started adopting them him*self*. Starting over. And over and over.

Watts stood from her place in the waiting room, her list fluttering down between the chairs.

Creed was standing in the emergency doorway, holding his gun hand steady.

Thinking about his last marriage, probably. Or his first.

Watts put her hand on his upper arm, saw her hand against the fabric. Pulled it back.

'We need to run some things,' she said.

He looked down to her from his remote place. The monk.

'The children in the . . . in his photograph, Tim, or his head, or wherever. They were his.'

Creed nodded.

'But they were *Indian*,' she said. 'And he isn't. He adopted them out, and then, I don't know. They're gone.'

Creed cleared his eyes, looked at her shoulder like he did when he was trying not to look anywhere.

'Yeah,' he said. 'They used to do that, I think.' He smiled, nodding. 'Was it a federal program, like the spotted owl?'

Watts looked past him, to Jim Doe, sitting alone in the rental car. Staring straight ahead.

'If it was,' she said, 'then all the owls are in there. And who adopted them.'

Creed nodded. They were standing together at the door, waiting for the moment to shatter, and then, hours too soon, it did. Someone coughed behind them. The attending physician, in from his tournament. Coating the palm of his hand with germs.

He looked from Watts to Creed and then at his chart.

Watts could see it. It was just numbers, letters.

'You might want to see this,' he said.

'What?' she said.

'The girl.'

'She's alive?'

'Asleep.'

'Well?'

'Like I said,' the doctor said, looking back at Room 181. 'You might want to see this.'

Jim Doe was watching the sunlight glance off the hood of the rental car when they came for him. The cuff of the leg of his pants hooked on the brake pedal, and he had to get out twice. His pupils were still tight enough that the FBI were shadows moving in the brightness, reaching for him. He had to bend over to smooth his pant leg back down. There was something solemn about the way the FBI were standing around the door of the car, waiting. They were too patient.

'What?' Jim Doe said.

Of all of them, Cody was the only one to shrug. There was a knot of blue over his upper lip, a cold pack in his hand.

'This way,' Creed said, stepping aside, and Jim Doe walked into that space, into the clinic.

'Sorry about the girl,' Creed said.

Jim Doe pretended not to hear.

She wasn't his sister, they didn't think. Not anymore. That's what Creed was apologizing for. Her doctor—the one who'd checked her in—had done his residency with a radiologist, in a part of town where CPS walked up to ten cases a day through ER. Child Protective Services, the agents each suicidal in their own way, and so easy to fall in love with.

'And,' Creed had said.

The doctor looked up to him.

'Just the facts, right?'

Creed stared.

The facts. He'd stuck the film of this Jane Doe's upper arm on the viewer. Her shoulder in it was shattered. They'd had to x-ray her from every angle, after Creed left her smoking in the bushes. Which was when he'd seen it, the doctor.

He traced the hint of a line in her upper arm.

'CPS,' he said, for Creed. 'I kind of . . . had a thing for this one agent, you know?'

'A penis,' Watts said.

The doctor nodded, not unproud. 'But she brought me the cases she needed, you know, *help* with. The cases that were hard to make. Because I could look closer, right?'

Jim Doe hadn't been sitting in the rental car yet, then.

They'd all been standing outside 181, ears still ringing.

The viewer was there on the wall because Calhoun Falls didn't have the funds to put one in each room.

The doctor touched the line in her arm, again. 'It's too *even*,' he said. 'Look at the edges. See how they're all shifted over on the top part, to the outside? What does that mean to you?'

'We don't have time,' Creed said.

'It means that this break wasn't *natural*,' the doctor said. 'To get something like this, you have to put the child's arm in something like a vise, then, right past the jaws of it after you've clamped them down, you tap the arm'—he did it, in the air—'like this, and presto, the lower part of the humerus shifts over, just enough.' He smiled, flicked the backlight off. 'And anyway,' he said. 'This one isn't even healed yet, all the way. It was done within the last year. Nine months, I'd say. Fresh. Clean.'

Cody had looked to Jim Doe then. For his sister in Nazareth, her arm shut in the door of the truck.

'She was two,' Jim Doe said.

Not *I wasn't even born*.

So she wasn't his sister.

But now there was something.

They led Jim Doe inside, crossed the waiting room, hooked around the admitting table, and the uniform posted outside 181 brought his hands together in front of his crotch. The kind of stance that made you look wider, more imposing. Feel it anyway.

He nodded to Jim Doe and Jim Doe looked past him.

She was under the sheets now.

The doctor turned himself sideways, followed his hand past Jim Doe to the bed.

'When we examined you,' he said to Jim Doe, like he was preparing an excuse. 'All your vital data, it came up.'

Jim Doe nodded. He'd had to fill it out, even: social security number, residency, DOB, tribal affiliation, height, weight, age, eye color. Nothing important.

'I mess it up?' he said.

The doctor smiled.

'I checked,' he said. 'No.'

Creed was standing behind Jim Doe now. He could feel the federal presence with the small hairs of his neck.

The woman, of course—Watts—she was across the bed from him already. Because she'd already seen whatever he was supposed to. Now all she wanted was his reaction.

'She's out?' Cody said, touching his mouth, his lip.

'Like a light,' the doctor said. 'One that's off, I mean.'

'Well then,' Creed said.

The doctor edged the sheet down off her new gauze shoulder pad. Jim Doe held his breath, because of how it looked. The size of the hole it would take that much bandage to cover.

She should be dead.

It was better this way, though. They didn't say it, but Jim Doe knew. It was better to have her to question, later.

The gauze was halogen white against her dark skin.

The doctor was moving slow, to not wake her.

He stopped at her iliac spine, the middle of her back bare.

And there it was, in the sway, in blue ink. Two words.

happy birthday

Jim Doe didn't get it at first. Not until Watts asked him.

'How old are you, Deputy?'

'Twenty-five,' he said.

She shook her head no, and then he got it: May fifth.

'Happy birthday,' she said, sweeping her hand out over the girl, and when Jim Doe turned, it was into Creed, and Creed wasn't going anywhere.

The tape hissed on the covers long minutes after the session was over. In the motel parking lot, a car pulled in, a car pulled out. Creed was staring at the pattern in the wall, trying to come to a decision: whether it had been faded like that when they'd glued it up twenty years ago, or whether it had been bright. Like there was more color before all this started, more life.

They'd listened to it four times, now, back to back.

He could say it himself if he wanted, word for word.

He didn't.

This Jane Doe had been number two for him. People he'd shot. It was funny: the second body was when they called him, sometimes. Maybe chasing these kind of freaks so long was turning him into one. Maybe he should have slashed a big *2* onto a piece of paper, dropped it out the window after her.

They'd been lucky, though.

If their plane had been delayed for five more minutes. If that motel jerk had knocked off ten minutes before the state trooper held the photocopied face up to the glass of his booth, his fingers splayed out over her head like she was a saint.

They were ahead of Him now, anyway. Maybe. His girl, this Jane Doe, was supposed to have killed one of them. She was like a landmine He'd left behind—planted—and they'd picked it up, tried to take it apart.

That would be Sheila's job now. Whenever the girl woke up.

Creed didn't envy her.

It couldn't be him, though. First, he was male, another father figure. Second, he'd shot her. Third, he didn't have the right degree, had walked into this particular parade before there *was* a fucking degree.

The kid rose, clicked the tape off.

Creed wanted to tell him about Steely Dan. Jessie Wiggs. Wanted to tell all of them.

happy birthday

The letters had still been raised from the needle. Under magnification, they were ragged, unprofessional, the gun probably rigged together like they do in county, from the shafts of ballpoint pens and electric motors from children's race cars. And you don't learn to make a gun like that unless you've spent time inside.

The best bet was Washington Correction Institute in Louisiana, or one of the two Tennessee lock-ups. Marion Isinger's one-time homes. The wandering inmate, in search of a cell.

They were still running the names. Now they were running different parameters, too—Watts's. Especially the Oklahoma angle. It made sense.

But *happy birthday*.

She was a gift to the Texas deputy. His sister after all these years, but not.

Had he left the room on some cue from her?

Denny from Latents called just before the ten o'clock news. He knew what had happened in that graveyard in Connecticut, could work it out in Claymation for them if they wanted.

'Clay-*what?*' Creed said.

'Like Rudolph, Santa.'

Creed didn't answer.

They were all watching him, Sheila and the deputy and the kid. Creed pulled the phone into the bathroom, closed the door, thumbing the lock in.

'Yeah?' he said.

The bigger set of tracks—the 13Ds, their tread common firehouse issue all over the country—had arrived at the church early.

13D?

'How tall was he?' Creed said.

Denny was getting to that.

13D, their Tin Man, it seemed, had arrived with dark, more than likely.

Outside the bathroom door, whoever was at the sink turned the water off, clicked the lights down behind them. Including the one Creed had been using. The filament glowed for a few moments, died.

Creed listened closer.

This Tin Man had had pizza delivered. To the agents at the church. Cheese, plain, no sauce.

The agents' tracks left the double oak doors, fanned out to both sides of the delivery car, and after whatever happened there, they walked back in, their tracks close now. As if one was carrying a flat box of heaven, the other reaching in.

That was when he got them.

Two shots, below the right eye of each.

The heels of his boots had pushed into the ground where he'd stood when firing, which meant he was solid enough to let the recoil pass *through* him, not mess up his next shot.

The pizza was unrecovered. Maybe he'd ordered it for himself.

'Then who checked in?' Creed said, already sure.

The radio checks were every other hour.

It was why they thought Agents Walker and Dunn had been jumped sometime after two.

'He did, Tim,' Denny said.

It was an embarrassment.

'We record it, at least?' Creed said.

Denny didn't answer. It wasn't worth an answer: of course not. The agents on the other end were being questioned. All they remembered so far, though, was Walker. His batteries had been low, so he'd been keeping it quick. They knew he was lying, but they thought it was because he was with Agent Dunn. Their batteries would be running low too. All night.

Creed changed ears.

At sometime after midnight, then, that was when the second set of footprints walked up. Away from a set of tire prints they already knew from the morgue. Amos Pease.

Walker and Dunn had been arranged for him, it seemed, their new, pineal eyes open.

And the Tin Man, his tracks were deeper now, holding water the next morning.

'He put his jacket on,' Creed said. Wanted to make a big impression. A fucking costume ball.

Like the first time Amos Pease had seen him.

Amos Pease ran from him at first, it seemed, but then they'd struggled—*father and son*, Creed thought—and then it had only been the Tin Man. It was the last thing Creed had learned at home: that you can't beat your own father up. And it's not just that he's stronger.

Amos Pease was unrecovered, too.

That's when the rain had come.

'So you don't know who dug the bodies up,' Creed said.

'Not Walker,' Denny said. 'And not Dunn.'

Creed switched ears again.

'Give me something I can use, Denny,' he said.

On his end, Denny leaned back in his chair. The springs, all the walls of his office an arm's length away. Creed had seen it.

'Well,' Denny said. 'This. I guess you don't have them there, but the photographs, the *casts* of 13D. They're anatomically unlikely.'

'Unlikely?'

It was the ball of his foot, the Tin Man's pivot point. It was too high up in the tread pattern. Meaning he wasn't as tall as a man with a 13D would be, statistically speaking. He was as tall as somebody would be who had to stuff the toes of their boots with rags and newspapers. Which wasn't tall at all. Like Watts had said: physically unimposing. Maybe even unappealing. Most of them were. Most *people*, in general.

Creed hung the phone up gently, so they wouldn't hear in the outer room, know he was just sitting there in the dark. Listening through the faded print of the walls.

Watts was telling the kid about the zodiac aliases in Tennessee.

Creed held his breath, waiting for the kid's reply.

It was so simple; all it took was someone like the kid saying it aloud: 'How long has he been doing this, you think?'

Creed opened his eyes in the dark, felt himself smile.

How long *had* he been leaving names?

Now they would have to pull all the credit card receipts for three weeks—a month—before each drop, for hundreds of miles in each direction. Because there would be more. Even eight years back, there would be more. And one of them would match the inmate lists, or there would be something in common between them and the other list they were running, of adoptive parents of Indian children who'd died—

Creed dropped the phone when it rang in his hands.

In the outer room, no one was speaking. Just someone from the floor, the receiver, his voice small but insistent.

Creed picked the phone up, held it to his face in spite of where it had been.

It was Quantico, whatever fuck-up they had on phone patrol.

'Talk,' Creed said.

The fuck-up slowed down, started over.

And he wasn't such a fuck-up, either.

'The Indian Child Welfare Act,' he said. 'That was nineteen seventy-eight. Before that, there were agencies all over the place adopting the children out. But, starting in seventy-eight, any child taken into state custody—'

'Any *Indian* child,' Creed said.

'Native American, yes. Any Native American child taken into state custody for whatever reason—did you know they can be indigent, when they're already indigenous?'

Creed didn't laugh.

The fuck-up heard it, went on.

'Well, starting in seventy-eight, the state had to give notice to the child's tribe, see? Like, give them first option?'

Creed nodded. He was holding the phone so still, afraid the connection would fail, that this would all have been a dream. That he'd fallen in here and hit his head on the can.

'And you know who they had to call?' the fuck-up said.

'Educate me,' Creed said.

'The BIA,' the fuck-up said. 'The Bureau of Indian Affairs. In Washington. They're federal, you know?'

Creed did: paperwork.

'Give me a name,' he said.

'Booth,' the fuck-up said. 'James Booth. In nineteen seventy-nine he adopted two Mennonite children, aged seven and ten.'

'*Mennonite?*' Creed said.

'Menominee,' the fuck-up corrected, making himself talk slower, more controlled: 'That's not what made him stick out, though, sir.'

'Death certificates,' Creed said.

Death certificates, yes. The two children.

They'd drowned on a camping trip in Maine. It was why he kept them in the woods—*back* in the woods.

'Where is he now?' Creed said.

'Here,' the fuck-up said, quiet like Booth might hear. 'Virginia, chief.'

Creed hung up slowly, watching the phone descend, his hand place it, the lighted pad of keys glow down.

happy fucking birthday.

They were going home.

31

6 MAY 1999

ROANOKE, VIRGINIA

THIS time when they went to the lake it was night, and the man didn't say anything the whole time, just sat in front and drove.

'He's letting us go,' Jameson said.

Jana was making herself smaller and smaller against the back doors.

At the lake they splashed around in the shallows like he said, pretending they were happy, and then Jameson was right, he did leave, the man—like he was the one trying to get used to it now—but there wasn't anywhere Jane or Jameson could go. They were too cold. He pulled back up into the other side of the parking lot and they hunched over in their towels, walked to him.

Two days ago he'd let them call their mother. Jana had told her everything all at once, in a spill, but then her mother had been talking while she was, while Jana was.

'She can't hear us, can she?' Jana said.

Jameson took the phone from her.

'She remembers what you sound like,' the man said. Like that was what was important.

In the van after the lake he made them both sit in back again, on towels.

Two nights ago, after the call to their mother, Jameson had woken Jana by shaking her, and pointed with his chin to two dark children watching them from the doorway. From the locked door. Jana had just looked at them, and they had just looked back.

Now they were going somewhere else, though, Jana, Jameson. The man kept slowing down then speeding up, like he was deciding.

He told them to be on their best behavior when they got there.

It was an old people's home, for grandparents. He led them dripping in their towels down the long halls of the second floor.

The door they stopped at said THE GARDEN OF EDEN. Jameson read it to her.

Jana shook her head no, held her fingers up to the letters: E-*N-I-D*. THE GARDEN OF ENID.

'Good,' the man said to her.

Inside, asleep on his bed, was an old man.

'Is he Indian?' Jana said. The face—dark; the lines in his cheeks. The way his nose hooked.

The man looked down at her again, then to Jameson.

'Do they have any Indians in Ohio?' he asked, then smiled: 'In *Columbus?*'

It was a quiz, not a joke. Jameson wouldn't answer, though. The man looked back to Jana.

'No,' he told her, about the old man being Indian. 'His . . . my mother was, though. Part.'

'. . . the part she sat on,' the old man said.

Jana clung to the man's leg even though she didn't want to, breathed into his pants. They were so clean. He lowered his hand to the top of her head. Jameson was all alone by the door. *Run*, she thought to him. *I'll hold onto him.*

But Jameson was just staring. His right leg shiny with pee.

The old man was watching them, each in turn, his mouth down in a frown. There was foundation pancaked onto his face. Jana knew it from her mother.

'Done there, Scout?' he said to Jameson.

'*Dad*—' the man said, reaching for Jameson. To protect him.

The old man was smiling, now, his face cracking in powdery lines, his real face pale yellow underneath. Then he started laughing in his chest. It turned into a cough, then a lot of coughing.

'You're not an Indian,' Jana said to him.

He looked down to her, his shoulders hitched for breath.

'Indians are nice,' she said, and then he really started coughing.

The man patted him on the back. Called him Dad some more, fixed his make-up from a compact in his own pocket, like he wanted to hide the yellow. Kept looking back to Jana and Jameson, apologetic, embarrassed, and for a moment Jana remembered Vacation Bible School, about Isaac and Abraham and God. How the man in the bed was God, here. And then Jameson was running, without her.

The man fell out the door in pieces, after him, slamming a nurse into the opposite wall of the hall, her tray everywhere. In the pee. All the pee.

Run, Jana said, in her head.

The old man was looking down at her, smiling around his handkerchief.

'You . . . you look—just like his mother,' the old man said, his eyes finally soft, watery, sick, and when he reached his hand out for Jana, like a tube she could crawl down to him, she held her hand out too, back, but it was for the fire alarm by the door. The whole world went red when she pulled it.

32

6 MAY 1999

FREDERICKSBURG, VIRGINIA

THEY had to take a commercial flight north out of Columbia, Cody and Creed and Jim Doe. There weren't three seats together, so Cody sat with Jim Doe, Creed just ahead of them, on the aisle. Watts was still checked in at the motel in South Carolina, waiting until Jane Doe was ready to play Twenty Questions with the federal government.

'Get some sleep,' Creed had said to Cody, when they were boarding, and Cody shrugged, and his shoulders, raised like that, made him feel fourteen again. In the presence of his father.

He didn't, though. Sleep. Couldn't.

For however long the flight took, Cody watched Creed, how he just sat there and stared, hardly even blinking. Like the rush and press of bodies up and down the aisle weren't even there for him. Like he was sleeping with his eyes open. And maybe that was the trick, to go dormant until shrugging into the Kevlar, settling the crosshairs on a set of shoulders in the distance.

First you had to think, though.

Cody was. About the list he'd found between the seats of the refrigerated waiting room of the clinic in South Carolina: a list made up of twenty-three entries—Watts's thumbnail sketch of the Tin Man. Her brain there in medium-point blue. That she'd numbered it was misleading, though; the space between the numbers was too large for a single digit to cover. In the bathroom of the airport, Cody had closed the door of his stall and restudied the list, trying to pick out which ones didn't fit. Where Watts's intuition was saying things she couldn't hear. It was an old exercise from the Academy: looking at old case notes when you already knew how the case had ended.

Think, Cody had said to himself, pressing his head to the back of the door hard enough that the barrel lock strained. What had she not seen, here? What was she *not* seeing?

Cody opened his eyes, ran down the list again, drawing a mental line at the bottom, after twenty-three, so that twenty-four—which she hadn't written down, just said—would be the conclusion, making the rest premises. He clicked back through the argument then, rereading each entry as a premise, working to support the adoption conclusion.

Seventeen was the first not to fit. About the Tin Man being a copycat. Unless he was being too strict with the term, limiting it to sociopaths: what about families? Is the abused son who grows up to abuse *his* son not a copycat?

Cody crumpled the list, pressed its sharp edges into his right cheekbone, a carryover from the standardized tests of high school, where scratch paper was the only acceptable noise you could make, and then was standing when he saw the divergence in Watts's list: twenty and twenty-one. She'd started going somewhere else then, going slow enough to even use periods at the ends of the lines, but then pulled herself back in, as if she *wanted* that blindness of going fast. Needed it.

Twenty read simply CREED. WAYNE.

Twenty-one was STEELY DAN. THAT LUMP IN HIS BELT, J WIGGS.

After that she retreated back to the safety of clinical evidence—Tuinol—then made the jump to control, education, adoption. Like that's where she'd been going all along. But Creed, Wiggs. There was no lump in his belt in the reports. Cody would remember.

On the plane, Cody checked the list in his pocket again, making sure of it.

It was why they'd taken him on: because he was a new pair of eyes on a case already eight years old.

Wiggs. Jessie Wiggs.

The file was twenty-one years closed already. By Creed. The requisition Cody filled out for it once they made Quantico never got processed, either; while they were suiting up, Denny came down with it folded in his hand, asked Cody if he had a minute, maybe?

Cody followed him down narrower and narrower halls.

'I should have been a jeweler,' he said to Cody, each of them turned sideways to fit into his office.

Cody nodded, not getting it.

'You're trying to be him, aren't you?' Denny said, when they'd sat down. 'Tim Creed?'

Cody watched the desk stand perfectly still before him.

'I don't know,' he said, finally. 'It's just . . . I don't know. He never—'

'Everybody makes mistakes, Agent,' he said, before Cody could finish. 'Even Timmy Boy.'

Cody just stared at him.

Denny leaned forward.

'You didn't know him twenty years ago.' Denny looked at the wall himself. 'Things were different then . . . I don't know. You know Marcia left him after that Steely Dan thing?'

'. . . Marcia?' Cody said.

'His first wife,' Denny said. 'Something like twelve or thirteen years. His personal best, I think.'

Cody kept listening.

Denny smiled.

'They didn't show you Wiggs's notes at the Academy, did they?' he said.

Cody nodded: he remembered them, projected up on the white screen—simple numbers, done block-style, the lines angling down to the left corner, indicating a right-hander used to arranging the paper sideways to himself.

Denny stood.

'He won't be down for you for a few minutes, at least,' he said. 'All that motor-pool shit.' He paused, then, looked to the side, then shrugged, giving in. To himself. 'I'll show them to you,' he said, one side of his face smiled up, narrowing the eye on that side.

Cody followed him down to Records.

'Denny Denny Denny,' the agent behind the desk said, and Denny nodded, led Cody to the back wall.

He pulled out the *Wiggs, J.* case.

'Tell me what you think,' Denny said. 'Before I show you what you've already seen.'

Cody blinked long. 'It's nothing, probably. Just what Wiggs had in his waistband, that's all. I mean—you're familiar with the case, I guess?'

'I was there the next day,' Denny said.

Cody processed this.

'It's just that Wiggs, from what that waitress said, he saw the gun on the *bed*, and *then* picked it up. But this was after they already thought he was carrying.'

Denny nodded.

'Data analyst, right?' he said.

Cody tongued his lip out, shrugged.

'What was it, then?' Denny said.

'Another gun?' Cody tried.

Denny shook his head no.

'Try a CB,' he said. 'Like a walkie-talkie. Mobile unit. Dinosaur-age electronic equipment.'

Denny pulled a series of large photographs from the back of the Wiggs box. The notes.

'What would that mean?' Denny asked. 'The radio?'

Cody was staring at him.

'That he was in contact with someone else,' Cody said.

That he wasn't alone. Hadn't been.

'He should have told you already,' Denny said. 'That's the only reason . . .'

Instead of finishing, he fanned the photographs out on a shelf.

'I'm sure he got the right guy,' Cody said.

'He was Tim Creed,' Denny said.

'Is,' Cody said.

Denny shrugged. 'He was different back then,' he said.

Cody looked behind him again. 'What?' he said.

'Nothing, really,' Denny said, nodding down to the photographs. 'Just this.'

Cody took one in his hands—number three—holding it by the edges as much as he could.

These weren't the notes he'd been fed at the Academy. He shuffled through the rest of them. What had been masked for the classroom was one word Wiggs had left at the upper left of each piece of paper, written in lemon juice or thinned-out model glue or water supersaturated with salt, so it left a residue: *Creed*. Transparent in the improper light.

'Why would they hide this?' Cody said.

'Would you have learned anything from his name being there?'

Cody closed his eyes, didn't know. But it didn't matter, either.

'They *did* run handwriting analyses against the notes Wiggs sent to the papers, right?'

'They didn't need to,' Denny said. 'Creed always got his guy.'

Cody stared at the box.

Had Wiggs even known about the gun before he walked into that motel room? Before Creed shot him?

'You should eat,' Denny told him, fading back to his office.

The next time Cody looked up, Creed was in the doorway. Filling it.

He looked from the box, the label, to Cody. Cody was comparing handwriting.

Creed stared at him just for a moment, not smiling, not anything, then underhanded the body armor across the room.

By two o'clock—no sleep, no talk—they had Fredericksburg PD scrambled, the SWAT van idling around the corner.

Jim Doe was in the car, in the backseat. A civilian, a federal prisoner. There weren't any handles there.

Their man was James Booth. He was fifty-seven, divorced. Had an RV sitting in his driveway, with the registration expired. Good tires, though. Good enough.

Creed pulled their radios from the padded box in the trunk, handed one to Cody.

Cody laid his gun on the roof of the car, action back, and strapped himself in.

Jim Doe was watching him through the window. He could feel it.

'We want him alive,' Creed said, just making sure.

Because James Booth probably still had the Isinger children tucked away somewhere. And whatever other ones.

Cody nodded.

From the dumpster behind Booth's house they'd recovered plastic forks and spoons—no prints—and pill bottles they'd had to call in: silybum marianum and thisilyn and lecithin and more. All the lipotropes and phospholipids the market had to offer. For liver damage. Specifically, the kind of liver damage associated with extreme chloroform abuse. 1850s-type stuff, before they knew it was dangerous.

Creed was breathing hard now, fully awake. Saying something under his breath that sounded like *Marcia*.

Cody tried not to watch him.

There was no doctor on the bottles, either, and the brown plastic was wrong, un-American. *Mexican*, one of the local detectives said, rotating it in his latex hand, tossing it once in the air.

Cody nodded. Watts had been right, just second-guessed herself away from it: number fourteen, PHYSICALLY INCAPABLE. Richard III, burying children under the stairs with his one good arm, a head full of reasons to be doing just that and nothing else.

'Hitler,' Creed said. About the pills.

Cody narrowed his eyes at him.

'He self-medicated, too,' Creed explained.

'So did Elvis,' Cody said.

Creed smiled.

This was what it was about.

They were in Booth's RV by now. They'd advanced feet at a time, their spotter talking into their ear about curtains, doors, sunlight. The sound-cover of a car passing—one of theirs. Every stray car in the neighborhood was official, now. And the few mothers that had been home, they were huddled down at the grocery store, under supervision, their cell phones in a plastic shopping bag, some ringing, some not.

Creed wasn't allowing anything to go wrong here. Not today.

The RV was clean, too. Like the spoons and forks. No maps of Kansas, no snapshots of children, none of the pamphlets they hand out at the state lines, about diverse cultures, some Indian dancer backlit by the dying sun, the feathers of his bustle shadow-black.

Cody looked up for the vent Jane Doe claimed to have used.

There was one. It bolted on from the outside, though, or else clipped in behind the carpet glued to the ceiling. Probably clipped, Cody thought. It made sense: you didn't want any extra holes in the roof of something that was supposed to keep the elements *out*.

Prints, though. They were everywhere, even a bloody one, a whole hand, on the backside of a cabinet door. The tech they'd brought was already crawling over it, for the mobile unit one street over. Saying how this place was a fucking museum.

Creed was smiling, leading with his gun, eyes open for trip wires, trapdoors.

Cody walked behind him, tried not to make it obvious that that's what he was doing, but then stopped, pressing the side of his head into his shoulder, to push the earbud in deeper.

The van was here, the one they'd ordered. It was painted UPS brown, and its left side wasn't sheet metal but fiberglass. It interfered less with the thermal imaging unit.

The agents in the van were reporting one person above ground. He was at the strongest heat source in the house, aside from the water heater: the stove. Cooking something he had to stir. *Noodles*,

Creed said aloud, and Cody nodded.

It was time.

He would come to the door with the spoon in his hand, no weapon.

Cody stepped down from the RV behind Creed, was crossing to the porch when the sound rose up out of his subconscious, out of his childhood: a waxy thrumming, dopplering in.

He turned just as two children—brother and sister, obviously, maybe eight and ten—exploded around the RV, barreling down the sidewalk, their improvised turbans whipping behind them, the cards taped to the frames of their bikes stroking the spokes like tiny, furious engines.

Creed already had his gun on them, his rear foot setting the way it had in Room 181.

Cody stepped into the line of fire without thinking, breathing in to take the impact—his chest, blooming out into the day—but Creed just said *bang*. Quietly. And for Cody to never do that again. Ever.

Strike two, now.

The children rotated their heads to Cody as they passed, and long after, crossing the neighbor's driveway, then settled their eyes on the house *behind* Cody. The door.

It was opening, moments ahead of the SWAT UPS guy. He was just stepping from his truck, hadn't even pulled his clipboard out from under the seat. And Creed had his gun out.

Cody drew his too, swinging his head back around, to the brown truck.

'*Down!*' he yelled, advancing, and Creed stood too still for an instant, then followed, fanning out to the side. As if the residents of this street didn't matter, were incidental here.

The SWAT UPS guy held his hands out, his package (ceramic pig pepper shaker, one small Class D mike glued just inside the nostrils—the only holes on the piece) dropping to the gutter.

Creed said it again, for Cody: '*Down!*' That he was getting it, what they were doing here.

The SWAT UPS guy went to one knee first, then the second, then his stomach, his fingers laced behind his head a little too well. But maybe you couldn't see that from the porch. His brown hat came to a rest in the gutter.

Cody swung his shiny new cuffs out from his belt, fixed the SWAT UPS guy's hands behind his back, and then, from behind, a voice: '. . . what'd he do?'

It was a fifty-seven-year-old man in a robe. He was holding a pan of noodles. They were steaming. The neighborhood was so quiet, his hands so white.

'It doesn't matter,' Creed said, directing the man back onto his lawn.

'The hell it doesn't,' the man—Booth—said.

Cody had his foot on the SWAT UPS guy's back now. He was apologizing in his head, for what it was worth. He wondered what they looked like on the thermal unit, right now.

Creed slid his gun into his holster with one hand—not snapping it, Cody noticed—and held his other up to Booth, approaching behind it, as if shielding Booth's view of what was happening.

He was talking low, too, confidential. Man to man. 'You heard about those rapes in the Heights?' he said.

Booth just stared, finally nodded.

Cody smiled on the inside: there were no serial rapists operating in the whole city. Not on their radar, anyway.

Creed had been doing this a long time, though.

Cody nodded.

Creed went on, for Booth: 'Okay, look. This probably isn't even him. We know that. But just this morning, Mr. . . .'

'Booth.'

'Mr. Booth,' Creed said, pulling him closer, by the shoulder—*controlling* the situation—'Another woman. In the Heights again.'

He motioned to Cody for the clipboard. Cody took a step closer to the truck, slid it out from under the seat, saw it for a flash—a reduced photocopy of the blueprints of Booth's house, all the exits tagged red, the basement neon pink—then passed it to Creed.

Creed ran his finger down an imaginary column, nodding the whole time.

'What time was she?' he asked Cody.

'She called at nine fifty-two,' Cody said. 'It couldn't have been twenty minutes before that. Said she was watching Oprah.'

Creed nodded, nodded, then tossed the clipboard back into the cab.

It clattered, settled.

Booth nodded, looking again at the SWAT UPS guy, facedown on the asphalt.

'But why was he *here?*' he said.

The SWAT UPS guy turned away, smart enough not to speak without his fake attorney present.

'Is your wife home, sir?' Creed asked.

'Not married,' Booth said.

'Daughter?'

Booth shook his head no.

'Did you order something, then, maybe?' Cody asked.

Booth shook his head no.

The square package was lying there between them all.

Booth leaned forward for it but Creed beat him, lowered his mouth to his collar, his mike, making it obvious that's what he was doing.

He called for the Bomb Squad.

Four minutes later, the local detective stepped forward, wearing one of the SWAT team's bulky flak jackets turned around backwards, and a black baseball hat on his head, backwards too. He looked the part, walking soft around the corner, so as not to shake anything.

The package was addressed to Booth, a contingency, but Creed wasn't risking it for some reason. Or thought it would be more real this way. Or maybe that Booth knew communications equipment, would understand that the ceramic of the pig was ideal, because it wouldn't dampen the sound.

'Have you been home all day, sir?' Creed asked Booth.

Booth looked to his noodles, nodded.

The white on his hands was latex. Disposable gloves.

Creed looked to Cody, as if for confirmation. Cody shrugged. It was a real shrug. Creed played off it, turning back to Booth as if with reluctance.

'I don't know,' Creed said, rubbing his mouth with his hand. Then giving up: 'He was targeting you for some reason, anyway.'

Booth stepped away from the curb, from this, from all of them.

Noodles were bland. Ideal for someone with a bad liver.

He let them search his house, nevermind a warrant. They were keeping him safe.

To keep it unsuspicious, it was just Cody and Creed.

At the door they asked Booth if there were any firearms in the house, or any pets.

Booth shook his head no. 'I told you,' he said, 'I'm alone,' and Creed nodded, and they stepped inside, into the living room, sweeping back and forth, photographing it all with their minds, to catalogue later. It was clean, just noodle containers, newspapers stacked on every horizontal surface, pictures of landscapes hung in bunches, wherever there was room. Next it was the closet. For the 13D boots that weren't there. Then they opened every door they could find, for a shrine, a mound of souvenirs, a collage of photographs. And then they got to the basement.

Creed looked back to James Booth, his hand still on the door.

James Booth looked down, away, to a drawer. Came up with a flashlight.

'You'll want this,' he said.

Cody took it, thumbed the switch, shook the batteries awake, and then Cody realized what James Booth had done: given the flashlight to the agent not already opening the door. Meaning now there was no excuse to stay in the kitchen, keep the door from closing.

He looked hard to Creed for what to do.

Creed just shrugged, played through. Made a show of tapping his earbud.

'Say again?' he said.

James Booth looked to him.

Creed looked around the kitchen, settled on the range hood.

'. . . interference,' he said, looking into the living room, then to James Booth. 'Mind if I step in there to hear better?'

James Booth stepped aside.

So now Creed was guarding the door. Keeping it from closing.

Cody shook his head, directed the light ahead of him, and went down.

It wasn't a basement, it was a cellar. The flashlight stabbed across it, searching for a wall, and as Cody stepped off the last wooden step he was thinking how he was holding the flashlight with his gun hand. How much empty space there was behind him now.

Creed listened to nothing in his earbud for fifteen seconds, taking long inventory of the living room again, then nodded, said it—*check*—and looked up to Booth.

'They don't know if it's him,' he said to Booth.

'Him?' Booth said.

He was still holding the noodles.

'That driver,' Creed said, waving the back of his hand to the front lawn, the street. 'Fuck it, though, right?'

Booth looked to the street, back to Creed.

They sat down in the living room, Creed pinching his slacks up over his thighs.

'Eat,' he said, nodding to the noodles. 'Don't let us—' but then the bud in his ear came alive. He held his finger out to Booth to wait, let his eyes unfocus, to hear better.

Booth's prints from the RV had come back. He was just James Booth, adoptive father of two Menominee children who had died. Drowned.

Creed breathed in to talk, keep gaining Booth's confidence, but there was more. The mobile unit had pulled a match for the bloody handprint too: Marion Wayne Isinger.

'Say again,' Creed said. Buying time. To think.

Marion Wayne Isinger.

Creed nodded, looked up to Booth.

'Looks like you're out of immediate danger, sir,' he said, then smiled, hooked his chin around at all the newspaper. 'Unless we call the fire marshal, of course.'

Booth smiled.

Creed stared at him.

'We ran your name,' he said. 'That's what they were just telling me—could you hear? I never can tell with these—' Creed pulled the earbud out, let it dangle, giving them privacy, isolating them. 'Understand, though, Mr. Booth. We were just looking for a reason the UPS would have been . . . *interest*ed in you.'

Booth nodded.

'I mean, shit. What I mean is we know about your kids,' he said, finally. 'I'm sorry. We weren't looking for that.'

Booth shrugged, turned to eyeball a shelf of magazines, each leaning on the next, the last with its face pressed hard to the wall, spine bent, broken.

'You want to know about the gloves, don't you?' he said.

Creed shrugged.

Booth's noodles were long congealed on the coffee table. He turned back to Creed. 'Say one day you get kind of, I don't know. Fired. This after months of missing time. Like an alien abductee.'

Creed nodded.

Booth laughed.

'Don't worry, Detective,' he said. 'I don't wear the gloves for the mother ship or any of that. But one day you open the door to your office and it isn't yours. And then, that same month, your children, they die too, then your wife leaves, and you look at your hands . . .'

'Midas,' Creed said.

'The opposite,' Booth said.

'Sometimes it just happens like that,' Creed was saying. And maybe meant, too. He stood. If he'd had a hat, it would have been in his hands. Cody appeared in the kitchen doorway, gave a quick *no* with his head. Nothing.

'We might need to check back in,' Creed said.

Booth nodded.

Creed stood, extended his hand, but Booth pretended not to see. Maybe.

Missing time. Marion Wayne Isinger.

They were leaving now.

'What happened to them, anyway?' Creed said.

'Them?' Booth said.

'Your children.'

Booth turned back to him.

'They died,' he said. 'I told you.'

'It doesn't say how, though,' Creed said. 'On our sheet.'

'In the water,' Booth said. 'Drowned. That enough?'

Creed looked around the living room, a mock gesture.

'. . . no pictures . . ?' he said.

Booth shook his head, chewed his cheek, and crossed before them, to the fireplace.

There was one picture facedown on the mantel. He righted it with his latex hand and Creed felt more than saw Cody look away fast: it was the two children, in the woods, in the same positions, the girl looking up to the boy, waiting for something, the ocean behind her. And they were alive, with *features*, filled in. Not white.

'Good-looking kids,' Creed said. One father to another. The same voice, anyway.

Booth nodded, his hand still on the frame. Still touching them.

'All children are, Detective,' he said. 'Some of them just stay that way forever.'

Creed nodded, ducked out as if in apology, and Cody followed, picking through the sun-bleached plastic deer in the yard that had held so much promise five hours ago. Jim Doe was sitting in the car waiting for them, his hands in his lap, face straight forward, stoic like a penny.

'It was empty,' Cody said. 'Just boxes. Boy Scout shit.'

Creed nodded.

Cody had got the same news already, in his ear. About Isinger.

'A table, at least?' Creed said, over the top of the car.

Cody nodded.

They bent themselves into the front seat.

'What's he doing with those gloves?' Cody said.

Creed was making a wide right, the car's headlights tracking across a glass building, lighting up the stairs, the desk, a plant. A mannequin, nude.

Jim Doe was staring at him in the rearview.

'We need to figure out where that picture was taken,' Cody said. Like he was just thinking aloud now.

Creed nodded. Jim Doe just stared.

'He likes the bodies, right?' Creed said.

Cody nodded. Jim Doe was smiling now.

'The cemetery,' he said.

Cody looked from him—Jim Doe—back to Creed.

'He'll never sign an exhumation order,' Cody said.

Creed opened his hand, closed it.

The backhoe was waiting for them when they got there.

33

6 MAY 1999

GREENVILLE, SOUTH CAROLINA

THE birds. When FBI Special Agent Creed shot her, the birds had flown up from the ground again, packing their small bodies into the sky, blotting out the sun so just slivers of light remained. She turned away from them, to a man leaning over a birthday cake, lighting the candle with his cigarette, and then she turned away again, so that her head was backwards, and then she screamed, and then she held it all in, because she was Daddy's little stone girl. That was what he called her. Not flint or obsidian or chert, but *mica*. Mica. Jane Doe. Dorothy. Sister Christian. That was why she'd cut the man in the Ninety-Six gas station: because he knew about the concert, about Night Ranger. That, if you're good, you get to go to one. That he'll take you to one, keep his hand on your shoulder as you walk through the double doors, maybe even let go for steps at a time, your back swayed, swaying.

One night, his arms black to the elbow with blood—Disposal—Amos had unfocused his eyes and told her about *his* concert, Def Leppard, his teeth across the 15-watt basement a delicate white half moon. It was his wolf grin. Maybe he was lying, maybe he wasn't. She had been twelve, then, resting her face in a square of hogwire. And he was Amos. His voice was even like a chant, rising and falling, lulling her into the coliseum after him.

Def Leppard was big, then. The biggest. Hello America. Rise up, gather 'round.

Washington D.C. did. Throngs of people you could unzip from

neck to crotch, to let the sheep slump out steaming at your feet, their blank stares thankful, blissed.

It was going to be Amos's first time, solo.

Father took his pills, taping two of the mail-order moss patches over his stomach. They were supposed to regulate the liver. Amos stood by him in the foyer, shifting from foot to foot, trying to hold his lips in no particular manner. Because this could be another lesson. They might just drive by the concert, to a woman gagged and bound in a storage unit on the other side of town. Meaning *she* would be his first.

The moss patches had a definite smell.

Mica tried to think of the beach; couldn't.

Amos removed a gall bladder, thumbed stones out of it like black-eyed peas.

'Don't stop,' Mica said across the basement.

He didn't.

Father had parked the van nine blocks away, legally, because a ticket under the wipers could be the one thing that gives you away. Walking away from it they looked back, too, to map out all the angles of approach or regress, to fix the van in their minds, so that if it looked any different three hours later, they could just keep walking.

But Def Leppard. It looked like it was really going to happen.

Father put on his black wraparound shades, so his hand on Amos's shoulder wouldn't look that out of place. There was loose fabric there, too. Enough to grab onto. And the jacket, it was a trick to unzip, hard to shrug out of.

He would find you, though, if you ran. Mica knew. From North Carolina, she knew. It was why she was still locked up.

'What did you get to use?' she said across the basement.

Because He'd give you one thing, and one thing only.

'A bar of soap,' Amos said, huffing air from his nose. 'Ivory.'

And you were supposed to make it look like an accident, too.

But first, the concert, standing arms-up with tens of thousands of other people, none of whom know that you're different inside.

Seething, cold. And the songs you already know. It's like the shapes of the words are in your head already, waiting for the band to fill them with sound. And then the girl stands up from the audience, twice as tall as the rest—on a guy's shoulders—and peels her shirt up over her pale breasts, and you realize you're alone, untethered, no leash, no hand on your shoulder, and you step forward. It's not that you haven't seen flesh before like this, it's that you've never seen it so *willing*. And you step forward, and you step forward, and then the head between the girl's legs resolves into a face, and he's looking at you look at her, and you know *who*, now. Because he's seen you when you didn't have a mask on, when the girl's flesh has washed it away, leaving the fifteen-year-old boy underneath, still eleven, watching a funnel drop from the sky. The Amos nobody can see, and live.

You wrap your hand around the bar of soap in your pocket, lower your head—in invitation, to the guy—and slip between the warm bodies to the wide, concrete hall, and from there to the first bathroom.

It's empty, just leftover pot smoke up near the lights. Perfect.

Fourteen minutes later, the girl's guy walks in, unsure why he's even there, probably. Unaware that you've *called* him here.

You stand at the urinal not peeing, your belt open but your pants buttoned, and wait.

He's behind you, leaned against the sinks, arms crossed, staring.

'Indian,' he says. A classification.

You turn, look through your hair at him—the *boy* Amos, staring.

'Lakota,' you say.

His hair is long too, but dry and brittle. Because his father doesn't wash it for him every other day in the sink, then sit him in the kitchen, inspect for split ends, take them off with a pair of professional scissors. Because his father doesn't love him. Or smell like moss.

'So you like white women?' the guy says.

You step closer, closer, shrugging, doing whatever's necessary to get within arm's reach, a little less. He's taller than you, so unafraid. He should never have kept his arms crossed, though. It'll take too long to untangle them.

'She's a whore,' you tell him—the girl—and just as he smiles, agreeing, you do it: whip around behind him, wrapping his arms up, his hair in there too, so he can't come back with his head.

You drag him into the nearest stall, kick it out hard, so that when it swings back, it'll wedge itself into the frame. Because you don't have time or hands to mess with the lock.

Four feet away, at the row of urinals, someone starts peeing.

Father.

He doesn't flush, doesn't leave, just listens.

The guy in your arms kicks the toilet paper dispenser, the metal wall, the toilet itself. Pushes you back into the wall, over and over, until you both fall into the sludge. *You like white women.*

The bar of soap is cold in your pocket.

How to get it, though?

And maybe you're crying, here. Unsure, panicked. But then a wide brown loafer comes down on the other side of the stall, standing on the guy's hair. Yes. Thank you, thank you thank you thank you. You let the guy go, let him try to stand, and then come back down with the Ivory.

The only place to put it is his mouth, his throat, then hold it there until he stops kicking. It has to get wet with his saliva first, so it can slip in, wholly block the airway. And then he's dead. Father steps away, appears in the door of the stall. Outside, Def Leppard is filling the world with sound. Pyromania. Burn this place to the ground.

'Thirty seconds,' he says, and you nod, remove the soap, pocket it again, because it's soft, made for prints. But it has to look like an accident. You stand, looking around—slam his head into the toilet bowl rim, faking a fall?—but then your wet hair touches your face, and you know, and it's perfect.

You bring your wet hair around to your face, making yourself look at the matter there, then place it in your mouth.

There's no sound anymore, just the taste. The idea.

You lower yourself to the dead guy as your gorge rises, and, right before you spill it into his mouth, faking the rock star death—which fits, here—you see his teeth, artificially white, from the soap, and long after you've walked away, the Def Leppard shirt slung over your shoulder, the girl's breasts pale above the crowd, the bathroom wiped down, the teeth remain, how perfect they were in death. How you wanted to lick them.

It made Mica aware of her own teeth in a new way, and she understood what had just happened: just like she'd told Daniel about the birds, now Amos—Amos *Please*, they called him, because he could get them things—had told her about the concert.

'When do I get to go?' she asked him, and he shrugged, looking down at his work, his hands *in* his work, his grin sharp enough that he didn't even need a knife, and then, his wrist a flash, he whipped something across the basement at her, a pancreas, a liver, and it stuck to her face, blocking her airways for a moment, and she breathed in to scream, couldn't.

Jane Doe started convulsing at 4:42. Watts was standing by her bed when it happened, the phone held to her head. She lowered it to her collarbone, looked down to Jane Doe, and thought it was a show at first, like with Lucas. But then she vomited into the back of her throat, respirated it, her eyes slamming open with the absence of oxygen. Watts hit the emergency button and the doors behind her burst open, spilling medical personnel into the room.

When they couldn't find the key to the cuffs, they cut them with a bone saw. It turned the blade blue. They rolled her over on her side, to void her throat, and started calling out cc's.

Watts stepped back to let them work.

They had Jane Doe sedate in fourteen minutes.

But then it happened again three hours later, Jane Doe's hand rising up from the sheets this time, to grasp Watts by the shirtfront, pull her down.

She couldn't talk, though.

Her eyes rolled back.

Had he poisoned her before sending her here?

Watts asked for the toxicology report, read it in the hall up and down. It was just a record of everything they'd given her after Creed shot her. The hospital double-checking themselves, making sure on this one. Because the FBI was here. Watts flipped back, to the original report.

Tuinol. Its components, anyway, its residue.

It's why they were here in the first place. Because nobody used it anymore.

She fingered the time stamp: thirty-two hours ago.

She walked down to the pharmacy.

Behind her, Jane Doe was asleep again, pushed under by Thorazine.

'Tuinol,' she said to the heavyset pharmacist.

He closed his eyes, recited for her its textbook chemical composition.

'Addictive?' Watts asked.

The pharmacist smiled, leaned back. Held his finger before him and bent it a few times, like it was doing early-morning calisthenics. 'This can be addictive,' he said.

'*Physically*, I mean,' Watts said.

Her gun was checked with security. That was probably a good thing.

The pharmacist shrugged. 'It would take—'

'Years,' Watts finished. 'I know.'

'I take it this isn't hypothetical?' the pharmacist said, leaning forward.

Watts shook her head no.

'Sure, then,' he said.

'But how bad would it be,' Watts said, 'withdrawal?'

'Depends on the dosage, I guess,' the pharmacist said. 'Like coming off of phenobarb, I guess.'

'That reduces seizures.'

'Unless you stop taking it.'

Watts stared at him.

She slid the original toxicology screen to him, flipped to the back page, *this* Tuinol's residue.

'Can you mix this?' she asked.

The pharmacist had already digested the report whole, in a glance.

'I get off at nine,' he said, standing.

'Not tonight,' Watts said, then waited.

Four hours later, Watts wasn't supposed to be in the room. But she was.

Jane Doe was awake.

She blinked long, breathed, looked up to Watts.

'They left the girl behind,' she said, her words almost slurring.

Watts had turned the news on special for Jane Doe. Inset over the Oracle anchorwoman's right shoulder—upper left corner of the screen—was a running clip of Amos Pease moving through the morgue like a machine, the bat limber by his right thigh, his hair draped over his shoulders.

Jane Doe touched her own hair.

'I told you he used to let me wash it,' Jane Doe said.

'No,' Watts said, 'you didn't.'

Jane Doe shrugged.

'You'll start to seize again soon,' Watts said.

Jane Doe looked up to her. The idea of the syringe of Tuinol. Watts knew she was understanding.

'So?' Jane Doe said.

Watts didn't look away from her. Studied her, even.

'You look just like your mother,' she said.

Jane Doe's face set itself.

'A couple in Kansas identified the picture we faxed over,' Watts said. 'Your parents.'

'I don't have a mother,' Jane Doe said.

'Mica Jones,' Watts said, reading off Jane Doe's vitals. 'Born nineteen seventy-nine, presumed dead when the storm came through Paradise in eighty-nine—'

'I only have a *father*,' Jane Doe said, then touched her neck tenderly.

'His name is Arthur "Hoot" Jones,' Watts said back.

Jane Doe shook her head no.

'They sent photographs,' Watts said.

Watts slapped a vinyl wallet down on Jane Doe's—Mica Jones's—tray.

Jane Doe still wasn't looking.

'It's starting,' Watts said, nodding down to Mica's right foot under the sheet: it was trembling.

Mica looked up to Watts then. A child, scared. And then she seized.

An hour and a half later, Watts was back.

They'd given her the lightest possible sedative this time.

She was looking at the first picture, the one of the man with the glasses, at the birthday party, pulling deep on the cigarette he'd just lit the candles of the cake with. It was real, from Paradise.

Watts fished a tube of lipstick from her purse, stabbed it to her upper lip and held it there.

'You okay?' she said to Mica, her mouth a fake O. For the lipstick.

Amos Pease was moving on the screen again.

Mica strained at her leather straps without ever making a fist, quite.

Watts calmly pursed her lipstick.

'Well, Mica,' she said. 'Can I call you that?'

Mica made it to her knees in the sheets, her arms angled down to the bed rails.

'He said you'd try—' she started, then closed her eyes, counted silently. 'That you'd try to—'

'Deprogram you?' Watts said, taking her words from her, denying her even that.

Mica Jones stared at her.

'Paradise,' Watts said.

Mica shrugged.

'Not really,' she said.

The image of Amos Pease went to commercial.

'I've got the rest of the pictures they sent,' Watts said.

'Why would I want to see them?'

Watts shrugged. 'They're fake anyway. Our behavioral unit put together a composite—'

'You can't be doing this,' Mica said.

Watts looked right at her.

'And . . . "Mica." You just said that in one of your seizures, I think. Or was it Michael? Someone you knew, once, maybe . . . ?'

Mica was staring at her.

'Guerilla psychology,' she said. 'They teaching this at Quantico now?'

Watts looked away, shook her head no.

'Learned it from *my* father,' she said.

Mica just stared at her. Her foot under the sheets was trembling again. They could both see it, couldn't not see it.

'Will you give me some?' Mica said.

Watts produced the syringe, eased it into the branch in the IV line.

'Depends,' she said.

The plunger was just out of Mica's reach.

'What do you want to know?' Mica said, breathing hard now.

'Everything.'

'That I can tell you,' Mica clarified.

'Jim Doe,' Watts said, like she was only just now considering Mica's question. 'Or, no, no. Why now? After eight years of nothing. Let's start there.'

Mica rested her head on her knees. The strap on the side of her bed closest to the window was evenly scarred: she'd been forcing her restraint down into the bed's track, then adjusting it—the bed—forward and back, forward and back. After a month, it might cut through the leather. It meant she had hope, still. That was important, was something that could be used.

'What did it say on my back?' Mica said. 'I could feel him writing it.'

'Happy birthday,' Watts said.

Mica smiled, nodded. 'That's what it felt like,' she said, her head jerking to the side once, without her. 'Here, okay? Say a man, a confused, scared, helpless man, injured in many ways. He kills himself one day. Just like that. Only he doesn't die. What does that mean?'

Watts didn't answer.

'That he's not a *man*, Sheila,' Mica said. 'That he's above all that mortal shit. That he's beaten it.'

'But you can't,' Watts said.

'But he did,' Mica said back, and held her fingers up in rabbit ears, rotating them slow as if tuning in a better picture, one Watts could see. '*Twice*,' she said. 'Just to prove it, I guess.'

'Where?'

Mica was having to hold her teeth together now, against the seizure.

'*Now*,' she said.

Watts tipped some into the line. A taste. Mica closed her eyes to take it, came back calmer.

'When you kill a small animal,' she said, 'or a bug, you don't feel any guilt, do you?'

This was the reasoning she'd been conditioned with.

Watts could almost hear it—Him.

'Because I'm not a bug,' she heard herself say.

Mica nodded, playing impressed.

'And boys,' she said. 'Take boys. Twelve-year-olds. What do they do when they realize they can kill bugs with impunity?'

Watts didn't answer, didn't have to. Could see it: the Tin Man rising from his attempted suicide, reborn. Going on the rampage his former self never could have.

Mica nodded. 'They feel bad about it, though, later, don't they?' she said.

'If they have a conscience.'

'Pretend they do.'

'He.'

'This is a parable, Sheila.'

Watts stared at Mica Jones.

'Yes,' she said. 'They feel bad. They atone.'

Mica nodded, kept nodding.

‘There it is,’ she said. ‘Everything.’

Watts could feel that her teeth weren’t together. Her lips were, but not her teeth.

‘Is a man named Marion Wayne Isinger in there anywhere?’ she said.

Mica smiled—real appreciation, this time.

‘Judas,’ she said, her tongue pointed at the end of the name, eyes sharp.

‘James Booth?’

Mica laughed. ‘Poor Joseph,’ she said. ‘The cuckold.’

‘And you?’ Watts said.

Mica smiled, shrugged. ‘Who was that Queen who cut the guy’s head off?’ she said.

Watts stared at her.

‘And him, Mica? Your father?’

Mica smiled, turned to face the window, her own reflection.

‘The Good Shepherd, of course,’ she said. ‘The Pied Piper.’

34

9 MAY 1999

FREDERICKSBURG, VIRGINIA

JAMES Booth knew it was a setup. The UPS guy's legs had been too white. There was no rapist, no threat. Just him.

Now he could feel them watching the house. The FBI. It was messing up his digestion. Even more than it already was messed up.

One morning he woke and the picture on the mantel of Donny and Dawn was at a different angle. He only noticed it because now, when he sat at the kitchen table, the five o'clock sun glinted off the glass, through the doorway, across the stove, and right at him. It was something he would have noticed, fixed. Maybe that was even why it had been face down before the FBI, he couldn't remember anymore. There was nothing he could do about it, though. He walked through the house in his robe, pushing off from wall to wall, the days smearing together.

That was when he began performing for them. Miming himself, doing his best imitation of the way James Booth used to be, the way he should be. The way he would have been. It started with an extra step between the couch and television set, but then, by that afternoon—the eighth? a Wednesday?—he was looking over his shoulder as he stirred his noodles, and then looking down into the noodles like he'd forgotten his line here, dropped it into the pasta, the imitation sauce.

He took his pills in the shower now, so that only he would know about them, and prayed another package wasn't coming from Mexico. Not now.

Every sales representative who called was federally trained: no, he didn't mind if they recorded this conversation. How else were they going to establish a baseline?

He blew into his gloves before putting them on, and didn't ball them into the disposal anymore.

Now that Donny and Dawn were looking at him from the mantel, everything was different. And maybe it was *them* he was feeling in the small hairs at the back of his neck. He hadn't opened the door to the RV in nearly twenty years, now, just kept rotating the tires every thirty-six months. The weather cracked them open like eggs. The freezing, the thawing, the sun, the wind, the dogs.

He didn't go into the RV because there was something about it. Something wrong. Like the pills. They made him better, though. They under*stood*. But the RV. He watched it through parted curtains sometimes, and then, even when he wasn't watching it, he was.

There had been a fine layer of bug matter on its windshield the day Donny and Dawn died, was the thing. A layer he couldn't explain. He'd just come to in the living room like every time, groping for consciousness, afraid to look at a clock, the calendar, see how long it had been this time.

It had been going on for four months, then. Narcolepsy, somnambulism, *some*thing.

Jenine was gone after the first month, too, letting her supervisor send her to senior citizen colonies all over the East Coast, her cosmetics display case on wheels behind her. The only reason they didn't make the separation official was Donny and Dawn. Because the state would take them away. But maybe it should have.

James Booth laughed, a bubble of noodle cheese rising from his lips, collapsing.

She'd thought he was drinking. That there was another woman, another family, that he had the time for bigamy somehow, God.

He didn't know what he had time for, really. *Episodes*, he called them, or tried to. But things happened. The odometer on his RV was rolling back into itself, like a row of eyes opening.

He began to believe Jenine.

That something was clicking in him, that he was climbing into the van in some altered state, taking Donny and Dawn with him, and driving, having grand camping expeditions. Donny had a whole chestful of Scout badges from it. James Booth cried when he looked at them.

'Am I . . .' he started, one day, to both of them, '. . . am I bad? Is Daddy bad?'

They were tan, from some other sun.

When he found them at the end of the four months—his last blackout—he knew they'd drowned because of the way their hair had dried in the bed at the back of the RV. And their clothes, they were still damp on the inside. All the important parts of James Booth died, standing over them, and then—not in a fugue anymore—he inserted the key into the steering column, into the ignition, applied the brake, the clutch, the gas, stretched his seat belt across his chest, and drove to some water he knew in Roanoke, and set the two of them afloat.

Boaters found them two days later.

James Booth was distraught. It wasn't an act. The police that found him had to call their staff psychologist, and the psychologist had to call in for sedation.

Two months after the double funeral—two anonymous Indians stepping off the bus at the cemetery, unable to say anything—James Booth vomited blood into the sink then raised his head to the vanity mirror, smiled. Because he wanted to die.

'Okay,' he said.

He packed up his house, arranged his food by perishable and non-, then ate the non- first, wanted to try to write a poem about that: eating nothing, disappearing. Nothing rhymed with *guilt* the way he wanted it to, though. There weren't any more sounds to balance it out, cancel it.

And then the pills came, in a plain brown box, the ink blotted. Mexico. Lecithin, thisilyn, gamma linoleic acid. A gift. And they weren't pills at first, either, but rubber gloves, a whole carton of them. They were just the packing material, though. And he didn't mean to try them on, either, but—and he'd read this in a poem once, he was sure—you never do. The color they made his hands, though. It was the same color as the children's skin had been, when he dipped them into the water, saying all the holy words he knew, like *sorry*, *love*, *goodbye*.

He didn't tell that to the FBI when they asked, of course.

Until them, really, he didn't even know why he wore the gloves, but then he'd looked past them for a moment in the yard, and seen the same paleness in that UPS man's legs, and felt a kinship there: that they were both pretending.

He'd almost smiled, and they'd almost caught him, but that would have been the easy way out—his shadow on the yellow grass showing dime-sized shafts of sunlight, the shots resounding down the narrow brick corridor of the neighborhood—and, after twenty years now, James Booth knew there weren't any easy ways out. Not for him, not anymore.

35

4 JULY 1965

TINKER AFB, OKLAHOMA

HIS mother was talking to him again. In her voice. It was 6:43 am, the sun just cresting through the window over the kitchen sink, the world out there starred and striped, full of flags.

'You haven't been up all night, have you?' she was saying, the ash of her cigarette long and impossible.

John13 looked up as if trying to organize her face into one he could recognize, know how to respond to: mother, post-toothbrush, pre-coffee. On holiday.

He smiled a smile he knew she knew, looked back to his receiver, waited for her shadow to fade back into the house, leaving only his, the outline of his headphones against the white utility wall crisp and necessary. He'd been up for thirty-six hours now, dialed-in, on-air. Not bad for a thirteen-year-old. He smiled. John13 wasn't his real name, of course, just an anagram of his ham call sign: 3O1JN. But *John13* sounded better, fit better. He'd even looked it up in the Bible. It was about Judas—another *J*. The first verse was about *J*esus knowing he had to leave this world now, go to his Father. But the end of 27 was his favorite: 'Do quickly what you have to do.'

John13 lived and breathed above thirty megahertz, in the two-meter band. The Mosley CM-1 receiver had been a gift his father bought him so he could stay in touch with his friends in Big Springs, or Corpus Christi, or Peterson, whatever base *their* fathers were moving to now. None of them knew enough Morse to get their general class license, though. John13 hardly remembered their names anymore.

His mother made him keep his radio in the utility just off the garage, so she could monitor who he talked to while she cooked. She'd even read his ARRL *Radio Amateur's Handbook*, to see what the fascination was, but then given it back in defeat. John13 had held his headphones out to her, but knew she wouldn't take them. Because of her hair, set every Monday at the parlor, and dyed once a month, away from the métis black she was ashamed of. It made John13 think of her underwear, whether she was still Indian there, and then he just had to make noises to not think anymore.

From the stove, she could monitor what he said, but not what he heard. Not who he talked to. And there was always Morse, and the various Pig Latins of Morse.

Back when John13 had just been technician class, dodging Vacation Bible School with the rest of the sixth graders, the thing to do was tune in the tower on base, cross their fingers for a drill. When they came, he could hear his father barking orders. It was a thrill to hear him like that—intense, as if each of their actions was important. It was nothing like when he got home, stepped out of uniform, turned back into a man.

That was when he was a child, John13. Before he put away those childish things.

Now he was general class, could go cross-country on HF.

Some nights he only got as far as Enid. GB4HK. It was the call sign of Jesse James. They talked in dots and dashes in the silence when the rest of the radio operators in Oklahoma were listening to Hurricane Donna, the Florida operators relaying messages up and down the coast, their voices urgent and frantic.

'How many you think?' Jesse James asked, in Morse.

Died was the missing word. Two dashes, seven dots: -•• •• • -••.

Jesse James was always asking questions like that.

'666,' John13 typed back.

Last night, all the people from base furtive in the dark, trying to get their flags up first, be the most patriotic, Jesse James hadn't come on until three in the morning. He'd had his repeater on.

'Where were you?' John13 asked.

'Out.'

'With a girl?'

Radio silence: yes. Jesse James was dramatic, supposed to be nineteen, trolling the junior highs after three-thirty, when they let out, his pocket full of dime store wedding rings, because twelve-year-old girls always want their first time to be special. John13 had been taking notes for three weeks now. Jesse James was teaching him anatomy, and methods of approach, and what books at the library had what pictures. John13 kept those notebooks in Morse code, so his mother couldn't read them. His father knew it, though—Morse. Sometimes John13 left his notebooks out on the kitchen table, daring his father to read them, to *know* him, but it never happened.

In the kitchen, his mother was explaining how he'd been up all night again. The static at two meters was hard to tease apart from her bacon, sizzling in the pan. John13 waited for his father's response: 'Want me to do something?'

'You got it for him.'

'I know.'

'Well.'

'Okay.'

Usually they never even got that far. John13 checked his leads again, and the legs of the table. Opened and closed his notebook. His mother was still talking.

'Maybe he'll forget about it when school starts.'

'I shouldn't have given it to him.'

And then he was there, right after his voice: Father.

'Brushed your teeth yet, Scout?' he asked, a hand dropping to John13's hair.

Scout.

He could feel his mother staring at his back too, could remember one of the games he used to play: tracking his father on base all day, praying for a drill, please, and, if there was one, then waiting for him to get home, to ask him what he did that day.

'Work,' he would always answer. Just work.

'Nothing special?'

'You know, the usual. Why?'

'No reason. Just thought I heard something.'

It was like his father was hiding it from him, the drills. Like he was having another life that he couldn't bring home. One that mattered.

His mother knew about the game somehow, too. Would apologize, offer John13 a second, secret coke. To make up for everything that wasn't there.

In September he was going to meet the rest of the base kids.

It would be better then. His mother said so. It would be better.

John13 shook his head no, he hadn't brushed his teeth yet, then pressed the leather headphones down tight, so they cupped his ears even harder. So he could *hear*.

Jesse James was gone by now, of course, at the garage he worked at between other jobs. Now it was just FD98I, out of Minneapolis. He was trying to loop around down through Atlanta, find something out about milk. John13 had missed the first of the conversation, didn't know what 'milk' was supposed to mean. He dialed deeper, listening for that one voice he knew he was going to hear, inarticulate and uncontrolled, but so full of emotion.

Harry Cary, his father had said when they'd dialed it in on accident, as if the name itself were magic. Harry Cary. That was four years ago, that first crystal radio kit: a diode, a coil; a brass ball for tuning; some caps. John13 knew nothing about baseball then. Just *Harry Cary*. The tone of voice his father reserved for it, for him, like it brought him back to him and *his* father, arcing a ball back and forth across some 1940s lawn, one of them too old for the war, one too young, everyone between their two ages dead or dying.

The crystal radio set was supposed to have made up for one of the dogs they'd had to leave behind, rather than pay to have transported.

John13 watched his father and grandfather in the tall, sepia-tone grass, and held his hand up for his father to throw him the ball, then ran away before he didn't throw it to him again.

But if he could just hear that voice again, find it.

Sometimes John13 would pretend Harry Cary was his grandfather. That somebody in his family had been able to *feel* like that.

He fell through the hash marks, listening for him.

His parents were still talking in the kitchen.

He closed his eyes, held his hand around the shape of a ball for a shameful moment, then closed it.

July Fourth was the one night of the year his father would drink. The only military holiday he wouldn't spend with the other officers. Because they couldn't see him like this.

John13 had spent the whole day on the air. He was a ghost, no sleep for two days now.

'Who were you talking to?' his father asked.

They were walking out the door, carrying the big cooler between them.

'Nobody,' John13 said.

'That Jesse James again?'

John13 shook his head no, didn't look up.

Their new dog Bert jumped up against the cooler, pulling John13's side down. He was Bert number four now, reborn in another pound after his father shot number three in the backyard, to teach it a lesson. This Bert couldn't come in the house.

'Back by ten?' John13's mother called out, through the screen door.

'What time's the show?' his father asked back.

'Dark,' she said. 'What, quarter of?'

'Make it eleven,' John13's father said. 'We might be tipping a few back or something . . .'

He made eyes at John13 about it, drinking. John13 felt his face try to smile.

His father's excuse for making him see the fireworks show was that he needed someone sober to drive the boat. It was supposed to be a thrill, to sit in back, the outboard's throttle in your hand, the nose lifted up against the water. It wasn't. Jesse James would know how to get out of it, if he were here. John13 didn't, so he rode with his father to the lake, their fourteen-foot boat trailing behind.

They got there an hour early.

'Why?' John13 asked.

They didn't have any rods or reels. The high-schoolers were skiing on the lake, holding the bar with one hand, their bodies bronze in the dying light.

'Why what?' John13's father asked.

'Why are we here so early?'

'To get a good place, son.'

Son.

They did, out where it was deep. His father had an old pumpjack gauge. They dropped it to seventy-five feet, reeled it back in.

'That should do it,' he said.

'*What?*' John13 said.

'You'll watch your tone, soldier.'

Soldier. Son. Scout.

John13 looked out across the water. There was a white hot line of light between him and the sun. Like it was pointing at him.

'I want to apologize,' his father said, an hour later.

'I want a coke,' John13 said.

His father put the heel of his hand on the cooler, held it down.

He said it again: 'I want to apologize.'

John13 looked up to him.

'Okay,' he said.

'You don't even know what for.'

He had eight beers in him now.

'The Mosley,' John13 said, looking away. 'I know.'

'You should be out—' his father said, so unable to form the words that he just held his hand out to the high-schoolers, their music, their *fun*.

'I know,' John13 said. 'I will. September.'

His father shook his head no.

'You have the rest of the summer,' his father said. 'To do whatever you want. Whatever a boy your age *should* be doing.'

John13 looked at him. There was a finality in his voice that hadn't been there before. Like he was preparing for something, talking himself into it.

'We should get Mom,' John13 said, urgently, standing enough to rock the boat.

His father smiled, an early bottle rocket glinting off his beer can.

'She doesn't know about this.'

John13 flinched when the bottle rocket exploded. His father's face was slack now, a mask, strings tied from his cheeks to his mind, so he could imitate a smile.

John13 went cold all over.

There was nowhere to run out here. Nowhere to go.

His father looked up to the puff of sparks. 'You didn't even ask for any fireworks, James.'

James.

John13 shook his head inside his head: *no*.

'What are you doing?' he said, his voice cracking down the middle, so that he could feel it in the underside of the back of his jaw.

'You'll thank me next year,' his father said.

'No.'

His father flipped the lid of the cooler back then.

It was the Mosley.

John13 felt himself breathing hard. Like it was from far away.

'*Dad*.'

His father's eyes were wet, the beer in him rising.

'See,' his father said. 'Look at yourself, son. It's . . . I don't know. Unholy. It's just wires and—'

'No.'

John13 was crying now, down the back of his throat.

His father hooked his chin back towards the ramp, said something else about the high-schoolers. Maybe the same thing.

John13 didn't look. It didn't matter.

'*No*,' he said again.

Now his father's voice was cracking, too. But he was laughing at the same time. 'I mean, James, *shit*. I expected to have to tell you to quit or—or else go *blind*.' He smiled, cracked a new can open. 'I guess this is the sixties, though, right? Maybe you'll just go deaf.'

Across the lake, all the running lights were fading off for the show. It was like candles in a church, a strong wind blowing through the open doors, sweeping across the pews, up to the altar. The cooler.

'Dad—' John13 finally got out, standing now, reaching.

His father smiled, gave him the beer. It was a ritual; John13 could see his father trying to hold his shoulders, his head, just like his father had stood when *he'd* offered the beer.

'Drink,' he said. 'You'll feel better.'

John13 held the can, looking down at it.

'Please,' he said, or tried to.

'Take one,' his father was saying. 'Your mother'll never know. You're almost a man now.'

John13 held the yellow can to his face, his lips, and let the beer crash into his mouth. After he swallowed, he pursed his lips and looked over to his father—*is this enough?*— then retched over the side.

His father smiled, patted him on the back, guided the can out of his hands.

'I know you hate me now,' he said.

John13 looked up at him through the bangs he was going to have to cut off for school. He shook his head no. His father was crying now, wrapping John13 up in his arms, pulling him close.

'I want everything for you,' he said.

'I have it,' John13 said.

'You don't know,' his father said back. 'I wish you didn't ever have to grow up.'

'Dad.'

'I wish it didn't have to be like this.'

His sweat was acrid, his jaw rough, nonregulation.

John13 tried to pull away, couldn't.

Son, Scout, Soldier. James.

He tried to pull away again then, and his father held him closer, closer, his thick body racked with sobs, the can at John13's lower back crunched, the beer slipping down the seat of his pants, and he saw his father for a moment the way he wanted to see him, on his drills, every motion efficient and sure—pure—his hands steady and right, because the world depended on them.

But he wasn't that person. Just on the radio.

'Dad . . .' John13 said, and his father held him out at arm's length, appraising him, looking for himself in his son, the muscles on one side of the back of his neck twitching, so that his head kept jerking that way.

'. . . son,' he said, then kept one arm on John13's shoulder, used the hand of the other to tip the cooler up to the edge of the boat, his eyes apologizing already at a furious pace.

John13 took one step back, away, and for one crystal moment the cooler—the *Mosley*—was perched on the aluminum lip of the boat, and John13 was making deals at a furious pace: that if it would just *float* in there, he would never hurt any living thing again, and he wouldn't think wrong thoughts, about anybody, and more, and more. But then it started leaning over into the water, turning all his promises the other way, inside out, until they were threats. He moved towards it without even meaning to, never saw the back of his father's military hand approaching.

It unhinged him, slapped him back into the other side of the boat, and the Mosley slipped into the lake.

Neither of them looked at it, just at each other. John13's left nostril leaking blood.

'You're growing up, now,' his father said. 'Can you feel it?'

John13 smiled, looked over at the shore. Some of the high-schoolers had a bonfire going, the sparks trailing up into the sky.

'Yeah,' he said, toeing a lifejacket.

His father smiled, then, extended a hand—something you do for a *man*—and John13 smiled back, but it was a different smile altogether.

'Do quickly what you have to do,' he said.

His voice was different, even. He could feel it, hear it, and then he was diving into the water after his radio, making no splash at all.

It was hanging eight feet under the boat, strung out from receiver to headphones, the headphones tangled in the hinge of the cooler, the cooler bobbing just under the surface.

John13 held the receiver hard to his chest, screaming bubbles, and then the fireworks exploded over the water, and it was all color, no sound. Beautiful with no oxygen, the surface of the lake on fire. Independence Day. He screamed, kicking for the boat, his eyes burning, but the slack he made in the headphone cord loosened the headphones from the hinge of the cooler. It corked back up, disappeared—his father, lifting it out, thinking it was him, John13. That he would be attached.

He wasn't. He was sinking, unable to let go.

Seventy-five feet. John13 reeled the headphones down to him, shoulders jerking when his eardrums burst, but he was going to die anyway, it didn't matter. The last thing he did was cup the headphones over his ears, to staunch the blood, to *hear*, and then it was days later.

The head of his bed was against the window, and it wasn't his window, wasn't his bed. The hospital, his mother talking to him. She sounded like her mouth was full of tinfoil. She was stroking his hair.

He was alive, the Mosley polished on the top shelf of the closet. Unmossy.

'Dad?' he said, when he could, and his mother explained how John13's father was living on base now, with one of his friends. That he might be there for a while. That it wasn't his fault, John13's.

John13 nodded.

He was alive.

Every time he opened his mouth, his jaw, his ear popped, the drum in there stretched too tight now, but trying to heal.

'It still smells like gunpowder,' one of the nurses said.

Like fireworks.

John13 stood at the window watching the base kids shoot off what they had left over, and flinched with each explosion. They were too far away to hear, but there was *some*thing.

It was behind the base, looming: a thunderstorm.

The barometer was dropping, and he could feel it now. In his inner ear.

'Gonna rain,' he said aloud, to nobody.

That night he stayed awake to watch the lightning play on the white walls, and then he was still awake when the storm broke.

It was two months until September.

The clouds were beautiful.

He was alive.

36

9 MAY 1999

FREDERICKSBURG, VIRGINIA

THIS time when the storm came it was silent, and Jim Doe was unafraid. He watched it develop in time-lapse—the anvil forming; sheets of hail in the distance; the rows of mammatus hanging onto the belly of the cloud like eggs. The sky going dusky green. The rope of a funnel wisping down, striking the ground, all the utility poles on the east side of Main bowing to it, every pane of glass in Nazareth shattering. It took only three minutes and thirty-two seconds. Jim Doe stood in the stillness it had left, walked into a living room. An aquarium of fish was watching him. It was the only piece of furniture left. Even the carpet was gone. Jim Doe touched his fingertips to the surface of the water, kneeled down to the glass, and then, through the backside of the aquarium, saw Him.

He was stepping through the ruptured buildings and tangled wire of Nazareth, dipping out of view for steps at a time. And Jim Doe knew what was going to happen, what was *happening*. He clambered out of the living room he was in, trying for *his* house, *her* room, the closet he knew she would have hidden in. It was at the center of the house, backed up to the chimney. He knew it—the place, the closet—because when the pilot light was out, the two of them would sit with their backs to the wall, for the heat, empty sleeves touching their hair, like all these invisible people were watching them, watching after them. But they weren't.

Jim Doe ran ahead of the fireman, was twenty-six again instead of eight, tall enough to *move*, do something, but all the old landmarks were gone—Nazareth was flat, a jumbled paste of concrete and rebar, attics not opened for fifty years. On the corner he found his mother, sweeping and watching a television program. It was *The Wizard of Oz*.

'Why does he have an axe?' she said, looking at the screen for a moment, at the Tin Man, and Jim Doe stumbled back, onto a couch with his father. His father had his face deep in his hands. His shoulder where Jim Doe touched it was cold. Jim Doe opened his mouth to ask them where his sister was, tell them how important it was that she be found, but right when he was about to shape her name, he realized that his father was holding his breath, to hear better, and his mother had stopped sweeping.

They were waiting.

He rose, pushed off a crumbled wall and into the street. At the other end, *he* stepped all the way into view, his yellow jacket unmistakable. Jim Doe turned, looked *up* to him, but the fireman was looking away, at all this devastation. Like it wasn't enough. Then he turned his head down to Jim Doe.

'Donde Indios?' he said.

He thought Jim Doe was Mexican.

Jim Doe shook his head no, said it even, that *he* was the Indian, and he was smiling, that this could be the source of everything—mistaken skin color—but it came out somehow as *Padre*. Father. And he was pointing to the remains of his own home. His sister's closet.

The fireman nodded, rubbed some black off his chin with his glove, then tilted his mask back, to breathe, and it was Creed.

Jim Doe sat up hard, his knee driving into the underside of the table he was at. The FBI table. The courtyard he kept going to because nobody smoked anymore and he could be alone there with the wire furniture and nobody asking him questions.

Creed.

When James Booth's children's graves had been empty, had he turned in anger a moment too soon? Like he already knew? Was that it?

Jim Doe shook his head: it was a circus, Quantico. All musical doors and eyes-only files. Jim Doe closed his eyes again, to see his sister again, to see Gentry again, Agnes, Terra, Terra Donner, sitting beside him, walking down the road away from the high school, and when he stood, a man was behind him he didn't know. Watching. Creed's age, maybe—retirement.

He was braiding blades of grass into a bowl of sorts. A nest.

He held it up for Jim Doe to inspect.

Jim Doe cocked his head in mock wonder, made to leave.

The man shrugged, looked suddenly around, at all the glass around the two of them.

'Wonderful day in the neighborhood,' he said, singsong, just loud enough for Jim Doe to hear as he passed.

Jim Doe looked over.

'What do you want with me?' he said.

The man pursed his lips like an apology, embarrassment. Offered the woven bowl to Jim Doe. When Jim Doe didn't take it, he flipped it over like a coin. Daring Jim Doe to snatch it from the air.

The man nodded.

'Right-handed,' he said.

Jim Doe balled the bowl back into grass.

The man smiled.

'Just wanted to see if you really looked like him,' he said.

'Who?' Jim Doe said.

'Jim Thorpe?' the man said, like it was obvious. 'Amos Pease. The *In*dian.'

'Well?'

'I don't know,' the man said. The agent. 'He's dead, I mean, right?'

Jim Doe stared at him, then pulled the door he had hold of open, a smile ghosting the corners of the agent's mouth, and his eyes.

Creed was watching Jim Doe through the glass when the phone rang.

'Yeah?' he said, looking to his door, where Doe would appear in two minutes, like clockwork, to ask if they were done with him.

'We got something, Chief.'

Chief.

It was the same fuck-up from before.

'You're calling me from down the hall?' Creed said.

Nothing. Yes.

Creed closed his eyes.

'Well?' he said. 'I have to guess here?'

'It just came in,' the fuck-up said, his tone more sheepish. No more *Chief*, anyway.

'Eggers, right?' Creed said.

The fuck-up waited, then said yes.

Creed shook his head.

'*What* just came in?' he said.

'I guess maybe it's been here for the weekend, really,' Eggers said. 'But in the sense that—'

'Would this be better if I came down here?'

'The axe,' Eggers said.

Creed leaned forward. The axe?

'The Tin Woodsman, right . . . sir?' Eggers was saying.

Creed went down there.

Eggers hung up as gently as possible.

'Sir,' he said.

'Tin *Woods*man?' Creed said.

'From *The Wizard of Oz*,' Eggers stammered. 'Isn't that why you had us flag any and all unusual occurrences involving axes?'

Creed narrowed his eyes, pinched the bridge of his nose.

'I don't know,' he said. 'This was Dr. Watts, maybe? Phoned it in?'

Eggers rotated his chair over to a set of files, thumbed through them, slid the form out. Nodded.

'I thought it was for all of you,' he said.

'Just tell me,' Creed said.

Eggers already had the manila folder on his desk. He peeled the top flap back.

'This is airport security, Hartford, Connecticut,' he said. 'An axe head, sir. The head of an axe, it seems. No handle. It showed up in a routine scan of luggage that had already been checked in.'

Creed smiled, remembered now: the alert Sheila had considered. It wasn't for *air*ports, but for uniform and costume shops. They were supposed to report anything fireman-related. Any unusual requests. Because of the 13D boot tracks in the Bethlehem cemetery.

'The axe seemed to have a sharp edge, sir,' Eggers said. 'That was the thing. More than ornamental.'

So security had opened it.

It was in a glass display case, with a folded flag, at which point they felt guilty about the intrusion, just noted the engraving on the plate set in the wood frame, the destination of the bag, and pushed it through. But then one of the guards saw it come *back* through, a few hours later. It was because one of the throwers cracked the glass of the display case, needed security there to unzip the bag. It was the end of the guard's twelve-hour shift. It was nothing but luck.

'. . . and?' Creed said.

Eggers looked up at him, his hands flat on the table.

'It was under a different name, sir,' he said. 'Same axe, same case, but a different name.'

Creed felt his face warm with pleasure.

'They took a picture of this commemorative axe?' he said.

Eggers slid it over.

Stamped on the blade—on the side *without* the station-house number—were two letters: *O* and *K*. Oklahoma.

The Tin Man's father had been a fireman.

'Now, Eggers,' Creed said. 'Just tell me the origin of that first flight matched the destination of the second.'

Eggers nodded, stood. He was as tall as Creed, maybe taller.

'Roanoke, sir,' he said.

Roanoke, Virginia.

It was only four hours away, if they didn't speed. But they would.

37

9 MAY 1999

ROANOKE, VIRGINIA

CREED inched the LTD through Roanoke, the engine still ticking, the temperature gauge deep in the red, ribbons of steam wisping up the windshield. Cody had kept one hand on his seat-belt button for three hours, now. There was no music: when Creed found Cody to tell him about the axe head, Cody had been back in the archives, *Wiggs, J.* spread out on the table.

'We found him,' Creed had said, instead of everything else he could have.

Jim Doe was in back, no seat belt, a small, broken bowl of grass balanced on the back of the front seat before him.

Creed had looked at him.

'That back there?' he said—the floorboard.

Jim Doe had nodded.

It was still green, the grass. Cody didn't ask.

They were only bringing Jim Doe because maybe the Tin Man wanted him. If it came to that, to talking to him through a bullhorn.

They didn't call ahead to Roanoke PD, because they didn't want them turning their sirens on, the Tin Man diving to ground.

Creed had turned theirs off five miles outside town, and set the bubble down onto the seat. Cody could feel the heat radiating off it.

Three times he'd tried to say Wiggs's name—*ask*—and three times he'd not been able to. He told himself there would be time later, though. Six weeks from now, when they were just getting the reports back they'd forgotten they'd ordered, about the chemical composition and geographic availability of the birdseed at each site; about the technology involved with the phone device they'd recovered from the phone booth in Bethel, whether it was military or civilian; about what names had turned up in the hotel registries the last eight years, around each body dump; about who, married or single, had applied to adopt Indian children—ever—and been denied; about the extended family and friends of whoever Marion Wayne Isisnger had vehicularly manslaughtered. And the prison lists, and that parole officer's list. And the phone book, probably, for good measure.

The name the Tin Man had used for his return flight from Hartford was George Williams. The phone number tagged onto the commemorative axe head was handwritten, the letters careful. There was an address on the lines below it: 2253 Terrace Green.

George Williams.

Creed trawled two gas stations before pulling into a third. There was a patrol car nosed up to the ice machine.

He went into the store, met the patrolman at the counter, and the patrolman left his honey bun by the register, forgotten. He stood taller when Creed was talking to him. It was something Creed could do, give. Or take away.

'So this is him?' Jim Doe said, from the backseat.

Cody nodded.

'Be careful,' Jim Doe said.

Cody kept nodding.

Creed climbed back in, shut his door just as the patrolman next to them was shutting his. It was one sound. Everything was in sync, falling into place.

They followed the patrolman through town, and as they did the agents Creed had left on the highway fell in. The line of black Suburbans and sedans was too long to make it through the traffic lights at once, but they did anyway. It was like a funeral. A half mile down, the Roanoke PD were even parked at angles in the intersection, letting them pass.

Creed shook his head, hit the wheel with the heel of his hand.

'I told him not to call it in,' he said.

The patrolman in front of them.

It was their town, though.

They turned their headlights off when the patrolman did. A helicopter was thumping the air far above them.

Creed held the wheel long moments after they were stopped. He looked over to Cody.

'It's not—' Cody started, trying to apologize for the *Wiggs, J.* box, for *doubting* him, but Creed shook his head.

They stood from the car, shrugged into the vests and earbuds, making sure the wires wouldn't tangle their arms. Dome lights were glowing on all around them.

Directly above them, a high-tension junction was humming. One agent was standing in the street, looking up at the wires, the helicopter.

'Well?' Creed said, to Cody.

Cody looked around at the night, nodded once, and they guided their doors closed with the palms of their hands, muffling the sound, then walked away, guns held at shoulder level, their earbuds whispering about cats and sewage entry points and parked cars and streetlights and Williams, George Williams, the Tin Man.

2253 Terrace Green was dark.

'The yard,' Creed said.

Cody nodded: it was immaculate, manicured.

There were no cars or vans in the driveway. No dogs.

Three houses down, Creed had called for radio silence. Now there was just static in Cody's ear, and then an urgent whisper—one of the local uniforms.

'. . . *here*,' it was saying.

'What?' Creed hissed.

'Crawford?' another local said, quiet too, as if using a soft voice was the next best thing to radio silence.

After a few beats, the voice came back. Crawford.

'Just a couple of kids,' he said, almost shy.

Creed stood from behind his row of bushes, looking down the road behind them.

'This is Agent Creed,' he said. 'Hold them.'

No response.

He looked to Cody, back down the road again, then to the house. He didn't look away from the house. They were going in anyway. Fuck it.

Cody held his gun like he'd learned, advancing slow, and the sound when it came was so familiar he thought it was just himself at first, his unconscious worming itself into the background for a few bars. But then, up and down the block, the rest of the agents started breaking cover, standing for visual confirmations, their mouths moving close to their mikes but the frequency already saturated. It was Steely Dan. Not in the air around them like it felt, either, but *on* it.

'Fuck,' Creed said, ripping the earbud from his head, taking off at a run for the front door.

All the agents moved in behind him, like an oil slick spreading.

The door was already open.

Creed crashed through, slamming it against the foyer wall, and Cody followed, aiming his gun at everything, his heart thrushing in his inner ear.

It was just a living room. Like every other living room.

On the backside of the house, a window broke—more agents pouring in—and Cody found himself breathing hard, reading tomorrow's headlines: the house, rigged to explode, forty FBI dead, the only thing left of them their torsos, in the shape of their vests. A field of turtle shells.

And the music wouldn't go away.

'What?' Creed said.

Cody looked at him, saw that he had his fingertips on Creed's chest, keeping him from stepping forward.

He shook his head no, nothing. That he didn't know.

They crouched down the hall into the kitchen, to the only sound in the house. It was noodles, on the stove, the blue flame licking up around the copper bottom of the pan. Creed dipped one out with the wooden spoon that was on the counter by the range. It was still stiff. He slung it across the room, closed his eyes to have been this close and missed him, then came back with the side of his gun. It splashed the noodles across the counter, the steam billowing past Cody.

Cody bent to the bag the noodles had been in.

'James Booth,' he said, up to Creed.

They were the same, bland kind.

Creed stared at the noodles then swiveled his head along the countertops, to the sink. A featureless brown pill bottle. Booth's brand—Mexican. Quercetin and silymarin and fenugreek and the rest. For the liver.

'He'll have more,' Creed said.

They moved out of the kitchen together, in stages, always keeping their right shoulders to the wall, so they could fire down along it if necessary. Creed breathed in sharp when an agent from the Fredericksburg field office stepped around the corner.

'Boom,' he said.

They both raised their guns, away from each other.

Cody was thinking of Jessie Wiggs, for some reason. His motel room door bursting in.

The other agent did some military hand signal to Creed. Creed nodded, Cody followed: a basement. It was right before the living room. The agent opened the door to step down but Creed placed his hand on the man's shoulder, stopped him.

'*What?*' the agent said.

Creed just shook his head no.

The agent stared at him for a few moments, then at Cody, but backed off.

'Flashlight,' Creed said.

The agent just stood there.

'There's enough to go around,' the agent said.

'Of me, yeah,' Creed said.

The agent surrendered his flashlight.

Cody followed Creed down.

The first thing they saw was the leading edge of a massive wooden table. It was stained, the round heads of the carriage bolts rusted. A gutter around the edge, draining into a pan. A floodlight above it. Opposite it was the gallery—a corner of the basement sectioned off with hogwire. It was wallpapered with clippings from the Bundy trial, from the Lucas trial. A grainy picture of Manson.

'A classroom,' Cody said, aloud. Just, instead of presidents on the walls, there were famous killers, and their victims. From all angles.

Deeper in, past the table, was a fifty-five-gallon drum, the lid clamped on, a vent hood rigged above it. Meaning noxious vapors—acid; disposal. Past it was a single-door freezer, with magnets stuck to it, seven—*Ursa Major*?—in the shapes of states. All the places the bodies had been left. Creed jerked the light away, raking it suddenly across two small bodies. When he moved his arm to bring the light back to see them better, Cody stopped it, said it with his eyes and his mouth: '. . . please.'

Creed looked to him.

The children had been standing in the same positions as the children in the woods, just no heads. *Yet*, maybe. No heads *yet*. Because they were on television every four hours, the heads, the Isinger kids. But then Cody became certain the bodies weren't there anymore, now that there was no light on them. That they were moving through the dark, around the edges of the basement.

He spun to a corner he couldn't quite see into, releasing Creed's arm. The light fell on the children again.

Department store mannequins. Practice dummies.

Cody dry heaved, threw up a weak line of vomit, tried to contain the splash between his feet, not pollute the crime scene any more than he already was.

Creed didn't say anything.

When Cody could look up again, the beam of light was fixed on the wall behind the children. There was a hole beaten through the cinderblock, some of the dirt behind it scraped out. To the right of it were thick black words: *I have several children whom I'm turning into killers. Wait till they grow up.*

'Son of Sam,' Creed said, like he was spitting it.

Cody nodded, wiping his nose with the back of his sleeve. The hole and the words, they were from the photographs of Berkowitz's apartment. The original inscription was signed by a *Mr. Williams*. One of Berkowitz's supposed splinter personalities. Or a joke.

'Here,' Creed said, playing the beam over.

It was the source of the Steely Dan: a tangle of wires and radio components tucked into the corner, a set of headphones hung over the back of an office chair on wheels.

Creed held the light there.

'He's been listening to us,' he said.

Cody stared at the equipment.

'The phone in Gentry . . .' Creed said, putting pieces together out loud, 'he really is a fucking lineman. Goddammit. That's how he knew our number, to call you, right?'

Cody stared at him, trying to put it all together too.

Behind Creed, four more agents streamed down the stairs, covering each other. They were like circus performers, a troupe of mimes in their black turtlenecks and identical blazers. Creed walked over, unplugged the radio-rig with the toe of his shoe. The backlights of the dials died down, then came back up, a battery kicking in. The Steely Dan wound down in Cody's head, came back, then went away again, Creed kicking the whole table over. Without the music, Cody could still hear the children down here, whispering to each other across the room.

Creed lowered his head. 'He has three houses, right?' he said, to Cody.

Cody nodded. 'That she knew about, anyway,' he said.

Creed pressed the side of his gun into his forehead, his forearms trembling, and then slammed his head up, bellowed for everyone to clear the house, *now*. That it was *his* crime scene, his responsibility.

The rest of the agents faded away. Because he was Tim Creed. But Cody stayed.

Creed crossed the floor to the refrigerator. The padlock was open, just hooked through the handle.

'It could be a trap,' Cody said, stepping back, shielding his face.

Creed opened it anyway.

In the refrigerator was the badly decomposed corpse of a middle-aged man. It had been a job to pack him in. Cody thought of a turtle, the belly-view of a turtle, with a glass shell. The man's hands were gone. There was a piece of paper. It was pinned to his cheek, the number eight. No blood from the puncture.

Creed slid down the one wall that was bare.

'Not seven?' Cody said.

Creed was just staring.

'Angel,' he said.

Cody looked at him, looked at him, then up to all the feet shifting above them.

'What do you want me to tell them?' Cody said.

'Tell them to wait,' Creed said. 'I have to think.'

'He's just fucking with you,' Cody said. 'Wiggs is dead.'

Creed looked up to him like he wanted to believe.

Cody looked away, holstered his gun, walked back up the stairs, but instead of retreating to the yard, crossed the living room, the boards creaking under his feet, Creed watching his footsteps probably, dust motes falling from each one, dancing in the weak beam of the flashlight.

The helicopter was burning the front lawn with candlepower up in the millions. It was seeping in around the top of heavy drapes over the front window. They covered the whole wall. Cody turned to look at the living room but the drapes stayed in his head, glowing at the edges. Or, *not* at the edges. Not quite.

The window wasn't that big from the *out*side, was it? The lines of light on either side were maybe two feet shy of the end of the curtain. Like the window was stopping there.

He rolled a glove onto his hand, blew the powder away, and felt the long rail the drapes hung from, for hidden wires. Nothing. Then he parted them. It was just glass on the other side, panes and panes of it. And light. An agent on the lawn nodded hello. Cody didn't nod back, just looked side to side now, for the chain, the wheel to roll all this fabric back.

He found it, pulled.

'What the—' he said.

It was the *rod* that was too long. Why there weren't any pleats or bunches or gathers. Why the drapes were stretched tight.

On either side of the window, the part of the wall the extra drapes had been hiding, were the duct-taped forms of two children, with drinking straws for breathing, the tape on the faces haphazard, so that the pasty white plastic of the mannequin skin glistened through.

'He tried it out here first,' Cody said to himself. He'd tried it out to see if it would look real to Isinger; real *enough*.

It almost did, too.

Cody unfolded his knife against his leg.

Maybe if they could figure out where he was *getting* these? Wasn't there some horror movie that happened in a mannequin factory?

He leaned against the wall, his latex hand glowing in the light, and cut a clean line down the top of the thigh of the mannequin nearest the door, trying to just get the tape, not the hard plastic skin. He did, though, get the skin. And it wasn't hard. It bled.

Cody tried to catch it, couldn't, and before Cody could even get his other hand up Creed was there, his thick fingers desperate, grubbing at the edges of the tape.

'. . . the other one,' he said to Cody, lifting his chin across the window.

Cody floated through the light—no sound, anymore—and peeled the tape back.

It was the girl, Jana. Jana Marx-Isinger. In a plastic mask cut from the missing heads of the mannequins downstairs.

He was crying now, he thought. Probably.

She fell into his arms and he held her, warmed her, carried her out onto the lawn with her brother, and all the men in black armor with guns and worse didn't say anything, just to call the mom, call the mom. Wish her up out of the sidewalk to run across the lawn for her babies.

Creed stood from the grass without his jacket—still wrapped around Jameson, the boy—and Cody stood with him.

The rest of the house was normal, just one room of communications equipment.

Creed let the techs have the basement. Cody watched him. There was blood on his shirt from Jameson's cut.

'We saved them,' Cody said. 'We won.'

Creed looked across the room at him.

'We got lucky,' he said.

'Still,' Cody said, touching the VCR with a latex finger. It was running, the heads turning. Cody turned the television on. *The Wizard of Oz*. He looked to the counter, memorized the number—*3386*—then stopped the tape. The weather rose up in its absence, muted. A wall of craggy clouds surging across some anonymous skyline over Kansas or Oklahoma or Texas. Cody left it on as a lamp, looked around.

The only thing different now was that he could see the mantle better. The shrine each family erects. The Tin Man was no different. On the mantel was the framed picture of a girl, a dark girl. Indian.

Cody rose to see her better but the phone stopped him.

Creed appeared in the hall at the second ring.

He nodded.

Cody picked up the receiver, understood *doubt* in a new, personal way; disorientation: it was Creed, on the phone. From 1978, probably. In Bismarck, talking to his wife Marcia from a hospital bed, saying her name at the end and beginning of each sentence, telling her that Jessie Wiggs was dead. That it was over, that he was through with all this now, once and for all.

Cody held the phone up to Creed and Creed took it, listened, and Cody lifted the picture from its place. There were no lines of dust where the frame had sat.

In his ear, one of the locals was calling for an ambulance. Crawford was down, had been for half an hour.

The two kids he'd called about. Working in tandem for their first kill.

Cody looked at the picture, held it up.

'I'm going to go ask him,' he said—Jim Doe—but Creed wasn't listening. Not to him. He just tossed the keys over.

Cody snatched them from the air and walked out, through the milling agents, through the hot beam the helicopter was lancing down. The lawn was trampled, a mess. Cody smiled: at least they'd messed up the yard some. Even if they didn't catch him. One of the agents rolled the wheel of his lighter for a cigarette and the flame jumped six inches, disappeared. He smiled, rolled the wheel again. Tonight, at least, they'd won. Cody followed the flashing red bulbs down the sidewalk, back to the car.

It was empty, the dome light shining on nothing.

Cody smiled in a way that hurt, sat on the curb and watched the LTD for as long as it took Crawford's ambulance to get there. He twirled the keys on his finger over and over, letting them slap his palm. He had the whole *Wiggs, J.* file in the trunk now. Creed had insisted.

Some of the prints from the house were going to match some of the unidentified ones from the RV, he knew, but it wasn't going to help.

And another person was dead, or dying: Crawford. And maybe Jim Doe, taken from the car.

Cody stood, finally unlocked the front door.

On the front seat was the age-progression of Jim Doe's sister.

He held the photograph up beside it in the dome light.

It was her. At fourteen.

He shook his head with the wonder of it all—this night, this case—then pulled the driver's side door to, to ease back, collect Creed, but stopped before he even had the key turned all the way over in the ignition: the dome light was still on.

He stood from the car, rounded the trunk to the passenger side door. It was half-open, barely caught. Cody leaned against it, closed it all the way. It came back, the dome light insistent.

Cody started laughing, then—for everything, for worrying about shutting a door when there was a man tucked into a freezer—then rubbed his eyes with the fingers and thumb of his right hand. The pressure tilted his head back so that he was looking up when it happened, his hand over his mouth by then, covering a yawn: the high tension wires suddenly flashed a reddish orange.

It was an explosion, a ball of flame, at 2253 Terrace Green.

But that wasn't why Cody Mingus fell down.

For an instant, when the light had reached that high, there was a man ratcheting himself down one of the wires a block over, a pendulous bag hanging from him like an egg sac.

Cody pulled out his pistol in the sudden darkness, held it up against the sky, and pulled the trigger, over and over, screaming, the shells clattering in the gutter.

PART THREE

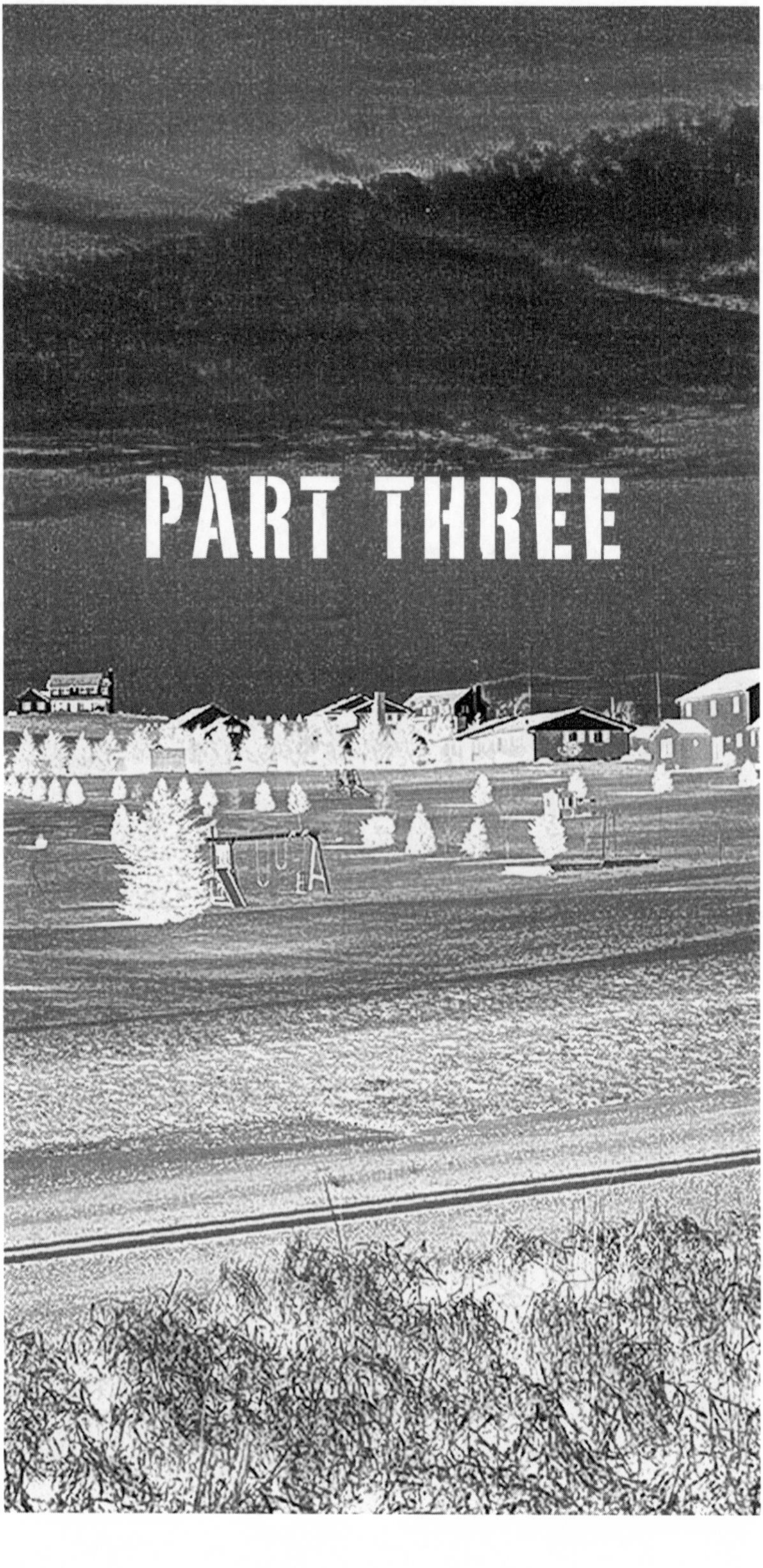

38

23 MAY 1999

GREENVILLE, SOUTH CAROLINA

MICA was telling Watts more about Amos. He was a saint, now. A martyr. Better than any of them. At his Def Leppard concert he moved among the unclean touching this lost one on the shoulder, then this one, each of them turning to ash in his wake. But then it was a Night Ranger concert, and Mica was up near the front, head angled to the stage, and when she looked around Amos was coming for her, his face serene, eyes set.

'That's because he's dead,' Watts said.

'Then I'm dying too,' Mica said.

Watts knew better than to argue this, to accept her reasoning, enter her world, validate it with participation.

'. . . we used to wash his hair together at the brown house,' Mica said.

Watts wrote it down: *brown house*.

'He had real Indian hair,' Mica said. 'That's what Daddy used to always say. Not like some of them.'

'Like who?'

'Daniel,' Mica said, after a few breaths.

Watts wrote down the name.

'Tell me about him,' Watts said.

Mica smiled, her closed eyes settling on something, someone: Daniel.

'No,' she said finally. 'Have you ever killed anybody, Doctor?'

Watts stared at Mica, shook her head no.

'Me,' she said, 'me, I'm a *natural*. Like Amos. All Father . . . ever—Daddy . . . '

She couldn't find the word, assign one term to him.

Watts pretended not to notice.

'. . . all *he* did was accelerate the process.'

'What about Daniel?'

'Daniel was fucked up anyway.'

Watts started to say something back but looked to the door for some reason instead. For Creed, maybe, risen from the house on Terrace Green. Her eyes were full, unprofessional. Mica raised the corner of her sheet to dab them, the chain of her restraints sliding across the hollow tubing of her bed. Watts lowered her face without thinking, barely caught the other hand. It had been coming for her throat, her windpipe. Her life. Mica fell back onto the bed laughing, the white gauze on her shoulder blooming red with effort.

'Head doctors always forget about the body,' she said. 'Ask Lucas.'

The door moved then, as if Watts had just looked a few moments too soon. It was nobody, though.

When she turned back to Mica, Mica's eyes were shut again, the pupils darting under her closed lids.

Watts shook her head, stood to face the window, just for the light.

'She's beautiful, isn't she?'

It was a man. Behind her. Not one of the doctors.

Watts choked on her own breath, tried not to clench her fists, give herself away.

'She's so . . .' she said, '. . . injured.'

'People, Sheila,' the voice said. '*People* are injured.'

'She thinks she's a natural.'

'Surely you understand, Sheila. They're *all* naturals.'

Watts turned around.

He was stroking the side of Mica's face. Five-eleven, maybe; six foot. Athletic build, that bran-fed kind of lean. Not young. Caucasian. Infertile, or impotent. Both. Wearing a simple Tin Man mask. Soft soles.

'I'm surprised this room isn't under surveillance,' he said. 'It's the perfect trap, isn't it?'

'Maybe it *is* under surveillance,' Watts said.

The Tin Man smiled behind his mask. They both knew she was lying.

'You want to know what I'm doing,' he said—calm, reassuring. 'To under*stand* me, right?'

'We do understand you.'

The Tin Man looked up, interested, his eyebrows already arched up in black paint.

'You're into . . . electronics,' Watts said. 'Communications. It's how you've been monitoring us all this time.'

'Okay. But that doesn't narrow it down very much, does it? I mean, this is the industrial age. The silicon revolution.'

Watts took a step forward.

'How do I even know you're . . . you?'

The Tin Man nodded appreciation.

'Well . . .' he said, massaging the chin of his mask. Then he looked over. 'Croatoan,' he said. 'How's that?'

'Croatoan?'

'Doesn't VICAP have a missing person's file, Sheila?'

It was rhetorical, the teacher leading the student to what they both already knew. Watts nodded, knew she was playing along, feeding him. But she had to keep him there.

'Go back to 1590, then,' he said. A group of colonist trash—'

'Roanoke,' Watts said.

CROATOAN had been carved in their absence, all that was ever found.

'Okay,' she said. 'You're you. Stealer of children, killer of cops. It's your big soliloquy now, right?'

The Tin Man managed a flourish with his arms, a little half-bow, his ankles properly crossed, and, his head dipped, caught something in Watts's purse. 'I'm sorry,' he said, reaching in, getting the gun first, dropping it onto Mica's sheets, then coming up with the recorder.

He held it to the slit of his mouth like a microphone, his eyes never leaving Watts.

She knew she was going to dive for the gun, knew she wasn't.

'A *thought* problem,' the Tin Man said.

'I'm not your student,' Watts said.

'Pretend, Sheila. And listen. A man starts a . . . an inland fish farm. Some boring, necessary fish. Use whatever one has emotional resonance for you. Whatever fish your father said he was going out for on Friday nights, when he was really meeting his mistress. Anyway. So this man, this *farmer*, he grows his first crop, has his fleet of tankers—he had a lot of investment capital, yes—his tankers truck the *live* fish to market. But when they look into the tanks at the end of the drive—you've guessed, haven't you?—an unacceptable portion of his crop is dead, Sheila. Belly up, as they say. And this happens year after year, run after run, no matter how much they modify the water solution in the tankers, no matter what they feed the fish en route, no matter *what* kind of tires he puts on his tanker trucks. Follow?'

Watts nodded.

'So, this man, then. His yield is all *fucked*. The return on his investments is becoming wholly unsatisfactory. The covenant between him and the—oh, you caught that? Covenant? Thank you. The *covenant* between him and the fish, he's keeping his side, feeding them, playing them songs at night on the underwater speakers, all that, but they're all dying in transit. Or, enough are dying, anyway. The question now, after all these years, is of course how can he keep his fish alive to market?'

Watts just stared at him.

'Try,' he said, looking at the gun with her.

'He . . . he . . .' Watts said, and then heard it, started hearing it: the static buzz that always preceded a code blue in this facility. The horn, the way it would draw the lights down in the room for a millisecond or two.

She was moving by the second, millisecond, airborne, reaching, sound all around, someone's heart stopping in another room, paper feet rushing across the floor.

It wasn't enough.

Instead of stepping back, or for the gun—the two normal responses—the Tin Man stepped forward, took Watts cleanly by the wrist. His hands were cold, latex.

He held both her wrists in one of his, his knee in the small of her back, and with his other hand pressed her face into Mica's sheets, brought his mask down to her ear, so he was lying on top of her.

'What does the farmer *do?*' he said.

Watts just shook her head no. Please, no.

The Tin Man leaned into her neck with his shoulder then, his free hand reaching for something else.

Watts recognized it when he brushed it against her neck: Mica's IV needle, still warm. Tuinol.

He inserted it cleanly not into the vein, but the artery, and held it there, getting the drip started, then rolling the wheel over, all the way open.

'. . . I don't know what he does,' Watts said.

'Do you need a *hint?*' the Tin Man said, his voice almost manic.

Watts nodded.

'Ask for it,' he said.

'Please,' Watts said.

'London, 1887, then,' he said. 'What did our boy Jack say in one of his letters? About the new century?'

That he was going to give birth to it. Or maybe that was from a movie.

Watts wasn't sure if she was talking anymore or not. The Tuinol. Just that much.

'Now, this farmer,' the Tin Man said, 'this *genius*. What is *he* doing for the next century?'

'Jack?'

'Me.'

Watts closed her eyes. 'I don't know,' she said.

It was what he'd been waiting for: acquiescence. Evidence of his superior intellect.

The sheets were grey for Watts now. Maybe she was laughing, or crying.

'I'll tell you what he does,' the Tin Man said, right in her inner ear. 'He introduces predator fish into the water, to keep the other fish nervous. To keep them vital, *alive*.' He stood from her. She couldn't follow anymore. 'My gift to the twenty-first century,' he said, as if disgusted with it already. Then Watts could feel him looking down to Mica. Or could feel like she was feeling it. 'My own little predator fish,' he said.

'Don't . . .' Watts said, trying to roll over.

The hole in her neck was the size of a drinking straw, and dilating. The blood from it was slick under her bra.

The Tin Man was standing, fitting a surgical mask over his cardboard one.

'It'll wear off before too long,' he said. 'You'll wake with a headache, Sheila.' Then he nodded down to the gun. 'Shoot me if you can,' he said, 'or'—smiling behind the mask, drawing Mica up to him—'just the next person who walks in in smocks. How's that?'

Watts swept her eyes over to the gun, the institutional sheets where it should be, but the room fractured along the way, at the molecular level, and in order to mend it she had to organize it first, catalogue it, give it a taxonomy. Yes: *order* it. She smiled, found the right hierarchical language system for the project, and started intoning names, the stem cells of names, which would tell the objects how to act, where to *go*, and it was only when she heard her own voice, how flat it was, that she realized she was already asleep. That was the only place she could know Latin. The dead tongue.

It swelled in her mouth and she rolled off the bed, clutching at the bright, loud IV rack, whispering to it to please be quiet, please please please.

39

25 OCTOBER 1966

TINKER AFB, OKLAHOMA

AT the MP gate Hari Kari stood at one end of the striped wooden arm, staring along it at the guard on duty. In fatigues in a concrete and steel booth.

'I'm leaving,' Hari Kari said.

The guard looked over at him.

'Again?' he said.

'Don't tell my dad.'

The guard stared at him, looked down the road into the base, back down it to civilian America. He stepped out. He was twenty-two, maybe. Eight years ahead of Hari Kari.

He stopped so that his shadow almost touched Hari Kari's feet.

'But we might need you,' he said, narrowing his eyes at the sky, the weather.

'There's nothing coming,' Hari Kari said.

The guard shrugged, chewed his cheek, adjusted his helmet.

'I can't stop you,' he said.

'I know.'

'Well then.'

'Well.'

Hari Kari turned, already walking away.

'Be good,' the guard called behind him.

Too late, Hari Kari said back. In his head.

He didn't want the guard to see him smile: three-quarters of a mile down, Jesse James was supposed to be waiting. The old gas station. It was shaped like a big A, all the windows shattered. The two at the top looked like eyes. Hari Kari thought about them a lot.

The note he'd left his mother said simply DON'T WORRY.

He stood at the abandoned pumps of the gas station a long time before stepping around, his eyes ready to take in the Chevy II Jesse James was supposed to be borrowing from the garage.

He wasn't there.

Hari Kari sat on the back stoop, in the sun, and waited. Like a little kid. It was something John13 would have done, if John13 would have risen from the lake, the baptismal waters shimmering off him, the air black with gunpowder. But he hadn't, couldn't. It took somebody like Hari Kari to live through that, his veins blue with emotion, with the sound of a single, impossible baseball rushing through the wires, into his head. His grandfather, his namesake, leaning back in his chair, clutching the air, screaming.

It meant to kill yourself, hara-kiri. Hari Kari just spelled it different because he'd killed himself and lived—rearranged the letters.

He sat behind the gas station until his skin was red, his nose blistered, and didn't eat the sandwich he'd brought, and when he woke it was dark and there was a rail of a man standing over him, the ragged ends of his hair lifting on the wind, curious.

Jesse James.

Hari Kari held his hand up for him to take, and he did, and Hari Kari rose into the night with him, settled into the bucket seats of the El Camino Jesse James hadn't told him about because he didn't want anybody to be expecting him.

'That's the trick of it, man,' he said. 'Moving undetected, like.'

Hari Kari watched Jesse James shift, steer, check the rearview.

He was real. Not even as old as the guard at the gate, either.

The CB radio under the dash rattled as they drove, had just been installed.

'Hari Kari,' Jesse James said, placing his hand on Hari Kari's knee.

The car had fins like the Batmobile.

'Jesse James,' Hari Kari said, and they leaned north together, left Oklahoma.

Hari Kari woke again in Colorado. The skin around his mouth was tight, dry. He touched it. Jesse James watched him touch it.

'Hungry?' he said.

Hari Kari nodded.

They rolled into a grocery store in some town nobody knew the name of, walked in, and Jesse James lined Hari Kari's shirt with strips of jerky and bags of chips and other bags of peanuts, then stood by him at the register, buying a pack of gum.

They ate it all in the parking lot, and it was the best food ever.

'What'd you tell your mom?' Jesse James asked.

'Not to worry.'

'That's pretty much like saying please worry, you know?'

Hari Kari chewed, chewed. He'd told the guard not to tell his dad, too.

There was a junior high girl walking across the parking lot. Jesse James saw him looking.

'Like that?' he said.

'No.'

'Yeah.' That smile.

Jesse James turned the engine over, rattled the pipes. The girl looked over.

'Me first,' he said, watching Hari Kari, like he was gauging his reaction. Hari Kari tried not to have one. The food was swelling in his mouth. The girl's name was Candace. Jesse James saying something about taking Candy from strangers.

It was three o'clock, maybe. He wasn't sure which day anymore. How long did it take to get from Oklahoma to Colorado?

'Sorry, pard,' Jesse James said, then, like he was talking down a long tube, and Hari Kari looked over to his side of the car. The sky behind him was black again. They were driving.

'Colorado?' Hari Kari said.

'Colorado,' Jesse James said. 'I can't get pulled over here.'

The mountains were cool, like when Hari Kari would stand in front of the open refrigerator, his mother napping, Father at work. The smoky cold air billowing out.

The cuffs of his pants were rolled wrong, though.

He looked at them as if they were betraying him.

In Colorado Springs Jesse James ran out of gas money, so Hari Kari called the Peterson BX. Where his friend RW's mom worked. Every base they went to, RW's mom's worked the checkout register.

'Your cute mother around?' RW's mom asked.

'She's outside . . . carrying stuff in. Is RW around?'

She gave him the address of their house. RW opened the door, looked up Jesse James's long legs to his unmilitary hair.

Jesse James smiled.

'Don't look,' he said to Hari Kari, and then palmed a white cloth over RW's mouth and nose. It left him sleeping on the tile behind the front door. Jesse James set him down soft.

'I told you not to look,' Jesse James said, already moving through the house, touching lamps and ornamental plates.

Hari Kari stood over RW, felt his own mouth.

They were off-base in twenty minutes.

'Utah,' Jesse James kept saying. '*Id*aho.'

Right before they got there they drove through a small town during the daytime hours, Jesse James taking pictures of all the honeymooners, explaining to Hari Kari what they were going to be doing to each other that night, and how. But then school was letting out. Jesse James smiled, nodding. Slung one wrist over the wheel, let the other fall to the side mirror, so he could lift the fingers, wave to the kids walking their sidewalks home. To the girls.

This time he put the white cloth in the center of a map, so that the girl who walked over to help was leaning down to *it*, asking for it almost.

Hari Kari helped put her in the bed of the El Camino, under the tarp that was already there. He was feeling like John13 again. Like James. His chin, trembling.

'Got something there, killer,' Jesse James said, spanning the distance across the console to flick something from the corner of Hari Kari's mouth, and, too late, Hari Kari saw the white cloth approaching, tried to hold his breath. Jesse James's other hand was already at the base of his skull though, pushing him forward.

When he woke, the girl was gone.

'Jennifer,' Jesse James said, her name. 'Now say thanks.'

Hari Kari threw up into his own lap. It was warm, like peeing.

Jesse James laughed.

'She wasn't *that* bad,' he said. 'Shit, man.'

They drove on, into Utah, Idaho, Montana, then turned south again.

Don't Worry, Hari Kari said to his mother.

Don't come look for me, he said to his dad.

Not now.

South Dakota was dry, Indian. Jesse James raced all the trains, pretending to be plowing through three-mile herds of buffalo, their endangered gore sloughing up onto the windshield.

Hari Kari couldn't control his pupils anymore. The chloroform. The skin around his mouth was red, peeling.

'America,' Jesse James said, holding his thin hand out over the dash.

Hari Kari nodded.

They were going home. Jesse James liked to say *Tinker*. It made his upper lip curl back off his teeth.

Hari Kari had lost count of the small towns, the junior high girls impressed by the black El Camino.

They stole a whip antenna off a tractor-trailer, and Jesse James wired it into their CB. The air was crawling with voices. Jesse James lowered his mouth to the mike, talked like movie stars to them, made up huge, illegal payloads for him and his sidekick to carry: elephants, Chinese vases, spongy metal from Roswell.

Hari Kari smiled. It made his face crack.

'And grasshoppers,' he said. 'For the reptile industry. Tell them what it sounds like. About that time the trailer broke and the sky went brown with them, like a plague.'

Jesse James keyed off, leaned forward so his chest was almost to the wheel, and watched Hari Kari.

'What are you going to do when you grow up?' he asked.

'What did you think you were going to do?'

'This,' Jesse James said.

Hari Kari looked at it, or tried to.

'I don't know,' he said.

That night—Kansas, maybe, or still Nebraska—when the bartender wouldn't serve him, he sulked back to the car. It was pointed right at the roadhouse. Jesse James walked out on the stilts his legs were becoming. In his shirt was a beer he'd smuggled out, in a glass.

'For my partner in crime,' he said, then faded away like he could.

Hari Kari sat with the beer in both his hands, staring into it.

A couple walked by, the woman hanging on the man. Somebody in a Chrysler had left their headlights on. If he held his breath, the music would almost make it to him. There was a storm coming, too—low pressure system, up from the Gulf. He could feel it.

He raised the beer to his lips, held the first drink in his mouth until it was warm, then forced it down, made it stay. Over and over, until it was gone. Because it was one his father hadn't given him.

It felt like he was going to fall into the sky now.

He smiled, held onto the dash just in case, and caught one of his fingers tracing the line around the glove compartment.

It opened.

In it were snapshots—him and the girl Candace, from Colorado, naked, entwined. And the rest of the girls too, him with each of them. A whole stack of Polaroids. He couldn't stop looking at them, at *him*, him*self*. Doing that. It was like stories he'd read of people who recorded themselves snoring, so they could tune back in to the sound, wake up when they started. Only some of them talked during the nights. And hearing yourself when you're not yourself like that. They didn't snore anymore because they didn't sleep.

'Try the chloroform,' Hari Kari said, nodding with the alcohol—everything funny—then laid his head on the side of the door so that his hair hung out. He was growing it long now, like Jesse James. An outlaw cut.

He put back just enough pictures that Jesse James wouldn't be sure if any were gone or not, and the rest he held inside his shirt, wet against the skin of his ribs, black side out.

The tower was the first thing they saw of Tinker. For three hours Jesse James had been talking nonstop, constructing Hari Kari's story for him—how he'd been camping out in the old gas station the whole time, eating birds and stuff. It was a lie, though: Hari Kari couldn't eat anything anymore. His legs were thinning down too, like Jesse James's. He felt spindly, immaterial.

'Okay,' he said, standing from the passenger side.

'Good old 3O1JN,' Jesse James said.

'GB4HK,' Hari Kari said back.

His veins were black now, no emotion. Something else: seeing himself in the pictures. He thought now that maybe the girls had been dead. The ones he was lying with, arranged with. In.

Jesse James kept it in reverse, backing up in the same tracks. It was one of his tricks—making the car look like it just got sucked up into the sky.

Hari Kari felt his way into the gas station, for the details of his story, but there was nothing. Just broken display cases, old calendars with slogans about Korea.

He left, dragging his bag, holding the pictures to his side like he was hurt there, and made it back to the MP gate without collapsing, or screaming, his mouth open wide enough that the lips curled back over his head, turning him inside out until there was nothing left. Just 3O1JN.

The guard in the booth was different.

'Oh,' he said. 'They're looking for you.'

'Where?'

'Colorado.'

Peterson.

Hari Kari nodded.

'Want me to call your dad?' the guard said.

'No,' Hari Kari said. Yes.

The guard's arm had a black stripe over it.

'Who died?' Hari Kari said.

The guard shrugged, looked overseas, to Vietnam or wherever. 'Everybody,' he said. 'Edgerton. You knew him?'

'Edgerton,' Hari Kari said.

'Tall, like me?'

'An MP?'

The guard nodded.

The one who'd told Hari Kari to be careful.

Hari Kari turned away.

'I'll call your dad,' the guard said.

'What's your name?' Hari Kari said.

'Roberts,' the guard said. 'Why?'

'You're going to die too, aren't you?'

The guard looked down at him.

His face was already exploding over a landmine, his hand a skeleton, the flesh burned off, his girlfriend crying, but relieved too.

The dirt by the asphalt looked baked, like it had been rained on eight days ago, ten.

A jeep was straining somewhere close, the teeth of its grill set. Father.

'He's going to make you trim that mop,' the guard said. *Roberts* said.

Hari Kari smiled: Jesse James's brown, medicinal bottle was in his bag.

'No,' he said. 'I think he's going to like it, really.'

40

24 MAY 1999

FREDERICKSBURG, VIRGINIA

CODY kept checking his gun over and over, until he had to go down to the street again, pace. Think. Jim Doe was gone, vanished, probably kidnapped. Mica Jones too, kidnapped again, and Watts, still half-overdosed in South Carolina, just a voice on the phone, trying to describe the Tin Man. Creed, upstairs in a hospital bed, one of his arms in a sling, one of his ears white with gauze, hamburger underneath. One of his eyes stained red.

The explosion in Roanoke had been from the stove, the burner they'd left on with no flame, no noodles, just gas. It had started in the yard, probably, one of the agents dipping his head down for a smoke, looking up too late at the orange tongue licking out of the house for his hand, his lighter.

There had been two walls between Creed and the kitchen.

The FBI made all the news broadcasts—the three tall letters on the back of their windbreakers bright in the swath of darkness Cody had cut into the middle of town, one of the slugs that was supposed to hit the Tin Man cutting his high tension wire instead, raining sparks, the Tin Man riding the wire down, all the way to South Carolina, to hold a needle hard into Watts's neck.

Cody told himself not to think about it. At the burrito stand on the street. Just for a minute, not to think about it. And the burrito stand, it was the best place for it. Because the girl working it just gave him burritos. Because the only thing she asked him was a thing he could handle: more cheese? He would have paid her anything. He walked into the shade of the hospital and ate his burrito and balled the wrapper up methodically and placed it behind the bush with the others he had been trying to mark time with, until some small nervous animal—a squirrel, a rat—had started taking the wrappers. So Cody was just replacing ones he'd already set down. Going nowhere.

He stood, trying to get his two-day slacks to hang right, and was considering another burrito when a man walked up to the stand. Cody corrected himself: *gentle*man. It was there in the way he held himself. He was nearly six feet. Late fifties, maybe more. Almost thin, just not quite. White; not nervous but quick with his movements all the same. Efficient, as if he were on a schedule, had a plan.

Cody swallowed. The man had been going towards the main entrance when the burrito stand presented itself. Or the girl working the counter? Was it her for him, too? But she was too old. Not twelve. Not Indian.

Cody didn't let himself look at him anymore, the man, just walked ahead, to the twin doors. It was the best way to tail someone who was always looking over his shoulder: stay in front of him.

Cody let two elevators go up without too much of a scene—one obviously grieving father, holding the elevator doors open, trying to do one more kind thing today, in trade—and then the man was standing beside him, the burrito still wrapped in his hand. When they both tried to step in at the same time, Cody deferred, let the man go first, followed.

'Up?' the man said.

Cody knew the voice, almost. Maybe. He nodded.

The man pressed *2* for himself and Cody stabbed *4*. It was maternity. They kept it on the top floor to make it harder to steal the newborns. There were cherubs around the button. The man smiled.

'Congratulations in order?' he said, '. . . Daddy?'

Cody kept looking at the button.

'A friend,' he said.

The man nodded. The interior of the elevator was burnished aluminum, or stainless steel: mirrors. Cody's face all around him, staring now at the man to his left.

The bell for the second floor dinged, but the horsehair crackle at the end gave it away as electric, an imitation. Supposed to engender trust, security. The sounds of childhood. Cody almost stepped off, out of habit.

'Two,' the man said, holding his fingers up in case Cody wasn't getting it.

Cody nodded, already reaching for the CLOSE DOOR button.

The man was watching him do it.

'How much did she weigh?' he said.

Cody narrowed his eyes, stumbling up corridors in his mind, falling down stairs. Five pounds? Was that normal? Ten?

'It was a boy,' he said instead, the doors thankfully hissing shut, and then he was staring at his own reflection again. Surprised he couldn't see through it.

In Maternity, he fell out of the elevator, rushing for the stairs. A woman was approaching with her newborn, the little grey security box on its ankle locking each door she passed. Cody had his hand on the handle of the door for the stairs when the lock clicked. The woman was walking slow, still bleeding probably.

Cody faked the best, most patient smile he could.

'How much?' he said.

The woman stopped, holding her baby higher, closer.

'She's not for sale,' she said, alarm in her voice, and then was backing up as Cody approached, shaking his head no, that's not what he *meant*, but then the door behind him clicked *un*locked finally and he stood between her and it. Took it.

The walls of the stairway were grey, layer upon layer, the banisters the same shade, the stairs themselves striped yellow and black. Cody took them four at a time, burst onto the second floor.

Creed was in 211.

Cody made himself just walk past the nurses' station. Because he still had his gun, was supposed to have checked it downstairs.

'Detective,' one of the nurses said, in passing.

Cody smiled, let them call him whatever they wanted as long as they didn't slow him down.

The man with the burrito wasn't in the hall.

Cody ran the last few feet, couldn't help himself, then touched the door with his forehead before entering.

The man with the burrito was there.

He was standing over Creed's bed.

'*Stop!*' Cody yelled, his voice strange even to him, his gun already out.

The man turned to him. He had the mask on. The one from the security cameras in South Carolina.

The man laughed, looked down to Creed. Dropped something light onto the foot of the bed. Onto Creed's feet.

Cody looked to Creed, unsure, wavering, and then the man slid the mask up, and Cody saw that he hadn't been scared at all. That he was liking this, even.

'You must be Mingus,' he said, tucking the mask under his arm. 'Special Agent Cody *Wayne* Mingus?'

The man's hand was extended—to shake? meet?

Creed was looking back to Cody, too.

Something rose under the sheets. At his hips.

The man with the mask under his arm raised the hand he'd had out, stepped back. Looked to Cody again.

'Either he's happy to see me, or that's there's a man-sized pistolero . . .'

Creed waggled it.

'Either way, you're fucked,' he said.

The man laughed, apologizing with his eyes to Cody. Cody lowered his gun.

'You know him,' he said to Creed. About the man with the mask.

'Martin,' Creed said. 'Ring any bells, kid?'

Cody sagged, recognized the voice he'd only heard in recordings before, at the Academy: Mr. Rogers. He'd almost shot Mr. Rogers.

Mr. Rogers nodded over to him.

'This the one who shot out the lights the other night?' he said.

Creed nodded.

On the television set hanging above them was *The Six Million Dollar Man*. Creed saw Cody watching it. Watching anything but what was happening here.

'Know what they call this episode?' Creed said.

'Lee Majors,' Cody said. It was all he knew about the show.

'"Killer Wind,"' Creed said. 'Martin's an expert.'

Cody looked back to Mr. Rogers. 'That's the mask?' he said.

'*Like* it, yeah,' Mr. Rogers said.

The one Watts had seen.

'What are you . . ?' Cody asked.

'Special assignment,' Mr. Rogers said, shrugging.

Cody smiled, looked away. Rubbed his mouth.

'Because I didn't replace you good enough,' he said.

'Because there's two of them,' Mr. Rogers said, 'or was, anyway.'

The Tin Man and Amos Pease.

Or now, the Tin Man and Mica Jones.

Cody looked back and forth from Creed to Mr. Rogers.

'I'm interrupting something,' Cody said then, getting it.

'Five minutes,' Creed said.

'It's about me, isn't it?' Cody said.

Mr. Rogers looked to Creed. 'I believe you now,' he said.

'What?' Cody said.

'Five minutes.' Creed held his hand up, all his fingers.

Cody holstered his gun, nodded, backed out, then couldn't help but fall down two flights of stairs, into the fake ambulance parked at the red curb, all the wrong antennae sticking out of it.

He stepped inside.

'You listening?' he asked.

The agent at the headseat wheeled his stool around, chocked the phones back to his neck.

'He asked us not to,' he said.

'But you're the FBI,' Cody said back.

The agent smiled.

Cody got into the headphones maybe two minutes after the conversation had restarted. He was on the stool now, leaning over the dials, the agent—Hendricks?—on break, if it came to that. In the gift shop buying something he could get a receipt for anyway, to prove where he was, when.

'—over there,' Mr. Rogers was saying. 'Nobody thought he could do it alone, Tim. It's not your fault.'

'Sheila's figuring it out too, I think,' Creed said.

'Of course she is. We train them to, right?'

'He thinks he's blackmailing us, maybe,' Creed said. 'That eight-note.'

'Sideways it's a butterfly,' Mr. Rogers said. 'Or infinity . . .'

'—or the Chevrolet bowtie,' Creed said. 'A fucking pair of reading glasses, Martin.'

Mr. Rogers laughed.

'Angel—' he said, not the first part of another word, but a word in itself, a name, but then there was no answer from Creed—or just Lee Majors, coming in loud suddenly. Too loud.

Cody backed half-out of the headphones, and then, suddenly, the van was all sound. Not electrical, through the wires, but *physical*, immediate: something had *hit* the van. Like a shot.

Cody rolled off the stool, holding his gun between himself and the sound. It had come from the roof, towards the front.

And then it started to drip and smear across the windshield: Mr. Rogers's burrito.

Cody didn't get out for twenty minutes, until Hendricks came back.

'You record it?' he asked.

'Funny.'

'What?'

Cody left him standing, went to the bank of payphones on the first floor, just stood there. Ten minutes later, he was outside 211 again, whipping back and forth.

Behind him, a buzzer went off at the nurses' station. Cody slung his eyes over. The nurse who'd hit the button turning the sound off was listening to the small speaker set in the wall. She looked up from it to Cody.

'He says to go on in,' she said.

Cody closed his eyes in pain, touched his fingertips to the cool wood of the door. The air in there was different: sterile, chilled. Intimidating. He made himself go in, opened his eyes on Creed. He was still watching *The Six Million Dollar Man*.

'A marathon,' he said, the clicker there in his good hand.

Cody looked up to the show, nodded.

'You don't have to tell me anything,' he said.

'Shut up,' Creed said. 'Sit down.'

Cody did, and instead of thinking whatever he was supposed to be thinking, he stumbled onto something one of the senior agents had said at 2253 Terrace Green, when they'd opened the door onto all the phone equipment: 'Well, we know he's not Amish.'

Cody had smiled. With Creed being carried out of the blasted house head first, half the city without lights, the Tin Man swinging above it like Tarzan, Cody had smiled. And the senior agent had seen it, corrected himself: 'Kevin Poulson.'

Cody had looked him up, Kevin Poulson: outlaw telephone hacker, finally caught for good in 1989, convicted on charges of interrupting federal communications, wiretapping, telecommunications fraud. And the senior agent—like Creed, Rogers—had known this on instinct, in a flash. Was able to make those connections, see those similarities. It had made Cody feel small. Like here. He'd pulled his smile down into his neck.

'What's that?' he said—at the foot of Creed's bed: some of the ribbon that came with some of the flowers. It had been braided into a bowl of sorts.

Creed looked down at it, dismissed it.

'So you know,' he said. Like it was nothing now.

'Why would they—*you*. Why hide it from us?'

Creed stared at him.

'Why do people usually hide things, Agent?'

Cody stared back at him. 'Because they're protecting someone,' he said.

'There you are, then.'

Cody nodded, wrung his hands some more.

'There was another,' he said. 'Working *with* Jessie Wiggs.'

Creed didn't correct him.

Cody smiled. 'And you knew,' he said. 'You all knew.'

'Think of it this way,' Creed said. 'Bonnie and Clyde. Take one of them out, the other's a nobody, doesn't have what it takes to knock the bank over, right?'

'Night Stalker,' Cody said.

Creed nodded. 'Or Corll and Henry or that shit in England or a hundred other cases. The killer isn't either individual, see, it's the *combination*. They feed off each other. If they'd never met up, none of the shit they did would have ever happened.'

'But they're both guilty.'

'But they're not always both *there*. So you do what you can, Agent. You're young. You'll learn this soon enough, I expect.'

Cody stood up, sat down again. Went to the door, to check the hall.

'Was that where you learned?' he asked.

Creed didn't answer. Yes.

'How did you know back then? That there were two?'

Creed looked over.

'In the Stone Age, you mean?'

Cody smiled.

'There were two series of notes, Agent. Both authentic, but dissimilar. *Divergent*, even. Ever seen that before? One body, two distinct, legitimate trails?'

'Why were they to you?'

Creed stared at him.

'That's the thing,' he said.

'I've seen the originals,' Cody said back. 'Photographs.'

Creed smiled, looked away.

'He was calling me out, I guess.'

'The second one.'

'The one we didn't catch.'

Cody nodded. In the *Wiggs, J.* box was the work-up of Jessie Wiggs, from the way his mother had spelled his name like a girl's on the birth certificate to the thirteen-year-old he was supposed to have impregnated in Oklahoma to 1963, when the Community Mental Health Centers Act let him and the rest back out to prey on society, live on its dregs. Somewhere in his tangled life was the shadow of the other killer.

'We never thought he could do it on his own,' Creed said. 'You never saw the women, right?'

'Photogra—' Cody started.

'You never *saw*,' Creed said.

Cody shook his head no, he never did.

'That file you've got on him,' Creed said. 'Steely Dan.'

Cody kept nodding.

'Ever count hotel receipts?'

Cody shook his head no.

'How many crime scenes were there, then?'

'Is this who you're protecting?'

'How many?'

'Six,' Cody said, then remembered the receipts: he'd leafed through them absently, because they were just for budgeting. Six *times*, though. He'd leafed through six folders of them.

'There were six files of receipts,' he said. 'It all matches up.'

Creed smiled from his bed.

'Thought you were top of your class.' he said.

Cody nodded.

Creed turned the sound back up, Lee Majors vaulting across some impossible distance, loud enough that the van down in the street might be having to roll the volume back.

'That burrito was for me,' he said.

Cody focused back in on him.

It was the only thing Creed had said about it, the eavesdropping.

'I can get you another one,' Cody said, standing, trying again to get his slacks to hang right.

Creed shrugged whatever.

'A marathon,' he said, nodding up to the television.

Cody was watching him.

'Why not just *tell* me?' he said. 'Instead of these games?'

Creed looked over at him for a flash, like an X ray.

'Because, Agent,' he said—the formal term, again—'you're smart enough to not make me break any of my promises.'

'People's *lives* are at stake here,' he said, then shook his head. 'You're being just like him, you know? Fucking riddles.'

'Guess that would make you me?' Creed said.

Cody turned, slammed the door hard enough that the minute hand of the clock on the wall dropped straight down, half an hour racing away.

Fuck it.

Cody walked past the staring nurses, Lee Majors on their set too, the music worming its way into his ears, his head in there nothing now but numbers—*6*, *6*, *6*, for eighteen, the number of years since 1981, since Nazareth.

Mr. Rogers was waiting for him at the car. In the car Cody had checked out from the pool.

'Ride?' he said.

Cody looked up the street some.

'How'd you get here?'

Mr. Rogers nodded, smiled.

'Talk, then,' he said.

Cody shrugged, unlocked both doors.

'I know what you're thinking,' Mr. Rogers said.

Cody looked across the bench seat at him.

'That he was keeping that Steely Dan angle to himself because he wanted to be the one to solve it. That he doesn't want not to be famous anymore. Not to be Tim Creed.'

Cody shook his head no. 'Maybe it's just personal,' he said. 'Between . . . the two of them.'

'Either way, the investigation isn't the priority, right?'

Cody took a wide left, accelerating towards Quantico. His desk, his computer: silence, privacy. Time. Something to hit, to shoot. Over and over. But Mr. Rogers was still talking, about if they could figure out why *now*, after eight years—or, going back to '78, twenty-one—then they'd have this guy, their Tin Man.

'Jim Doe was six then,' Cody said. Just driving.

Mr. Rogers looked over.

'More like four, right?'

Cody did the math, nodded. 'His sister, then.'

Mr. Rogers nodded.

'If you don't mind,' Cody said, steering with one hand now, one wrist, 'why'd you leave? The case, I mean.'

Mr. Rogers stared straight ahead.

'Between us?' he said.

Cody nodded.

'I didn't want to burn out like him,' he said—Creed.

Cody nodded, could see it too, but then before he could say anything back, the radio under the dash crackled awake. Cody rolled his window up to hear: there were more. Bodies. Children.

He hit the dashboard with the heel of his hand.

They were in Wilderness. Wilderness, Virginia. Not an hour away.

'That's where Jesus went,' Mr. Rogers said, steadying himself as Cody turned.

They were there in forty minutes, taking over.

It was Donny and Dawn. Cody could tell right away. Because they were so desiccated, because, figuring backwards from rebar in the leg to fiberglass molding to industrial glue was *this*, the first attempt: the bodies of two children, dug up, preserved, then hung from a tree with twelve-pound test, so that, from a distance, for a moment, they would look alive.

The boy was the only one still standing after eighteen years. Or, hanging. Just one arm, a wrist, like he had something to say. Their clothes rotted off long ago, the threads looted for bird nests.

Mr. Rogers was just standing in it, nodding.

'He put them here so he could see them,' he was saying.

Cody looked around, for a window, a tower, anything, and what he saw was a high-tension power line. Maybe the same one that cut through Roanoke. He was breathing hard now. Fast.

'We need to get employee history for whoever had the contract for this county in the early eighties,' he said, as if in a dream, looking up at the wires. 'He used to sit in his bucket up there and watch them.'

And then Mr. Rogers saw it—them—among the leaf litter at the children's feet. The bones of their feet: patches. For Survival, Fire-Building, Water Safety. He picked one up with the end of a pen, for Cody.

'These are official,' he said. 'The thread—that's why they lasted.'

Cody was looking past the patch. To Mr. Rogers himself.

Mr. Rogers smiled, nodding.

'You think it's me,' he said.

Cody just stared.

'I fit the profile, right?' Mr. Rogers said, settling the patch back down. 'And what better cover?'

Cody stared.

'So now, just when things are really heating up,' Mr. Rogers continued, 'I pull a few strings, get myself reinserted into the investigation . . . ? For the thrill, of course. The *voyeur* in me.'

Cody nodded.

'And then this, these,' Mr. Rogers said—the patches. 'When you already know I had my own Pack.'

Some of the troopers were listening in now. Their hands to their weapons, the cameras behind them dimly curious.

'Good . . .' Mr. Rogers said, looking at the troopers too. 'I see why

Tim likes you. But, Special Agent. If I fit the profile, doesn't he too, then?'

'He was in the house when it blew up. When I saw . . . him, the Tin Man, up there.'

Mr. Rogers nodded, nodded.

'Guess you caught me, then,' he said, shrugging, raising his hands, offering the gun strapped to his ribs.

Cody took it, and it was too easy.

'Just a precaution,' he said.

'Completely understandable,' Mr. Rogers said.

'Maybe we should go to the office,' Cody said.

Mr. Rogers nodded, and, before they stepped into the car—Mr. Rogers still in the front seat—Cody looked back to the children one last time, thinking about how if this was the first one, they might not even get called, not until the others started turning up, and then he got it, what Creed had been saying, who he had been protecting all these years: whoever had *survived* Steely Dan. Because there shouldn't be *six* sets of receipts, not if Creed got called after the *second* body—the day of the *third*, if Cody was reading right. The only explanation was another victim, somewhere.

He sat down into the car with Mr. Rogers, turned the key.

'What was her name?' he said, softly. 'Number seven?'

Mr. Rogers smiled, impressed.

'She was really number five,' he said.

Cody was waiting to drop the car into gear, waiting for a name.

'I wouldn't tell you if I was him,' Mr. Rogers said.

'And because of that, maybe you would,' Cody said back.

Mr. Rogers nodded, tapping his thigh with the palm of his hand.

'Maybe it's me *and* Tim, think? Covering for each other, trying to keep the investigation interesting . . . ?'

Cody stared straight ahead.

'Angeline Dougherty,' Mr. Rogers finally said. 'Tim called her Angel, I think. She's part of why Marcia left him, y'know. Maybe the biggest part.'

Cody put the car into gear, climbed back up onto the blacktop, and then, miles later, a blue emergency phone whipping past, he felt his head jerk with awareness—in James Booth's basement again—and stood on the brakes, all the honking cars driving past, flashing their lights.

Mr. Rogers was looking at him, waiting.

They reversed to the emergency phone.

Cody got out, walked around the front of the car where Mr. Rogers could see that he had his gun out, then leaned down to the receiver.

The emergency operator connected him to the switching station in D.C. in five minutes. Because they were only using landlines, now. Cody told them to shoot him through to James Booth, but they sent him to the van on the street in front of Booth's house instead, and the agents wouldn't piggyback him into the house—to *Booth*—without Creed's approval.

Cody slammed the phone down. Again and again.

Mr. Rogers was watching him, a thin smile.

Cody still had the gun by his leg, held tight. He got the operator back on the phone, gave her his badge number, intimidated her into giving up James Booth's home phone. But there weren't any numbers to dial. No keypad. The operator kept saying how the phone was for emergencies only. Cody agreed, but told her this was, then said that if she didn't want to get in trouble for doing it herself, to just let him. To just connect him to the number on the back of the prepaid calling card he'd dug out of his wallet. The operator didn't say yes or no, just went away. The next voice was customer service. For the card. Cody waded through the robots and finally gave a customer service rep Booth's number, the number on the front of his card, and the operator thanked him, shunted him back into the automated system. Another robot came on, female. The card was down to one minute. Cody told her to go to hell.

Booth picked up on the fourth ring.

'They had a friend, I think,' he said, instead of hello. 'Donny and Dawn. Right? Older, male?'

'Who is—?'

'The Ghost of Christmas Past, Booth,' Cody said. 'Special Agent Cody Mingus. I was there the other day.'

Booth hesitated, placing the voice maybe, then did: 'The kid in the basement,' he said.

'Yes. Now, they had a friend, right? A special friend?'

'They were *children*, Special Agent.'

Cody closed his eyes, held his hand over them. Didn't have time for this cat-and-mouse shit. Maybe thirty-five seconds, to be precise.

'Their scoutmaster,' he said.

'Stanny?' Booth said. 'Now you're going to pick on him?

'I just want to talk to him.'

Booth laughed.

Twenty seconds.

'Was he affectionate to them, Booth? In a fatherly way?'

Fifteen.

Nothing.

'Booth?'

'It wasn't him, Agent Mingus. He loved them. He was even trying to get in the program, before his wife—'

'Program?' Cody said.

Ten, nine.

'To become an adoptive parent,' Booth said, defensively. 'He would have been perfect. I mean, for Indian kids. Because the Scouts—'

The mechanical operator interrupted, suggesting the many ways Cody could recharge his card. He hung up, looked to Mr. Rogers, framed in the side glass.

Because the Scouts were all about Indian shit.

41

26 MAY 1999

DEDHAM, MASSACHUSETTS

JIM Doe wasn't sure how long he had been awake. How long his eyes had been open. What he was seeing, even: moving, motion—*water*. A boat. He was on a lake, at night. And not alone.

Sitting opposite him, in fatigues, was a man in a Tin Man mask. *The* Tin Man. Jane Doe to his right, her hair down, her shoulder still bandaged, spotting.

'Look who's back,' Jane Doe said.

The Tin Man nodded his cardboard face.

'From the dead,' he said.

His clothes, Jim Doe's clothes, they were wet. Cold. And his chest, his whole torso, it was burning. He scrabbled back against the side of the boat, clawing at his shirt.

On his chest and stomach were blood blisters, each an inch wide. A small, round Band-Aid over his heart. He felt suddenly hollow.

'—what?' he said.

Jane Doe held up the leads, the wires. At the end of each of them was a sensor. Stolen from a hospital, ordered from a medical supply catalogue, built, *some*thing. The kind of little pads you put contact jelly on, so they'll stick, get a good read.

And his burns, they were electrical. The fiberglass of the boat wavering like the water, little distinction between the two.

'What have you got me on?' he said.

'Oxygen,' the Tin Man said, like it was obvious. 'Adrenalin.'

He touched his heart to show, and Jim Doe saw for a flash the needle he must have used. Like the kind you get rabies shots with: eight inches long, beaded at the tip like the fang of a snake you never want to see.

He held his hand over the Band-Aid delicately, cupping the pain so it wouldn't spill over.

'No . . .' he said, blacking out again.

'He's not like Amos, is he?' Jane Doe said.

The Tin Man snorted, a laugh. 'Amos wasn't like me like that either,' he said.

On the backside of his eyelids Jim Doe saw the tentacle that had wrapped around him, pulled him under, the digestive acid in its suction cups burning into his chest, marking him. And it led to the water, the tentacle, and all he had then was an auditory flash, of somebody talking into his head somehow while he was under. Telling him things. Asking him if he could see the pretty lights yet. The fireworks. Independence.

When Jim Doe opened his eyes next, either an hour had passed, or a day. His clothes were dry, anyway; stiff. His wrists duct-taped. The Tin Man and Jane Doe sitting just where they had been.

'Why—' Jim Doe started, cramped, started over: '. . . what, *what* are you doing to me?'

The ears to either side of the Tin Man's mask moved. It meant he was smiling.

'Thought you'd never ask,' he said.

Jim Doe looked up to him, still holding his stomach.

'I'm making you in my own image,' he said.

'You're . . . killing me.'

'But bringing you back.'

'You can't—'

'I *did*.'

Jim Doe breathed, breathed. Soon the sun would be up. He could smell it, the way the air chilled just before dawn, especially out on the water.

'How long?' he said.

The Tin Man shrugged, cast his eyeholes out across the lake, at some early morning troller.

'About twenty seconds,' he said. Then looked back. 'It's more symbolic, really. A ritual, you know? The rites of manhood . . .'

It made his ears move again, with pleasure.

'I'm just catching you up, I guess,' he said. 'With me, I mean.'

'Why?'

The Tin Man stared at him, as if gauging whether Jim Doe was ready to hear or not.

'Why *me*, then?' Jim Doe said.

The Tin Man still just stared.

'You should be cataloguing the shore, deputy. Charting the stars. Listening for foghorns, watching the flow of traffic, tasting the salinity of the water. Guessing at what kind of fish are under here.' He trailed his fingers over the edge of the boat to show, flicked them into the air.

Jim Doe shook his head no.

'Because if it's small-mouth bass, Deputy—*James*—then what state does that suggest? Or wall-eye? Pike?' He spread his arms out. 'This . . . is this even a natural lake, or a reservoir? Spring-fed or run-off? If you put your ear to bottom of the boat, can you hear the turbines of a dam . . . ?'

Jim Doe nodded. 'So I can report back where we are,' he said.

The Tin Man nodded his blank face. Jane Doe shook her head, looked away.

'So you're not going to kill me,' Jim Doe said.

The Tin Man's ears again. Smiling. 'Oh,' he said, 'don't worry about that, James. You will be dead, soon.'

'Until you bring me back again.'

Bingo.

Jim Doe shook his head no. Please, no.

'I can't—' he said, 'you don't—'

The Tin Man shut him up. Just an outstretched hand, palm-up.

'You're twenty-six,' he said. 'Starved-down some, but still.'

'I'm not like you, though.'

'I wasn't like him, either.'

'Who?'

The Tin Man's mask gave nothing away.

'Your . . . grandfather,' he said, then laughed, to himself, said it to himself: 'your blond, blond grandfather . . .'

'You're not my—'

'No, Luke, I'm not. Yet.'

His voice was low and corny.

Jim Doe stared at him.

And then he said it, the Tin Man: '. . . to her, though, I was.'

Jim Doe uncoiled himself from the cooler he was sitting on, made it to within inches of the Tin Man's mask before whatever he was tied to drew him up.

The Tin Man never flinched. Had measured it off already—the distance, the whole conver*sa*tion.

'Why her,' Jim Doe said, collapsing into himself. 'Why us?'

'Why you,' the Tin Man corrected.

Jim Doe felt himself look up.

The Tin Man shrugged. 'For a long time I thought it was Amos. That it was going to be Amos. You should have seen him, James, he—'

'Jim.'

'—he was perfect. All that anger, but calm, too. Around the eyes. No matter what he was doing.'

'Ten o'clock,' Jane Doe said, from the front of the boat.

The Tin Man's head swiveled around to the lights she was talking about, and he tracked them—stop, go; stop, go.

'Trot line,' he said, finally. 'Probably illegal. We don't need to worry.'

Jane Doe nodded, went back to watching.

'Amos,' Jim Doe said.

The Tin Man nodded, as if he were watching Amos Pease kill all over again.

'He's indiscriminate,' he said. 'That's the thing. Do you know what I mean?'

Jim Doe just stared.

'Like that Gentry,' the Tin Man said. 'He didn't have to do that, James. Or that mechanic up in Kansas. So I had to let him go.' He shrugged. Like this was just one of those things.

'But *you*,' he said. 'You, James. Tabula . . . how would you say it? Tabula rosa, I guess. Red slate, I mean. Blank red slate.' He smiled, touched the mouth of his mask with his hand, drew it away, confused for a moment. 'Like those Big Chief tablets, James, remember?'

'I'm not like you,' Jim Doe said.

'I wasn't like me when I was your age either, James.'

'I'm not going to be, either.'

'That's your choice, of course. All I can do is the . . . nurturing part. The environment part. Provide these little'—looking down at the leads—'experiences. But of course it's up to you in the end, James. I wouldn't have it any other way.'

Jim Doe stared at him.

'Did you have a choice?' he said.

The Tin Man had some kind of involuntary physical reaction, then—touching his side, his ribs. He relaxed out of it, stretched his neck, his chin rising, sharp.

'Was it your father?' Jim Doe said, pressing.

The Tin Man shook his head no.

'My father was perfect,' he said. 'It wasn't his fault.'

'Then your other father.'

The Tin Man nodded, said it again: *my other father*.

'Why isn't he here?

'Because I killed him, James.'

Jim Doe stared at him.

'And didn't bring him back.'

'Didn't want him back.'

'And you want me to be you.'

The Tin Man nodded.

'I'm tired,' he said. '. . . all the killing, the games, the FBI . . .'

'Then let it end here.'

'It's bigger than us, James.' He smiled, like it was funny: 'The cycle of violence, as it were. It is the best way to live forever. Through your work.'

'Father,' Jane Doe said, 'we'd better—'

'*Don't*,' the Tin Man said, so sudden and harsh it was like the mask's eyes actually narrowed.

At the front of the boat, Jane Doe swelled up, deflated. Sat.

'Sorry,' she said. 'It's just—'

'It's just *nothing*,' the Tin Man told her. No lips.

Jim Doe kept watching her.

'I thought she was . . .' he said. 'Nothing.'

The Tin Man nodded.

'You want to know what happened to her,' he said. 'Where she is.'

Jim Doe wouldn't let him see his eyes. 'Yes,' he said.

'How bad?'

He looked up then.

'I'm not going to kill for you,' he said.

'You'd be surprised,' the Tin Man said back. 'But, for now, just yourself.'

Jim Doe stared at him. 'Is she—can I . . ?' he said, tried to say.

'You have to be baptized into it, James. Knowledge. Made worthy.'

'I don't want to die. Again.'

'I'm right here, James.'

'I know.'

They stood together then, the boat moving under them. All that water. Jim Doe shaking his head no, but taking the small, white pads the Tin Man gave him, rubbing them in different places than he was already burned.

'Good . . .' the Tin Man said, extending an index finger to press one of the pads down better. Jim Doe caught his wrist, though. Shook his head no.

'Okay, then,' the Tin Man said—*not* Father, not ever that—and told Jim Doe to open the cooler. Jim Doe did. There was a battery—for him?—and two bowling balls.

He looked back up to the Tin Man.

'Put your fingers in them,' he said, cutting the tape at Jim Doe's wrists, and Jim Doe shook his head, did. Stood, the leads fixed to his chest tugging for a moment when the Tin Man plugged them into some homemade extension.

'That's direct current,' Jim Doe said, about the battery.

'Would you rather it alternate?' the Tin Man said, raising two fingers of his right hand, to flip and flop them back and forth, *show*, but Jim Doe just shrugged, cutting him off.

'So when do I know?' he said.

'About her,' the Tin Man said.

'About her,' Jim Doe said.

The Tin Man nodded, looked wherever Jim Doe was looking, at nothing, and said it: 'Amos has her.'

They locked eyes again.

'Amos is dead,' Jim Doe said.

Now the Tin Man just shrugged, mocking—a child, caught—and Jim Doe kept staring right at him. Because in that mask his peripheral vision would be limited. Meaning he wouldn't see the bowling balls coming together until it was too late.

He didn't.

They were each eight-pounders—ladies'—so Jim Doe could get his fingers stuck, not have to hold on. And they only hit each other after they hit the Tin Man, the left one shattering into the dust.

Through it, Jim Doe watched the Tin Man spill over the side of the boat, slinging blood from his mouth in a delicate arc across the water, and he smiled, said it to him—*Father*—and then heard more than saw the wooden oar Jane Doe was swinging, the butt end under her arm, because she only had one good arm. It was enough, though. The next thing he knew was water, and the last thing he knew was water, the balls dragging him down, the rope at his waist holding him up, and then he was dying. Again.

42

26 MAY 1999

DEDHAM, MASSACHUSETTS

SEVENTEEN Prairie View Lane. Not a light had gone on or off all night, since Creed had rolled up, Martin in the car with him, unretired.

'Sheila should be here,' Martin said.

'She will be,' Creed said.

Her plane had set down thirty minutes ago.

Seventeen Prairie View Lane was the home of a Richard Beaux. He was one of the eight linemen who had worked for CP&L Co-op in and around Wilderness, Virginia in the early eighties. The only one who died in 1991, the year the first pair of bodies turned up, in North Carolina. It wasn't his house, though, was the thing. The house was still owned by a Stani Kiozelsky—the only variant of Booth's 'Stanny' Martin had been able to pull out of any of the Scout registries for the East Coast. Only Stani Kiozelsky didn't exist as far as the Scouts were concerned, hadn't since an order of patches in 1981. To this address. They were the same person.

Creed looked at the sky, a plane lifting off into the coming light.

'Fuck it,' he said, and disabled the dome light, opened his door.

'Maybe this'll prove to him I'm not the Tin Man,' Martin said.

Creed hissed a smile: Cody. Agent Mingus.

'I should have let him shoot you,' he said.

'He's the next thing, Tim,' Martin said. 'Our replacement.'

Creed grunted. Cody *had* given them *Stanny*, then *Stani*, then *Stani*

Kiozelsky, then connected them with Richard Beaux, then just stared at Creed when Creed told him to listen to the tapes of the Isinger kids' sessions again, and again. That they needed him as an analyst there worse than they needed him as a field agent here.

'This is because I took his gun,' Cody had said, nodding at Martin without looking at him.

Creed hadn't had to nod for the kid to get it.

It didn't matter now, though. They were here, walking up the sidewalk, spacing themselves properly. Their guns not even out, because he wasn't here. Nobody was.

'Nice lawn,' Martin said.

Creed walked across it, his heels leaving crescents in the dew, then listened before he knocked, then listened to how the knock sounded, trying to gauge furniture, carpet or hardwood, any open spaces above the entry.

Nobody answered.

Creed pushed the doorbell, looked to Martin.

'Well,' he said.

Martin shrugged, looked in the flowerbed behind them, passing up one rock, another, then finding the right one. He carried it back to the porch.

'Hide-a-key?' Creed said.

'Sort of,' Martin said, and knocked out a pane of the front window with it, then reached through for the deadbolt. Creed watched behind them for any lights going on, any cars idling, because they couldn't afford getting this called in, having to explain that they didn't have a warrant because somebody up the warrant-chain would have called to verify something, and then the Tin Man would have been there, listening.

They walked in behind their guns, trying to make themselves both small and large at the same time.

Creed nodded right and Martin took it—the kitchen.

In the living room, Creed tried the television, but it wasn't set to weather. Hit redial on the phone, but it was voice mail. He didn't have the code.

He looked around, at the normal couch, the normal fireplace.

In the master bedroom, Martin was being Martin—looking for any 13D footwear.

Creed stood in the kitchen, trying to orient himself. To the house in Roanoke. How this house would have to be a version of the other one. He nodded: there, by the sink. The pill bottle. They were different though. *American.* He balled them in his hand, buried his hand in his pocket.

Maybe this was just another house. Another breaking and entering. The government doing what everybody thought the government always *did.*

He could feel Martin standing behind him now.

'No basement,' he was saying.

Creed lowered his head, slammed his open hand onto the countertop.

This was *supposed* to be him.

Martin was going through the pantry now, for noodles. He threw one pack down onto the counter. Different brand. Creed laughed with his eyes closed, so that he almost didn't hear it: the doorknob on the front door, turning.

He was there when the door opened, his gun leveled on Watts.

'You,' he said.

Watts looked past him to Martin.

'Keep from blowing this one up, Tim?' she said, closing the door behind her.

Martin laughed. 'The three wise men,' he said.

Watts hooked her head to one side, flashing her gauze.

'Three, anyway,' she said. 'Where's Agent Mingus?'

'Listening to the tapes,' Creed said.

Watts shook her head no.

'I called,' she said. 'He's not at home or the office.'

'Between, then,' Creed said.

Watts knew, though. 'I would have thought it was him too,' she said, hooking her chin to Martin. 'If I didn't know him, I mean.'

Creed looked at her.

'I'll buy him a fruitcake,' he said.

Watts stared at him, shook her head.

'A table dance, then,' Creed said.

Watts smiled.

'So this our guy?' she said, looking around at the house.

'You tell me,' Creed said.

'Tell me his name again?'

'Stani,' Creed said. 'Kiozelsky.'

Watts nodded, walking into the living room, then her back went straight.

'Say again?' she said.

'Stani Kiozelsky,' Creed said, spelling it out.

She turned, to face them both.

'Stani,' she said. 'It's a Russian diminutive for Stanislav. As in Stani*slav* Kiozelski, with an *i*. It was one of the aliases of the . . . what? Yes. The Red Spider, Tim. Martin. Lucian Staniak. Remember? *Stanislav Kiozelski* had been one of his aliases in 1966, in Poland. In 1967, at the age of twenty-six, he was charged with the brutal murders of six women.'

'Like Wiggs,' Creed said.

Watts nodded. 'And who just turned twenty-six?' she said.

That Texas fucking deputy.

'Shit,' Martin said.

It sounded wrong, coming from him.

'And letters,' Watts was saying. 'He even wrote letters to the paper . . .'

Creed was looking away.

'How much time do we have?' Watts said.

Creed shrugged.

Ten minutes later, they had an apple box in the living room, dragged out from one of the closets in one of the bedrooms. It was full of school annuals.

'Look for Oklahoma,' she said.

Creed did, Martin still on the phone, reading the prescription off the pill bottle to Eggers or some other fuck-up.

There wasn't a Beaux in either of the two Oklahoma yearbooks, or a Kiozelski, or a Kiozelsky, or a Dahmer or a Bundy or a Berkowitz. A lot of Williams, just no Georges. All the portraits were looking to be unmarked, too. No thought bubbles or devil goatees or erased glasses or anything.

'It's like he just bought them at a junk store,' Watts said, flipping to the *back*-back pages, for an inscription. She held her hand before the blank paper like a game show hostess: nothing.

'He would have been a loner,' Creed said.

'. . . and white,' Martin added, over the phone, a joke. 'Twenty-five to forty-five, forgettable—'

'*Okay*,' Creed said, slamming closed the year he was on.

Watts just looked at him.

'There has to be something,' she said, settling all the books up in a row so their spines were bowed up. Martin was watching the street now, the phone pulled to the window.

Watts selected out the two Enid Plainsmen ones again.

Creed took the one she had had, gave her his.

'Look at everything,' she said.

They sat on the floor and turned the pages slow, one by one, studying the faces, the styles, the cars the cigarettes the sideburns.

Behind them, Martin finally hung up.

'Well,' he said. 'We know why now, now.'

Creed looked up to him. He was holding the pill bottle up, between his thumb and forefinger.

'It's end-stage stuff,' he said. 'Morphine derivative. Practically heroin, in oral form. Not for the symptoms anymore. Just the pain.'

'He's feeling mortal,' Watts said, turning, turning.

Martin nodded, turned to the window again.

'That's not your rental?' he said.

Watts nodded without turning, explained: 'They were, I don't know. A convention or something. Booked.'

Martin smiled, a thumb at one corner of his mouth, index finger at the other, so it looked like he was holding his face like that. 'But still,' he said.

'Do you want the keys?' she said to him, impatient, then tossed them over, still poring over the books. 'Same old Mr. Rogers . . .' she said through her hair. He was gone already. Distracted by the ordinary, like always.

'What about this?' Creed said, a minute later maybe.

It was all the clubs—FFA, WrenchHeads, Sewing Circle, etc.

Watts took the annual, rotated it to herself.

It was the Amateur Radio Club, standard black and white, one-time-or-bust, whether you're smiling or not. Two rows of four-eyes, one behemoth receiver before them, like an altar. Instead of their names, it was their radio handles. Because they were the kids whose names you didn't know.

One of them had been altered, however. Lightly, in pencil. The one that ended in *JN*. The first three letters were under lead. They would be there, though.

But there were extra letters, too, smaller than the rest, written almost as an afterthought, it seemed, an *o* and an *a* wedged between the *J* and the *N*, for *JoaN*. And after that, *Gay*, and *Croft*. Joan Gay Croft.

'Who the fuck's that?' Creed said, without looking up.

Watts didn't answer, didn't know.

They called D.C. again, for the route-through to Eggers.

'Croft,' Creed said into the receiver. 'Joan Gay.'

Eggers paused, paused.

'Sir?' he said, finally.

'Croft,' Creed said again. 'Joan Gay Croft.'

'You all right?' Eggers said, like he was whispering into his headset.

Creed closed his eyes.

'Listen carefully, now. Please. Croft, Joan Gay.'

It took Eggers forty-five seconds.

'I don't know,' he said. 'Her name comes up, let's see . . . there. Okay. It's something about this tornado in nineteen forty-seven.

April . . . *ninth?* The article's from the tenth, but it says "yesterday." Okay. Yes. There's this big tornado that goes from Whitedeer, Texas to White Horse, Oklahoma. Big one, or a lot together. Kills a lot of people in Woodward, anyway. That's Oklahoma, just barely. That's where she lived. Joan Croft.'

'Joan *Gay* Croft,' Creed said.

'Gay, yes,' Eggers said. 'Initially, she's reported among the missing, presumed dead, flung out in a field for the birds, all that. But then her . . . sister. Her sister Jenny there. No. The neighbor. The Crofts' neighbor, after the girls' parents are killed, the neighbor takes the girls to the hospital.'

'Okay,' Creed said, his thumb already rubbing on those first three marked-out letters.

'Let's see,' Eggers was saying, humming with the scroll bar. 'Joan Gay Croft. Four years old, light blue eyes. Anyone with information . . . Here. She's in the hall of the hospital, overspill from the ER, I guess. Waiting. And then either one man in khaki or two, they're not sure, but he comes in, looks around, and tells her her father's waiting for her.'

'But not the sister.'

'The father was dead, though,' Eggers went on. He paused then, confirming maybe, reading ahead. 'Okay. Yeah. That was the last anybody ever saw of her.' He waited then, breathing into his mike. 'The Tin Man, sir,' he said. 'He can't be *that* old, can he? This was nineteen forty-seven.'

Creed didn't say it—*maybe he was immortal*—just hung the phone up.

Beside him, Watts was looking around the half-darkened living room.

'Weird,' she said.

Creed looked up from the black tip of his thumb, trying to follow where she was looking.

'What?' he said.

The letters were numbers: 301. 301JN.

'Most people have more pictures,' she said, 'right?'

Creed looked again, nodded: yes, they did.

All this house had was one. Small, framed, at eye-height by the doorless entry to the kitchen, so you could see it each time you passed. For your pills.

Creed rose to it.

It was a man and a woman holding hands, at some black and white time of the past. A cheap Polaroid. Creed took it down, to see.

'That him?' Watts asked, and Creed finally answered: no.

He had to sit down, though.

The way they were holding hands. The mountains past the parking lot. Rocky Mountains.

'It's me,' he said. 'And Mar—Marcia.'

1965.

He picked up the phone again.

Outside, Martin Rogers stood on the porch long enough for his eyes to adjust to the predawn darkness, then smiled to himself: that *couldn't* be what they'd rented Sheila. A *van?*

It hadn't been there before. He would have seen it. And there wasn't any dew on it, like everything else.

It was just sitting there.

Special Unretired Agent Martin Rogers rotated his left shoulder so that the seam on the top of his suit jacket just touched his ear. It served to push the handle of the gun under his arm forward, loosen it. He didn't take it out, though. Just the cuffs.

The van was directly across the street.

Martin Rogers stepped down off the curb—motion, inside, in the cab?—then became aware of the keys in his left hand. Sheila's keys.

He brought them into view as if seeing them for the first time.

There were two, flat on back, toothed on the other.

He looked from them to the van, the line it cut against the pale brick of the house behind it.

Ford. The van was Ford.

He let the keys fall between his fingers: Ford keys were double-sided.

It wasn't Sheila's rental. She'd parked farther down, maybe, like she would have thought to, so as not to get a lot of strange vehicles bunched around 17 Prairie View.

Martin Rogers thought of a ribbon—it was always a ribbon—a ribbon looping in and out of other ribbons, so that they made a checkerboard like his mother's baskets, only this wasn't a basket, just a sheet of repeating squares that, when you backed off far enough, curved up into a saddle, which was the shape of space-time, if it looped back on itself like Martin knew it did.

On one of the squares, one of the sections of sidewalk just before the nose of the *Ford* van, was a girl. Facedown on the concrete.

Martin Rogers looked back to the house, to the window nobody was standing at, then to the space behind the steering wheel of the van—empty—then back to the girl.

Her black hair was pooled around her like blood.

Martin Rogers cocked his head to the side.

The leading jaw of the cuffs in his right hand, under his right index finger, fell open, swung in place.

She wasn't moving.

'Hey,' Martin Rogers said, his voice sudden and loud in the street.

Nothing.

The engine of the van was still ticking, and then he saw it, he thought: the chrome handle of the driver's side door. It wasn't all chrome, but black in places. Blood. He looked from it to the girl, pictured lifting her from the concrete, the front half of her body missing, her insides trying to hold to the sidewalk. Because that was all he could see, was her back. All he was *sure* was there.

In the driveway behind her, there was a piece of tickertape fluttering from the antenna of some parent's family car. A ribbon, writhing in the wind.

Martin Rogers smiled, took a step forward, then another, and, four feet short of the girl, the cuff jaw still defined by his index finger, he said it again: 'Hey.'

Nothing.

He could throw Sheila's keys at the body if the keys weren't already in the road.

He thought too of the wire structure *under* the road, cross-hatched, all the right angles, the geometry, the checkerboard.

'FBI,' he said, finally, to the body, the girl, the *morning*, and before she could move or not move, something in the van did.

Behind the wheel now was a cardboard mask, not smiling.

The Tin Man.

Martin Rogers opened his mouth but that was as far as he got: standing before him suddenly, her knife deep in his solar plexus, was the girl, risen. Looking him in the eye.

'*FBI*,' she said, close to his neck, his ear, 'take this with you,' and then pulled the knife up, hard. Martin Rogers felt it lodge against the base of his sternum, the point against his spine, maybe, all his organs falling away to either side, and all he could think of was the knife itself, how it must be a filet-job, thin, sharp, flexible. How she used it like an extension of her own hand.

He smiled.

'And you,' he said, '. . . don't want you . . . for*getting* me . . .'

His own hand had come up to hers, the pain, on instinct, but then there had been more instinct. Of the cop, not the man: his hand was on her wrist, the cuffs under it, the other end on *his* wrist.

The girl shrieked—it was the first time Martin Rogers had ever thought of a sound like that, as a *shriek*—and fell away, but he came with her, fell on top of her, the knife going deeper still, the tip breaking against his vertebra with a sound he heard, yes, but from the wrong side of his eardrum.

They weren't leaving the house now. Watts rubbed the bandage on her neck and watched the sun break against the backside of the curtains and tried to figure everything out all at once: that the Tin Man had been with Jessie Wiggs in 1978—Jessie Wiggs, from Enid. Meaning the Tin Man was close, maybe. *Then.*

On the plane up from South Carolina, she'd taken Mica Jones's parable apart again and again, word by word, until she realized what a parable *was*: something real, just stripped down to archetypes. If she wanted to understand it, she had to build it back *up*, like a facial reconstruction, when all you have is the skull, and have to then start modeling clay—flesh—onto it, until you have a recognizable person. Something you can *use*.

It started in Oklahoma, anyway. That was the first layer of flesh she had: the Amateur Radio Club member 301JN Creed had found. Joan Gay Croft. Maybe that was his handle on the air. But the parable: in it, 3O1JN killed himself. Twice. So, failed suicide attempts. Watts plundered her coursework and reading, just came up with popular knowledge bullshit: that the attempts weren't successful because they were really just communications, pleas for help. But what if, here, they'd been real? What if he'd really wanted to die?

Then.

Then 3O1JN would rise up the first time, feel fortunate perhaps. Like he's been given a second chance. He might even feel compelled to atone, make things right that were wrong before, that made him kill himself in the first place. To be a better person. But then the second time. When you come back a *second* time, it's no longer fortune. Depending on the individual—*confused*, *scared*, *helpless man*, *injured in many ways*, Mica had said, and, probably, isolated, prone to fantasy escapism, the seeds of delusion, creating a world system convincing enough you can *believe* in it—'fortune' becomes 'charmed': immortal, invulnerable. A god, to whom humans would be infantile. Insectile. Like Mica had said too: bugs. But 3O1JN killed them, perhaps out of juvenile fascination. Maybe withWiggs. The *girls* were his bugs.

Watts stood up, started for the window, for whatever was taking Martin so long with the Firebird she *hadn't* wanted, but then stopped.

The annual, the yearbook.

She went back to that, tore the Amateur Radio Club page out—fuck evidence—and guessed at an age for 301JN, and leafed back to the fifth grade, the sixth, and there he was, looking back up her: James

Kulpin. Same glasses, same hair, same forgettable smile.

She said the name aloud, just to see if it was real, then passed the page to Creed, still on the phone with Eggers.

Now all they had to do was catch him.

Watts forced her hand through her hair.

James Kulpin. Who had a picture of Creed and his first wife somehow, on their honeymoon. In 1965. When he was supposed to have been in Oklahoma, his father dressed up in a yellow slicker, beating him with a fire hose, raising a red axe against the world.

Watts started over, trying instead to force Kulpin's life events into the typical pattern associated with serial killers. The isolate childhood: his ham radio kit. Discovering that alternate means of gaining and maintaining power, however brief, exist, are out there: his first suicide? his mastery of knowledge, or, in particular, mastery of knowledge of the history of violent crimes? The creation of an alternate, social identity—a mask—to hide the true self: all the names, the aliases, the George Williams and Richard Beauxs and the victim names already filtering in from the dump-sites. The animals, though, the neighborhood pets locked in abandoned refrigerators, the frogs burned with matches, where it was supposed to start, those first, hesitant explorations into murder, the fascination which would manifest itself with the placement—arrangement—of birds left around the children who weren't children. Maybe Kulpin had lived near a park as a child, or somewhere with statues. White statues. Pigeons. Watts held her eyes closed tight, trying to see him, but couldn't. Just the kid in the radio club, the most average kid in America.

And then Creed starting writing on a pad—what they were knowing about Kulpin. Watts made herself not look, not crowd him. Went further into the *hypothetical* Kulpin, the one who could grow up into a Tin Man in the national news. She forced the kid in the radio club into the cookie-cutter developmental stages: if the culmination of all this was the murder spree in 1978, typical of the early to mid-twenties, then, right before that spree, there would be an inciting incident. A murder to imprint upon. She smiled: all she had to work with was . . .

She opened her eyes: him*self*. Like Mica had said.

Kulpin's imprinting murder had been himself.

She was breathing hard, now: this was not typical, not even close.

Slow down, she said, inside. Slow down. Go back to the stages.

There were so few examples after the killers' twenties. Lucas, Lake, a couple more. Because most of them got *caught* on their first big spree. Burned out. And Lucas, and Lee: they didn't really ever escape their twenties, even, just dilated that first spree out. The Green Man, though. The Boston Strangler. Watts nodded: if Albert DeSalvo was really him, then he'd done the one thing all the killers were *supposed* to do, eventually—dealt with his inner demons enough via violence that he quelled them, then, simply, retired. Went on with his life. Kicked the addiction. Found alternate means of power.

Maybe, yes.

Maybe this is what Kulpin had done: killed or helped to kill those six women, then stepped back into the normal life. But Mica was still talking: *They feel bad about it, though, later, don't they?* The boys, with their bugs. Watts nodded, again, heard Mica again: *They feel bad. They atone.*

Guilt.

Kulpin had been guilty, felt he had to atone.

How do you atone for six women, though?

She sat with the question and then finally got it—you *atone*, you pay your debt to society. In, say, the socially accepted institution of *prison*. She dug the list from her purse. He was there, had been all along: Kulpin, James. In for possession of stolen goods in 1979, then released in 1980, when his lawyer produced a receipt for said goods.

One year for six women. Two months for each life.

Watts shook her head, knew she wasn't even talking about Kulpin anymore, maybe, but an idealized killer, for the classroom. For an article. The hypothetical Tin Man. And don't even call him Kulpin anymore, but Boanerges. One of the sons of thunder, from the Gospel of Mark. A comic book superhero's nemesis, except their superhero—Creed—was sitting in the evil villain's lair right now, staring at a picture of a woman he'd already lost.

Watts stood, looked around. Held her forehead in her hand.

Creed stood behind her.

'Is Marcia okay?' she said.

Creed nodded.

'And Kulpin?' she said.

Creed gave her the list. It was sparse: father a fireman in the Air Force, out of Big Springs, Texas; mother Canadian, out of Manitoba; the two of them married in North Dakota. Unremarkable childhood, only two arrests in his twenties, before he disappeared—one for wiretapping, in Colorado, and the other when a patrolman came back from coffee to find him, Kulpin, sitting in the back of his locked car, waiting to go to prison. They were trying to fax the old inmate records over, whatever they had.

'His mother died?' Watts said. 'She was young, right?'

Creed turned the envelope over he'd been writing on. It was the father and mother—more: the father, still alive somewhere, and the mother, dying of lupus in 1977, dead by '78. Her obituary, though. Eggers had found it somehow already: a thumbnail sketch of her childhood in Woodward, Manitoba, how devout she was, loved, et cetera, but, tagged onto the end of her obit, a note about her son, still recovering from his attempted suicide. In the lake.

'This doesn't happen, Tim,' Watts said, finally. 'There's no precedent, no protocol—they don't start killing again, later in life.'

Creed nodded.

'It's like he's *two* killers in one . . .' Watts said. Then stopped, looked up. 'Maybe he is, too,' she said. 'How many children did Wiggs father?'

'Fourteen,' Creed said.

Watts closed her eyes, shook her head no.

'Fifteen,' she said. 'Kulpin makes fifteen, God. Reproduction. Offspring. It's a form of immortality, right? *Literal* self-actualization. Just as Jessie Wiggs is living on through him, now—Kulpin, the other killer inside Kulpin—so does Kulpin hope to live on through *his* son.

To reproduce, the one thing he physically, biologically *can't* do, Tim.'

'Jim Doe,' Creed said, the phone still in his hand, Eggers talking from it, his voice small, distant, saying something about James Booth having just killed himself, but then drowned out suddenly by metal on metal. In the street.

Watts fell to the window, the small-gauge hole in her neck suddenly more open.

It was a black van, its reverse lights on.

It had just torn its passenger side mirror off on a brick mailbox

Behind the wheel, a mask was coming down over an unremarkable face.

Watts screamed, everything happening at once: the van smoking its tires backwards, its nose whipping around, Creed falling out the front door. Watts drifting across the living room, gun held high.

Directly across the street from them, Mica Jones was hunched over Martin like an animal, her hair falling all around them, but then the van's headlights lit her up, and Watts saw: Martin's hand was in her mouth. She tore it—her mouth, her *teeth*—away when she saw them, stood, and ran for the van, moving out of her coat, her shoes, clawing in through the driver's window. The Tin Man's window.

Behind them, Martin opened his mouth to say something maybe.

The stump where his thumb had been was pumping thick, red blood, and when whatever Martin was going to say started to come Watts was just shaking her head no, no, she didn't *want* to hear, please, and then Creed had his car moving before her door was even closed. It clipped another car, slamming shut, the glass shattering inward.

Creed still had the photo in his hand, too. Of Marcia. And didn't even know it.

The road before them was straight forever, and flat, the van receding into the day, its brake lights flaring for a moment at an intersection, then pulling through.

Creed didn't even look, just followed, some early morning traveler clipping them just behind the passenger side rear wheel, spinning them slowly sideways, Creed hand-over-handing the wheel.

They came to a stop maybe five feet from the figure in the road. The form. The person.

It was Mica Jones, on her knees.

She'd been shot again, in the same shoulder, the blood pooling around her. Watts thought of Ophelia for some reason. From *Hamlet*. And smiled. Mica Jones did too, her throat lumping up behind it. Martin Roger's thumb fell out, nail first, blood stringing behind it.

Creed stood, walked up to her, his gun loose by his side, and Watts was already screaming inside, again, still, and then Mica Jones brought her good arm up from the jacket she was draped in, the cuffs still on her wrist, flashing silver, and there was the gun Watts had known she'd have, and Mica Jones was hardly even awake, hardly even alive.

'*Tim!*' Watts yelled, just as his own gun was coming up, to Mica Jones's face, her mouth, and he looked over just long enough for Mica Jones to pull the trigger against him.

The hammer fell on nothing.

He had *wanted* them to kill her, James Kulpin. He'd wanted it.

Watts was shaking her head no against the dashboard, Mr. Rogers still talking to her from his place on the sidewalk, about how it was a wonderful day in the neighborhood, his voice soft and lilting, like they could come with him too, if they wanted.

43

2 SEPTEMBER 1977

PUEBLO, COLORADO

JESSIE Wiggs was Burt Reynolds dressed up like Rod Stewart, ducking out incognito for a little rest and relaxation. It was long overdue: he'd been a choirboy now for three and a half years. He wore the Jackie O shades all the way out of Oklahoma, keeping the speedometer nice and legal. The car was candy apple red—a bad idea, he knew, but it was the only one in the yard with t-tops. They made the girls who walked over from the sidewalks feel less threatened. Like he didn't have anything to hide. Like they could get out whenever they wanted.

School had started last week.

Jessie knew because he'd found himself taking the long way back to his mother's place, found himself brushing his hair for the drive, sitting far down in the seat, one arm stabbed up at the windshield, slung casual over the wheel. There were newspaper clippings of him on the telephone poles, though. His face, the three kids he'd fathered so far, only one of the mothers legal, now. The other two would be in a year, though. Soon he'd have his own James Gang. He laughed, dialed it back to a smile, then just pursed his lips, kept his right hand on the floor shifter, his left on the wheel. Fuck Enid, then. It brought the smile back, thinking of Enid as female, a woman. Oklahoma slipped away faster and faster.

In the tachometer housing was the snapshot. His ticket; the carrot.

It had turned up in his mother's mailbox two days ago, taped between two of the same postcard. Of Pueblo, Colorado. They'd been glued back to front, so they looked like just one. It was too thick, though, uneasy to bend. Jessie opened it standing at the mailbox, and the nostalgia washing up from the snapshot had been so thick he'd had to grab onto the shaft of the red flag to stay standing: it was Candace, or Christine, maybe. From Colorado, anyway. Her skin was grey in the picture, but she'd coughed herself awake at the end, he remembered. Candace, yes. With the healthy set of lungs. Twined in there with her was John13, or Hari Kari, or Bodhisattva, Whoudini, or whatever the kid had been trying to get everyone to call him after that. *Deflowered*, Jessie said.

Initiated.

Broken in.

But fuck him too. He was dead now anyway. Jessie's mother had showed him the article before work one day: the kid swallowing pounds of birdshot then walking out into the reservoir, his hair a spoked disc on the surface of the water for a few steps, then not anymore. Four people had watched him do it, raised their beers to him. They only told the cops about it because they'd built their fire too big that night again. They traded the kid's suicide for a warning citation. Jessie had nodded to his mother, touched the paper with his middle finger, told her *See?* You *can* work with the law.

The note on the back of the second postcard said simply HAVING FUN IN PUEBLO. WORKING AT SCHLESINGER'S NOW.

Candace.

Jessie pulled into and out of the diner parking lot all afternoon, suddenly frantic about the snapshot: was it an angry boyfriend? big brother? father? husband? But how would they have *gotten* it? That was the thing. *Candace* shouldn't even have had it—nobody should have. They were gone, used up. Except for the one the kid took. Jessie clearly remembered looking for that one, in every crevice of the car, for weeks. It was from when they'd swung through Enid, just before Tinkerbell Base. Angel. He'd wanted to show her that one. Wait for her to get older then show her, see if she remembered.

The only answer was that, now that the kid was dead, he was Jessie's helper. Doing things for him from the other side. Helping him out.

It felt good, but he didn't want to see him, either, his stomach distended with lead, his skin flaying away from his face.

Before he went into the diner to see her, Candace, he made up a system of hand signs he could talk to the kid with. Most of them just meant *thanks*, and *yes*, and *I remember*. He could do them all under the table without anybody seeing.

Inside, too, he recognized her immediately. Smiled.

'Smoking?' she said, just that. Her voice flat.

'Sure,' he said. 'Yeah, smoking.'

It was like it was all meant to be.

'You know you're parked in handicapped,' she said, taking his order, and Jesse James shrugged.

'I'm an *outlaw*,' he said, trying to remind her.

She stared at him over her pad, like it was almost clicking.

He sat there the rest of the afternoon, eating, walking the line of booths to the bathroom, to throw up in the urinal. He'd never taken a grown woman like this. Even if it was Candace. Should he say some line? Maybe if she could just see him in his car. If he could get her out there to see the mannequin he'd found naked on the side of the road.

It took him two more hours to decide, and then he said it: 'Oklahoma, right?'

She nodded, poured.

'You?' she said back.

'Once upon a time,' he said. 'I think we used to play you in football or something.'

It was like he was invisible to her—like in her head she'd cut a Jessie Wiggs–shaped stencil out of corrugated cardboard, sewed a couple of elastic straps to the back for her forearm, then used it as a shield, so that anybody who looked like him just wouldn't exist. Or maybe it was just that he looked like Rod Stewart now.

'Christine,' he said to her.

She smiled.

'Candace,' she said.

'Candy,' he said.

He asked her if she'd ever ridden in a Trans-Am. She looked out at the parking lot, back to him, and that was all it took: she was the same junior high girl who'd crossed the sidewalk to him thirteen years ago, because his hands were too big to get the pocket comb he'd dropped between the seats.

Candace.

Her shift was over at six, and he walked her out of it, to his car, to the hotel, and when it happened—when she saw him in the cheap mirror, recognized him—it was all okay, because she just went limp, pliant. Like she remembered. Had been conditioned.

Jesse James smiled, laid her back on the bed.

She was too old, but he made do. He could close his eyes, and, if he pushed hard enough, reach the girl still inside her.

Candace Crocker.

She was number one.

He left her in the room, her clothes opened around her like when you butterfly a shrimp, and she *thanked* him, for *leaving*, and he looked back, took a picture of her in his mind for later, and smiled, walked away, sat in the car. There was another snapshot under the wipers, on his side.

Two days later, he was in Utah, reading about Candace.

She was dead.

He made a hand sign under the table—*please*—then chatted up MJ Harrison. Her earrings had gotten her kicked off the junior high cheerleading squad. Jesse James had liked them, though. Wanted to see them up close. But she was married now. With children. And he had to tell her over and over that he wasn't who he was, and still, she wouldn't serve him, so he had to wait for her in the parking lot. It was the same, though; in the motel room her body remembered what her head didn't want to.

Jessie tried looking back at her like he had Candace, but MJ was balled up, sobbing.

'I'm sorry,' he said.

She didn't look up.

After that, he decided to make it better, *nicer* for them, so he scored some Tuinol, tapped it into their drinks. Jesse James.

MJ turned up dead too, though.

Jessie drove faster. Quit bathing.

The next snapshot that shouldn't have still existed was Jennifer Korell. He shook his head no, no no no, then holed up in a truck stop diner for two days, until he started seeing himself out at the pumps, his long blond hair lifting in the wind, his hands in his pockets. He was waiting. For himself. He made a hand sign under the table. When he got to the car, there was a belt-CB waiting for him.

It was the kid, talking to him from the afterlife.

'Her name was Jennifer Korell,' the kid said.

'I don't want to,' Jessie said.

'Her shift starts at eight.'

'But you died.'

'I can't die, Jessie. Don't you know that?'

After that, they were in contact always. Jessie never even talked into the radio anymore. He just wanted to be back in his mother's garage, or in the shop, scraping gaskets, or anyfuckingwhere, please.

Jennifer Korell.

He held her down by the wrists and cried as he did it to her, then stood, saw himself crossing the parking lot to this room, the blade flashing by his leg.

'You can't do this!' Jessie yelled.

He just kept on coming.

'I'll tell,' Jessie said.

'Your mother?' the kid said back, from Jessie's belt.

Jennifer Korell was already dying. Slow.

Jessie Wiggs shook his head no.

That night he wrote all the letters all at once, addressed them to the newspapers of the different cities he'd been in already, the ones he thought he was going to, then the next day, bought a fabulous red top hat, sat in a booth to have his picture taken, and, when the hat blew across the parking lot, slipped the letters into a drop box. He'd written like the kid would have, if he were still alive. He was telling. All the hand signs he made were to himself, now.

The next girl was Wanda Richardson.

Jessie got the mannequin from his trunk, dressed it up like her, left it in a motel room.

It didn't work, though. Nothing did.

He drove, and drove, then read one of the letters he'd written on the front page of a paper, circled it in red, left it in Wanda's diner, *P L E A S E* spelled out beside it.

Nobody was listening.

The next picture was Angeline Dougherty. Back in Colorado.

Jesse James stood at an island of pumps at some sprawling truck stop, filling the car up, the weight of his thirty-four years heavy on him now, like car batteries tied to his neck, but then a twelve-year-old girl stepped out of her father's sedan one island over and Jessie watched her cross the slick concrete for the restaurant, stretching her legs as she walked, and he smiled, relaxed his hand on the pump, so he wouldn't finish before she was gone, so she could stay like that forever, for him.

44

27 MAY 1999

ROANOKE, VIRGINIA

JIM Doe woke behind a mask, tried to cough, couldn't: there was something down his throat. A tube. Through the eyeholes he could see it was clear, the tube. A great proboscis, bleeding him dry. He pulled it out, pulled it out, fighting it hand over hand, then threw up onto the backside of the mask. It slid down his chin, into his shirt.

A hospital. He was at a hospital. In a hospital. The smell.

And it was night. And he was alive.

His shoulders hitched forward, his chest caving in as his trachea contracted involuntarily, still pushing the tube up, out. The memory of the tube, the shape. It lay in his lap twisted into a snake, hissing air, oxygen. He was alive.

He brought his hand up to his face, to clear his eyes, but something was wrong with his fingers—they were numb. But then it wasn't his fingers, it was his face, the mask, the rubber before it. He pushed with his feet, back into the wall, and brought his other hand up as well, and it only came so far, was holding something: a plastic cylinder. His thumb positioned at the button. The nurse button.

Jim Doe looked through the twin eyeholes of his mask at the vertical rectangle of light in the door, the slim window crosshatched with steel filament.

'A hospital,' Jim Doe said, out loud, and then the white slit of window broke in two. A head leaning down through it, a face: an old man. Sallow. Jaundiced. *Yellow*. Even the balls of his eyes.

Jim Doe felt his own face again, peeled it off with one hand.

It was President Lyndon B. Johnson. Or Spiro Agnew. Nixon. A bank robber mask from the movies. An old man mask. Like the old man leaning forward before the door.

'You're not him,' Jim Doe said.

The man laughed, fell off the edge of it into a series of coughs that hunched him over further and further, until a thin line of wet descended from his face to the soft tile of the floor. He broke the line with his hand, flashed his eyes up. Smiled, all gums, no teeth, so his mouth was hollow. Jim Doe looked away, back.

The old man was talking now.

'. . . she comes by at three and then four-thirty,' he was saying.

Jim Doe looked to the narrow window again, pictured the third shift nurse, touching her forehead to the glass for an instant—bed check—looking only for the outline of an old man lying face-up in bed, like he was supposed to be, like she would want him to be, his nose pitted and over-large, one of the three male body parts that never stopped growing.

It was what the mask was for.

This was a nursing home.

The Tin Man had left him here, Jim Doe. It didn't feel like part of the plan, either, just something he'd made up at the last possible instant. It was so unelaborate was the thing.

'. . . where is he?' Jim Doe said, pulling himself up with the rail of the bed.

The old man stared at him.

'You can't stop me,' Jim Doe said.

The old man laughed, choked a cough down.

Jim Doe stepped down with his left leg, steadying himself on the IV rack, and when it went he went with it, crashing to the floor.

'I never expected you to come up from that lake,' the old man said, smiling his black smile, shaking his head with wonder. 'You fucked everything up, you know.'

'Who are you?' Jim Doe said.

'Call me—' the old man started, coughed. '. . . call me Grampa.'

Jim Doe shook his head no, was already trying to pull himself up onto the bed again.

The old man tilted something across the room so it caught on the foot of the bed, stayed there. A crutch.

Jim Doe watched it.

'*Who are you?*' he said again.

The old man shrugged. 'Three fifteen,' he said.

'I don't care,' Jim Doe said.

The old man shrugged. '. . . makes two of us then,' he said.

Jim Doe sat on the edge of the bed, pressing his palms down, pushing with his arms, then brought one of them up—his right hand. The nurse button. He looked from it to the old man.

'Push it,' the old man said. 'She'll come get you, yeah, hand you over to the . . . I don't know. Proper people. Maybe they'll even believe your story after . . . what? twelve hours? fourteen?' The old man smiled. 'Unless they look at your arms . . .'

Jim Doe did: bunched in the crease of his left elbow—because he was right-handed—was a series of holes. Fresh, probably just skin-deep, no scar tissue even, the scabs still soft, but still. Anything he said the track marks would unsay. For a while, anyway, until his blood work came back clean, except for the lactic acid leftover from the ephedrine or adrenalin or whatever the Tin Man had used to bring him back the first time, the second.

He looked up to the old man.

'Better than being here,' he said.

The old man nodded.

'Damn straight,' he said. 'But still, maybe you best just put that mask on, Scout. Three-twenty.'

Jim Doe shook his head no.

'. . . *where is he?*' he said again, trying to stand.

The old man did something with his lip, his dry, raspy tongue. He was smiling with his gums again. 'He wanted me to tell you something,' he said, punctuating it with a cough.

Jim Doe looked up to him.

The old man shook his head no. Looked to the mask again.

Jim Doe took it, turned it upright, his vomit slipping down into the sheets. He breathed once, twice, then fitted it over his head, down onto his face. It was already warm, slick.

'Shit,' the old man said. 'That what I look like?'

'Tell me,' Jim Doe said.

The old man coughed some more, some more.

'I don't know what it means,' he said, half-breathless.

'*Tell me*,' Jim Doe said.

'It was about how a man,' the old man said, 'about how a man, a boy, a son, he can't have two fathers. If that means anything to you.'

Behind the mask, Jim Doe closed his eyes, and thought of all his father's names—*Horace, Horse, Hoss. Dad*—and about how many cars a person would have to steal to get back to Texas, how many states he was going to have to cross. How he was going to get out of the nursing home without being seen, his one crutch glinting in the harsh light, the thin lips of his old man mask set, unable to smile.

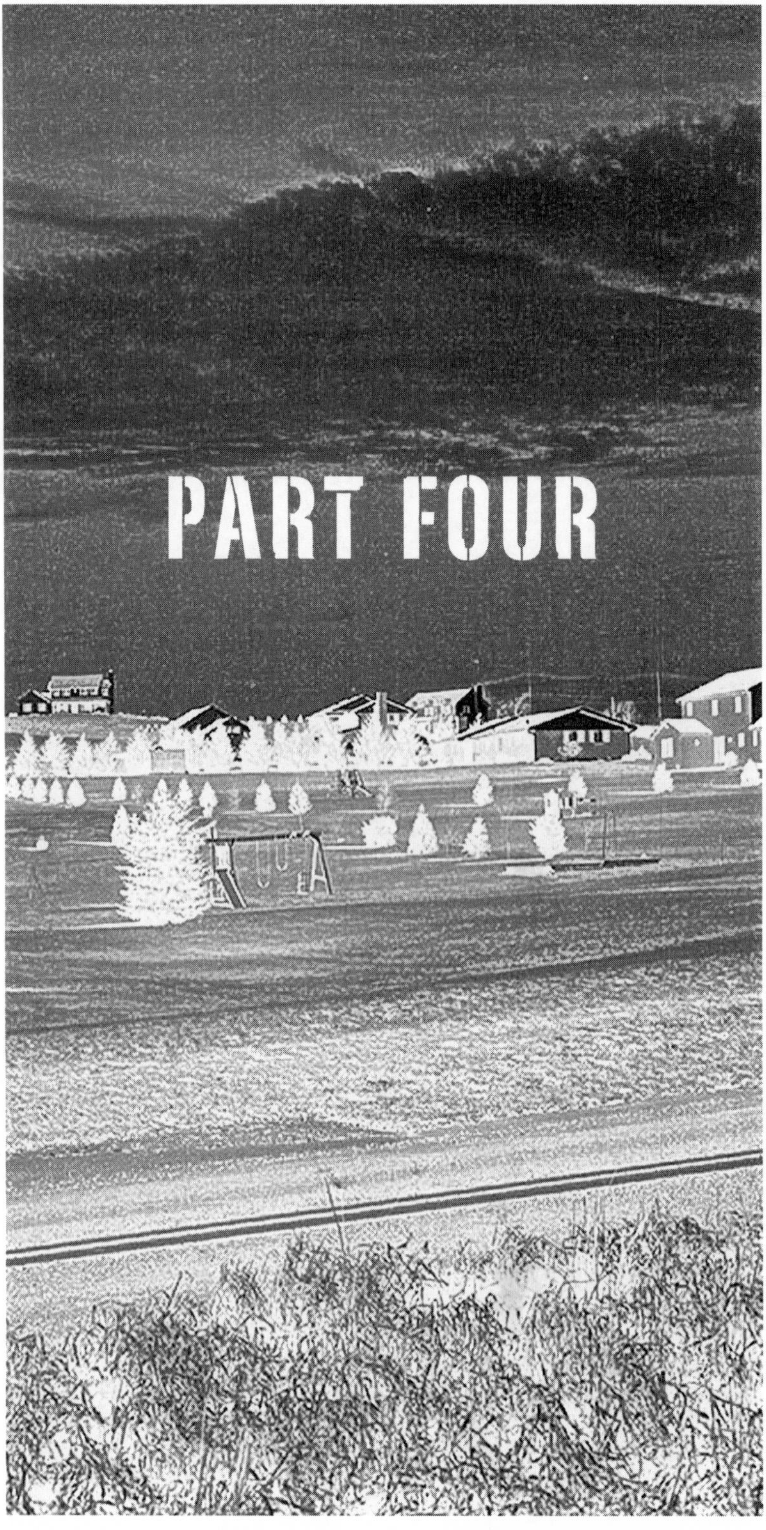
PART FOUR

45

29 MAY 1999

LYDIA, KANSAS

THE birds. Maines and McKirkle didn't know Garden City, or where the tax assessor's office was supposed to be, the Paddyshack or whatever the hell it was, but the birds. They'd heard about the birds—a black column standing up over Mosley Debs, and lying down beside him.

'Milo?' Maines said, when they pulled the truck up to the edge of the yellow tape, the seed crunching under their tires.

McKirkle took the cup off the dash, spit into it.

'So he's out here again,' he said, setting the cup back on the dash. Maines took it.

The Indian, Jim Thorpe. Still stealing the bodies back.

'He's dead,' Maines said, moving his head forward and back, like he was trying to work something down his throat, slow.

'Then it's the old man himself,' McKirkle said.

McKirkle breathed out through his nose. 'Boston Tea Party,' he said, resetting his hat on his head, from front to back. Kansas.

Maines looked at him.

'All the white guys dressed up like Indians,' McKirkle said.

'Thought that was the Village People,' Maines said.

Already, on the radio on the way in, there was word of more scaffolds outside town. More dead kids. Maybe the ones from here.

Maines stepped down from the truck but McKirkle sat there a moment longer, watching a small brown bird plummet from the sky.

In the east, the birds were just poisoned enough to get them blind and addicted. Here, they weren't blind, just dead.

Whoever'd done this was getting the mix wrong.

McKirkle stepped down too.

Aside from the chance of picking up that deputy's trail again, making him stand up for Tom Gentry, or that Donner girl, they were there out of respect for Debs, from when he used to sheriff Lamb County. Before Kansas got into his blood. Before his blood got into Kansas.

Maines was squatted down in the dirt, balancing a grain of sorghum on the blade of his pocketknife. It was tinted pink, powder-coated.

'Been treated,' he said.

Herbicide, pesticide: either bagged or about to have been bagged. It narrowed the list of where it could have come from—one of the research or production facilities; a warehouse; train depot. The bed of some farmer's truck.

They were trash birds anyway, the ones that came to eat. Their insides already black.

Maines flicked the grain of sorghum up, let it fall.

Later the coyotes would move in, for this feast of bird-flesh, then slink off into the night to chew their intestines out, die alone instead of in a pile like this.

The officers ringed around the yellow tape were watching them. Behind the officers, kids.

The Paddyshack was all shot to hell. From the inside.

'Well?' McKirkle said to them.

'I wouldn't go up there,' the closest officer said.

McKirkle looked over to the Paddyshack.

'You're sure it's him?' he said.

The officer nodded.

Debs. The officer was sure it was Debs in there.

Maines looked back at the birds once more, then took his hat by the crown, holding it down against all the bird shit in the air, and stepped across the loose dirt towards the door of the small shed.

Debs had been like this since last night, maybe.

McKirkle shook his head in disgust.

'Got Rosy down here for him yet?' he said, to the nearest officer. Rosy Debs.

The officer flashed his eyes at the shed then looked away: no.

McKirkle shook his head. 'Your funeral,' he said.

'Promise to sing?' the officer said back.

McKirkle had to stand still a moment to be sure he'd heard right. He looked up at the officer in wonder, the mirrored sunglasses straight out of a movie. McKirkle reached up calmly, removed them, threaded one of their arms into the pocket of his shirt.

'You better hope he shoots me,' he said, then, turning for the shed.

Maines was already almost to the door. McKirkle stepped up just as the wood jamb splintered out: Debs, shooting blind.

The cooler wasn't cool anymore.

Sheriff Mosley Debs, formerly of Lamb County, was lying back on one of the fold-down shelves, his khaki uniform black with blood.

'You through there?' Maines said.

He hadn't moved.

All anybody knew was that it had happened sometime last night— the two short bodies, stolen back. There had been no lights to speak of, no cars, no screams. Just the open door this morning, the air inside the same temperature as outside, the two dead Indian children who weren't children gone. Again.

'Oz,' McKirkle said, then spit, rubbed it in with the toe of his boot, rolled the cylinder of his revolver over one cartridge, to get away from the blank he always kept under the hammer, just to watch people think they were dying.

Maines held his hand out: no.

But Oz. It was what the papers were calling Kansas, especially after last night, up across the border: McCook, getting leveled by an F3. And the storm was moving south now, fast, the sky already blue like monkey fur.

Maines picked up Debs's hat, from the floor, set it up on a shelf, crown down.

'Well then,' he said.

'Was it him?' McKirkle said.

Debs looked over his gun at McKirkle, the finger nervous on the trigger. It wasn't until he smiled that McKirkle moved, two-stepping to the side, the shot opening up another hole in the wall, a column of dusty light pouring in, on fire with fiberglass from the insulation.

'We're not going to shoot you, Mose,' Maines said. 'So you can just quit this, if you want.'

Debs fired again. It was just sound this time, the slug whining through some hole he'd already made in the wall.

'*Was it him?*' McKirkle said, again.

It wasn't clear whose blood that was on him, even. Just that he'd probably woke to a stray dog licking him. It was dead on the other side of the cooler, anyway.

'It doesn't matter that he took them,' Maines was saying.

'. . . Rosy,' Debs said. Just that. But the way he raised his head to his hand, at a fly—that he'd *felt* the fly—Maines understood: he had been scalped. His hair lifted.

Debs saw him see it.

'It's not that,' he said, finally. Lowering his forehead to the barrel of his gun.

McKirkle shook his head no.

'Who was it?' Maines said, again.

Debs looked up.

'A ghost,' he said. 'That Indian. The dead one.'

Jim Thorpe: Amos Pease. Or somebody in a black wig. At a tea party.

Maines looked to McKirkle and McKirkle nodded, left a cigarette smoldering in the sawdust.

As they walked away, smoke was already billowing from the door.

The officer standing there coughed, shielded his pale eyes, looked to McKirkle and Maines.

'He'll be out directly,' Maines said.

The officer touched the butt of his gun, but McKirkle shook his head no.

'Do it the hard way,' he said. 'Maybe you'll learn something on accident.'

Maines stared at the officer for an extra second, making sure it was taking, then turned back to the truck just as a bird fell at his feet, convulsing.

He took a long step for it—the bird—but then McKirkle had him by the sleeve before he could bring the heel of his boot down.

'What?' Maines said, jerking away, his mouth full of spit.

McKirkle lifted his chin to the police barrier, all the twelve-year-olds watching them.

Maines touched the tip of his hat to them, in acknowledgement, then held the hat away from his forehead as he leaned forward to trail a brown line of spit to the ground. The kids were all watching him, or looking away, the bird forgotten, so that when McKirkle stepped on it longways, pushing all the blood to the head like you can do with a caterpillar, none of them heard. It splashed ahead of Maines. Like they were walking through it. A rogue muscle twitched on his cheek. It was almost a smile.

46

29 MAY 1999

McCOOK, NEBRASKA

THE fireman. He was moving along the edge of town in the boots, his heart slapping the inside of his chest, his facemask down. Blood seeping from his right ear, under his collar. It had started in Liberal, when he first heard the tornado—throaty, pure—then saw it on the news over the counter like a delayed visual, then walked calmly across the parking lot, drove all night and stood into the humid calm after the storm, his clothes simple, the axe in the trunk. He rubbed mud onto it before approaching the yellow tape, and they let him in, and he walked deeper and deeper into the broken concrete and shattered glass, until a fireman waved him over, to help pry a garage door up.

As he walked over he rubbed the mud off his axe.

The other fireman saw it, registered it, looked up.

'Where you from?' he said.

'*Hölle*,' he said. Hell.

He left him under the garage door, moved on in the too-large yellow jacket, the readjusted helmet, the numbers on it matching all the other firemen's numbers now, the fingers of the gloves thick and warm. He flexed them as he moved, kept himself calm by thinking of Martin Rogers, so serene with the steel inside him, all the plans to make Tim Creed shoot him evaporated, all at once. But there had been no other way. A cat darted in front of him, stretched out and long, barely touching the ground, still distrustful of the sky.

It was always like this.

He smiled, *saw* his smile on the backside of the heat-resistant plastiglass: sharp, hungry.

He watched the cat run.

The residential area crumbled all around him was Gatecrest Estates. It had been on the brick pylons by the road, along with a generic coat of arms as emblem, all the heraldry looted, used up. American.

They deserved the storm. More.

The fireman stopped at the entry sidewalk of a collapsed house. The red flag on the mailbox was still up. He lowered it, approached the house, opened the door, ducked in. It was quiet, wet. His thick fingers located the phone cord, followed it into the kitchen. It ended at the wall, the jack. So he followed it the other way, across what had been the hall. It went under the closet door. He tapped on the knob with the sharp end of the axe. Nothing. He opened it.

It was a father and a daughter. Maybe two daughters, it was hard to tell. A storm radio hanging on the wall, copper pipes coming up through their thighs and feet, from when the house shifted over, fell off its supports. Three feet. It was enough. Above them were all their winter jackets, and, beside them, two books: the Bible, and a phonebook. He took them both, sure it meant something, that it was his mother, *leaving* it for him, but then made himself breathe, breathe. Just look at the white pages.

He sat down across from the partial family—one of them alive, maybe, still bleeding, at least—and looked up and down the columns of names. Six. There were six families with Indian names. Probably more, hiding under *Smiths* and *Johnsons* and *Morrisons*.

But there was no time.

He flipped to the middle section of the phone book, the simple town map, and matched the names he'd torn out with Gatecrest Estates.

Two of the families lined up, then. To the east. Next door to each other.

He thanked the father, slid the phonebook over, placed the Bible perfectly on top of it, like it had been, and closed the door.

Outside, a highway patrolman was standing at the mailbox, leafing through the unmailed mail, his gun heavy at his hip.

'Federal offense,' the fireman said, nodding down to the opened mailbox.

The patrolman looked up.

'They in there?' he asked, looking down to the mail, the return address: '. . . the Cranigers?'

The fireman shook his head no.

'See that cat?' he said then.

The patrolman looked up, shook his head no.

'It was beautiful,' the fireman said, looking up the street. To the east. 'Well then,' he said, touching the brim of his helmet with his thick fingers, and the patrolman nodded, reading the next piece of mail, holding it up to the sky, for light, and it took the fireman forty-two minutes to get to the rear retaining wall of Gatecrest Estates, because the patrolman was going from mailbox to mailbox behind him.

He waved to him before stepping over the low wall.

The patrolman never even saw.

The two Indian houses were trailers. The storm had missed them somehow. There was a low lodge set between them. Dug into the ground. The fireman took his glove off, touched the top blanket covering the lodge. It was hot, full of breathing. He nodded, looked behind him, to Gatecrest, then went to the front door of the first trailer, stood back against the railing of the porch after knocking.

A girl answered. Eleven, maybe twelve.

The fireman raised his facemask.

'Just checking,' he said.

The girl stared at him, looked behind her, then back to him. Her eyes were flat black. The cat that was beautiful when running rubbed up against her leg, out the door. To the fireman's right boot, the pieces of the other fireman that were still there. It started licking, its rough tongue sending shivers of sound up the fireman's leg.

'. . . Ray?' a boy said then—younger. Eight, nine. Dark.

The nice fireman smiled, didn't look away.

'What?' the boy said.

The fireman was shaking his head no, nothing—*just that you remind me of someone else*—then looking down to the sweat lodge one last time, then stepping through the door.

47

29 MAY 1999

GREENVILLE, TEXAS

HORACE was making tea in the early morning dark, listening to the big trucks whine past, for Dallas. It never stopped and he never understood. The house he lived in with fourteen other men—six of them pipe-fitters like him, two from the same shop—was shaped like a wide horseshoe. It opened onto the interstate so that the packed-dirt courtyard filled with sound. Originally, it had been a trailer, the ranging tenement, but the trailer was buried deep in the tarpaper now, like a seed, a memory. Each room that was added on was another two hundred dollars a month for the owners. They'd only stopped at fourteen because they didn't want to buy a bigger water heater. There was no common room anymore; it had been rented out to number fourteen, a man named Jackson whose family was supposed to be on the road behind him, once he sent word of work. There was a kitchen, but most of the men just had hotplates or cans of Sterno in their rooms. Four toilets, two showers. At night, Horace could pick out the recaps from the still-new tires, just by their hum on the asphalt. He talked to Jackson about his family and Jackson would talk until daybreak.

Horace dipped the tea bag into the hot water in the pan, let the string trail over the edge so that the paper tag at the end touched the open flame, flared up like a match head, the cotton string smoldering up to the metal lip, but never over. It was a game. While the tea steeped in the windowsill—so as not to heat up the room this early in the morning—Horace walked out to the fence behind the house to pee. The fence was staggered metal and wood posts—two metal, then a wood. Across the back of the house, there were three wooden posts. They were the only green on the lot anymore, the Johnson grass and careless weeds tall there, and greasy.

'Booting out,' number six called from his post, careful not to look over.

The Johnson grass.

Horace nodded. It was—early—the heads angling out, ready to drop their seed. It would be poison for about three days, now. You'd have to eat a lot to kill you, though, and there maybe wasn't enough here. Horace shut his eyes. When he opened them, he was alone. He was number four. Early on, he'd traded two months' rent—back when it didn't include utilities, when he was fresh from Nazareth, the clothes he'd worn to commencement still folded in a bowling ball bag—for help framing the four rooms on the southeast side. The owners thought his name was because he was running from the law. That he might as well call himself Johnny Lam or, because he was Indian, Billy Runs Away, Timothy Hides-a-Lot. He was dark from working in the yard at the shop, the radio on, acres of hot pipe arranged around him, their threaded ends jagged, their bellies incubating generations upon generations of rabbits. The first thing they would smell would be rust.

Horace kept the fence around the yard patched, so the coyotes couldn't get in, wait the rabbits out, their breath polluting the mouths of the pipe. There was nothing he could do about the hawks but throw bottles and washers, though. At first the way they clanged down the tin roof of the shop would draw the men inside to the fourteen-foot door, their welding caps tilted back, but now they knew. It was the best place to be during an eclipse, though—the shop. All manner of goggles. You could stare at the sky for hours. Horace was always expecting someone to come falling out of it.

He went inside for his tea. This was his eighth day now without coffee. And the tea, he was making it weaker and weaker. Soon it would be water.

Out on the interstate, a milk truck was passing, all chrome and recaps. Horace stood over his pan watching it, the steam sliding up the thin panes of glass, and when it was gone, the milk truck, there was a shape in the window. Over his shoulder.

He didn't turn around.

'Wayne Bo moved out three months ago,' he said. 'And he was down in twelve, anyway.'

'I'm not here for Wayne Bo,' the man behind him said, and Horace stopped breathing, smiled: Jim.

'Come to arrest your old man?' he said.

'For living here, yeah.'

Horace took the pan in one hand, lifted the bag out, his hand shaking around the blackened string as he trailed drops across the floor, to the trash can. It was lined with a plastic shopping bag.

'Jimmy,' he said.

Jim Doe was just staring at him. Like he hadn't been expecting to, maybe.

Horace stood, to let his son sit on the foot of the bed, then made him a cup of tea, then himself one. They drank and didn't watch each other any, or too much.

'You're missing,' Horace said.

Jim Doe smiled, nodded.

Horace looked at him—dark from the road, gaunt.

The tea was hot, too hot, but they drank it anyway. With both hands.

Down the hall number nine creaked from his bed to the toilet, the fabric of his shirt scraping the wall the whole way.

'He killed me,' Jim Doe said.

Horace stared at him, then.

'You're Blackfeet, though,' he said.

Jim Doe nodded, smiled like he'd spilt something.

Horace looked out the window, at the interstate, the trucks sweeping by like leaves on the back of a dirty river. A barn swallow flitted to the porch, left without touching its mud nest. It had been six years, now, since the graduation ceremony. Or seventeen. He looked just like her around the eyes.

'What do you need?' Horace said.

'I know what happened now,' Jim Doe said.

Horace turned to him.

Together, they didn't say her name.

'He took her,' Jim said.

Horace leaned back against the dresser.

'I think I can find her,' Jim Doe said. 'Him, anyway.'

'Where?' Horace said.

'Nebraska, right now,' Jim Doe said. 'That storm last night.'

Horace stared at the floor, tracking himself across it by the tea drops: window to trashcan, day after day, week after week.

'He follows the storms,' Jim Doe said. 'I can track him that way.'

Horace nodded, his head heavy, the world suddenly big. Breathed out through his nose.

'But—' he said, 'He . . . I saw her in the closet . . .'

'You didn't,' Jim Doe said. 'You just remember it that way. I did too.'

Horace looked hard at his son.

'It's not just that you want her to be alive,' he said, almost a question.

'I can find him,' Jim Doe said.

Horace looked at his hands.

'What do you need?' he said.

'A truck,' Jim Doe said. 'Some money. One of your old ID cards, maybe.'

'I know this Arapaho down at the liquor store. Almost your age. Tell him I sent you.'

'Okay.'

Horace nodded.

'They let me take the parts truck home now,' he said. 'White supercab out there.'

Jim Doe didn't have to look outside for it.

'They'll know,' he said.

'It got stolen,' Horace said.

Jim Doe smiled.

Horace motioned for him to stand, then turned the bed on its side. In one of the hollow legs of the bed, behind a patch of fur that looked vermine—security—Horace pulled out an old piece of leather, like something he'd tanned himself. It was folded over. He lifted the flap. Inside was the stub of the check insurance had given him in 1982, and, rubber-banded to it, the cash.

'She can help you now,' he said.

'Dad . . .' Jim Doe said.

'I don't have anything to buy anymore,' Horace said.

Jim Doe didn't say anything.

'And clothes,' Horace said, opening the drawers, stacking work pants and work shirts up. All of them. He was breathing hard now, fast, his hands sure. 'You want me to come?' he asked.

Jim Doe looked away, at the supercab. He was just pretending. Horace let him.

'I think about her a lot,' Jim Doe said.

Horace nodded.

Jim Doe turned to him.

'Mom too, I mean.'

'There's a whirlwind out there,' Horace said, smiling his whole-face smile. It was a movie line.

'I know,' Jim Doe said, and, because they were Indian, they didn't shake hands, and, because they were men, they didn't hug, or even touch, just looked at each other through the windows each of them had, one in the side of a sprawling house, the other in the side of a truck, moving away.

Minutes after his son was gone, Horace said his daughter's name, once, his lips moving faster than the word itself, and then he put on his sunglasses, walked to work.

48

29 MAY 1999

WHITE HORSE, OKLAHOMA

FUCK Tim Creed. Cody had said it to himself like that the whole flight west: fuck Tim Creed.

Listen to the tapes.

Cody had. Over and over and over. The child psychologist talking to them for hours, the girl never talking until the doctor asked them about the other children.

'The Sandovals?' she'd said. Just that.

Cody looked them up. It took four hours, his eyes shot through with blood, mapping the screen red, but he finally found them. In White Horse, Oklahoma. Last year. Two Comanche children at the end of an article listing the facts the papers always loved: a strand of blond hair run through the metal of a fire hydrant; all the boxed meals of a grocery store moved one shelf down, all the gas pumps reset to $55.55. Two children found a mile outside town, in the cellar of a house that used to be there, forty-odd years ago. The storm had even stacked firewood on top of the ancient cellar door, so the children couldn't get out, and lined the walls with canned goods and bottled water.

Cody forwarded the link to Eggers, down the hall, then walked out the door, to the airport, for Oklahoma, the Sandovals, to get their testimony, *any*thing, anywhere but here, the office, but then Creed was crashing through the parking lot, backhanding cars out of his way, and Watts was right behind him, not smiling: Dedham. Massachusetts.

Mr. Rogers. That was the twenty-sixth.

Cody followed them inside, ran the name *James Kulpin* for ten hours, and the parents too, and found the only link there was: that Myna Janks, Kulpin's mother's maiden self, was out of Woodward, *Saskatchewan*—not Manitoba—and Woodward, *Oklahoma* was the main town the Joan Gay Croft tornado had hit. And then he ran the stats on the Saskatchewan Woodward. It was thirty-five point seven percent Mennonite. So he ran *Mennonite*. It went back to 1536, all the usual boring religious stuff—anabaptist, evangelical, insular. They were practically Amish. Meaning that agent in Roanoke had been wrong, the one who knew Kevin Poulson off the top of his head. And then Creed was there, staring at the window, asking Cody where he had been going in the parking lot that day.

'White Horse,' Cody said. 'Oklahoma.'

Creed nodded. It was where the 1947 tornado had quit. Whitedeer, Texas to White Horse, Oklahoma. Like it knew even then, wanted that symmetry.

'You should go,' Creed said.

'But—' Cody started.

But they already *knew* who he was.

Creed just stared out the window, his hands in pockets.

Two hours later, Cody cornered Watts in the hall about it. Watts was wearing black, for Mr. Rogers's closed casket service that the whole building was draining down to. She stared at him.

'After—in the ambulance after we found her again, Mica Jones.'

Cody nodded, following.

'He said it could have been you, Agent Mingus. If you would have been there. That it could have been you.'

Cody stopped nodding.

'He never had any children,' she said, then shrugged. 'He's protecting you.'

'But it's bullshit,' Cody said. 'Oklaho—'

'Would you rather go to the service?' she said. Of the agent he'd put on the news as the possible Tin Man.

He was on the plane west in two more hours, saying it still: Fuck Tim Creed.

He called Eggers from the air, had him look for something else: any other children missing, presumed dead during or after a tornado in 1998. There were none. None reported, anyway. Cody thanked him, hung the phone up on the back of the seat in front of him, and closed his eyes.

The Tin Man would be desperate this year, then. Kulpin.

Maybe that was another reason things were happening. Besides that he was dying, and that Jim Doe was twenty-six, and Marion Wayne Isinger had been paroled. And that he was *wanting* them to happen.

Cody stood in the road in White Horse, opened the broken gate leading up to the Sandoval house, and stepped up onto the porch. There was a flyer on the door, a note at the bottom, in a female hand, telling someone to meet them there. The flyer was for May thirtieth, tomorrow. A pow-wow. 'The only place to be if you're Indian.' Then something *written* in Indian. In Comanche. Letters, not pictograms.

Cody took it with him, went to the second address he had, that Creed didn't know about: 192 Ochoa Place, in Enid. A nursing home. Garden of Enid in granite or weatherproofed foam letters by the emergency driveway.

It was the last residence they had listed for Kulpin's father. Maybe there would be a note about where any records were forwarded. That they hadn't been able to find over the phone. But, looking at the patient list they'd faxed over, he saw another name he knew: Angeline Dougherty.

He found her in her room, and understood immediately why he shouldn't be there. Why Creed didn't want him to be: her throat was still cut. After twenty-one years. Other than that, she wasn't even old enough to be in assisted living. Other than that and whatever emotional damage there was. She had been beautiful once, though. The kind you look away from. Cody sat down opposite her chair, waited for her to look up, for her to look up and have her head loll off, backwards, her neck yawning up at the ceiling. The scar was that wide.

She shouldn't have lived. Not when there were people out there dying from taps on the head. Mosquito bites.

The first thing Cody said to her was that he was sorry.

She looked at him for a long time about it.

'You're not old enough,' she said, finally, her voice mechanical, tracheal.

Cody looked out the window, at an old man trying to line up on a croquet ball, everyone on the lawn watching him, teetering between life and death.

'I just wanted to ask,' he said, not not *not* looking at her, 'I just wanted to ask why you, Ms. Dougherty.'

She smiled.

'Angel,' she said.

'Angel,' Cody whispered back.

She waited until he raised his eyes to her to talk.

'Tim knows I didn't tell him all of it, doesn't he?' she said. It took twice as long as normal for her words to form.

Cody nodded.

'It was because my mother was still alive, Agent . . . ?'

'Cody. Mingus.'

'Agent Cody Mingus. Surely you understand?'

Cody shook his head no.

'Jesse James,' she said, as if that was enough.

'You mean Wiggs,' Cody said. 'Jessie Wiggs.'

Angeline Dougherty shook her head no.

'The outlaw,' she said, as if the girl-part of her was still in love with him. Had been. She looked out the window. 'In nineteen seventy-eight, Agent Cody Mingus, my mother was still alive.' She smiled. 'I was *Elise* that year—Tim told you this, I'm sure. I was Elise because I was the one who saw Gil Rames shoot that girl in the Prospector, remember?'

Cody nodded, didn't remember.

She had been in some kind of witness protection. And she'd called Creed *Tim*.

'How did he find you, then?' he said. 'Wig—Jesse James.'

Angeline Dougherty shrugged. 'We had a system,' she said. 'My mother, me. She made all the cookware parties, I mean. Went to them all. I can't imagine what her kitchen must have looked like. I kept up with which parties were where. We had a system.'

Cody waited, didn't even know what to ask anymore.

'I couldn't tell Tim, because then she would have found out. And that would have killed her.'

'Your mother.'

Angeline Dougherty nodded, her head moving too far for a second, it seemed, the world tilting with it.

'Because I was fourteen,' she said, quieter. 'And Jesse, he used to drive this, I don't know. These cars for his garage. You've got to understand, Agent Cody Mingus. Do you know what it's like to be fourteen and have an eighteen-year-old pay attention to you?'

Cody shook his head no.

'You do anything for him,' Angeline Dougherty said. 'Even things you can't remember.'

Cody looked out the window again.

'He called it his reunion tour,' she said. 'When he found me, I mean.'

It was a funny thing to her. Absurd.

'It *was* him, though,' Cody said. 'Jessie . . . *James*.'

'You don't forget, Mr. Mingus.'

Cody nodded, nodded. 'When he . . .' he started. 'When you were fourteen. Did you know any of his associates, maybe? Friends? Anybody you saw him with regularly?'

'Just us,' Angeline Dougherty said, lost inside herself like she was when he first walked up. 'It would have killed my mother.'

Past the open door of Angeline Dougherty's room, old people were shuffling down the hall to the cafeteria one after the other, their eyes fixed on the distance, their teeth set: one foot, then the other; one foot, then the other. Until a few years ago, Kulpin's father had been one of them, pausing maybe a moment too long in her doorway to catch his breath. Look at her. Had he known, though?

Cody wrote his number on an open notebook on Angeline Dougherty's nightstand.

'If you think of anything,' he said.

She smiled. 'I think of everything,' she said, her lips thin, her voice small like a girl's.

Cody sat in one of the vinyl chairs of the dayroom with his head in his hands until he could think again, then stood, called D.C., for Creed, or Watts, watched the television while he got patched through. It was the news, and the news was the weather: a low-pressure system, the one that hit Nebraska last night. It was falling down the map towards Kansas now, Oklahoma, Texas, and, down in the lower right-hand corner of the screen, there was a cartoon tornado, words underneath it, too small to read. The Big Bad Wolf, probably. Here to blow all the houses down.

Cody held the phone to his chest and stepped closer, and then the shot behind it was Nebraska, a mobile unit. A real tornado, twelve dead, and one—an Indian woman, a mother, her picture inset—dead in the living room of her own trailer, two children missing. Because he was desperate.

Cody lifted the phone back to his ear when there was somebody there. Creed.

'You can stop looking,' Cody said. 'I know where he is.'

It was starting again.

49

29 MAY 1999

ARAPAHOE, NEBRASKA

HE was the one in the brown hat, the booth by the window. Where he could see the car.

'Your ear,' the waitress said, touching her own, to show.

It was bleeding, yes.

'That low-pressure system,' he said, still watching the car, the windows of the car.

The waitress looked out with him.

'You're not from around here,' she said. 'Your ear'd be bleeding all the time, I mean.'

James Kulpin touched his ear, the warmth there.

'Suppose so,' he said.

There was blood in his throat, too. If he smiled, his teeth would be red. Everybody in the diner, though. They were all full of blood, ready to burst.

'You're not married,' he said to the waitress.

She looked around at him.

He was looking at her now, too. All of her.

'Sherry,' he said.

She kept looking at him, then down to her badge, her name.

He hadn't done anything wrong, that was the thing. Nothing really improper.

He took his hand off his cup, opening it in invitation: yes, please. Now.

She came back, poured.

'You've *had* children,' he said.

The coffee spilled over in his saucer.

'You're not a stormchaser,' she said to him.

He shook his head no: I *am* the storm.

In the backseat of the car he was driving this week, the shape—the shadow—of a head crowned, breaking the line of the dash, then slipped down again. He didn't even know their names yet. It was better that way, sometimes. This time.

'Volunteer,' he said, holding his cup to his mouth.

The girl in the car had a Band-Aid on her inner arm where the needle had been. The boy just had a small hole. James had had the Band-Aid ready for him, peeled, adhesive side up, but then had become fascinated with the hole itself, and with the prospect of the boy waking, realizing his sister has a bandage, he doesn't. What it might mean to him.

The waitress—Sherry—left, watched him from behind the bar. Forgot about him. He could see it in her body posture. When his coffee was gone again, turning his liver even blacker, he held the cup up, said it under his breath: 'Gwynn.'

She came.

It had been so long since he had taken an adult like this. The slow way. From the inside out.

From his booth he could see the Arapahoe water tower.

'Why do they spell it with an *e*like that?' he said, pointing with his chin.

She couldn't see it standing up.

This was what it was all about: she had to sit down, across from him. Look up, give him her profile.

'Isn't that right?' she said.

James Kulpin shook his head no. Drank.

'The Arapaho—no *e*—that wasn't even what they called themselves, I don't think. Just like the Sioux weren't the Sioux to the Sioux—'

'But they—' Sherry said, looking to the water tower again. 'What were they, then?'

James Kulpin smiled.

'What *are* they,' he corrected. 'The Lakota, the Nakota, the Dakota, the Yankton, and then down to bands, and tiospaye . . .'

She was just staring at him.

'Or the Navajo,' he said. 'They're the Diné. Ojibway itself just a corruption of Otchipwe, which is just Anishinaabe the way somebody else said it.'

'Who?'

'In their case, the French,' James Kulpin said. 'But Navajo. It's what the Apache told the soldiers the Navajo were. It means something like 'those who raid in the fields.' The ones to the east, that were contacted first, always got to name their enemies. Like Sioux. It means a lot of things—rude things, things I won't repeat—but it all comes down to enemy. That's what they were to the Anishinaabe.'

'The Ojibway,' Sherry said.

James Kulpin lifted his cup to her. 'Good,' he said.

She was watching him, both her elbows on the table.

'How do you know all this?' she said.

He smiled. 'I'm a student of the Americas,' he said.

'You should be a teacher,' she said.

He shrugged, looked to the car.

'When's your shift over?' he asked her.

'Why?' she said, her elbows drawing in—a natural reflex: protect the soft organs. The breasts.

'I'll tell you about the Gros Ventres in Montana,' he said. 'The fatbellies.'

He did his hand in a waterfall over his stomach, out farther and farther.

'Two hours,' she said. 'Sorry.'

James Kulpin rotated the coffee in his cup. It was poison.

'I can wait,' he said, making his voice shy, then nodding out to his car. 'Anyway, I should wait until dusk. It keeps overheating.'

'And the roadblocks,' Sherry said, standing, nodding as she stood.

James Kulpin nodded, still looking outside.

'And the roadblocks,' he said, nodding with her.

It was so easy.

She had two kids, Ben and Mark.

'What time's their sitter have to go home?' James Kulpin asked.

'They're with their grandmother,' Sherry said.

In the parking lot, the automatic lights were coming on one by one, moving across the asphalt from east to west. It seemed backwards, but wasn't. Not on this small a scale.

'Benjamin and Marcus,' James Kulpin said.

'Just Mark,' Sherry said.

He took her order pen from her pocket—that close to her right breast, his fingers shying away, almost, revulsed—and traced a florid *B* onto a clean napkin. It was the kind that opened a chapter in an old book, would be as tall as the paragraph, almost. Have the head of a dragon if it was a medieval story.

'It's beautiful,' Sherry said.

Smitten was the word.

He rolled his sleeve up, showed her the *Donny* he had drawn on his upper arm in the bathroom half an hour earlier, then rubbed light, faded. He acted like he couldn't look at it too long. She noticed. While she noticed, he unaccidentally put the wrong end of the pen into his mouth, wetting the tiny ball with coffee.

When he put the pen down to trace an *M* by the *B*, it gave out.

Sherry stood to get one from the cup by the register but James Kulpin shook his head, produced one himself.

'Here,' he said, taking the top of her hand. 'Like a tattoo.'

The muscles in her arm tensed.

'It'll come off,' he said.

She didn't say anything. He didn't let go of her hand.

'Marc . . .' he said, as he drew, connecting each letter around her wrist, like a bracelet, or a cuff. On the inside, where the skin was thin, where all the veins were, the letters were blocked-in. It took a lot of ink, more concentration.

'. . . beautiful,' Sherry said, extending her other hand.

'Show them,' James Kulpin said. 'They'll love it.'

He did the complete BENJAMIN around the other wrist. It took twenty minutes, almost. By the time he was done, she was already groggy from the first one, the secobarb in the ink seeping in, collecting in her eyelids.

He held her hand to keep her from swaying back too far.

Waitresses. He owed that to Jessie, at least.

'Donny,' Sherry was saying, slurring.

James Kulpin nodded.

'He was my Ben,' he said. 'My Mark.'

'I'm sorry,' Sherry said, not having to ask. Maybe unable.

'I can tell you about him,' James Kulpin said. 'It.'

Sherry smiled, one pupil larger than the other.

'Gwynn,' he said. 'Can I call you Gwynn, Sherry?'

Sherry shrugged, nearly vomited.

James Kulpin almost laughed, pulled her closer.

'I can tell you the way it really was,' he said. 'But, well. I may have to kill you.'

Sherry—*Gwynn*—laughed, her head lolling back on her shoulders, her teeth a perfect line of white in her mouth.

James Kulpin watched her, falling in love all over.

'Okay,' he said. 'But you remember anyway, right? It was nineteen eighty. We'd been married nine months. The human gestation period. I was just out of prison then.'

You were still being a good boy, Gwynn said.

She was dead. He had just killed her. His wife.

'Yes,' James Kulpin said. 'I was trying, at least.'

They were crying in the hall, together. Holding hands, praying. The social worker hadn't even come by herself, had just sent a letter. Later, he would look back on it, that moment, and know that that was where it all started. Where it all started again. After he was through with that life. But then Booth walked in, no doorbell, no knock, and just stood there in the entryway.

'Stanny?' he said. '. . . Gwynn? I'm sorry—what—?'

Booth who had two beautiful children.

After he was gone, Gwynn sat on the couch with her tissue box, patting her face, not rubbing, because she didn't want wrinkles.

'Karma,' she said, laughing to herself. 'I must have done something in my past life. Y'know, to not deserve children this time around?'

James Kulpin shook his head no. It wasn't her.

But he had gone to *prison* for all of it, that was the thing. Done his time, served his sentence.

Two months later, Gwynn threw herself into Vacation Bible School, holding the children there close, tight. Stanislav Kiozelsky dropped her off every morning, picked her up for dinner every night. She glowed. He hated himself.

After her first week, she volunteered to help another church.

'You too,' she said, as he drove her from church to church. 'You should do it too, I don't know—*some*thing.'

Stanislav Kiozelsky nodded. The world was going grey for him again, monotone, and he was letting it. Concrete maybe, that was the color. Like prison. But then, coming home from a church he didn't know the denomination of, a shade of brown separated itself from the rest. A color he knew, remembered: khaki, with a red bandanna. A Scout, walking alone on a sidewalk. James Kulpin felt his face change, under the skin.

Two weeks later, the handbook committed to memory, he offered to help with Troop 4302, however he could. Cook, clean, carry. Booth vouched for him. He had two children, and Jenine. Jenine who was happy, selling outlandish shades of blue eye shadow to senior citizens.

At night, the James Kulpin locked inside the Stanislav Kiozelsky heard himself crying.

'What's wrong?' Gwynn asked, because maybe it would be something easy: job, car, lawn. It wasn't, though.

'Nothing,' he told her.

Two days later, Stanislav Kiozelsky found himself walking through the gaming store, though. Just to see how available stuff was. Acetone. Sodium hypochlorite. The components of chloroform.

He never meant to use it, either. Not really. He told himself it was for home defense, and constructed elaborate scenarios involving himself, the brown bottle, a wily intruder. But then, one day—too soon, too fast—there was Booth on his own couch, the skin around his mouth red from the rag.

Jenine was gone for the weekend.

'I'm just taking them camping,' James Kulpin said, looking sheepishly out to the RV. 'Mind if I take your rig?'

Booth just lay there.

James Kulpin powdered the sleeping pills into Booth's open mouth, warmed the water in his own, dribbled it down Booth's throat, their lips almost touching.

'Thanks,' he said, locking the door behind him, the curtain already drawn.

Donny and Dawn were waiting for him in the RV.

'He said no problem,' James Kulpin said. 'And have fun. Not to eat too many marshmallows.'

Donny looked up at him from the thin, lumpy mattress.

'He doesn't want to go, does he?' he said.

Stanislav Kiozelsky shrugged it off. 'Some people just don't like the outdoors like the rest of us,' he said. 'Don't hold it against him.'

'Can I do the tent this time?' Dawn said.

Stanislav Kiozelsky nodded, started the truck.

Yes.

Later in the summer, he'd start picking Gwynn up on the way out of town too. Tell her that Booth and Jenine wanted a romantic weekend, maybe. That they were having problems. Not to call them, or say anything about this later.

Gwynn, though. She would have believed anything, just to pretend for two days.

'This is what it's supposed to be like,' Stanislav Kiozelsky told her.

Gwynn nodded, her eyes wet, almost spilling over.

Stanislav Kiozelsky put his hand on her knee.

'Picturebook,' he said.

'Picturebook,' she said back.

It was the perfect summer.

'So he wasn't even yours,' Sherry said. *Gwynn. Gwynn said.*

James Kulpin angled his head, looked at her.

'No,' he said. 'He was mine. My Donny.'

'But—'

He still had her hand. He applied pressure to the nerve center just below the web between her thumb and index finger. She felt it, didn't understand it. Looked at her hand.

'So I guess your friend found out?' she said.

James Kulpin just studied his car in the parking lot some more. Shook his head no.

'Then . . . ?' Gwynn said, unable even to form the question, get it out.

James Kulpin.

'And then,' he said, looking right at her. 'Then, dear, you let him into the trailer, I guess.'

'. . . *him?*' she said, trying to remember.

'Marion,' James Kulpin said.

Marion Wayne Isinger.

Stanislav Kiozelsky had just stepped out, down to the creek, to get some water to boil, for breakfast, but had found a fire down there, still smoking, ringed with beer bottles. He poured dirt over the ashes until it was gone, cool. Later he would wonder if it had been Marion's fire, if they'd crossed each other on the trail, each watching their feet, trying not to trip.

It didn't matter. Soon, nothing would.

When he came back to the RV, the trailer, the door was locked.

Stanislav Kiozelsky smiled—*the kids*—then knocked, not wanting to wake Gwynn up yet.

Marion Wayne Isinger answered.

James Kulpin dropped his water.

'Jimmy boy . . .' Marion said.

'. . . John Wayne,' James Kulpin said back.

It was their usual greeting.

'Didn't know you were . . .' he said, searching for a word Gwynn wouldn't know: '*public*, again.'

There was blood on Marion's forearm. And a heat from the trailer.

'Public,' Marion said, tasting the word.

James Kulpin closed his eyes, opened them.

'Where are the children, Marion?' he said.

'Kids . . .' Marion said, shrugging, doing that thing with his lips that made them look like a sideways question mark, his dimple the period.

'And Gwynn,' James Kulpin said, looking down. The compulsory question.

Marion smiled, released air that might have been a laugh, in another world.

'That her name?' he said.

James Kulpin closed his eyes, then, trying to start the day over, all over. Make it be one where he didn't need water, didn't *need* breakfast. Where he could just stay in bed with Gwynn and listen to the children—his *family*—sleeping, on pallets, on tables, all around him.

'How did you find me?' he said, to Marion.

'Rock,' he said.

The parole officer. One of Marion's new clients, probably.

James Kulpin held his hand over his mouth, so Marion wouldn't see his chin tremble, hear his voice cracking.

'Let me in,' he said.

Marion shrugged. 'Yeah,' he said, 'everybody needs a turn, right?'

Inside it was what he'd already seen in his head: Gwynn, her sweat pants torn off, her face bleeding. She was awake, though.

Stanislav Kiozelsky knelt by her, cradled her head.

'. . . he has you confuse—' she started, coughed, said again: 'He thinks you're from the prison he was in,' she said, trying to laugh, in spite of everything.

James Kulpin nodded.

'I am,' he said.

Gwynn looked up to him, breathed in sharp. Shook her head no, no, even said it some.

'. . . what for?' she said.

James Kulpin smiled, shrugged.

'Not what they think,' he said, his voice changing. He looked down to the head in his hands. To Gwynn. 'You know I love you,' he said. 'And that I thank you for . . . this. All of it.'

Her hands found his wrists, held on.

'Stan—?' she said.

James Kulpin shook his head no. Stanislav Kiozelsky, he was dead.

Her grip wasn't strong enough to stop his hands, one at the forehead, one at the base of the skull. The sound of her neck filled the small, metal space.

'Holy fu—' Marion said, behind him, clutching his chest.

James Kulpin stood, then, the head of a tent stake suddenly in his palm, the dull point hard under Marion's face.

'You killed her,' he said.

Marion shook his head no.

'Jimmy boy . . .' he said.

James Kulpin pushed the stake in, further, until a line of blood slipped down Marion's throat.

'The children,' he said. 'Tell me you didn't hurt the children, Duke.'

Marion smiled, relief washing across his face.

'Of course . . .' he said, choked. 'My fucking heart, man.' He touched it, through his chest. 'They're *kids*, Jimmy. What do you think I am, man? A monster?'

James Kulpin smiled, just his mouth.

This was the first place Marion had come, he knew, Gwynn the first woman he'd seen. Rock was already dead by then, a hundred, spectacular ways.

'No,' James Kulpin said, 'monster?' then reached back into the drawer for a steak knife, to finish this thing.

Marion was shaking his head no, though. The front of his still-unzipped pants darkened.

'Jimmy,' he said, was saying. 'No, you don't—*Jimmy* . . .'

James Kulpin stopped, the tip of the blade to Marion's right lung, from the back. Where he stabbed him when he found him over Gwynn. So it would be a slow, suffocating death. One he could watch before he called for help.

'You ruined everything,' he said to Marion.

'The kids,' Marion said back. 'You'll never find them, Jimmy boy, shit. Not if I'm dead . . .'

And that was the way it was: in trade for where the children had been tied, so they wouldn't have to watch their mother's rape, Marion walked one way, James Kulpin the other. To Donny, to Dawn. Only Marion had lied. They *were* in the direction he'd pointed, yes—the water, a little upstream, by that tree with the swing—only they'd each been held under too long. Donny's khaki shirt blended with the brush just as it was supposed to, too. James Kulpin carried them back one at a time.

Sherry laughed, cried. James Kulpin was observing her.

'. . . and you just—?' she said, flipping her hand up in the air.

James Kulpin emptied his pen into her coffee.

'Drink,' he said.

She did. It turned her lips blue. Like Gwynn's, in the bathtub he'd kept her iced down in for a week, waiting to see how Booth would respond. What he would do. How he would go about blaming himself.

'C'mon,' he said, to Sherry. 'I'll take you home. To your mother's.'

'After you *kill* me,' Sherry said, staggering up. He steadied her. People were watching.

'After I kill you, yes,' he said.

His coffee cup behind him was already clean, no prints, the two dollars of his tip the same. Sherry's tip. He left it anyway. There was a fingerprint on the convex side of his spoon, right thumb, perfectly centered. A gift, for whoever found it.

In the parking lot, he draped Sherry's arm over his shoulder, carried her to the front seat of the car.

'Mommy's here,' he said to the children.

They didn't stir.

He set Sherry in the front seat, covered her with a blanket some, up to the shoulders, then slipped Gwynn's ring from his pants pocket, forced it over Sherry's bloated finger, knew he was going to have to snip the finger off when it was time to take the ring back. But that didn't matter. She was necessary; he wouldn't make it out of Nebraska without her. And still, it would be close. There had never been roadblocks before.

He shut and locked Sherry's door, then opened the back.

The girl slumped out. He lifted her back in, held her head up by the chin as he cut her hair with a pair of scissors he'd bought two days ago. It turned her into a boy, almost. Close enough.

Next, he got into the driver's seat, pulled his own seat belt across his chest, and eased out of town, down 83, into Kansas, his ear bleeding freely again. The line for the roadblock was miles, bumper to bumper. James Kulpin sat in it with the news on, the window down, because fathers don't like to run the air conditioner when the car's idling.

'Who you looking for?' he asked the young officer who approached his door forty minutes later.

'Two children,' the officer said, shining his light into the backseat.

James Kulpin looked back to them too. Sleeping.

'Do I need to wake them?' he said.

'Name,' the officer said.

The plates of the rental car would come back to an Evan Louis Fuller, the name Earle Leonard Nelson had married under before his beautiful, abortive rampage. James Kulpin smiled, shrugged. 'Robert Frank,' he said, on a whim. 'Like Anne.'

'Anne?' the officer said, suddenly alert.

James Kulpin pretended not to notice.

'That Jewish girl in the attic,' he said, overloading the small man's mind, accessing the part of his animal brain that still remembered high school English class, would whisper that this guy wasn't lying.

The officer nodded, maybe.

'Not important,' James Kulpin said. 'My wallet was in my real car, y'know?'

The officer looked along the side of this car.

'How'd you get this one, then?' he said.

'Gwynn—my wife—already had it,' James Kulpin said. 'Loaner, from the body shop. But, these two, Ben and Marcus. They've been with me the whole time . . .'

The officer smiled, shook his head no, then the beam of his light caught James Kulpin's neck. The blood from his ear.

'You okay?' he said.

'I've still got my family,' James Kulpin said. 'Yes.'

'So you're from McCook?'

James Kulpin nodded.

'You're who we're looking for then,' the officer said. 'Older gentleman, two children, eight and ten. Boy and girl.'

James Kulpin closed his eyes, bit his lip. As if with relief.

'Their names are Ben and *Mark*,' he said. Two *boys*.

The officer shined his light into the backseat again.

'. . . and Mark's eleven,' James Kulpin added.

'I'm going to need you to—' the officer started, but James Kulpin already had Sherry's hands fished out from under the blanket, the ring winking in the battery light.

'Ben,' he said, *read*. 'Mark.'

The officer directed his beam in, hooked one side of his mouth into a smile.

'Thought it was the other way around,' he said. 'Aren't the kids supposed to get her name tattooed on *their* arms?'

James Kulpin shrugged. Sherry was stirring.

'Her brother—who thankfully doesn't come by anymore—learned to do tattoos somewhere. Probably jail. It was a birthday gift two years ago.' James Kulpin smiled. 'I would rather have had a VCR or something, but'—looking west, to McCook—'guess that doesn't matter anymore.'

The officer nodded, nodded, then finally swept his beam down the hood, directing James Kulpin on, into Kansas.

James Kulpin raised his hand in thanks, pumped the window up so he could hear the radio more, and drove.

They'd even had his description this time. A composite, at least.

He was impressed. Tim Creed was doing his job. But then another thing came over the radio, tagged onto his description now, onto his name: Gilles de Rais. The child killer of child killers. An abomination. It was supposed to explain the Tin Man to America. The newsreader wasn't even pronouncing it right.

James Kulpin George Williams Hari Kari John13 Richard Beaux Stani Kiozelsky Mitchell Saginaw Dwayne Laramie Mr. Rogers Byron Calle Whoudini started screaming on the inside, then, until he threw blood up into the back of his throat. He held it for two miles, finally coasted over, staggered out, fell to his hands and knees by a fence, then looked back to the car for long minutes, standing still, giving them a chance to drive away, save themselves. They didn't.

'Hey,' he called out to them.

Nothing. Just wind.

He shook his head with wonder, got back in, rolled the news up louder, for detailed descriptions of himself, more insults, then heard it, what they were saying, had been saying: the children, their names. Robert Twice and Rayanne Johnston. The highway patrolman they had patched through was explaining how they were cousins, the two, Bobby and Rayanne, but had grown up enough that you could call them brother and sister, if you wanted.

James Kulpin let the car slow some under him.

You could call them that, yes. If you wanted.

He looked in the rearview at the two children—the *cousins*, who weren't even brother and sister, weren't even *right*—and didn't look away.

They were asleep, still.

He almost wished he didn't already know their names.

50

30 MAY 1999

WICHITA, KANSAS

CODY had been awake for forty-eight hours, maybe: up all night at Quantico, then crossing time zones for White Horse, for Enid, then Creed telling him to meet him in Wichita. To pick him up at the airport.

Cody wished he smoked, or read, or did anything besides walk back and forth past Gate 12B. It had been four hours already. He called Watts, to confirm that Creed was in the air.

She didn't answer, didn't care, just told him to listen: James Kulpin's mother, the Mennonite, she had some Indian blood in her, way back. Between an eighth and a quarter. Meaning James Kulpin was half of that.

'So?' Cody said. 'We already know he's into—'

'*Black*foot Indian,' Watts said.

Cody looked across the miles of carpet, then got it: Jim Doe, he was Black*feet*. It had stood out in his file.

'Same tribe?' he said.

'Just different countries,' Watts said.

'So that's why he wanted him,' Cody said. 'Because he can restore the blood—carry it on, but better, purer.'

'Something like that.'

'Shit.'

It didn't matter now. Jim Doe was probably buried wherever Amos Pease was. Because Cody hadn't let him come into the house in

Roanoke with them.

He hung up, leaned on the booth, the index finger of his right hand pressing into a wad of bubblegum for maybe twenty seconds before he realized what it was.

He whipped around, to the news. Always the news.

This time it was for him, though, a grainy, distant shot of two plaster-white children, no faces, even. They were standing half-under the shade of a rest stop. Posed against the poles. Not like before.

Cody staggered back, into somebody's coffee, then turned, ran.

Trego Center. The words at the bottom of the screen had been Trego Center. Fuck Creed. He'd been saying it so long now, it felt natural.

He slammed the rental car straight up out of Wichita, the road peeling up behind him.

It didn't take long to find the rest stop, either. It was white-hot with light, and helicopters, and miles of emergency vehicles, well-wishers, rubberneckers. There were even flowers in the road. Just one bunch, like they'd fallen out a window. Cody eased around them, walked up to the yellow tape, badged the highway patrolman. He let him in.

'They alive?' Cody said.

The trooper lifted his chin to the sheer plastic tarp they'd thrown over a metal lean-to. It gave it translucent walls. Flashlights moved on the backside of it like bugs.

Cody nodded, tried to prepare himself, then started pushing through the milling bodies until he just wanted to draw his gun, make a corridor. But then one appeared on its own, for just a moment, and at the end of it was a tall, narrow Indian, his hair shaggy and dull, eyes hidden, and Cody said it without thinking: 'Amos.'

The Indian looked up, back through the bodies, and it wasn't Amos Pease.

Jim Doe smiled at Cody.

Cody felt all the water in his body rush to the back of his eyes. Fought through to Jim Doe.

'You're alive,' he said.

Jim Doe shrugged, unbuttoned his shirt, pulled it down. The area over his heart was black with broken capillaries, and yellow in the center, where there were two ragged puncture holes.

Cody looked up to his face.

'He thinks you're his son,' he said.

'I know,' Jim Doe said, then dragged his eyes across the ground, up to the makeshift tent. 'They won't let me in,' he said.

Cody shook his head, led Jim Doe over.

'We got that girl again,' he said, on the way.

Jim Doe shook his head. 'She's alive?' he said.

And then they were there, at the wall of plastic. There wasn't a door, just a place to pull it apart. Another trooper standing there.

'Move,' Cody said, his badge up.

The trooper looked at him for a second more, back to the badge, and stepped aside, but then stopped Jim Doe, his gloved hand hard to Jim Doe's bruised chest. Jim Doe came back with an elbow to the trooper's chin, then the trooper came back with his gun, and Jim Doe came back with one too, spirited up out of his pants.

Everybody in the tent was quiet. Two papier-mâché children sitting on the picnic table, one of their heads lifting to this.

'No no *no!*' Cody said, stepping between Jim Doe and the trooper.

'You're not from here, Agent,' the trooper said through his teeth. 'We know how to deal with Indians out here.'

Cody just stared at him, then lowered his head into one of his hands.

'Touch him again,' he said, not looking up. 'Touch him again, and I shoot you. In the face. We know how to deal with locals, see?' He turned to the paramedics in the tent with them. Then to the kids.

'Two minutes,' he said. 'They're all right?'

The lead paramedic shrugged, raised one of the children's arms, let go. The arm stayed there.

'He dosed them with something,' he said. 'You can't talk—'

Cody just opened the flap in response. The tent emptied.

He turned to Jim Doe. Jim Doe was already looking at the children.

There was a bucket for each of them, with warm saline water and washcloths. The medics had been wiping the white off them. Jim Doe took a rag, held it to one of the children's lips—the girl—and cleaned them. Her shoulder was already bare. Jim Doe looked down, to the cloth, then up to Cody, offered it to him.

Cody took it, unsure how hard to press, or where, but tried—*like washing the dead*, he thought—and Jim Doe stepped around to the other side of the picnic table, took the rag from the boy's bucket, and started rubbing a soft circle in the middle of the girl's back.

Cody stepped to the side, saw the blue letters starting to emerge—*S A R*—but then Jim Doe quit, had to close his eyes for maybe a minute. The girl he had been touching was crying. Like she was in there, somewhere. Like she knew.

Jim Doe turned, lifted the tarp, went out the side opposite the flap.

Cody followed.

They were going deeper into the pasture behind the rest stop. Away from the light.

Cody stayed two steps behind.

'You know what it means,' he said—flinging his hand back at the rest stop. The first three letters of his sister's name.

Cody nodded: that Jim Doe's sister was like *that* girl—white, posed. That she hadn't been able to pretend Jerry LeChapeau was her brother good enough, or for long enough.

'Creed's in Wichita,' Cody said, just to be saying something.

Jim Doe just stared at the bank of clouds to the south, lightning branching sideways in them, the sound rolling across the grassland.

And Watts was on her way. Cody didn't say it, though. Because it didn't matter.

'You were going to Nebraska,' he said, instead.

Jim Doe nodded. 'He's not there anymore,' he said. 'I don't know how he gets there so fast. Before the rest of us.'

'He's Mennonite,' Cody said.

Jim Doe looked back at him. Like that meant something, but he couldn't quite register it. 'Where are you going now?' he said.

'You should be in a hospital,' Cody said.

'Later,' Jim Doe said. He was looking at Cody again, waiting.

'Dodge City, I think,' Cody said, finally. 'It's nothing, probably. Two kids he almost kidnapped last year.'

'They got away?'

Cody nodded, Jim Doe too.

'They used to shoot a lot of people there,' Jim Doe said. 'Dodge City.'

'You trying to talk me into it?' Cody said back.

Jim Doe smiled. Beside him, on the low fence he had walked up to, was a smudge of white. Cody rubbed his mouth with the palm of his hand.

'Dodge City,' Jim Doe said again.

'Only place to be if you're Indian tonight,' Cody said, and Jim Doe's head snapped up. As if he was suddenly not trusting Cody.

Cody shrugged, pointed Jim Doe down the fence. They looked out into the immediate pasture together.

'He must have . . . done it out there,' Cody said, and Jim Doe nodded, and then, for an instant, the helicopter's blades dipped, its spotlight swaying over into the scrub, burning a halo around the naked body of a woman, her wrists blue like ligature, her throat cut wide, a number pinned to her cheek: *9*.

51

30 MAY 1999

DODGE CITY, KANSAS

IT was like he had been here before, Jim Doe, in another lifetime: the parking lot of a pow-wow. Walking among the cars to the exhibit building, his sister touching each *S* in the license plates, him touching all the *J*s. Amarillo, it had been Amarillo. The stands were wooden, loud.

'. . . cost anything?' Cody was saying beside him, trying to wake up.

Jim Doe nodded, easing the supercab down another narrow aisle of cars.

'Two, three dollars,' he said, then found himself slowing, looking at each car. It was like he'd seen them before too. Then he got it: Garden City, the basketball game.

'What?' Cody said, trying to see too.

Jim Doe just kept watching, waiting, then, eight minutes later, there it was: a red handprint on the driver's side flank of a lowslung sedan. A dog standing by the trunk.

Jim Doe stopped, nodded over the dash.

'He smells them,' he said.

'Them?' Cody said.

Jim Doe looked over, didn't have to say it.

He stepped down with a screwdriver. The dog flitted away, appeared in a different corner of their vision: downwind.

'Coyote dog,' Jim Doe said to Cody. 'See how it moves?'

Cody nodded.

Jim Doe stood behind the car. There was the stump of a key in the trunk latch. Again. Jim Doe shook his head, looked up. It had been a straight line down from Trego Center. Not just for them.

'Not a rental,' Cody said, touching the metal of the trunk.

Jim Doe nodded.

'But we know he's *in* a rental,' he said.

'He likes them alive, right?' Cody said.

Jim Doe just stared at the trunk, trying to imagine what—who—was in it. His sister's name was all he could see, written in blue ink on Rayanne Johnston's back.

'Hey,' Cody said.

Jim Doe looked up: a tall man with a single braid, walking the way they'd just driven.

'Don't badge him,' Jim Doe said.

The man watched them the whole time he was walking, looking once to the sedan to see if he knew it.

'Relative?' Cody said, still watching the dog.

Jim Doe didn't answer, just held the screwdriver by the shaft with one hand, drove his palm into the butt with the other. The flat tip of the head was right on the key. It pushed it further in. Jim Doe hit it again, again, then had the screwdriver deep enough to turn. The trunk clicked open. The air in it was fetid, thick with decay.

Jim Doe reeled back just as the rain started again—thick, heavy drops.

'Shit,' he kept saying.

Cody had his gun out.

The trunk slowly overcame the extra weight of the screwdriver, opened.

Cody approached behind his gun, his sleeve over his nose, then threw up onto it, around it. Slung it off into the packed dirt. He was laughing, though. At himself. Jim Doe looked at him. Cody pointed loosely to the trunk with his gun.

Jim Doe made himself step closer, look in.

It was a doe, her glassy green eyes staring up.

Jim Doe shook his head. The water was running off him now, the wind lifting everything in the parking lot it could, bending all the antennae over, spinning the exhaust turbines on top of the exhibit building.

'Doesn't mean he's not here,' he said, finally.

'Doesn't mean he is,' Cody said, slipping his gun under his jacket again.

'But they are,' Jim Doe said. 'The Sandovals, right?'

Cody looked at him, looked away.

'You think he'd come back for them.'

Jim Doe shrugged.

'They weren't hard to find,' he said.

Cody nodded. '. . . he'll be the only white guy in there?' he said.

Jim Doe smiled.

'Ever been to a pow-wow?' he asked Cody.

'I didn't even know there were Indians anymore until last month,' Cody said.

Jim Doe smiled, led.

'Me neither,' he said.

Inside it was all feathers and colors and sound and fry bread, dark faces smearing by, children weaving through legs, glass cases of turquoise, trash on the ground. Jim Doe remembered his sister for some reason, holding onto his shoulder so she could take off her shoes.

The tall man with the long braid was standing with a group already, near the doorway to the arena. He lifted his bottled water to Jim Doe, marking his entrance. And Cody's. That he'd seen them at that trunk. Jim Doe looked away. Everybody else was looking at him too. Because of Cody. His black jacket and black slacks, the tie. Jim Doe talked to him without looking at him.

'You've got throw-up on your sleeve, FBI,' he said.

Cody looked down.

'It's rain,' he said.

'Doesn't smell like rain,' Jim Doe said.

Cody raised it to his nose, pulled it away fast.

'Stay here,' he said, already taking his jacket off, walking to the restroom signs.

A twelve-year-old boy was standing by a pillar near Jim Doe, had been.

'You his boyfriend or something?' the boy said.

Jim Doe looked down at him.

'Maybe I'm in federal custody,' he said.

The boy laughed around his fry bread, nodded to the front doors.

'My dad says America stops there,' he said.

Jim Doe smiled.

'Where can I get some of that?' he said—the fry bread.

The boy didn't stop eating.

'Can't,' he said. 'It's my grandma's.'

Jim Doe pursed his lips, looked away, and the boy was gone. Not even a crumb left behind. He shrugged, turned to the sound of tin bells on moccasins, but they were everywhere, some event just starting, or ending. Jim Doe stepped into the flow of people ducking into the arena, and, as he walked, kept touching his mouth with the topside of his thumb. And watching people over his hand. Looking for a little girl in bare feet but looking away at the same time.

The rain was pounding the metal roof of the exhibit building.

Jim Doe turned his face up, to let the sound wash over him at least, to try to gauge the wind up there. As long as it was blowing, they were okay. It was when it stopped, that silence when you realize something's missing, not there anymore. And you hide. He walked counterclockwise along the fringes of a round dance, trailed his hand over the table tops, touching the grey fur of animals he'd never seen, couldn't imagine. At one point a girl—five, maybe—latched onto his finger, led him to a set of earrings she'd found, then looked up at him, saw he wasn't who he was supposed to be. The vendor looked at Jim Doe as if he were still supposed to buy the earrings. Jim Doe stepped away, back, tried to stand so he wasn't tall, so the FBI couldn't see him across all the dancers, with their bustles and regalia and false heads.

Soon the boy with the fry bread was back. A new piece, still warm, shiny.

'How much?' Jim Doe said to him.

The boy just laughed again.

'Looking for a couple of kids,' Jim Doe said. 'About your age.'

The boy took a bite, chewed it, gauging Jim Doe.

'Tin Man,' he said. About Jim Doe. That that was his pattern—two kids, Indian.

Jim Doe shook his head, rubbed his chin.

'I'm more like the Scarecrow, I'd guess,' he said, smiling. 'Their name is Sandoval.'

'You related?'

It wasn't the boy talking, but a grown-up version of the boy, standing suddenly beside him.

Jim Doe shook his head no.

The man stared at him.

'Why are you here?' he said.

'I'm not who you think I am,' Jim Doe said.

'You're not Indian.'

Jim Doe tried to step away but the man took him by the shoulder, spun him around.

Jim Doe came back with the screwdriver, was hardly even aware of it in his hand.

The man smiled, nodded. All his suspicions confirmed.

'You brought the FBI here,' he said.

Jim Doe looked at the screwdriver in his hand.

'Their name is Sandoval,' he said. 'I just want to talk to them.'

The man stared, stared.

'Will you leave then?' he said.

Jim Doe nodded.

The man shrugged, lifted his chin to the registration table.

'Check the entry sheets,' he said.

Jim Doe didn't turn his back on him. The man led the boy away, guiding him by the top of the head. Jim Doe blew out the air he'd been holding in, closed his eyes, opened them, and turned, for the registration table, but found a paint-black face right up to his, the top bisected from the bottom by a white line that rose to pull across the nose. A fancydancer with a coyote head on his own. Like the dog in the parking lot had stood up, followed him in. Their noses were tip to tip, their faces mirror images.

'Sorry,' Jim Doe said, trying to slide past.

The dancer had his wrist, though. The one with the screwdriver. Jim Doe could feel the hand trembling. Deep, near the bone. He jerked his hand away, rolled off, into the crowd. The dancer watched him, not smiling.

At the table the entrants were all on separate clipboards. All he had to do was pick the right age-bracket: boys, twelve and under. Sandoval, Gregor. He held his finger on the name.

'They already went?' he asked.

The woman behind the table nodded.

Jim Doe showed her where his finger was on the list.

She smiled. 'Bear boy,' she said.

Jim Doe stared at her.

'. . . little black bear,' she said, then smiled, looked over to the far corner, the one most opposite the front door. 'Under the stands,' she said. 'He likes to scare the girls, that one.'

Jim Doe nodded thanks, turned to go. Felt the coyote dancer pacing him, moving through the people like he was moving *through* them. At one point Jim Doe stopped, to catch him, make him stumble two steps ahead, look over, but it didn't happen.

The stands. Just go to the stands.

They were wooden, like Amarillo.

Jim Doe turned sideways to fit past a table and something snagged the back of his hand, stuck: a porcupine quill. From someone's traditional dress. Jim Doe unhooked it from his hand, looked around, couldn't find who.

Forty steps later, he was to the stands, and the old woman had been right: there *was* a bear under them. He could make out occasional patches of fur moving behind people's calves, eyes darting, nervous. Gregor Sandoval.

Jim Doe sat down on a seat three up from the rails, waited to feel the fur brush the leg of his pants. The second time, he caught it, but then it strained away. He lifted the bristles of black hair he'd kept, let them fall.

Next time, he held the porcupine quill down through a slit, waited for it to get pulled in. It did, all at once.

The fourth time, he was lying on his stomach, waiting.

'Greg,' he said.

The bear grunted, pawed.

'There's a man with a coyote head on,' Jim Doe said. 'He's behind me, I think.'

The bear looked, then backed up, to where Jim Doe could just make out his face.

'Greg,' Jim Doe said again. 'This man. Do you know him?'

Now the bear withdrew all the way, into the trash that hadn't been cleaned up from the rodeo or the monster trucks or the Ice Capades.

Jim Doe stood, walked to the stairs leading to the corridor under the stands, and took them, but slid through the rails halfway down the ramp. Under the stands too. He barely fit. He didn't look at the bear, just kept his eyes forward, sat down beside him, hugging his knees.

'You're from Oklahoma,' Jim Doe said.

The bear didn't respond.

Jim Doe closed his eyes, opened them back up.

'The man who put you in that cellar, Greg,' he said, like he didn't want to be saying it. Reminding.

The bear grunted, drew in smaller.

'. . . that's where bears live, right?' Jim Doe said. 'In cellars, dugouts?'

The bear's two small eyes looked over at him.

Jim Doe nodded.

'I'd like to be a bear too,' he said, 'maybe. Teeth, claws . . .'

The bear was still watching him, then not. Looking forward again, at a pair of bare legs walking along the third rows of bleachers. The third slat of light. A girl, maybe twelve, her calves smooth.

Jim Doe smiled, looking from the legs to the bear, then nodded ahead, like *do it*, and the bear smiled too, and only when it started to move forward did Jim Doe look at the legs again, and feel everything that was inside him drop, give just a little: her feet, no shoes.

Sarina.

It was too late already to stop the bear—Greg—from scaring her away again, back to Amarillo. Anything might break the moment: touching her, calling her, looking. Not looking.

Jim Doe drew himself in like the bear had, becoming smaller, an egg of himself, afraid, and when he looked up again the bear had pulled up short of the third slat of light. Like he knew not to touch her too.

He looked back to Jim Doe, saying something with his eyes.

Jim Doe just shook his head no. Please. Something. And then the girl with no shoes was there, between the two of them.

'He doesn't talk anymore,' she said to Jim Doe, about the bear. Greg. Gregor.

Jim Doe nodded.

'Natalya,' he just managed to say. From the list.

Russian front names, Mexican lasts: Indian.

Natalya held her hand out to him.

Jim Doe took it, just so that if she got pulled up into the sky, he could go too, this time.

Doe had been right: the left sleeve of Cody's jacket was ripe. He held it in the sink and just let the water run over it. Nobody used the sinks to either side of him. Not because of the smell, but the shoulder holster. Cody made himself look down, look down. Make no eye contact. But then it started anyway, maybe *because* he wouldn't look at anybody: a broad man in a bright shirt stood up in front of the urinals, as if he were rising whole from the rusted grate of the drain.

Cody leaned over to see him better in the mirror, then did it without even meaning to: made eye contact.

The broad man cocked his head, as if asking what Cody wanted. He didn't say anything though—just stood there listening to his cell. It was clapped hard to his ear, and he was leaning into it to hear better, starting to smile wide. It wasn't a good smile.

The man talked so that Cody had to hear: 'I don't know,' he said, panning around the bathroom. 'A full, blood, Indian, you say?' The way he hit each letter of the sentence, the term, made Cody play it back, get what he was supposed to get.

He smiled, then: *F,B,I.*

'Looks more BIA to me . . .' the man said, approaching Cody in the mirror. When he got within arm's reach, he palmed the mouthpiece of the phone, held it down close to his bright shirt.

'Special Agent Cody Mingus?' he said.

Cody looked around. Everyone was listening.

He nodded.

The man smiled again, deeper, shrugged, held the phone out. 'Think your cover's blown there,' he said.

Cody reached for the phone without thinking, and, once it was in his hand, recognized it: his. Fallen out of his jacket while he was cleaning the sleeve probably, skating across the small tiles, following the incline down to the drain.

The back of it was tacky against his palm.

'Yeah,' he said, into the mouthpiece, his eyes closed against this bathroom.

'Where are you?' Watts said.

Cody turned the water off.

'Kansas,' he said.

'You didn't get Tim,' she said.

'I know.'

'Can you talk?' Watts said, after leaving room for Cody to explain. Room he wasn't using.

'I can listen,' Cody said back.

'You've got the deputy sheriff,' she said.

'Yes,' Cody said, trying to towel the sleeve of his jacket dry. The paper towels just crumbled over it.

'Good,' Watts said. 'Listen. We've been wondering how he gets to the storms so fast—'

'If he's not really a fireman.'

'Which I think we can assume.

Cody nodded, worked his arm into the wet sleeve, switched ears to get the jacket all the way on.

'I'm going outside,' he said.

'What?'

'Nothing.'

'Agent Mingus?'

'How does he get there so fast, then?' Cody said.

Nothing, nothing. They weren't even supposed to be talking on a cell phone. Cody looked at it to be sure it was still on, then shook his head: the battery light. With his charger in the rental car, parked in a ditch in Trego Center.

'I don't have much longer,' he said.

'It's the German,' Watts said. 'He's been telling us all along. The Mennonites, they speak German.'

'Since fifteen thirty-six, yeah.'

'No,' Watts said. 'If you would have looked deeper, you'd have seen it. They had to move around a lot to avoid persecution. Along the way they picked up German, and then never let it go.'

Cody cocked his head then, sure there was some breathing on the line. Not him, not Watts.

'Did you route this?' he whispered, like that would help.

Watts wasn't listening.

'Tim thinks we can—' she said, got cut off.

'What?' Cody said.

After a long delay, just one word came through—'services'—then Watts was gone, the phone dead. That breathing still there.

'I can hear you,' Cody said, into it.

The breathing stopped, then the voice came through, soft, close: 'Careful, now.'

Cody held the phone before him and just looked at it for long moments, until he realized the smokers to either side of him had become quiet, were directing their faces out to the parking lot. Cody looked with them, just saw it: the coyote dog, only it was running along the roofs of the cars, maybe. Standing by Jim Doe's white supercab, like it was looking in.

Cody stepped out into the rain.

One of the cigarette men looked at him, then shook his head no. Cody went anyway, splashing after the dog. His whole jacket was wet now.

Because the dog was running on the roofs, it could move faster. And because it had four legs. Cody had to grab onto side mirrors to turn, and hood ornaments. The ones that came off in his hand he threw after the dog, didn't even know why he was chasing it, this dog, this coyote. Just that he had to. And then, suddenly, it wasn't a dog anymore: two cars over, the coyote head was still maybe two feet above the cars, but floating between them.

A man, with a skin on his head, his face painted black.

Cody fell back, saw the man's smile halogen white against his skin, then Cody was running, the coyote chasing him, the cigarette men at the wall watching and smoking, like this had all happened before. Cody ran and ran, covered in mud now, and one trunk he grabbed onto opened, and it was the one he'd already seen, with the dead deer, only the trunk was filling with water now. It made the deer look alive again, its eyes wet all over. Cody pushed away, ran harder, deeper into the parking lot, then slowed to a stop, breathing hard.

His gun.

He turned around, holding it, and the coyote ducked behind a car again, disappeared, looked up four rows over. As if waiting for Cody to see him. Cody didn't let himself run this time, just walked, pushing off from car to car, his steps loud now, the rain coming down harder, desperate, like it was trying to outrun something behind it: the hail.

It came down the size of marbles maybe, dancing off hoods, windshields shattering across the parking lot. Cody shrugged his jacket up over his shoulders, kept walking to where he'd seen the coyote head.

It was still there. On the ground, empty, black mouth pulled back into smile.

Cody knelt down, nudged it with the barrel of his gun, then stood.

He was being watched. Even out here he could feel it, with all the sound.

He turned slow, three sixty, looking between all the cars, cataloguing each side mirror, each vinyl roof, then moved onto headrests—the *insides* of the cars—and that was when he saw it: the car right beside him. There were two shapes in the backseat. Two small people, looking at him. Two children. Not moving.

He fell back against the opposite car, his gun splashing at his feet.

He fumbled for it, found it, lost it, found it again, and stood behind it, inching forward to the driver's side window, the hail sound muted now by the rush of blood in his head.

There *were* two small bodies in the backseat, belts across their laps, duct tape across their chests. Two children, their heads too large, their eyes sewn shut.

Cody threw up again, couldn't stop, pulled himself up with the door handle.

It swung open, the door.

The smell.

He covered his mouth with his sleeve again, made himself look inside—evidence—and settled into the driver's seat, sideways, never not looking at the children. Because if they moved.

And then he heard it, processed what he was hearing: footsteps, where he'd just been. A voice, saying *niction*, *niction*. The butt of some stick or lance coming through the glass on his side, taking him in the side of the face, so that his head spun around, the blood from his mouth slinging across the rearview mirror, across the reflection of the children, sitting there with their hands in their laps, waiting. It didn't knock him out, not all the way. The side of his face was across the passenger seat, and he could see, then, slowly, hear: the bits of shattered glass. They were falling into the door, and then the door was opening.

'Careful,' he tried to say. Maybe did.

For a long time then there was nothing, just a breathing, above him, watching, but then across the parking lot a truck started.

The form—the presence above him—laughed in his chest, leaned down to Cody's ear, said it again, but Cody heard it different this time: *nick shun*. And then he was alone for long minutes, until the truck pulled up behind the car, its headlights on. From the way the door closed, as if on a great, empty space, he knew it was the supercab. That that's why the coyote had been standing by it.

'Nichs hun,' he said, trying not to forget it, then the back of the front seat folded over him, pushing his face deeper into the fabric, a seat belt clicked, and he knew the children were crawling out, that by opening the door he'd released them into the night, and then, with that word—night—he got it, the word, the words. They were German, easy German, maybe even Mennonite German: *nicht schon*. What the Tin Man had already told him once, on the phone: *not yet, no*. Not yet.

52

31 MAY 1999

DODGE CITY, KANSAS

CODY woke in a robe of some kind. Brown—buffalo, maybe. Or bear. Wool. It had been draped over him, some of the long hair snagged in the CB unit under the dash.

Standing in the open door of the car was a twelve-year-old boy. He was eating a piece of bread with one hand, holding Cody's gun against his hip with the other.

Cody moved, flinched from the pain, then pulled himself up with the steering wheel.

'I'm guarding,' the boy said, his words clipped like Cody had already heard, last night, in a hundred Indians' mouths.

'. . . me?' Cody said.

The boy shook his head no, pointed the gun down to the robe.

'It's four hundred dollars,' he said.

Cody looked at it.

'Yours?' he said.

The boy just stared at him, chewing.

Cody took the fur in his finger, pulled the robe onto his lap.

'Trade?' he said—the gun for the robe.

The boy stopped chewing.

Somewhere in the parking lot three doors shut like firecrackers popping. A handful of white birds exploded into the morning.

'Okay,' he said, the boy.

Cody handed the robe over, took his gun by the barrel, rolled it around, already checking the clip.

'You should let my grandmother look at that,' the boy said, pointing loosely at the side of Cody's face.

'Maybe I'll just go to the doctor,' Cody said.

The boy shook his head, disappointed. 'She's a nurse, I mean,' he said.

Cody closed his eyes, exploring his face with his fingertips. It was open on the left side, and swollen. The muscles of his neck all strained, one side of his tongue chewed, the inner wall of his cheek ragged, the hair around his ear matted with blood. And the car. It still smelled of decay. Cody made himself look in the rearview mirror, steeled himself for it, but the backseat was empty, the tape that had been holding the children up even gone. Probably never there. And outside the open door, in the mud: no coyote pelt. All the tracks rounded off, vague.

Cody smiled, shook his head, leaned back into the seat like he was driving. The keys were even there, dangling from the ignition. A gift. He twisted them back, to dial in the news, see where the storm was last night—the Tin Man—but there was a tape in already. Cody looked at it as if committing it to memory. Just the shape. Because he wasn't sure what he wanted it to be.

But then it poured in from the back dash: Steely Dan. *The Royal Scam.*

Last night *had* happened.

He stood up, steadying himself on the car.

The parking lot was blowing trash, now, clumps of oil-stained grass; dirt. No Ford white supercab, just the occasional car, a wall of RVs on the east side. Cody walked into the exhibit building. It was the same as the parking lot: empty, abandoned. Like the fair had moved through, or the zoo. Cody picked through the trash to the bathroom, looked at his cheek in the mirror and tried to wash the dried blood off with water, where he could. Where it didn't hurt. For the first time in hours, then, he thought of Jim Doe. How he hadn't been there by the pillar when Cody'd walked out of the bathroom.

Cody shook his head at this—himself—then splashed enough water on his face that he had to close his eyes. When he opened them, there was a man in the mirror. A narrow man, this time, in a grinning Indian baseball cap. A Brave, maybe. The man was grinning the same. He was just moving through, didn't want to talk. It was like Cody wasn't there, even—like the narrow man was an automaton, on a track in the floor, that came in from the door, looped over to the urinal, then met back up with itself. Cody stepped in behind him, followed the narrow man on his silent walk back through the arena, to a door off one of the corridors on the other side of the arena.

It opened onto the area walled in by the RVs. A camp, the ash of last night's fires blowing, making everything pale. People asleep all around, unmoving. Pompeii. Husks. Cody picked through them, heard a rustle behind him—three grey figures, lifting, rising into a truck—then nothing.

Cody sat by a dead fire until the people around it stirred. They just looked at him, nodded. He nodded back.

'There was a storm last night,' he said. Not because he knew, but because there had to have been. And that's where Jim Doe would be. The Tin Man.

The woman looked away, to the west.

'We heard,' she said.

'What station?' Cody said.

She smiled.

'Moccasin telegraph, FBI.'

Cody looked away, with her.

'My friend was here,' he said.

She didn't say no.

'Bluff City,' she said, then laughed with her shoulders. 'It's just a town, though. Not even that.' Then she shrugged. 'Not anymore, anyways.'

'Nicht mehr,' Cody said, still thinking in German, from last night.

But then the woman answered.

'That's what I said,' she said, still looking west.

Cody turned to her.

'You're Indian,' he said.

'You FBI,' she said. 'Don't miss a thing, right?'

'How much does a buffalo robe go for?' Cody asked.

'To you?' she said back.

Cody smiled, looked away. To Bluff City.

'Three and a half, four hours,' she said. 'If you got a car.'

Cody nodded, almost in wonder.

'Yeah,' he said. 'I've got one.'

He took the car he'd come to in because the keys were in his pocket, then rolled into Bluff City just after nightfall, his phone too dead to call Creed in Wichita, Creed sitting at some phone Cody didn't even have the number for, anyway.

The Bluff City water tower was leaned over, like it was trying to look at something on the next street. The tornado had set down on the south side of town like a drill, then just stayed there. The dead weren't even counted yet.

Cody let his eyes adjust then walked in. The rain coming down was soft now, easy. Like the storm was apologizing. In the streets, men in homespun, simple clothes were wheelbarrowing shingles and galvanized drainage pipe to dump sites set up at the corner of each street. Like ants. Cody watched them for long minutes, until one of them got close enough to ask a question.

'You're Mennonite,' Cody said.

It wasn't really a question.

The man looked at him, his eyes fierce for a moment, then appeasing.

'What can I do for you?' he said.

Cody looked around, at Bluff City. How hard it had been trying to be something else, something bigger.

'You're not from this town,' Cody said.

The man shook his head no.

'We do what we can,' he said, his lips thin from the weight of the wheelbarrow.

'Which is . . . ?' Cody said.

'What Jesus would have done,' the man said: 'Help.'

Cody let the accusation glance off. Was the water tower leaning farther, now? He thought of Narcissus, for some reason. Looking at his reflection in the surface of the water.

'I'm sorry,' he said, finally, releasing the man. He watched him go. Tried to understand, couldn't; moved on.

Finally, after the paramedics had been pointing to him for some time, a trooper approached him, the catch peeled off the hammer of his service revolver.

'I'm not him,' Cody said.

'Who?'

'You know who,' Cody said, letting gravity unfold his ID. There were men in fatigues crawling over everything. The National Guard. 'Already?' Cody said, about them.

'They were on maneuvers already,' the trooper said.

'What about the Mennonites?' Cody said, watching the trooper's face now, for a reaction.

'A godsend,' the trooper said. 'Around here, anyway.'

'Around here?' Cody said, looking—the water tower?

'They're based out of Wichita,' the trooper said, like it was obvious.

Cody gave him his full attention, then.

'The *religion?*' he said.

The trooper smiled, his radio crackling.

'Mennonite Disaster Services,' he said. 'Thought you were FBI?'

Cody shook his head. 'Me too,' he said. 'Were they here first?'

The trooper nodded. 'Always are,' he said, looking importantly up to Cody for a moment. 'Sometimes even before, you know? You see them pouring into town, you go crawl under the bed.'

Cody closed his eyes, trying to imagine a way out of this, or into it. There were none.

'How do they know?' he said, finally.

The trooper spoke quieter now, shrugging like maybe he didn't believe it, even. 'They call him Jésus,' he said. 'Jésus Baptìs, I think. Because they—'

'—don't know where he comes from,' Cody said.

'Or where he goes,' the trooper added.

'Shit,' Cody said.

'What?'

'Have you accounted for all the children yet?'

'We're trying,' the trooper said.

'Try harder,' Cody said, already walking away, his black overcoat whipping around his legs. It was standard FBI issue. Under it, his suit was four days old now, maybe more. It hadn't been clean since the day before Enid, anyway, before Angel Dougherty. It made him feel like the angel of death, all in black, his collar blown up half across his face. The way the Mennonites were watching didn't help dispel the feeling, either.

Under his overcoat, in the slit he could reach through to his real pocket, he had his hand around his gun.

Jésus Baptìs. For someone with the initials JK.

The firemen that were already there had pink crosses on their helmets, and sleigh bells, tied to the second buttons of their jackets, on the idea probably that the Tin Man wouldn't be able to find pink tape *and* sleigh bells in the same store. Not this early in the season. And the bells were probably a certain size, too, some particular, midwestern timbre.

One of the firemen approached Cody. He sounded merrier than he was.

Cody didn't look right at him while they talked—at the pink cross—just kept scanning the debris.

'All your guys are accounted for?' he said.

'To the man,' the fireman said.

Cody nodded. 'Don't let me interrupt you,' he said.

The fireman shrugged, looking out, at the job ahead of them.

'Want a bell?' he said.

In the fireman's gloved hand it was silver, shiny.

'Sounds like Christmas,' Cody said.

'To him,' the fireman said, already walking away.

After he was gone, Cody stood with the bell in his hand, looking at it, then back up to the retreating fireman: he hadn't even asked for Cody's ID. Cody smiled, shook his head, pocketed the bell.

'Where are you . . .' he said as he walked, angling to what looked like residential.

It was full dark now, flashlight beams crisscrossing the sky.

Cody stayed close to the walls, moved, moved, following first one fireman, then another. They were just shoring up walls. Calling out for people under the sidewalks. Walking around the bicycles and barbecue grills hanging from the overhead wires. Directing people to the community center. Cots were on the way, and a Red Cross truck, and ambulances, and portable phones. There were so many non-emergency personnel, even aside from the Mennonites. Too many to track. Instead, Cody did what he thought the Tin Man had to do, when he first rolled into these towns: dug up a phonebook, ran his finger down the columns, for the Indian names.

There were four, at least. The rest had Anglo names, or weren't listed.

Three of the four lived on the same road, though.

Cody tore the page out, took it to a man standing in a bathrobe, no shoes.

'This,' Cody said, pointing to the Indians' names, their addresses.

The man lifted his hand to the east.

'Redtown,' he said, laughing at it. At *some*thing. It was forced, though.

Three families.

Instead of going to the end of the block, Cody just walked through a destroyed house, trying hard not to step on the toys there, like that would curse him. Or curse him more.

The trailers were all still there, too. Candles flickering in the windows.

Cody knocked on the door, stepped back.

A man with a black crew cut answered.

'Yeah?' he said, looking at Cody's black clothes.

'FBI,' Cody said.

The man laughed.

'That's the first thing you have to say now, right?' he said.

Cody just stared, holding the bell in his pocket silent.

'Children,' he said, in explanation. 'We're just checking—'

'Tin Man,' the man said. 'Yeah, yeah. Shit. They're already down there, man. Safe.'

Cody looked at him, making sure he'd heard right.

'Down there?' he said.

The man nodded. 'When we saw it coming, y'know. All the kids. The Army put them all in the basement at the library. Just to be sure.'

The Army, the Guard. But they hadn't gotten there until *after* the storm.

Cody looked back, towards town.

'The library,' he said.

'So they could do their homework,' the man said.

Cody chewed his cheek.

'It's June,' he said.

The man just stared.

'Can you tell me where the library is?' Cody said.

He was here, then. The Tin Man. Or had been.

Cody stopped the first Mennonite he came to.

'Jésus Baptìs,' he said.

The Mennonite stood from his work, stared at Cody, then hooked a long index finger downstreet, downtown. Cody nodded thanks, walked on. People were crawling over the debris on fingertips, the water tower watching them all, peering closer and closer. Where Jésus Baptìs was supposed to be, Cody found his first uncounted dead. He was sitting in a car, in the driver's seat. Cody turned to wave somebody over, but then stopped, with his hand in the air. Looked back to the man.

He didn't have any shoes on. Jeans, a T-shirt, but no shoes.

Cody stood, suddenly: or *boots*.

It was a fireman, stuffed into the car, hidden. His pink-striped helmet moving through town without him, sleigh bells jingling. The Tin Man wearing his boots.

Cody started shambling, running, in every direction—back to residential, maybe, *any*where, wherever *he* was, or might be—but then tripped on a dress or skirt. Rolled over to untangle it from his shoes. It was when he saw he wasn't alone.

Standing over him was a fireman. The fireman.

He was smiling.

'I didn't expect you here so soon,' he said, offering a hand to Cody.

Cody hesitated, then took it, just to have hold of the Tin Man at last.

He hauled Cody up.

'The children?' Cody said.

'Safe,' the Tin Man said. Kulpin, James Kulpin.

'You're not getting out of here,' Cody said. 'Whatever you do to me.'

The Tin Man shrugged, like it didn't matter anymore.

'Take me in, then,' he said, offering his wrists.

'The children,' Cody said.

The Tin Man smiled again.

'The children,' he said, 'yes,' turning his head slightly away from another fireman, angling across the road a few yards up.

Cody shook his head without letting his eyes lose Kulpin for a moment.

'Where are they?' he said.

The Tin Man shrugged.

'I could show you,' he said.

'Your ear's bleeding,' Cody said.

The Tin Man raised a gloved fingertip to it—his ear, brought it back red. Nodded: yes, his ear *was* bleeding.

'My eustachian canal,' he said, walking ahead. 'The valve between the inner ear and the back of the throat? Gone.' He smiled. 'Usually the blood just drains down into my mouth.'

'We know what you're doing,' Cody said.

'Oh?' he said, still walking, stepping between two houses, still mostly standing.

'Jim Doe,' Cody said. 'It's all about him. You want him to . . . kill you. Like you did for Wiggs.'

The Tin Man didn't say yes or no, just moved his head, as if in appreciation. Or thought.

'Sometimes,' he said. 'Sometimes I think it's best if I *don't* take them, y'know?'

Cody was staring at his back. 'You look so normal,' he said.

The Tin Man turned, flashing a conservative smile. 'So do you,' he said.

'Where are they?' Cody said.

The Tin Man stepped back, presenting a window. A basement window.

'Now,' he said. 'You go make sure they're all right, I walk.'

Cody shook his head no. 'You never walk,' he said.

The Tin Man smiled. 'I can walk on anything, Agent Mingus. Haven't you heard?'

'You're not—' Cody started to say, but then something was happening: the Tin Man was *climbing* him, inserting something into his neck. A needle. It happened so fast. Cody got his hand up like he meant to, in defense, but there was no gun, just a bell, a merry little sound, jing-jing-jingling.

The Tin Man laughed.

'*Jetzt*,' he said, into Cody's ear.

Now.

Then Bluff City drew itself down to a pinpoint of light and stayed there for Cody didn't know how long. Time didn't really matter anymore. It was soft, something he could move in, in whatever direction. But then he stood up from it. The two children were lying unconscious by the basement window. Cody smiled, collected them in his arms, and stood, walking with them back into the street. To give them to somebody. As he walked he kept thinking about where Jesus was born. That he'd walked on water.

The street was empty, everyone collapsed onto some emergency in residential—a woman trapped under a couch, under a roof; a boy sucked up into a chimney. One of a hundred possible things, the thousand impossible. Cody smiled, thinking about it, then tried to separate the new sound he was hearing from all the other sounds. It was a sound he knew, but from a long time ago.

His neck was bleeding, from the needle. He could feel the blood.

And the facemask. His breath collecting on the backside of it.

Tuinol. That was what he had. It was like sitting in the dentist's chair. The children were light under his arm, sacks, their heads lolling, faces hidden by their hair. One of them was moaning, it was hard to tell which. Cody stood for a moment, just listening, to them at first, how they were *alive* this time, unstolen, then to the sound he was used to but couldn't remember. A plastic sound. And then he wasn't alone on the road anymore: someone was standing at the other end of the street.

Cody smiled, laughed: Jim Doe. Here.

He couldn't sneak them out, this time, he wanted to say, holding the children up. *We saved two of them.*

Jim Doe was just staring at him. Like he wasn't recognizing him. And then Cody got it—the sound: rain, falling on him, but not getting him wet. Hitting his raincoat. He looked down, to the side: he was yellow. The Tin Man had dressed him reflective yellow. And his head, the reason it wasn't moving right, it wasn't his strained neck, it was the helmet. Why he had a facemask. It wouldn't shake off.

He took a step back from Jim Doe, shaking his head no, but it was too late, the moment sluggish: Jim Doe's hand was already exploding in flame. The only safe place to shoot Cody, too, was in the chest, between the children.

It didn't make any sound, even, just heat, pushing him back, back, the children sloughing down the side of his leg, one of them catching on the top lip of his boot, then not.

This was it.

He felt his mouth grinning—to finally get to *rest*. Not have to *think*.

And then Jim Doe was standing over him. Cody was either seeing him or hearing him or smelling him, he could no longer separate his senses. All at once, maybe.

Jim Doe fell to his knees, tried to cradle Cody's head.

He was saying something but there were no words, just the water tower behind him, its knee folding out at last, the head crashing down to the street face first.

Cody thought he could feel the rain, finally. In his wound. In the hole in him.

He wanted to tell Jim Doe everything, but the two times he opened his mouth, nothing came out. And Jim Doe was trying to listen.

'. . . Jesus,' Cody said, laughing, inside at least. 'Jessie—Jesse James . . . good buddy. Jesse James.'

It was funny, perfect, right.

Cody leaned back then, to see over Jim Doe's head. The sky, dark, no stars, just cold lines of water lancing down. Up through them, impossibly high, a small plane moving through the thin air like a silver cigar, like a steely dan, Watts inside, thinking about him, maybe, Cody, Agent Mingus, middle name Wayne. Thinking about him as if he were alive.

53

31 MAY 1999

BLUFF CITY, KANSAS

JIM Doe had heard about Sheriff Debs on the way into Bluff City, seen him rising from the smoldering sawdust, his skull slick and red, then angling his gun up at the officers outside, his wife stepping between at the last moment. And then, just outside Wichita, filling up the 1982 town car he'd bought at the pow-wow, for all the money he had left from his father, there face-up on the newspaper rack was the picture nobody'd had for seventeen years: a fireman walking through a broken town—McCook—a dark-haired child under each arm. Like a hero. Like Cody. Buffalo Bill.

He'd thought it was him, the Tin Man.

It *had* been him.

Jim Doe stood from the body just for an instant before the wall of water took him from behind, slinging him over Cody, into the side of a van. Then he stood from that too, watching the waters recede, paramedics swarming the scene, each other, the yellow slicker washing back and forth between them, the red washed off.

Jim Doe stood for long minutes, waiting for someone to walk up with handcuffs. It didn't matter who. But Cody had been alone, it looked like. No back-up, Creed still sitting in the airport, Watts still on the phone.

It was only when he tried to nose the gun back into his waistband that Jim Doe saw more than felt his forearm: it was wrong, broken. One bone or both; both. He dropped the gun. Walked away, not saying *Dorothy* anymore but *Agnes*. That he still had one good arm, one good hand.

From a phone booth in Oklahoma, just east of Sand Creek, Jim Doe called Monica again. She wasn't there.

'Yeah?' a voice said. Deep, male, tired: Creed.

Jim Doe swallowed.

'Kind of figured you'd call here,' he said—Creed.

Jim Doe still wasn't saying anything.

The town car was idling behind him.

Creed laughed, far back in his throat it sounded like.

'He was wearing a yellow jacket,' Jim Doe said.

Creed didn't answer.

'Who?' he said.

Jim Doe closed his eyes, lied: 'Him.'

'Did he get more kids?' Creed said.

'No.'

'Agent Mingus?' Creed said then, forcing it. Like he'd already gotten the call.

'We lost each other in Dodge City,' Jim Doe said, finally.

'Dodge City,' Creed said back to him.

'Where's Monica?' Jim Doe said.

'Ask her,' Creed said.

Jim Doe didn't, just listened, then, from closer somehow—not wherever Creed was—Monica: 'Hi, Jim.'

'Mon,' Jim Doe said.

'Anything Castro County can do for you today?'

Jim Doe smiled. It was her receptionist voice, the one she saved for when she had to cover someone else's shift.

'Jesse James,' Jim Doe said, to both of them.

Creed was the one to answer this time.

'Wiggs,' he said.

'Wiggs?' Jim Doe said, back.

'Steely Dan,' Creed said. 'Why?'

'I don't know yet,' Jim Doe said.

'He's dead, you know,' Creed said.

'Does that matter?' Jim Doe said.

Creed laughed, just a little.

'What in particular do you want?' he said.

There was no other way to say it: 'His handle,' Jim Doe said. 'His call sign.'

It was what Cody's *good buddy* had to have meant—trademark Rosco P Coltrane. He couldn't talk on the CB without saying it.

'His call sign,' Creed said.

Jim Doe nodded.

'Give me a minute here . . .' Creed said.

'Jim?' Monica whispered, while Creed was looking. As if Creed couldn't hear.

Jim Doe didn't answer.

Creed read the handle out like all old men do: 'Gary, Baker, the number four—that's *four*—Harry, King.'

Gary Baker for Harry King.

It was like a celebrity endorsement.

'Why are you doing this?' Jim Doe said, instead of thanks.

'Did the kid not tell you?' Creed said.

Jim Doe shook his head no. 'What?' he said.

'He wants you,' Creed said. 'This . . . this Kulpin. James Kulpin. You're the only one he'd ever let get close enough to—to—'

Jim Doe said it after he hung up: 'I know.'

It was the only reason Creed had even talked to him.

He drove the town car to the highest rise he could find, killed the lights, dialed low on the citizen's band, and started saying it over and over as he went up through the channels—*GB4HK*—holding the mike left-handed, backwards.

It only took ten minutes to get an answer.

It was what he'd already been saying: *GB4HK*. Like a question.

'James,' Jim Doe said.

The Tin Man laughed into his mike.

'I could say the same thing about you,' he said.

'Where are you?'

'. . . it's like,' the Tin Man said, was saying, 'it's like, I don't even know. Do you know sunspots, Jim? Maybe you're just bouncing your own signal off one here, just talking to the way you're going to be. Me.'

'Sarina,' Jim Doe said, in answer.

'Yes,' the Tin Man said.

'They're using me to get to you,' Jim Doe said.

'You're smarter than them, though, Jim.'

'Where are you?'

The Tin Man keyed off for a few moments. Jim Doe stared him back on.

'I could tell you,' he said—the Tin Man. 'But I'd be gone.'

'Where?'

'The storm, Jim. Come on.'

'You don't know where it's going to hit.'

'I've got a fair idea, you could say.'

'This is never going to work if I'm not there,' Jim Doe said.

Again, the Tin Man keyed off. When he came back on, then, he was different. Strained.

'Read the Bible much?' he said.

'I'm Indian,' Jim Doe said.

'I know,' the Tin Man said. 'But Jesus. You know where he was . . . con*ceived*, right?'

'Bethlehem,' Jim Doe said.

'*Listen*,' the Tin Man said. 'Think.'

'This is a joke, right?' Jim Doe said.

'Only in the sense that everything is,' the Tin Man said.

'Where, then?'

The Tin Man laughed: 'One more chance, James.'

'Now you're the one talking to yourself.'

'And you're the one wasting time. Now. Nineteen forty-seven. That too.'

1947?

'A white horse rides through,' the Tin Man said.

'This is bullshit.'

'Not to you, James.'

Jim Doe lowered his head to the mike, thinking it—*1947*, *1947*, *1947*—and then there was Cody, in White Horse. Oklahoma.

'The Sandovals,' Jim Doe said.

'Good,' the Tin Man said. 'But go over Woodward instead. Back over.'

Jim Doe looked there, to White Horse—northwest. North. The other way was south. Towards Texas. Through Woodward. He breathed out, got it: *over* Woodward. To Whitedeer. Where the tornado had started in 1947. Like some decades-long weather pattern was repeating itself, coming full circle, but there was a circle within *that*, too: where Jesus *wasn't* born, where he was con*ceived*—in a straight line down through Whitedeer. To Nazareth.

'Tonight?' Jim Doe said.

'Does it matter?' the Tin Man said back.

Jim Doe held the mike to his chin, shook his head no.

The Tin Man didn't come back, *good buddy*. Just left it at that.

Jim Doe sat there a long time, looking south, to the bank of clouds still sweeping down into Texas.

Nazareth.

He shook his head, got back onto the blacktop, and kept the town car to a reasonable sixty, whipping past the old Indian man on the side of the road before realizing who he was. He hit the brakes then, the tail end of the car rising, putting all the weight on the front discs. In the mirror, the old man was walking, trying to catch up with the car. When Jim Doe turned to look over his shoulder, he was alone. An old Indian trick. He shook his head and pulled forward, into Texas.

54

31 MAY 1999

BUFFALO, OKLAHOMA

HE was throwing up in the ditch again. Amos. Pills, pills, the great heaping handfuls he had swallowed when Father was there at the pow-wow last night, unbidden, unexpected, the water beading off his suede jacket.

'Amos,' he had said, in his too-soft Mr. Rogers voice, like he was surprised, like anything with him could ever be chance, but then before he could say the neighborhood part—blinding Amos in the head—Amos had swiveled away, into some Comanche regalia from a wet cardboard box, then, from across the arena, his way out stepped into view: the other him, the one that had split off, chased him up out of Texas. He was there.

Amos smiled, his face heavy from the black paint, his fingers dully pushing the floating bits of bone around under the skin of his side, like a Ouija board, the blood welling up as high as it could around the line of fist-sized hematomas. At least Father had left him his teeth. His smile.

But he had power now, too, tied to his belt: the scalp of the fat sheriff who had tried to kill him, the sheriff he'd already killed once, that he'd found in the morgue with the other dead. People hardly ever died all the way, though. Not him, not Father, not the Texas deputy, not any of them.

He threw up in the ditch until he was throwing up blood, and then he touched his side, and it was blood too.

He still had the leggings on from last night. His face, too—he didn't know if it was still black. Probably.

All it had taken to lose Father last night had been touching the Texas deputy on the wrist. They looked enough the same that Amos was able to slip away, take the deputy's truck even, *proving* they'd traded places, and then it was just driving, driving, driving. Taking these last children home, to Nazareth, because once everything was done, finished, he would get to go back to Pawnee City finally, sit in his car in his mother's driveway until she walked out late in the afternoon, found him there, led him to the front door again, where he could explain about Amanda. Let her tell him it was all right, that having one of them back was better than not getting either.

But Nazareth. First Nazareth.

Amos stood, pulling himself up with the seatbelt of the supercab, and folded the seat down to look at the children for a moment, see if they were still belted in or had gotten up on their knees again to watch out the back window. They were just sitting there. Amos nodded, blacked out on his feet then came back an instant later, a half-step ahead of himself. Something had changed, though: on the seat, under the papers that had been there, was another paper. A picture: Sarina. Her face, the FBI's picture of her face. How she had looked at first.

Amos fell to his knees, smiling.

Sarina. There. Sitting the backseat too.

He put her back together as best he could, the front seat folded forward, his numb fingers tying the picture over her face with a long piece of robbed string, doing it over and over, getting it just right, *perfect*, so that her mouth would match up with her mouth, so she could talk to him again, like in the basement, telling him the impossible: that she'd already been there five *years*.

Amos laughed, heard himself laugh too, like he was talking to himself through a long and complicated pipe, and then, because he hadn't been paying enough attention, his world collapsed all around him: on his shoulder, suddenly, was a hand. In a glove. Amos turned, his mouth already shaped like a scream, and it was a fireman.

Amos slid down the side of the truck, his breath coming in gasps, then not at all.

The firemen knelt after him, cupped his gloved hand over Amos's mouth.

Amos's shoulders caved in around the hand, his back bowing into the shopmade running board of the supercab.

'. . . you okay?' the fireman was saying.

Behind him was his truck. Not a regular fire engine, but a red one-ton GMC. For the chief. There was another fireman behind the wheel, doing something with the radio. Both wearing the yellow jackets.

Amos shook his head no, no, he wasn't okay. Ever again.

The fireman took his hand anyway, pulled him up.

Running behind them now was a river of water, crashing down a draw, higher than the fence.

Amos smiled.

'I couldn't . . .' he said, '. . . the truck.'

The fireman understood: the water was too deep to cross. And it was. But the truck was pointed the wrong way, too. Like it had already crossed.

He walked closer to look, at the water.

Amos Pease followed.

'Did you see my . . . the children?' he said, softly, and the fireman turned to him, to the jump seat of the supercab, and Amos felt the air on his teeth and knew he was smiling.

'What about them?' the fireman said.

'They're dead,' Amos said, blood running from his mouth now.

The fireman took an involuntary step back, into the running water, to see Amos better maybe, re*hear* what he'd said, but then the water grabbed at him, hungry, his right arm clutching up for Amos's. Amos let him hold on for a moment, long enough for the river behind him to become a different river, different water, and then he stepped forward, the water up to the fireman's waist suddenly. He was shaking his head no. Amos started shaking his head no too, that he understood, but then he stepped in deeper, up to his knees, the fireman off his feet now, his only anchor Amos.

'Don't worry,' Amos said, 'I've done this before, see,' and then let the fireman go, the barbed wire strands on the backside of the ditch either cutting him into sections or holding him there for the water to wear away, Amos didn't watch.

He went to the back of the fire-engine red truck.

There was an old yellow jacket there, a helmet standing rainwater.

Amos put it on, the water running down his broken-in side, the skin drawing up from it.

There was an axe, too. And the door of the truck opening, closing.

'—he . . . he fell *in*,' Amos said, into his chest, trying to get the stresses right, then showed the axe. 'I think we can reach him with this, though.'

The other fireman was already at the water's edge, stepping in up to his waist.

Amos set the outside of his foot against the outside of the fireman's heavy boot, then held his hand out, for the fireman to pull against, so he could reach deeper.

The fireman took it without thinking, and they edged out into the current, until Amos felt his foot sliding over an inch at a time.

'He's down there,' Amos said, lifting his chin to the fence, the fireman's weight pulling him in two.

'Where?' the fireman was saying, screaming.

'Here,' Amos said, bringing his other hand around to the fireman. It was the hand holding the axe, far down the handle. The point-end caught the fireman in the chest, and he looked down at it, up to Amos, and then disappeared.

Amos nodded. This was what he was made for.

They wouldn't find these two until tomorrow, if then. And by then it wouldn't matter.

He pushed the truck in behind them anyway, then dry-heaved again, birthing a small bitter pill into his throat, one he didn't remember taking. He chewed it, the powder numbing his gums, and looked around. The world was still grey, pale.

He was going to make it, too. Only a few more hours.

He sat down in the front seat of the supercab, still in the yellow jacket, the yellow hat. In the rearview mirror the children were just staring, waiting.

'We're almost there,' Amos told them, in the calmest voice he had.

Something moved in the backseat, though. *Was* moving.

It was the boy—Jerry, Jerbait?—trying to open his eyes, flakes of black skin falling down onto the tops of his arms.

'You're not him,' he said. Father.

Amos smiled, opened his mouth, to say something—ask if he wanted the sirens on, maybe—but then saw her again, Sarina, sitting beside the boy, the photograph still tied over her face with the long piece of string. Her hands were moving in her lap, nervous. Amos stilled them.

55

31 MAY 1999

JERICHO, TEXAS

FOR his grand finale James Kulpin became Richard Beaux again. The dead one, walking around. He laughed: a *zombie*. Who Jesse James the Scurvy Brother had been writing to in the newspapers, in 1978. But James Kulpin hated Steely Dan, only played it for Creed. To keep Jessie Wiggs alive for him, the way Creed had kept him alive for James Kulpin, when Kulpin was twenty-two, watching a motel television. By then he'd convinced himself all the pictures he still had were fakes—actors, mannequins, props. Part of Jessie Wiggs's elaborate set of manufactured psychoses. But then Tim Creed the mankiller killer had materialized on the ten o'clock news, growling into a microphone. Matching *up* with one of those pictures. Making it real all over. More real.

Richard Beaux shifted into sixth.

He was in a lineman's truck again. It felt good. He even had the lights up top on, because nobody would stop a lineman in this weather, not even one from Oklahoma. And the only person who could report it stolen was in the bucket, staring at the sky. His hands tied behind him for good measure, but he wasn't going anywhere. The one good thing he'd had—besides the truck, the company coveralls, the insulated boots—was a ski mask. One with a big oval for the face. It hid the blood seeping from Richard Beaux's ear. And the fabric didn't get in the way at all: with the windows down, he could sense the pressure like a bird, maybe.

It was definitely Castro County, anyway, or close: Lamb, Parmer, Deaf Smith.

At the swinging yellow light in Jericho he killed the truck, listening. To the sky.

But then another truck drowned it out, right beside him, going the other way but not: stopped. A lineman.

He nodded to Richard Beaux.

'She won't go?' he said—the truck.

Richard Beaux shook his head no, that wasn't it.

The other lineman was reading the Oklahoma off the door. He looked from it up to Richard Beaux. James Kulpin. The Tin Man.

'Volunteer,' he said.

The other lineman looked around.

'For what?' he said.

'What's your call?' Beaux said.

The lineman shrugged, bifocaled down to his clipboard.

'Usual,' he said.

Beaux nodded, like that was one thing he understood: the usual.

He started his truck.

'It's about to storm down there,' he said, nodding south, southwest.

The lineman hooked his elbow down his door, ratcheted his head out, to look.

'Ugly as hell,' he said. 'But shit. Sun won't heat it up till this afternoon, I don't figure.'

Beaux—*Kulpin*—nodded, let a wave of nausea wash over him, radiating out from his liver. It was coated in chocolate. Punishment.

'You all right?' the lineman asked, aiming a cigarette into his lips.

Kulpin ignored the question: he was the Tin Man. Of course he was all right.

'Some of them bad boys,' he said, nodding down to the supercell, already changed from half a minute ago. 'They make their own heat, y'know? Like from the inside . . .'

The lineman shrugged like it didn't really matter, he was going to be out in the shit *any*way, then rolled the wheel on his lighter, leaning his face over for the delicate flame, and Kulpin said it: 'I'm the Tin Man.'

The lineman didn't flinch, just inhaled deep and closed his eyes, holding it in. 'Say again?' he said.

Kulpin just kept looking south, his arms folded over the wheel. He shrugged like it had been nothing. 'Those'll kill you,' he said—the cigarettes.

'Like I'm gonna live that long,' the lineman said, leaning into the clutch, straightening his arm for first gear, lifting his other hand to his eyebrow in farewell, the remnants of a military stint, maybe. Or time spent under a wide-brimmed hat.

James Kulpin nodded back, straightening his own arm against first, and eased away, smiling, free of guilt, because he'd told somebody where he was going, who he was.

It was their own fault if they didn't stop him.

56

1 JUNE 1999

DIMMIT, TEXAS

IT felt like high school again, for Watts, sitting with her shoulders drawn in, in the front seat of a pick-up truck, going to another place she knew nothing about: Texas. Because something was supposed to be going on there.

The two Rangers escorting her up from Lubbock had barely even introduced themselves.

'Let me guess,' Watts said. 'You always get your guy?'

The taller one, the driver—McKirkle—had smiled behind his hand, shrugged. 'Sometimes they hear us coming, ma'am,' he said. 'Just take care of it for us, y'know?'

Ma'am.

The one with the handlebar moustache, Maines, had reached for the handle of her overnight bag then, his motions stiff, jerky.

Watts stepped out of the airport. The sky was green, sick. All the way to Nazareth, which was dead, nothing. No Tin Man, no Jim Doe. Creed was supposed to meet them there, in some church parking lot. Another church parking lot.

'You sure?' Maines asked.

All there was was a church van, layered in paint.

They sat watching the weather develop for two hours, until McKirkle leaned over to the dash, spit into the cup, and nodded west. Maines's moustache moved like a smile, maybe. Watts leaned forward, to see too, and for a moment forgot how to breathe: a funnel was forming, the clouds above it rotating slow, immense. A hole they were going to fall up into.

'We should—' she said, didn't know *what* they should do.

McKirkle was shrugging it off, though, and then, in the road before them, St. Joseph, a truck stopped and a boy in a sleeveless shirt and backwards cap stepped down from the cab, reached behind his seat, and came up with a slender rifle. He lifted it against the sky, pulling the trigger again and again, against the storm, and all at once Watts understood the world for a moment, and this boy's place in it. Hers. That this is what you did.

The cloud took its funnel back, too.

Watts's eyes were wet.

'How many'd you count?' Maines was saying.

'Sixteen,' McKirkle said.

They were talking about the boy's gun, missing the boy completely. How he'd looked down the line his barrel made, like it mattered.

The truck started between McKirkle's thumb and forefinger.

'Browning,' Maines said as they pulled away—the *kind* of gun that held sixteen shots, no more, no less—and Watts wanted to scream, didn't. Just asked where they were going.

McKirkle nodded up, to the retracted funnel.

'It's already been here,' he said. 'Few years back.'

'Nineteen eighty-two,' Watts said.

McKirkle nodded. 'Why you think that water tower's so white?' he said.

'So?' Watts said.

Maines smiled, spit.

'It's never been to Dimmit, best of my knowledge,' he said, hooking his chin west again.

They were talking about it like it was *one* storm. As if it had a memory.

'What about my partner?' she said.

'FBI?' Maines said.

McKirkle smiled, accelerating. 'He'll see it,' he said.

Twenty minutes later, Sheila Watts nodded: he *would* see it, God.

It was moving through Dimmit, one of the four grain elevators going end over end down the main street, its seed pitting everything that was.

'Jarrel,' McKirkle said, to Maines.

Maines spit, nodded, and then the truck started moving across the highway, sideways. The seed was like marbles.

Watts thought that maybe she was screaming, but couldn't hear it above the wind. The definite fact that their windshield was about to shatter in on them.

McKirkle smiled.

'Welcome to Texas, ma'am,' he said.

The numbers and letters written on the dust on the dashboard—where she'd been instructed *not* to touch—was the license plate of the stolen line truck. Watts knew it had been a real call when the lineman on the other end said he was calling from Jericho, looking hard over his shoulder the whole time, smoking like a train. The James Kulpin she almost knew would go far out of his way for a town called Jericho. But here. He was having to come *here* to see the walls come tumbling down. And they were. It was like the buildings were exploding.

'You think?' McKirkle said, pointing a meaty finger through the windshield.

Maines leaned forward, tipping his hat back.

It was a white bucket truck, parked on the railroad tracks, like it had driven down them to get here.

'Could be,' he said.

'Well,' McKirkle said, looking to Watts. 'You want him, right?'

Behind the truck was the tornado. But it was ropy thin, already dissipating, spinning out. The sky was full of newspaper, now, and leaves, and plastic shopping bags, and grain, and, every few seconds, a parking curb, a mailbox, a chimney. Softer things.

McKirkle killed the truck, let it coast up onto what had been a lawn. Both doors opened. The three of them stepped down. The first thing to hit Watts was the smell—the musty insides of trees, not open for two centuries probably, before Texas was Texas. And under that the stagnant water of iron pipes. Whatever had been fermenting at the bottom of the grain silo. Blood.

Watts stepped where Maines stepped at first, the ground too still for all this to have just happened, and then all three of them saw it at once: a yellow figure moving among the ruins, away from them. A ghost.

'Time to meet the fucking Wizard,' McKirkle said, spitting a lone, brown line down into the ground by his boot, his hand already rising with his gun then coming up fast, his body slamming down into a crouch: helicopters.

Watts turned her face up to them.

The National Guard, already on emergency alert. Setting down around Dimmit like Valkyrie, to ferry off the dead.

Watts palmed her gun, kicked out of the shoes she'd worn on the airplane, and followed the Rangers.

Creed stepped down from the helicopter, already rolling out into the field, to make way for the ones behind him. In 1971, the joke had been that it was easier to just step out of the transport and into your body bag. Creed looked over his shoulder on accident for a moment, at the line of soldiers, and had to look away then.

The car he'd finally rented out of Wichita was in Bluff City now. His hands were shaking like 1978 too, standing outside the motel room door of Jessie Wiggs, and on the lift over he'd kept having to close his eyes, so the guards wouldn't see inside him. Because they would have just gone ahead and jumped.

He had the slug from Wiggs in the chamber now. Again. For Mr. Rogers. For Cody. He kept imagining scenarios where Kulpin would have the drop on him, from behind, and Creed would just smile where Kulpin couldn't see, then shoot through his own spine at Kulpin's softer parts. At his face.

He walked what was left of the roads with his tie loose and the gun by his side, daring Kulpin to step out.

He wondered if he and Marcia had driven through here on their honeymoon.

He tried to count the dead, but they were too many: the sixteen children they knew about, the rest they didn't; the parole officer and his family; the Colesons, in Bethel, Tennessee; the two officers there; the man in the refrigerator in the basement of Roanoke, and the other lab specimens before him; the agent in Roanoke. James Booth, walking to the store for bread or milk or something normal, then seeing an RV coming down the road for him—same make as his, same model—and stepping out into the road before it, *for* it.

It was best that Sheila was in Nazareth still. He didn't want her to see this, see him.

A parking curb fell from the sky, stood end-up for a moment in the asphalt, then the concrete crumbled away, leaving just the rebar underneath. Creed watched it, and the space after it—a corridor cutting across three blocks, impossible when the houses had been standing—and there, small, moving, was a man not in fatigues, and not in a yellow firecoat. An Indian, which was what Kulpin was probably dressed up as now, after scalping that sheriff in Garden City.

It would be his last disguise.

Creed held his gun low and paced the Indian north, drawing closer and closer to him, stepping through the remains of one house after another. The air was humid, thick. It kept pressing on him. It didn't matter, though.

One house he walked through still had the television on, sideways, the picture rolling, the horizontal shot.

Lying alongside it, as if to see better, adjust, was a man, dead.

On-screen, through a telephoto lens, was Creed in his faded charcoal suit, just walking into the living room. Everything else in color but him, his clothes.

He stood, panning for the camera, the great antenna standing up from a news van, but the town was too broken to make out any metal that didn't fit. A guardsman approached, looked from the dead man to Creed.

'Here's one,' Creed said.

He was wearing his badge in his shirt pocket.

When he stepped down onto the next street, the Indian was gone. But moving too. Just ahead, to the side. Creed walked at an angle for the next street, to walk up behind the Indian, but the displaced roof he stepped onto to get across groaned.

Creed stepped down.

There was a boy under there. Dark, probably Mexican. His upper half was pressed under a crossbeam, his right leg jerking, pedaling a spot smooth in the dirt.

Creed looked from the boy to the next street, twice, then finally holstered his gun, leaned under the roof. It smelled like pine, and there was still fiberglass glittering in the air.

'Here,' Creed said, touching the boy's leg in case the boy couldn't hear, or was in shock, but the instant he touched the leg, it slithered away, and he saw: the boy had scraped the dirt and grass away from *under* the beam, worked himself in from the other side.

Creed stood too fast, into a ceiling sharp with roofing nails. Each was maybe a quarter-inch too long, or else the air-hammer had been jacked up too high, driven them too deep. They pushed into him and he pulled away on instinct, even after he knew what they were, and rolled, shooting holes in the board. Beams of lights formed along the path his bullets had taken. They all came back to him.

'Pretty,' somebody said from the darkness around him.

The boy. He was ripping silver strips of duct tape from a roll, hanging them from the underside of the roof.

From another darkness then, a girl stepped forward—fourteen, maybe. And definitely Indian. Something in her hand, trailing string.

'You wouldn't shoot a girl now,' she said, like she was ducking into the words. 'Would you, Mr. Creed?'

The boy on the other side laughed.

'You're—' Creed said, tried to i*mag*ine. Them. The children.

'Paul,' the boy said, about himself, then nodded to the girl. 'Gina.'

'. . . Roanoke,' Creed said. The thing trailing facedown from the girl's hand was an *Oz* mask. The Tin Man. Something else too: stabbing up from the center of her palm so that the needle nestled into her wrist, a syringe of amber liquid. The Yellow Brick Road. For Creed. And the mask.

'Good,' the girl said, stepping forward.

'No,' Creed said to her, raising the gun again, his good slug screaming out over Texas now like a cartoon, pushing a bit of shingle before it. '*No*,' he said, again, the skin of his finger on the trigger going white with pressure, all that blood rushing to the hollow space behind his eyes, in his throat.

'You're supposed to save us,' the boy said, about the girl, and she just smiled, kept coming.

Amos heard the shot and died a little more inside, so that he was just black flakes now, ash, balled up in a broken chimney.

Go, Amanda said, beside him, but he was shaking his head no.

He was eleven again, his face soot-black.

He was holding his sister's hand, too.

But Father. He knew where they were, where they'd been. This was the part Amos screamed about on the inside: how had he *found* them?

Beside him, Amanda was crying clean lines into her face, because she knew too, remembered.

Go, she said again.

Amos shook his head no.

He won't find us this time, he said, whispered, thought.

She had been the first one he stole back, buried in the sky. Now she was here, in the chimney with him, hiding. Telling him to *go*. Amos held onto her hand tighter instead, looking at her from all the angles at once, and it wasn't until he looked down through the open flue to see the two of them together that he became aware of a third person in there with them. A boy, his blond hair obvious in this black place.

Sandy.

Amos turned to his right to look at him, see him at last, and then closed his eyes: the blond hair. Father had walked right up to it, then away, a child holding onto each hand, Pawnee City wasted all around. Amos remembered feeling vaguely sorry for the boy, then—Sandy—that his father wasn't sending a fireman to get him too, that he wasn't that special, but he hadn't looked back, either. Until now, Sandy bleeding down his chin, backed as far into the chimney as he could get. Safe because of his hair. Not Indian.

Go be a football hero, Amos said to him, in goodbye. *Take care of my sister—*

She was gone, though. Already. Amanda.

He'd seen the marrow slip from her femur, even, how it almost held its shape for an impossible moment. It had made his own leg hurt in a new way, and he'd held onto that for as long as he could. Promised to make it all better someday. Now. All he had to do was find him, stop him; run.

Amos Pease stepped out of the chimney with purpose, and there was a woman waiting for him: the FBI doctor. Sheila Watts.

'You're supposed to be dead,' she said.

'I am,' Amos said back.

The doctor looked at him for too long. Like she was looking through him, down a tunnel of his years. She was sitting on a sideways cabinet, her hands holding each other in front of her knees, like an aborted prayer, or one she was standing up out of.

'He says you're a natural,' she said.

Amos looked away. 'None of us are, really,' he said. 'Some are just better than others. At this.'

'This?'

'Killing.'

The doctor nodded.

Amos saw that there was a small-caliber handgun hanging from her hands, too. She was just holding it with both of them, pointing a finger down each side of the barrel. So, not a prayer, a demand.

'You have killed a lot of people, Amos,' she said, finally.

Amos nodded, held his index finger up.

'One more,' he said.

The doctor locked eyes with him.

'Patricide,' she said.

Amos Pease smiled wide, his teeth perfect, and corrected her—'*de*icide'—and then over her shoulder, a broken, patchwork man took shape, movement the only thing separating him from the background, the foreground, the midground, his green and black and olive drab fatigues a dull kaleidoscope, about to shift over again, with the sound of aquarium rocks.

'Ma'am,' he was saying, but the doctor wasn't looking at him, just at the girl holding his hand, unsure. Ready to run.

'She says he's got her brother,' the man said, and the doctor rose after him, her gun still out, and only after they were in the street, receding, did the man look back to Amos, nod, and say it with his lips like it was a beautiful thing: *patricide*.

Father.

Jim Doe was crouched behind a wall, afraid to look around it, sure there was going to be a tall woman, sweeping. A man, settling down into a couch. A girl, flying through the air.

His right arm had been inside his shirt, throbbing, but it was hard to balance like that, so now he had it out again, used it without thinking to shield himself from the sound coming in from the sky, building like a freight train, like it was coming back, for him. But it was just blades, in the sky. Gunships, helicopters: more. The green men were jumping out of the cargo doors before the wheels even touched the ground. Barking orders, each of their movements coordinated, precise, necessary.

Jim Doe leaned back against his brick wall, still holding his hand up. If he let it down now, again, he would have to scream, or bite his tongue in half. It was infected, too, of course, his arm: lines of red reaching up his arm, tracking back up the veins, for his heart, so that in the last moments he could push with his heels, like it was something he could back away from, keep backing away from.

But he wasn't here to feel sorry for himself.

There was a name on his lips, there since he'd heard that the storm was hitting Dimmit, not Nazareth: Danny, Danny Boy, Danny B, for Ballinger. He was the only Indian in Dimmit anymore.

Jim Doe knew him from when he used to come see Horace when Horace had been in town. They would never say anything, really, just sit, Horace's daughter taken, Danny's ran away. But then, six years ago, the daughter had turned back up on the deck of his trailer, running away from somewhere else now, a kid on both hips, each with Danny's Roman nose. Looking at them standing in line at the grocery store was like a row of Indian-head pennies. Jim Doe remembered being vaguely embarrassed by them just after high school, for some reason. And now he was embarrassed by that.

They lived on the north side of town, up Eighth.

The Tin Man wouldn't find them right off, either, because there weren't any animals or colors in their last name. He would find them, though: everybody knew Danny Boy, not so much as a person but as a silhouette of a person, stood up against the wall. A shadow by the door of the post office, rolling a toothpick across his lower lip, eyes hidden under the brim of his hat.

Jim Doe stood, walked down the middle of Bedford.

His gun was still in Bluff City, washed away, but it didn't matter. He would bite James Kulpin in the neck if he had too, then lance his heart with a needle, bring him back just to do it again, and again. Never let him say *Sarina*; make him say it with every breath. But then a thing happened, two things: Bill McKirkle and Walter Maines. They were standing outside a blown-in house as if waiting for someone to emerge. Like Noah, sending his bird ahead, watching for it to come back.

They saw Jim Doe at the same time he saw them, and then it was a foot race, the kind from the movies, where everything gets in your way, complete with dead ends and blind alleys, and, here, national guardsmen standing up from the busted sidewalks like cardboard cutouts on an obstacle course. They lunged for Jim Doe and Jim Doe swiveled away, ran, ran, until one soldier got his fingers around Jim

Doe's forearm, where it was broken. The soldier was an officer—tall, thin, greying. In control.

He looked down to Jim Doe and said his name—*James*—then looked up to the Rangers, just taking long steps mostly, not even having to run. Jason Voorhees, Michael Myers; worse.

Jim Doe shook his head no, no, clawing at the officer's fingers, the officer the whole time unfolding a flyer from his shirt pocket. Jim Doe could see it through the backside. It was him, his name: *Doe, James Alan*. His picture.

The officer looked back to him, confirming, and then fell forward, first to his knees, then over frontwards, onto Jim Doe.

Behind him was Amos Pease, dressed up like a fireman. Like the Tin Man.

'You know where you're going?' Amos said, his lips the same color as his skin now.

Jim Doe nodded, once.

Amos Pease smiled, then, started laughing, and flitted away like a bat, like a rag doll, the two Rangers pulling their long-barreled guns now, leaning after *him*.

Jim Doe stood, the officer sloughing off him.

Amos Pease who had shot Tom Gentry.

There had even been something tied to his belt, tied to his belt with its own *hair*.

Jim Doe reached for the gun he still didn't have, looked down to the club his arm was now, then north again, four lots up, to Danny Boy's, the ramshackle house and the trailer growing into it, the plywood-roofed walkway between them getting more boards each year, until it was almost a hall, something you'd need a lightbulb for. The only thing that had even kept it partially standing was the cracks Danny Boy'd left in it when he built it, beer in hand: the wind had blown *through* in places, instead of against. It was the best defense, the only defense. A judo house.

Jim Doe stepped forward, fell against a vertical slab of sidewalk, and stood again, *made* himself stand, the back of his shirt turning to ribbons against the rough concrete, the scraping sound of the fabric suddenly gone, then, when he had his balance. *Too* gone. Eighth Street was emptier than anywhere he'd ever been. Blasted clean, the trees barkless even, fingers reaching up into the sky, their hands just under the earth.

Jim Doe walked forward as best he could, a newspaper clinging to the shin of his pantsleg, and then, two houses closer, saw him for an impossible instant, framed under the tilted eave of a tilted house: James Kulpin, in a grey out-of-place suit, federal issue almost. A gun in one hand, a girl in the other, her brother hanging on. The face on his face was silver, cardboard, unsmiling. And the girl, the Ballinger girl. Kathryn, maybe. Tall, now. Taller than she should be, like at the end of a movie. And her brother. Jim Doe could only think of him with *J*-sounds: James, Jimmy, Jim. His lips moved behind the sound, trying to catch it, *them*, but when he stepped up onto the packed dirt of the lawn they disappeared, into the wall of a house. Danny Boy's house. The labyrinth.

Jim Doe walked up between the railroad ties embedded in the earth, knocked on the door.

It fell in, away from his hand, leaving him holding just a brass doorknob, turning it over and over like he should *know* it, and, after that, it's all legend, more or less. Of Jim Doe feeling through the house to the kitchen, finding there a fireman, a soldier, a forensic psychologist for the FBI. Two Indian children, drugged, limp. Three guns, each trained in two places at once, and then a third place, too: a man standing suddenly in the doorway by the refrigerator, looking down first for the children who are just dark arms reaching from the hall now, holding him up, then raising his face, to see where he is, saying it under the silver tape across his mouth—*Oz*—and he's the only one still in shades of grey here, his ears moving in a smile as the guard places his gun against the cardboard forehead, the man placing his gun on the guard's forehead in return, so that it's a dance, the end of a dance, two impossibly tall Texas Rangers stepping into the room too, behind *their* guns, seeing only the mask, the man behind it finally spreading his fingers, to show that his gun's *duct*-taped to his hand, then lowering that hand, that gun, to show the Rangers who he is, and isn't, the forensic psychologist only getting it when a clean tongue of flame licks down the man's pantsleg, spitting a .45 caliber slug, his right dress shoe blossoming flesh, *color*, the guard smiling about this, nodding once, in appreciation, the moment after that branching fast, desperate. Jim Doe looking up to a freight car in the sky above, tumbling end over end. The Texas Rangers filling the door behind him, over him. The guard extending a hand to the fireman, no glove, and the fireman reaching for it, his fingers trembling, letting the girl he's holding roll away, to Jim Doe, who holds her close enough and tight enough to feel the gun smuggled into her waistband.

He takes it just as the fireman touches fingertips with the guard, just as the fireman pulls the guard forward, away from the boy he has, but the Rangers above Jim Doe don't understand, or do, but open fire anyway, the fireman standing into their bullets like he wants them, and, for an instant, when the first round doesn't knock him back or even hit him, Jim Doe knows the fireman, Amos Pease, is one of the old-time Indians who couldn't *get* shot, but then the next slug opens his sternum, and the next spins him around like a marionette, and the next punctures both lungs, and the Rangers are still firing into him and taking fire from somewhere themselves when the tornado hits all at once, Jim Doe pulling the girl as close as he can—*saving* her—and firing from her midback, at the guard, the Tin Man, the walls of the house falling away, the long, black finger of God pointing down at the seven of them, Jim Doe saying it in his head: *now*.

7 JUNE 1999

DEDHAM, MASSACHUSETTS

JAMES Kulpin's father finally showed up at a post office box back in Dedham. His pension checks came there. He picked them up once a month. Creed stood in front of the post office and looked both ways. His foot was in a large plastic boot, now, the bones all shattered, and his undershirts were still red from the roofing nails in his back, and even when he sat too still and had to think about it, he still couldn't shoot that girl.

The nursing home was one block down from the post office.

Kenneth Kulpin was on the first floor. Taped to his door was GARDEN OF ENID. It was cut out from a placemat. The place he'd been before this place. He was sitting in a wooden chair, rocking his body back and forth, his hands under his legs, from the outside, his eyes yellow, breath poison. He saluted Creed with a nod, called him just *FBI.*

Creed rubbed his eyes. He was here to tell Kenneth Kulpin what the papers were already saying, even without the bodies: that the Tin Man was dead, along with everyone else on the east side of the house—public enemy Amos Pease, aka Jim Thorpe; FBI martyr Dr. Sheila Watts; intended victim Raymond Ballinger, legal name Raymond Dance, after his father. What the papers weren't saying was that ballistics had matched the two slugs William McKirkle had mailed them in a bloody envelope to the ones Watts had had on file. And that the two children who'd been propping Creed up were missing, and that nobody was looking for them, because they didn't have names, really. Just Paul, Gina. A set of parents out there somewhere who thought their children were still buried in the sky.

Creed held onto the doorjamb, to take the weight off his bad foot.

'He's dead, right?' Kenneth Kulpin said, finally, leaning forward, his body hunching for a cough that never came. Was too deep.

Creed looked at him. He'd asked for this assignment, really. Flown out in his black suit, from Watts's memorial.

'Yes,' he said.

Kenneth Kulpin didn't look away, just ran his index finger and thumb down the side of his mouth, stretching the cracked lips open, cleaning the corners, wiping it on his polyester pants.

'You don't have any children, do you?' he said.

Creed just stared at him.

Kenneth Kulpin shrugged.

'You *were* a son, though.' He smiled; it made him cough something wet into the palm of his hand. 'You ever look at those old-timey pictures, FBI? Of the saints, I mean. The men who painted them were children themselves once, is what I'm saying. Before they were sinners.'

Creed looked to the door, an old woman in ruby slippers hobbling past, for dinner. In the Green Room.

'I imagine they were,' he said.

Kenneth Kulpin smiled.

'But where did they get the *idea?*' he said, holding his hand out before him, upright, the index finger raised, pulling the rest up. A John the Baptist gesture. Of objection, or blessing. Either way, Creed wanted to leave, suddenly. Needed to.

'Not from the saints, anyway,' he said, half-laughing, rising from his chair.

'Because they don't exist,' Kenneth Kulpin said.

'Something like that.'

'That's what I'm saying, FBI.'

Creed looked down to him.

'What?' he said. Had to say.

'That those men who painted the saints had been *infants*, had been carried by their fathers out the front door, only, when the father saw the sun hitting the child's face, closing their eyes, he *opened* them, FBI. By placing his head in the path of the light, becoming a shadow. But . . . the way it must have looked to them, the infants, can you see it? Your father, the most important person in the world, the giver and taker of life, the sun behind his head, making his hair glow. Beautiful, FBI.'

Creed stared down at him.

'You never stepped out of the light, though,' he said.

Kenneth Kulpin laughed through his nose.

'I loved him too well, FBI.' He looked up at Creed one last time. 'Is that wrong?'

Creed walked to the door, stood in it for a few moments, then said it without turning around: 'Our people—we thought what he was trying to do was what you said. About fathers and sons. Replace himself. But he wasn't.'

He could hear Kenneth Kulpin behind him, waiting, his ancient heart laboring.

'It was just his third suicide,' Creed said, then. 'Facing the executioner and living.'

He set a bottle of pills on the cabinet by the door. The ones from 17 Prairie View, by the sink.

'They're sugar,' he said. 'Candy. Eat as many as you want.'

And then he left.

They knew more, though. That was the way it always worked: everything locked into place once the killing was over, the killer dead. Like the six-month psych evaluation that had filtered in from Louisiana, the *tape*, inmate James Kulpin talking into it while the staff psychologist was out of the room, or on the phone. Talking to Creed, telling him that if he just would have turned around in that parking lot in Colorado in 1966, he would have seen him crying in the front seat of an El Camino—Kulpin, the child.

The FBI had let Creed have the only copy.

It was still in the glove compartment.

In the parking lot, Creed stood with his back to the sun, looking at his shadow, then the sky, and then the cell phone he'd just started carrying. It was ringing, numbers forming in the little viewscreen.

Baltimore. He knew the area code: Marcia.

The only good thing. He smiled, lifted the phone to his ear, and when it wasn't her—when it was a man—his first thought was James Kulpin.

'Sir?' the man said.

Creed looked to the east.

'Eggers?' he said.

'. . . sir,' Eggers said again.

Creed was on the next flight out.

It had been a routine traffic accident on a routine day, a routine ambulance screaming Marcia to her routine hospital bed in ICU.

Creed held her hand and she looked up at him and died.

He'd brought the honeymoon picture with him too, the one from Colorado, from Kulpin.

He took it with him out of the hospital, turned down the sidewalk, and saw his shadow again, the sun glowing around his head, and then his phone started ringing with condolences. He left it in the trashcan, kept the picture until the end of the block, then left it too.

9 JUNE 1999

NAZARETH, TEXAS

DANNY Ballinger was building another house, closer to Nazareth. Swaying on the ladder, his beer can glinting the sun across the scrub. There were cars all around the place. Volunteers. Indians. Jim Doe was pulling up on the swell of land just above them every day now, waiting for Kathryn to walk out, *live*.

Two of her ribs were broken, he knew, on her left side. It was how far his left hand had reached around her. The doorway was all that had kept them there, and McKirkle, keeling over onto them like a shelter, his leg shot out.

Jim Doe's arm was still in a sling. He might never use the hand again, with the bone infected. It would be worth it, though, if Kathryn would just walk out, look at the sky.

'You there?' Monica said, over the radio.

Jim Doe looked down to it, keyed it open once: yes.

'Thought you'd want to know,' she said back.

Jim Doe nodded: Sarina. The labs had finally released her. After the storm she'd been sitting in the backseat of the supercab, her hands in her lap, waiting. Her face tied over her face.

At Danny Ballinger's house, someone was standing back by the burn barrels, watching Jim Doe. When he called somebody else, from inside the house, Jim Doe slipped down into neutral, coasted back a few yards. Started the truck.

'You don't have to come,' he said into the mike, to Monica.

She didn't respond.

An hour later, he was there, down a series of pump roads and less to a bare spot in the earth. Horace was already there, sitting in the white supercab. Jim Doe nodded to him, and they stepped out at the same time.

'So,' Jim Doe said to him.

Horace nodded.

It was all they could do, really.

Sarina was on a scaffold, strips of cloth tied all over it, and feathers, and pages from books, and a brass doorknob. Standing off a ways were the Blue Kettles.

'They're just going to tear it down,' Blue Kettle said—the scaffold.

Jim Doe looked up to it, blowing, and shrugged.

'Fuck it,' he said, 'right?'

Blue Kettle rolled his old tongue out between his worn teeth, smiled, and patted Jim Doe on the shoulder, and then left it there when Horace started singing, upwind.

He was five-eight now, maybe, and dark from the sun in Greenville, and singing with his whole body, his hands balled into fists by the sides of his legs.

'. . . real Indian song,' Blue Kettle was saying, nodding.

It was Johnny Cash, the man in black.

Jim Doe moved his head with it, his throat, felt more than saw Blue Kettle take his wife's hand, lead her out a ways, and pull her close, their feet shuffling through the dirt in a two-step, or close enough. The woman was crying, too. Because she was happy; because she was sad. Jim Doe looked away, to Sarina, then to the mini-truck pulling up.

Terra. Terra Donner.

The week-old shoe polish on her windshield said she was eighteen. Graduated.

'You look like my sister would have looked,' Jim Doe said to her.

'I guess I can't help that,' she said.

Jim Doe closed his eyes, opened them, and Horace sang Johnny Cash for Sarina until the rain came, the drops so far apart at first they were just balling up in the dust.

'Your hair's longer,' Terra said, threading it behind Jim Doe's ear for him.

Jim Doe didn't stop her.

'How was prom?' he asked.

'Just prom,' she said.

They were sitting in the small cab of her truck, now, their breath sticking to the inside of all the glass, closing them in.

'I don't know if you want to hear this,' she said.

Jim Doe looked over to her.

'It's about Molly Jankins,' she said.

Jim Doe said the name over and over in his head until it clicked: Molly Jankins. The senior who died in the Corvette. In 1982.

Terra shrugged.

'It's just that . . . Mitch was back in town the other night. Drinking.'

Mitch Morton. The driver of the Corvette. The one who lived.

'What?' Jim Doe said.

Terra wouldn't look at him.

'He thinks he saw her now,' she said. 'Your . . .'

Sarina.

'. . . why he wrecked,' Terra finished. 'She was in the road or something.'

Jim Doe smiled: so it had come this far now. Had been that long ago.

'Your dad,' he said. 'He doesn't much like me.'

Terra shrugged. 'He doesn't like a lot of stuff,' she said.

Jim Doe nodded, his head moving forward into this. The idea of this.

In front of them, the Blue Kettles were pulling away without honking, just Blue Kettle, clicking his lights off once, then back on.

'I think maybe they're ghosts,' Jim Doe said.

'I think maybe we all are,' Terra said.

Jim Doe nodded.

'You ready?' she said, nodding out to Horace.

Jim Doe looked to him, still standing there.

'Yeah,' he said.

'It's wet out there,' Terra said.

Jim Doe shrugged, walked through it, and started his truck, following Terra Donner at a crawl back to Nazareth, driving out of the rain at one point like pushing through a wall, coming out of the carwash. He rolled his window down then, trying to steer with his knee but drifting, drifting, and when he got straightened back out he saw her: she was walking in the ditch, along the road that went away from the high school. Kathryn, Kathryn Ballinger. She was carrying her shoes. He pulled alongside.

'Hello,' he said out the window.

She didn't look at him.

The rain was maybe four minutes behind them now.

'Where's Danny?' he said.

She looked over at him then.

'Did you know his name was Raymond?' she said. Her brother who died. Not just *Ray*, but *Raymond*.

Jim Doe held his lips together, nodded.

Kathryn kept walking.

'Those two—the police,' she said. 'They're at Granddad's house.'

'McKirkle,' Jim Doe said. 'Maines. Bill and Walter.'

Kathryn nodded.

'They were out there,' she said. 'Asking about you.'

Jim Doe looked ahead of him, to Nazareth, and understood: she'd seen them, what they reminded her of—the storm—and just slipped out. For town. This morning.

'Your granddad's going to be worried,' he said.

Kathryn shrugged. She was twelve, maybe.

Jim Doe slowed the truck.

'Ride back?' he said.

A truck-length up, maybe, she stopped. Waited for him to pull alongside, the passenger door already open.

'I'm not supposed to,' she said.

'But it's me,' Jim Doe said.

'That's what I mean,' she said.

She got in anyway.

'They had to tell you something,' she said. 'That's all.'

Jim Doe rolled his window up, trying to think what they could have to say to him.

'You were coming to tell me?' he said.

Kathryn smiled.

'To run,' she said. 'Yeah.'

Jim Doe smiled with her.

They pulled up to the strangely-angled frame of the new Ballinger house fifteen minutes later, the rain coming down hard. Bill McKirkle's truck was there, Walter Maines probably driving. They hadn't been there at lunch. Meaning maybe they'd been looking for him all day, had finally looped back around to here again.

'Granddad's around back,' Kathryn said then, before she got out of the truck, reached up and hugged Jim Doe awkwardly on the neck, all in a jerk. Jim Doe placed his left hand on her back and she arched away from it, still hurt.

'Kathryn—' he said, and then she was gone, running barefoot through the mud to the house that didn't even have a roof yet. Jim Doe shook his head, looked at McKirkle's truck some more. The windows weren't fogged. Meaning they'd been here a while. Waiting for him.

'Drive away,' he said, to himself, but, instead, reached under the seat, for the pistol Garza had said he was going to pretend he didn't know about.

The hammer was resting on an empty chamber, so Jim Doe rolled it over one, nestled it into his waistband, then left the truck running, stepped down. Around the house, from the back, voices were approaching. Danny Boy's easy lilt. Jim Doe lowered his head, untucking his shirt to hide the handle of the gun. Because it was foolish.

But then he heard the end of whatever Danny Boy had been saying.

He was thanking someone.

Jim Doe felt the smile on his face come down to just muscles, skin.

In trade for the thanks, for helping frame the house, maybe, a voice started in with a joke. An Indian joke, Kathryn listening from inside, melting from board to board, moving effortlessly through what would be walls in a few weeks, holding her face in a way that Jim Doe didn't understand: her eyes serious, jaws slightly open, lips in an oval. Her trying-to-hide face.

Jim Doe looked behind him, to all the cars nosed up to the foundation.

There were six, just the usual—plus McKirkle's truck, and his own—but then, at the end of the line, through the drizzle, there *was* another car. One that hadn't been here at lunch either. White, business. Like from a fleet.

Jim Doe flattened himself against the unfinished house, not even sure why he was doing it.

It was the car, the voice, the joke: insurance.

Jim Doe felt the gun fall into his left hand.

Kathryn was beside him now, her face between two close boards.

The insurance man was paying for Raymond.

Jim Doe was breathing hard, the world slick grey all around him.

He was eight years old again, crouched behind a wall, listening to his father take a check for Sarina. Listening to the same joke as then.

It was the one about the Sioux guy walking into a bar with his three-legged dog, the bartender asking what's up with that dog, the man saying it's *special*—the other night it saved the man's wife and kid from his truck after it rolled over and started burning—then the bartender asking if that was how it lost its leg, then?

Jim Doe closed his eyes, trying *not* to breathe now, and then Danny Boy and the insurance man rounded the corner, walking close to the wall, for what little shelter the eave gave.

The insurance man was wearing a black raincoat, holding his briefcase over his head, talking from underneath it. But then he saw Jim Doe, and his face changed.

'. . . a dog like that,' Jim Doe said, stepping forward, remembering the joke at last, 'you don't eat all at once,' and Danny Boy looked between the two of them and tried not to but started laughing anyway, even with Raymond dead. Maybe because. Slow at first, then more.

Jim Doe felt a smile flicker across his face too: he had his gun hard against James Kulpin's teeth, his arm locked behind it.

'James,' the insurance man—the *Tin* Man—said, 'think.'

'I have been,' Jim Doe said.

'The rest of them,' Kulpin said. 'The kids. Somebody said it like this once to me. Without me, you'll never find them. Not if you do this . . .'

Jim Doe stared at him, hard. Started to lower the gun just as Walter McKirkle crutched around the far corner of the house.

Kulpin looked over, smiled.

'If you would have done it,' he said. 'You would have been just like me, James.'

Jim Doe felt himself smiling back.

'Wrong,' he said. 'I'd be *alive*,' and then raised the gun back up, pulled the trigger, once.

The back of the Kulpin's head misted out into the rain and he stood there a few moments longer, his smile cut into his face now, ragged at the edges, and then he fell. Jim Doe stood over him, waiting for him to rise. Because he might. But then three feet away, her face splattered red, Kathryn turned to look behind Jim Doe. Jim Doe turned with her. It was Walter Maines, water running off the brim of his hat.

He looked from Jim Doe to the dead insurance man Kulpin was.

'You're looking for me,' Jim Doe said.

Maines shrugged, looked through the house at somebody, then nodded. 'Your FBI buddy,' he said, shaking his head at the uselessness of it all now. 'Tim Creed. His wife was killed.'

'He wasn't married,' Jim Doe said.

'They thought it was an accident, at first,' Maines went on, then shrugged, spit. Rolled his cheek between his teeth.

From the other side of the house, McKirkle spoke.

'Guess you done it now,' he said—the insurance man.

Jim Doe smiled. His left hand was trembling, seconds after the act. It was moving up to his chest, too. Trembling.

'You remember when it hit Nazareth?' he said. 'The tornado?'

McKirkle nodded, spit. 'Nineteen eighty-two,' he said.

Jim Doe looked south.

'Five years after that,' he said. 'Junior high. Four eighth-graders killed themselves, in one month.'

'So?' Maines said.

Jim Doe shrugged, threw his gun down onto the insurance man.

'Some of us wait a little longer, I guess,' he said, looking at each of them in turn before stepping back into the rain, falling into a primer grey Bonneville Brougham with chrome mags and a trashbag side window. It started under his fingers like it had been waiting for him, and he slung the nose around, fishtailed to the end of the drive then stopped there with his eyes closed, hard. Seeing Sarina for the hundredth time, in the backseat of Horace's supercab. How he'd thought for an impossible second that she was alive. That it had all been worth it. But it was, now.

He'd held the gun to the Tin Man's mouth because it was his left hand, and he didn't want to miss. Couldn't.

It had kicked all the way into his childhood. And deeper.

He smiled, Jim Doe, apologized once to Terra, like she could hear, then hauled the wheel to the right—north—and when the brown and white feather the Brougham's owner had hooked onto the radio knob at some last minute started blowing from the rusted-out floor, Jim Doe took it off, looped it over the rearview, and the first thing he drove through was Castro County, faster than any Corvette had ever gone, and the second thing he drove through was Texas, his mirror full of cowboys, gaining, the ends of their reins in their teeth, the twentieth century falling away, and the third thing he drove through was a fine layer of birds coating the road, lifting into the sky behind him, countless.

ACKNOWLEDGMENTS

so many helpful people. star-agent Kate Garrick, for reading and believing in these things I write. taking time out of her day to get back to me that day. editor-extraordinaire Shawn Coyne, for taking a chance on a super-unknown, then teaching me what a thriller is, what it isn't, what it can be. working with me through the drafts; trusting the story, the prose. Brenda Mills, for reading the words as I wrote them, 1100 miles over my shoulder. publicist Tammy Blake, for getting this out there in the world, me with it. copyeditor Shauna Toh, for reading deep between the lines, for things like cadence, rhythm. editor Chris Min, for juggling many manuscripts, never dropping even one. Timothy Hsu, for the cool cover, the cool fonts. Ted Genoways, for saying to me once, 'Rugged Land.' the National Endowment for the Arts and the Writer's League of Texas, for groceries, gas-money. my wife, for making me move from these keys to the table every once in while, to eat, be human, then holding my hand when my fingers start trying to write on the tabletop.